Dandyflowers
Laura's Voice

By Jordan T. Maxwell

I0571501

Dandyflowers ~ Laura's Voice

Published in the United States of America

ISBN-13: 978-1-7364136-2-3

Chapter 01

"Sophia Elizabeth Young, if all you are going to do is mope; go outside and do it! At least you'll get some fresh air." Carol Young said hoping to be heard by her angst-ridden daughter who was sitting dejectedly on the couch. Sophia, the name her daughter shared with her maternal great-great-grandmother was not happy and it showed.

A week after they had moved from Springfield to the little northern Missouri town where they now lived, Sophia had a very uncharacteristic explosion of anger when the house they were now living was referred to as "home".

Sophia, with tears streaming down her face, had yelled, "I'll never call this place home! Never ever!"

She stormed off to her room and slammed the door.

Carol knew that when you're nearly fifteen any change; no matter how great or small, was fodder for heartache.

"Fine." Sophia said in a flat, miserable tone.

After her mom had played the first, middle and last name card, she knew it was a done deal and there was no use arguing.

"Here." Her mother pressed something into her hand. "Why don't you go get yourself something?"

Sophia shoved whatever her mother had given her into the back pocket of her jean shorts, opened the front door and bounded down the front steps to the sidewalk to head down the street to…

"To where?" Sophia thought, then turned left and started walking.

The soft "thwap" of her flip flops hitting the bottoms of her feet was her only companion.

"You will get used to this new place." Carol called from the front porch as Sophia headed out into their new neighborhood.

"Humph!" Sophia grunted, but only she was aware of it.

~ ~ ~ ~ ~ ~

After living in the same house, on the same street, in the same town and going to the same schools with the same friends her entire life; Sophia Elizabeth Young had been abruptly and unceremoniously uprooted and transplanted to a small town two hundred fifty miles from the only life she had ever known.

The move had hit particularly hard as Sophia had to give up her hard-earned spot on the cheerleading squad. As an incoming freshman, she had secured a spot on the Kickapoo High School *varsity* cheerleading squad, something that was extremely difficult to accomplish. In fact, she was only the second person to ever do it. The first had been when Brad Pitt went to Kickapoo High.

Now, instead of being on the sidelines cheering for the Kickapoo Chiefs, Sophia would be "the new girl" sitting in the bleachers at the little high school in the little no-name town where she would be starting her freshman year.

Glancing back over her shoulder and down the street at the house where she was being forced to live, she sighed and asked herself, *"Why did Dad have to become the Postmaster here?"*

~ ~ ~ ~ ~ ~

The house was older, but it had been well-kept. According to Mr. Rick Fleet of "Houses from Fleet Can't Be Beat" real estate fame, who had been serving the real estate needs of northern Missouri since nineteen ninety-seven, the house had begun life as a bungalow. At some point, a wide porch and three rooms had been added to the front and down one side, making it a full-grown house.

Sophia vaguely remembered Mr. Fleet saying that a previous owner had purchased the adjoining lot, tore down the old house that was there and built a large combination garage and shop. The garage was on the street side of the building and could easily hold four cars instead of just their minivan and her dad's small pickup.

The shop portion was a large vacant space that could easily hold four more cars. Her father had covered the windows with brown paper right after they had arrived telling her he was working on "something special" and that she would really like it once he was done. When she had asked about what he was working on, neither he nor her mother would say anything except for, "We will tell you when we tell you and not before!"

Mr. Fleet had talked at length about the large amount of "green space" that ran the length of the lot between the house and the garage / shop. Her father had jokingly asked if the selling price of the property included a new lawnmower to take care of all that "green space". Mr. Fleet had laughed, only saying, "You never know!"

When her parents had signed the papers and took possession, there had been a brand-new forty-eight-inch, sixteen horsepower John Deere riding lawnmower sitting in the garage! Her father was ecstatic! Her mother was pleased. Sophia could not have cared less.

~ ~ ~ ~ ~ ~

Sighing forlornly, she turned and began walking toward the business district, if the stores she had seen there could actually be called a "district".

Sophia walked for several minutes and was so deep into her internal ruminations and external texting to her friends Audrey Noble, Leah Sterling and Laney Williams about how bad her life had become; she walked right into an old mailbox.

The mailbox had been painted an unusual shade of dark green and was sitting outside a building touted to be the town's library. Boldly stenciled in large egg yolk-colored letters on all four sides were the words: Library Book Dropbox. This is <u>NOT</u> a mailbox!

"Great!" She thought sarcastically as she quickly scanned the street to see if anyone had seen her mishap. *"They can't even tell the difference between a book drop box and a mailbox in this stupid little town!"*

Fortunately, although not surprisingly, the sidewalk was empty, so only she was aware of the incident.

To her right, in the library's window was a poster and Sophia stepped closer for a better look. The poster promoted a book that had been written by someone named Erin Ivey and a quote was printed across its top.

An attic is an interesting place to visit; it holds treasures and secrets. Sometimes the secrets <u>*are*</u> the treasures.

"That sounds really interesting." Sophia thought. *"Too bad I had to move to the middle of nowhere to find a book I might want to read."*

She learned that copies were available inside the library. Curious and always on the lookout for a good book, she stepped away from the window and pushed open the door.

The library was a single large room crowded with shelf after shelf of books. Sophia thought the building had been "repurposed" as it had the look and feel of an old grocery store. It had large street facing windows and a dual door entrance that appeared to have once had automatic door opener pressure mats in front of them on either side of the threshold.

Sitting at a desk just inside the door was a woman, presumably the librarian, busily pecking away at a computer keyboard; the soft and consistent clicking was the only sound in the building. Sophia read the name plate attached to the front of the desk. The librarian was named Paris Olden Spencer and her back was to the doors. She was so focused on her work that she never noticed Sophia's arrival.

"Um…hello?" Sophia said.

The woman, Ms. Spencer, physically jumped and turned to face Sophia with her hand on her chest.

"My word! I didn't even hear you come in! I really need to get a bell for those doors!" She said.

"Sorry." Sophia said, successfully holding in a laugh at the woman's startled reaction. It was the first time since the move that she had actually felt the urge to laugh.

"I'm Paris Spencer by the way. I'm head librarian, well, the only librarian at the moment, janitor and jack of all trades!" Paris Spencer said.

"I'm Sophia Young. I just moved here." Sophia said.

"Oh, so are you the new Postmaster's daughter?" Paris asked.

"Great, not only will I be 'The New Girl', but now I'll be 'The Postmaster's Daughter' too." Sophia thought. *"Could life get any worse?"*

"Yeah, that's me." Sophia said in a flat monotone.

"What can I do for you, Miss Sophia Young?" Paris asked.

"I am looking for a book." Sophia said.

"Well, you came to the right place; we have lots of books!" Paris made an exaggerated sweeping arm movement toward the shelves. "I can get you registered for a library card in no time at all!"

Her gesture made Sophia chuckle despite her mood. "That would be great, but I was wondering about the book on the poster in the window; do you have any of those available?" Sophia asked.

"I believe I do! Just one second." Ms. Spencer leaned down, retrieved a book from under her desk and handed it to Sophia. "That is the last one."

Sophia took the book and read the dust jacket's teaser. It appeared the story was one about the author's father and a part of his life he revealed to her right after she had gotten engaged.

"How much is it?" Sophia asked.

"I've never actually bought a book in a library before." She thought.

"They are fifteen dollars." Paris Spencer said. "And all the money made from the books sold here at the library, Erin is donating back to the library!"

"Have you sold very many?" Sophia asked.

She slipped her hand into her back pocket to fish out the wadded-up bill her mother had given her. After leaving the house she had looked at what her mother had given her and was surprised to see that it was a twenty-dollar bill.

"That one is the last of two hundred fifty copies!" Paris said pointing to the book in Sophia's hand.

Sophia handed Mister Jackson to Paris Olden Spencer, librarian, janitor and jack of all trades, who in turn counted out five ones and handed the change back.

"Thank you!" Paris said. Then asked, "Are you coming to the signing?"

"The what?" Sophia asked looking up from her perusal of the book.

She had become fascinated with the book's cover which showed a dandelion that had gone to seed and some of its white fuzz was being blown into the air.

"I asked if you were coming to the book signing." Paris said.

"When is it?" Sophia asked.

An actual book signing was something she had always wanted to attend but had never had the opportunity.

"Sunday the twenty-sixth starting at two in the afternoon; we're using it as a kick-off for the new school year." Paris said. "School starts on Monday the twenty-seventh you know! Wow, only nine days of summer left! Well, at least for you kids. I had my last first day of school a couple of years ago."

"What do you mean?" Sophia asked.

"I was a guidance counselor for this school district for…oh my goodness…for forty years. Then I retired, got bored and took this job!" Paris said.

"Wow!" Sophia said. "That's a long time to work at the same place."

"Well, right out of college, I worked at another school district before coming back home." Paris said cheerfully. "But that is ancient history. How about we get you signed up for that new library card?"

"Sure!" Sophia said.

Paris handed Sophia a pen and a single page application form that asked all the usual questions like name, date of birth, phone number, grade in school (if applicable) etc. The one question she couldn't answer was her street address. When she confessed her problem, Paris Spencer chuckled as she quickly added the house number, the words "West Third", and zip code to the application.

"In little towns like this one, everyone knows everyone." Paris said. "My friend used to live in your house, so I know the address."

She gave the application a cursory look, then quickly entered Sophia's information into her computer. With a few more keystrokes, a printer came to life somewhere underneath the desk.

"Here you go!" Paris said handing Sophia a freshly printed plastic library card complete with a bar code along the bottom edge. "We are finally coming into the twenty-first century."

"What do you mean?" Sophia asked.

Paris laughed. "With that card and the Libby app, you can now download e-books and audiobooks to your computer, tablet, smartphone or any other electronic device."

"Good to know." Sophia said while resisting an urge to roll her eyes.

"I've been able to do things like that for a long time in Springfield, but the Libby app...?" She thought.

"Is this book, an e-book or audio book?" Sophia asked.

Paris Spencer clicked the keys on her computer's keyboard and looked at its screen.

"It will be!" She said.

"What was the name of that app again?' Sophia asked.

"Libby." Paris said. "L – I – B – B – Y."

Sophia's fingers flashed over her phone's screen. In less than two minutes she had downloaded, installed and set up the account that would give her access to thousands of books thru the library system. She then searched for the book, but the words "Available Soon" hovered just above the greyed out "Borrow" button.

"At least I now have the app." She said as she turned her phone to show Ms. Spencer. "I'll keep checking to see when the audio book and e-book of this is available."

"Let me know when you can download it, would you?" Paris asked.

"I will!" Sophia said. "But now I need to…" She nodded toward the door. "You know…"

"Don't be a stranger!" Paris said. "Come back and see me sometime."

"I will." Sophia said.

She left the library and returned to her walk and her mental grumbling. She only stopped thinking about the unfairness that had beset her life when she came to the end of the block and the business located there.

Chapter 02

Morton's was a restaurant that had a large, somewhat sun faded sign proclaiming it served the best milkshakes in town. Considering it appeared to be the only place that served ice cream in the place Sophia had begun calling "Podunksville"; she supposed their claim was true. Armed with that knowledge along with the remaining money in her pocket, she opened the door that had been booby-trapped with one of those annoyingly old-fashioned jingly bells that Paris Spencer, librarian, janitor and jack of all trades would undoubtedly like, and stepped inside.

The décor was one straight out of the nineteen fifties; chrome and silver-grey Formica topped tables, stools and chairs topped with red vinyl and a black and white tiled floor made up the restaurant's interior. There was even a jukebox sitting at the far end of the dining room with little bubbles floating up through tubes in front of the neon lights that lived on its face.

Patsy Cline was just finishing up her lament about her inability to dream sweetly about some lost love as Sophia closed the door, which reactivated the annoyingly cliché bell.

She knew how Patsy Cline felt; she'd spent every night since the move missing her home and her friends. On more than one of those nights, she had cried herself to sleep.

"What can I get for you honey?" A voice asked.

Sophia jumped nearly as hard as the Spencer lady had at the library; she had not noticed the woman standing behind the counter. She slid onto one of the chrome stools that were affixed to the floor and spaced about two feet apart down the length of the counter and sat down.

"A strawberry milkshake would be good." She said.

"Small, medium or large?" The lady asked.

"Medium I guess." Sophia said.

She had spent most of the twenty her mother had given her on the book that was now laying on the diner's countertop. She was certain the remaining five dollars would more than cover the cost of a milkshake.

"If this milkshake costs more than five bucks, I will just run away and never come back!" Sophia thought.

"Don't believe I know you." The woman said as she went about fixing the milkshake. "I'm Marion by the way. I run this place; took it over from my mother Fran, but that's ancient history."

"The Fifties are alive and well here in Podunksville." Sophia thought as she considered the woman whose hair was platinum blonde and towered above her head in a beehive hairdo.

"No, I don't think you would know me. I just moved here not too long ago." Sophia said.

"Ah, so that's who you are. I was wondering when I get to meet some of the new folks!" Marion said.

Sophia cringed internally waiting to be called "The Postmaster's Daughter", "The New Girl" or some other equally annoying label, but Marion said nothing as she placed a large scoop of vanilla ice cream into a shiny metal cylinder. Two heaping spoonsful of fresh strawberries were added along with some milk from a plastic jug she had gotten from a small refrigerator under the counter.

"I hate it." Sophia said flatly.

"The house or the move here?" Marion asked and slid the metal cylinder on to the blender that roared to life sounding like a dentist's drill on steroids.

"Yes." Sophia answered in the same flat tone.

The blender assaulted the strawberries, milk and ice cream until Marion deemed it complete. Once done, she poured the contents into a tall, tapered glass and after adding a straw, she placed the concoction in front of Sophia along with a couple of paper napkins.

"How much?" Sophia asked.

"That one is on the house, honey!" Marion said.

"What? Really?" Sophia said.

She had never had anyone do anything like that for her before.

"Yes, really. And this little town's not so bad either; you just give us a chance." Marion said with a wink and a smile before focusing her attention on wiping down the counter.

"Thank you!" Sophia said.

"You're welcome, honey!" Marion said.

"Sophia." Sophia offered.

"What's that?" Marion asked.

"I said 'Sophia'. My name is Sophia Young. I'm the new Postmaster's daughter." She grimaced internally at her words.

"I can't believe I just said that." She thought.

"I'm pleased to meet you, Miss Sophia Young!" Marion said, then returned her attention to wiping down the counter.

Sophia appreciated the cold treat that sat before her. It was the thickest shake she had ever had in her life! Her first several attempts to get a taste were frustrating; each time she tried to suck up some of the concoction, the plastic straw completely flattened out. Out of sheer desperation, she removed the straw and licked the ice cream from its end. It was delicious!

"Here you go hon...er...Sophia." Marion said handing her a long-handled spoon. "I always forget to put one in the glass. You'd think after fifty years I would remember!"

Sophia giggled at Marion's admission, then began the task of devouring the milkshake in earnest.

"Well, at least you can laugh, and you do have a pretty smile!" Marion said, then went back to wiping down the already spotless counter.

"Oh!" Sophia groaned a minute later and pressed her hands to her temples.

"Brain freeze?" Marion asked knowingly.

"Brain freeze!" Sophia confirmed in pained tones.

Marion filled a glass with warm water and handed it to her. "Here, drink this."

Sophia drank the water. After the second swallow, the throbbing in her head disappeared.

"Thank you, that helped a lot." Sophia said.

"It always does!" Marion laughed. "And if you don't have warm water, press your thumb on the roof of your mouth. That works pretty good too!"

"I'd never heard that before; thanks!" Sophia said.

She returned to her milkshake and in short order, it was a fond, sweet memory that ended with one last gurgling slurp.

"You really took care of that." Marion said and took the now empty glass and spoon from the counter.

"It was really good!" Sophia said. "Thank you!"

"You are welcome, Miss Sophia!" Marion said. "Come back and see me again sometime!"

"I will!" Sophia promised and spun herself around, slid off the stool and headed to the door.

"Did you forget something?" Marion called after her.

"I don't think so." Sophia said.

Marion held up the book Sophia had bought at the library.

"Oops!" Sophia said as she retrieved the book. "Thanks!"

"Don't forget to come back and see me!" Marion said.

"I won't!" Sophia said with a smile. "I love strawberry milkshakes, especially free ones!"

Marion laughed and shooed her out the door with a wave of her hands!

Sophia exited the restaurant and resumed her walk. As she did, she was amazed at the people of the little town. Whenever someone passed her in their car, pickup truck or in one case, on a small red and white tractor, they would wave and smile. The same thing happened whenever someone was in their yard as she walked past.

"Wow!" She thought after each gesture of friendliness. *"Nothing like that ever happened back home except in our neighborhood."*

~ ~ ~ ~ ~ ~

The business district gave way to residences and soon Sophia was walking down a street with neatly kept lawns and large trees much like the street where she now lived.

A well-used basketball bounced across the street and lodged itself in a storm drain just in front of her. Across the street, she saw a little girl of about six staring wide-eyed looking at the runaway ball.

"My name is Sandi." The girl said, then her eyes widened comically before she added, "But I'm not 'posed to talk to strange people."

Despite her mood, Sophia laughed out loud and said, "I won't tell on you!"

"Can you get my ball for me?" Sandi asked. "I'm not 'posed to cross the street without my mom or dad either."

"Sure!" Sophia said still giggling about the "strange people" comment.

Squatting down in front of the storm drain, she grabbed the ball; it took one mighty tug to free it from where it had wedged itself. Once it was loose, she bounced it once on the street, then served it volleyball style back to its young owner.

Sandi caught it on the bounce, smiled and waved her thanks before running back into her yard where she and several other little girls were playing kickball.

"Don't kick it so hard Cindy!" Sandi said. "My ball almost got eated by the storm drain!"

Cindy apologized then Sandi added, "My sister told me about a movie that showed a clown that lives in storm drains! If you see a red balloon by one…RUN!"

The kickball kids reminded Sophia of her former neighbors whom she used to babysit at least once a week. In fact, the remaining money from her last baby-sitting job was wadded up in her pocket along with the five ones left over from the twenty her mother had given her.

Homesickness struck her hard; she choked down a cry that was suddenly trying to escape from her mouth and she felt tears well up in the corners of her eyes and her throat tightened.

"Man, this sucks big time." She thought, then quickly moved down the sidewalk as the hot tears began to slide down her cheeks.

Two blocks later she discovered a small park that was placed neatly between two large houses. It appeared a house had once been located there, but at some time in the distant past, it had been replaced by the park.

The Coombs House Park, as proclaimed by a large bronze sign that was in need of polishing, was fronted by an old, tall, trumpet vine-covered red brick and wrought iron fence with a double gate guarding its entrance. To the left of the gate was a second bronze plaque with a bias relief showing a two-story house that had been built in eighteen forty-nine.

The plaque said that at the time of its demise, the Coombs House was one of the finest examples of an antebellum era home in the entire state! It had been the home of several generations of the Coombs family who had made a sizeable fortune running a brick factory.

The house had been badly damaged by a tornado in the late nineteen forties. Instead of repairing or rebuilding the old house, the Coombs family had the large lot cleared and used an estimated ten million red bricks to build the park.

"Wow! That's a lot of bricks!" Sophia thought.

She entered the park through the wrought iron gate that squawked in unoiled protest as she opened it. The park was bordered on all sides with a red brick wall twelve feet high and two feet thick. It was also covered with an abundance of the pungent trumpet vine and every twenty or thirty feet, there was an arched window guarded by more wrought iron bars.

The entire floor of the park was paved with the same red bricks that made up its walls; their tops were rounded and smooth from the rubbing of countless park goer's shoe soles. The bricks that made up the unique park were inscribed with the words, "Coombs Brick Works est. 1847".

Just inside the double gate was a large red granite rock at least ten feet high. At its top, a fountain of clear water exploded into the air causing a rainbow effect when the sun's rays caught it just right. The water cascaded down the red rock's sides and into the reflecting pool that surrounded it.

Secured to the rock was another bronze plaque, this one wore a coat of green patina, which detailed how the large red granite boulder was brought to the park on August 11, 1947 in honor of the one hundredth anniversary of the founding of the Coombs Brick Works. Surrounding the fountain was an abundance of benches that had been strategically placed where the numerous trees would provide the most shade to anyone visiting.

A mother with a little girl who looked to be three or four years old entered the park through the main gate just as Sophia had done moments before.

"See Eva, the big rock is still here!" The woman said to the little girl.

The little girl, Eva, erupted into happy cheers and began clapping her hands.

"It squirts told water!'" Eva announced.

Sophia had to chuckle; little kids always made her laugh!

Eva and her mother made several trips around the granite rock fountain stopping many times so Eva could put her hands in the fountain's water and splash.

"You sure do love that fountain, Eva!" Her mother said with the smile that seemingly all mothers had when watching their child being truly, unabashedly happy!

"I does!" Eva said before smacking her hand into the pool of water once again. "It's my favoritest place in the whole world!"

"Who loves _you_ Eva?" Her mother asked.

Eva squatted down and put her wet hands on the ground leaving their tiny outlines on the red bricks. She grinned! Then she launched herself upward as hard, fast and high as her little legs would let her.

"Allbody does!" Eva exclaimed.

Chuckling, Eva's mother asked, "Do you want to go get some ice cream from Marion?"

"Yes!!!" Eva shouted.

"Well, let's get going then!" Eva's mom said.

"Bye Durl!" Eva said to Sophia as she took her mother's hand to, presumably, head to Morton's for ice cream.

"Bye sweetie!" Sophia said watching the mother and daughter head to the gate.

Once she was alone again, Sophia removed a walnut-sized lump from her front pocket. It was a toy locket that had come from a fast-food restaurant's kid's meal. Most girls going on fifteen years old wouldn't be caught dead with such a childish toy, but Sophia was no ordinary almost fifteen-year-old girl, and the childish aspect of the plastic locket is what made it so very special.

Tossing the basketball back to Sandi and her friends had brought on a fresh torrent of memories and homesickness. Sandi, who wasn't supposed to talk to "strange people", was very much like Caitlyn Smart, a little girl Sophia had known since her parents had brought her home from the hospital nine years ago.

As Sophia was getting in their van to leave for the last time, Caitlyn ran up and pressed the locket into her hand and made her promise not to forget her. The tears flowed from both girls.

One of the photos inside was of a two-year-old Caitlyn sitting next to her infant sister, Mackenzie. She was holding a grape Tootsie Pop in her left hand and was lightly touching Mackenzie's head with her right. The smile of the new "big sister" was precious, to say the least.

Opposite the early picture of the sisters was a recent one of a now nine-year-old Caitlyn. The photo was a simple black and white and Caitlyn's hair had been styled so one long strand curled down the right side of her face and under her chin. She looked much older than nine. It gave a preview of the stunning beauty she would become in a few short years.

When Sophia looked at the picture of the bright-eyed little girl, a single tear rolled down her cheek. She wiped it away with the back of her hand and she recalled her neighbor from the time she had already started thinking of as her "other life". She slumped with her back against the bench and remembered when she had babysat a three-year-old Caitlyn.

~ ~ ~ ~ ~ ~

"Where's Mighty Mac?" Sophia asked when she entered the Smart's kitchen.

It was unusual to be asked to babysit just one of the Smart girls, if watching them while their mother was in the next room working on her scrapbooking was really babysitting, but Sophia didn't mind. The Smart's usually paid her ten dollars for her time and when you are nine years old, ten bucks was a small fortune!

"She's at her grandmother's house so it'll just be you and Caiter-tot today." Tammy Smart said. "Mac is teething and is a little grumpy. I think it will be easier for you if she's not here. Actually, it will be easier for all of us if Mac isn't here."

"Caiter-tot" was the name her mother called Caitlyn because of her nearly endless desire for the little potato plugs.

"Hi Sofa!" Caitlyn said bounding into the kitchen. "Let's play!"

She grabbed Sophia's hand and literally pulled her into the living room. Her pronunciation of her name as a piece of furniture always amused Sophia.

The morning went by quickly. Time flies when there are tea parties to be thrown for Barbie and all her friends, books to be read and videos of a curious little monkey and his friend, the man with a big yellow hat, to be watched. As George was being suited up for his trip into space, Caitlyn abruptly dozed off. Sophia quietly slipped back into the kitchen and fixed them both some lunch. A fifteen-minute nap would be good for both of them.

~ ~ ~ ~ ~ ~

"What you doing Sofa?" Caitlyn asked as she came into the kitchen.

The fifteen-minute nap had lasted closer to thirty. She probably would have slept longer, but when her video ended, the player automatically shut off and the television switched on. Some television judge was issuing a lengthy diatribe to a television defendant and that had awakened Sophia's charge.

"I am fixing you and me some lunch." Sophia said.

"Can I help?" Caitlyn asked.

"Sure!" Sophia said. "You can set the table."

Caitlyn eagerly took the heavyweight paper plates from the counter and precisely placed them on the kitchen table. She crossed the kitchen to the drawer where the silverware was kept and retrieved two spoons, two forks and two knives and skillfully placed one of each next to each plate before returning to Sophia's side.

"All doners!" Caitlyn announced.

"You are a good helper Caity-pillar!" Sophia said using the nickname she had come up with for her neighbor.

"I am a Caiter-tot, nots a Caity-pillar, Sofa!" Caitlyn reminded her seriously.

"I'm sorry Caiter-tot, I forgot." Sophia said. "And I am a Sophia, not a Sofa!"

"I forgotted too." Caitlyn said then changed the subject totally. "I don't know why people think those are pretty." She said pointing to what was in Sophia's hand.

"What?" Sophia asked.

It amazed her how Caity could switch topics so quickly, sometimes even in mid-sentence.

"Those aren't very pretty." Caitlyn said pointing at the long green vegetable Sophia was preparing to slice. "I don't know why they are called cute-cumbers."

It took nearly five minutes before Sophia could even speak. Every time she tried; giggles issued forth in place of her voice!

~ ~ ~ ~ ~ ~

As she looked at the plastic locket, the tears flowed.

"I want to go home." Sophia said morosely to no one as her tears returned in force.

Chapter 03

Sophia was stretched out across the porch swing to the right of the front door with her flip flops lying askew on the recently painted wooden floor below her. In the time they had lived in the house, Dan Young had begun renovating many things; his first project was the porch.

~ ~ ~ ~ ~ ~

Part one of the porch project was new paint. He had repainted the railing and the posts a bright white when Sophia and her mother made a trip to stock up the pantry. When they had gotten back, he said he had been really busy painting while they were gone, but to Sophia the porch looked the same as when they had left. She suspected the only thing her father had been busy doing was taking a nap!

However, when she sat on the porch railing, she found out he *had* been busy. Fortunately, the paint he had used was latex and the blue jean shorts she had been wearing were easily salvaged with a couple of washings in extremely hot water, an abundance of soap and the liberal application of elbow grease.

Later that afternoon he painted the porch's floor a battleship grey. To Sophia it looked more blue than grey, but it did contrast nicely with the rails and posts. While he was painting, the front door was not usable, so they had to use the door that opened into the laundry room instead.

After applying the last coat of paint in front of the front door, an event of such magnitude Dan asked Sophia and her mother to stand on the sidewalk to watch, they went to the laundry room door and found that although unlocked, it was stuck shut and would not budge.

The Youngs did the only thing they could do; they locked up and went to a place called Show Me Pizza. One of the mail carriers had told Dan about it saying that it used to be called the Burger Palace, but when the new owners bought it, they changed it to a pizza place, much to the irritation of most of the long-term residents of the little town.

When they were seated, Sophia was given the responsibility to pick out what they would have for supper. She ordered a large ham and pineapple pizza.

"Yes, pineapple DOES belong on pizza!" Sophia had said just before she took her first bite.

Part two of his home improvement project was the addition of new L.E.D. lights to the porch's old fixtures and the installation of a sensor that activated them whenever it detected movement. For the first three nights, any time a car drove down the street, the front porch glowed brightly. After the third night and several adjustments with a tiny screwdriver, the lights only came on when there was movement on the steps leading up to the porch.

The third part of his project was the addition of a large outdoor fan to the center of the porch's ceiling just in front of the front door. Dan and Carol had used the fan several nights to stir the breeze when they were sitting in the porch swing. It had made being outside comfortable. Sophia had not joined them; she sequestered herself in her room.

The last part of the makeover was the screening in of the porch which would make sitting outside in the summer less "buggy". He had installed screen panels on the inside of the porch railings. He was currently in the process of building and adding screen panels between the top of the railings and the porch's ceiling, but he was at a standstill because he had run out of screen. Sophia had heard him tell her mother that he would be done with that part of the project by the end of the week as long as the hardware store's order came in on time.

~ ~ ~ ~ ~ ~ ~

Dan Young mounted the steps and crossed to the swing where Sophia was sitting. He raised her legs, sat down and put her feet in his lap. She gave him the quick, disdainful glance that only teenage girls who are in a bad mood can do. She saw that he was wearing an actual mail carrier's uniform; something he hadn't done in quite some time.

Once he became the Postmaster, his uniform had become a button-down shirt, necktie, slacks and dress shoes. She remembered a conversation he and her mother had at supper sometime the week before where he had said he was going to be going with both city mail carriers to learn their routes.

"City mail carriers?" Sophia had thought at the time. *"This place is about as much a city as a kiddy pool is an ocean."*

"So, how was your day Sophia?" He asked.

"The same as yesterday and the day before that and the day before that and…" Sophia said in a flat, subdued sarcastic tone before being cut off in mid-sentence.

"Sophia, that's enough!" His tone was stern.

Normally, Sophia and her father had a close, conflict-free relationship, but since the move, she had not had much to say to him. He knew she was angry, and he knew *why* she was angry, but his patience was beginning to wear thin.

"I know you don't like that we moved. I know you miss your friends and I know that you are upset about having to give up your cheerleading spot, but I am getting tired of the attitude and so is your mother!" He said. "This is home."

"No!" Sophia said. "This is where we are *living*, but it is definitely not home!"

"We've been here for over a month." Dan said.

"I don't have to like it!" She said flatly without looking at him.

"No, I suppose you don't." He continued. "But staying mad isn't going to change anything except maybe the lining of your stomach."

"Huh?" She said looking at him.

Sometimes her father was very obscure with his comments.

"Sophia, if you keep on being mad you just might give yourself an ulcer, and that would be no fun at all no matter where you were living." He said.

"Humph." Sophia snorted, folded her arms across her chest and looked at the house across the street.

"What's that?" Dan Young pointed to the book that was on her lap unopened and unread.

"A book." Sophia said in the same flat tone.

As a rule, a new book was something she would devour as quickly as she had the milkshake earlier that afternoon. However, she had read no more than the teaser on the dust jacket.

"Where did you get it?" He asked.

Sophia sighed dramatically. She hated it when she was mad at him and he forced her to talk.

"I bought it at the library. I guess the author is from here or something and there's going to be a book signing." She said. "The lady at the library said they are using it as a kickoff for the new school year or something."

He took the book and perused the dust jacket just as she had done earlier that day.

"Sounds interesting. When is the book signing?" He asked.

"The Sunday before school starts." Sophia said. "I think she said it starts at like two o'clock or something."

"Are you going to go to it?" He asked.

"Might as well, it's not like there's anything <u>else</u> to do here."
Sophia said returning her gaze across the street to where two red squirrels
were chasing each other up, down and around an oak tree.

"Sophia Elizabeth Young, there is *plenty* to do here!" Dan said
sternly.

She cringed internally. Her father, like her mother earlier that day,
had used her first, middle and last name; it was definitely game over.

"Dad..." She started to speak in a plaintive tone, but he cut her
off.

"No!" His voice was level, but firm. "Your mother and I have
given you plenty of space and lots of leeway since we moved here."

"But..." She started to say. She was stopped again from
speaking; this time with a raised eyebrow and the beginnings of "The
Look".

Sophia had received "The Look" just three times in her nearly
fifteen years of life and it was something she did not want to see again.
She had asked him about it once and he had laughed when she called it
"The Look". He told her that she should call it "The Green Wire" instead.
When she asked why it should be called that, he told her the green wire
was the one that was used for "grounding"!

"But nothing!" He said in the same firm tone. "Since we've been
here you've done nothing but sulk and complain about everything."

"Dad..." She began again in an attempt to plead her case, but she
was silenced with a single raised finger.

Dan Young's eyebrow remained raised. Now his index finger was
raised as well; Sophia knew she had pushed him to his limit of grace
regarding the move, and now there would be a penalty to pay.

"As it seems you can't find anything to do but pout; <u>I</u> will find
something for you to do." He looked hard at his daughter; although he
was not actually angry with her, he was trying to give that impression.
"Most, if not all, of your moving boxes are still in your room unpacked,
right?"

"Yes." She had been waiting for the proverbial other shoe to drop
and here it came.

"Well, after today they <u>will</u> be unpacked, and your things <u>will</u> be
put away. Then you can break the boxes down and put them in the office.
Understand?" He said.

Sophia knew there was no arguing with her dad. Once he had
decided something, changing his mind was very nearly impossible.
Besides, she knew she had really been pushing it with both her parents.

"Yes." She said as her eyes began brimming with tears.

"Get to it then." He said.

Sophia picked up her book, slid off the porch swing, slipped on her flip flops and disappeared into the house.

After she had gone inside, Dan sat watching the two squirrels that were still racing up, down and around the large oak tree across the street, scolding each other in chittery squirrel speak.

He had had to endure several moves with his family when he was growing up, so he knew how Sophia was feeling. But unlike his father's moves; ones made to find the job that might finally get them ahead; this move was one that would allow them to become debt-free in just over a year.

Taking the Postmaster's position had increased their income by many thousands of dollars and the equity from the sale of the Springfield house had outright paid for the house whose front porch he was now sitting. They had taken out a small loan to pay for the improvements they wanted to make, but that loan and the remaining balance on what they owed on the minivan would be paid off in fourteen months.

Dan and Carol dedicated themselves to putting the nearly thirteen hundred dollars per month they had been paying on a mortgage into Sophia's two 529 college funds. They could put eight thousand dollars into each of them every year and get a nice tax deduction in the process! If things worked out like they hoped, Sophia would be able to graduate college without any student loans hanging over her head.

As upset as Sophia was about having to forfeit her spot on the cheerleading squad, Dan was doubly upset. When he realized what she would have to give up, he considered not accepting the new job. After many sleepless nights and many, many long discussions with his wife, co-workers and even a friend who was one of the guidance counselors at Kickapoo High School, he had accepted the job.

His one regret was that he had not included Sophia in the discussions even though it had affected her more drastically than anyone else. He hated that she was upset, but sometimes doing what was best was not always the most popular decision. Besides that, he knew his daughter, and he had predicted that within two weeks of starting school, their new home would begin hosting the new friends she would make just like they had done in their old home in Springfield. With what he was working on, he knew their home would be "the" place for her friends to hang out!

He returned his attention to the squirrels. They had momentarily stopped chasing each other so they could chatter at and scold another who had come down the tree from a higher branch.

The interloper was smaller, but it was colored the same shade of red. After a moment of being yelled at by the bigger ones, the small red squirrel ran back up the tree and disappeared into a hole in the tree's trunk.

"Looks like someone else got sent to their room." Dan said to no one.

~ ~ ~ ~ ~ ~

Sophia's room was in the older part of the house at the end of a short hallway just off the living room. When she had complained she could hear the television when she was in her bedroom trying to go to sleep even when her room's door was closed, her dad had told her that he would put in a door to cut down on the noise.

While taking some measurements, he found the hall actually contained a pocket door. After freeing up the door pull that had been covered over with a coat or two of varnish, he gave it a couple hard tugs and the old solid wood door popped loose and slid easily from its hiding spot inside the wall. When the door was closed, it diminished the sounds from the rest of the house enough to where Sophia did not notice them anymore. It also allowed her to cross between her bedroom and her bathroom in any state of dress or undress as she saw fit.

Once the door had been rediscovered, her parents had said she no longer had a bedroom, but now she had a suite! Having a bathroom that was totally hers was one of the few things she actually liked about the move, but she would gladly give up that particular luxury and return to her old house, her old friends, her old neighborhood, her old school and her old life.

In one corner of her bedroom were two stacks of boxes that had brought all her worldly possessions from Springfield.

"Kind of pathetic." Sophia thought as she walked over and looked at the cardboard towers. *"Everything I own can be moved in fifteen cardboard boxes."*

Anger suddenly flared inside her and without any real thought, she kicked the taller of the two stacks of boxes and two things happened rather quickly. First, a sharp pain shot through her big toe and foot; kicking boxes fully laden with dense objects such as books while wearing only flip flops was not the smartest thing she could have done. Second, the recently assaulted stack of boxes teetered back and forth before toppling over with a loud, thunderous "THAWUMP" as they hit the floor and wall!

"What was that?" Her mother called from the living room.

"I should have closed both doors." She thought.

"My boxes of stuff just fell over." Sophia yelled back. "It's fine."

But it really wasn't fine; her big toe was throbbing, and she wondered if she had broken it! As for the boxes, they were all still taped shut and nothing had fallen out. Her "breakables" were in a separate box that she had slid under her bed. Other than her toe, no real damage had been done.

Begrudgingly and with a slight limp, Sophia finally began the task of unpacking. Fifteen minutes later, all the boxes were empty, all her belongings were put away and her toe had mostly stopped hurting.

She ripped the brown packing tape from the bottoms of the boxes and flattened them out before taking them to the room her father was converting into an office.

He had begun the task of stripping the paper off the walls right after he had run out of screen for the porch project. The office wallpaper project had become more of a chore than he had anticipated; he had not expected to find seven layers of wallpaper on the old plaster.

Now that he was down to the last layer, it was evident that the room had once been a child's room or more correctly, a baby's room. There were pictures of pink and blue wooden blocks and various pastel-colored teddy bears all over the last layer of wallpaper.

Sophia sighed, tossed her broken-down boxes on top of the pile that was already there and returned to her room. With the boxes gone, she noticed that her room was quite large; a lot bigger than her room in Springfield, but again, she would gladly trade the larger room and a private bath to go back to the house she would always call home.

"I'd even sleep under the stairs just like Harry Potter if I could just be home again." Sophia thought, remembering the storage area under the stairs at her old house.

She looked around her new room and noticed that where the stack of boxes had fallen, the wallpaper next to the baseboard was pushed in and had torn vertically several inches up the wall. Remembering how heavy the boxes were, she was not surprised that it dented the wall.

"I probably will get "The Green Wire" now." She thought matter-of-factly.

Chapter 04

What caught her eye was a tear in the wallpaper. It was a straight, non-ragged rip that looked like it had been made using the edge of a ruler. Two feet above the indentation and at least that far across from it was a protrusion nearly the same size as the dent next to the baseboard. After exploring the area with her fingers, Sophia realized that the wallpaper was concealing a small door.

"What in the world?" She thought.

She retrieved the electric blue Buck pocket knife her father had given to her just before her first actual non-family camping trip the summer she turned twelve. It had been a church mission trip to the Blue Ridge Mountains in eastern Tennessee where she had kissed a boy named Melvin or Marvin or something. The kiss, unlike the boy's name, was memorable only because it was her first one, but nothing more.

She used the Buck to follow the original tear up the wall, then across to the protrusion. She made a second cut of the same length down the wall and across to her starting point. When her boxes had fallen over and hit the wall, they had pushed the door's lower-right corner into the space behind it causing the upper left corner to protrude out. Using the knife blade as a lever, she popped the door open without any real difficulty then looked inside.

"This is so cool!" Sophia thought. *"Finally, something interesting happens in Podunksville!"*

The space contained two old boxes stacked on top of each other. The top box advertised that is had once held twelve quart-sized canning jars. When she removed it from its tomb, she noticed how light it was, then brushed away decades of dust, dirt, grit and grime from its top, and looked inside. What she found were two film canisters. Based on their size, they were most likely eight-millimeter. Sophia knew about the pre-video, pre-digital format from the media class she had taken in summer school just before she started the sixth grade.

"Was that really three years ago?" She asked herself. *"I guess time flies when you're <u>not</u> having fun."*

The lid of the first canister, which was labeled "XMAS 1968", came off with an audible pop. Inside was a black ribbon of film tightly wound around a small reel. Sophia slowly and carefully unwound the first few inches of the movie, held it up to the overhead light and looked at some of the frames. Although each frame was small, she could make out the face of a young, blonde-haired woman standing next to a Christmas tree with two small children at her sides.

"I wonder who they are?" Sophia thought before carefully rewinding the celluloid strip back onto the reel.

The second film canister had a label that appeared to say, "Easter 1954", but it was written in pencil and had faded to nearly unreadable over time. Inside, Sophia found another ribbon of black film wrapped tightly around a reel. The overhead light revealed a young girl wearing a frilly white dress, white gloves and a white, wide-brimmed hat. The girl was smiling and after studying the images, Sophia could see that she was missing most of her front teeth.

"I wish I had a movie projector." Sophia thought.

She rewound the old film, replaced the canister's lid and turned her attention to the second box which had begun its life as a White Owl cigar box. She brushed off the accumulated grunge and opened the lid where her knowledge of old media again paid off as she found ten reels of audiotape. Like the film canisters, the tapes were labeled with old brittle masking tape with cryptic numbers written across them.

"Without a reel-to-reel tape player, these won't do anyone any good." Sophia thought.

She set the boxes aside and returned her attention to the space behind the wall. Other than the outline of dirt where the boxes had sat for years, there was nothing else she could see. It didn't help that only one of the three bulbs in her ceiling fan's light fixture was working, so she retrieved a small, extremely bright L.E.D. flashlight from her nightstand. It instantly revealed more treasure in the long-forgotten space.

On the right side of the opening was a dusty charcoal grey case. After a couple of tugs, she was able to wiggle it free. As with the boxes of film and audio tapes, Sophia first had to clear her latest find of its accumulated dust, dirt, grit and grime. Once she had dusted the case off, she popped the two round black snaps on the lid and flipped it open.

A wall charger, microphone and a user's manual fell out and landed on the floor. Along with those items was a black cord with a sliding switch on one end. At the top of the sliding switch was the word "ON" and on the bottom end was the word "OFF". On the opposite end, was a plug like you would see on the end of a set of earbuds.

"A tape recorder! A reel-to-reel tape recorder! This is so retro!" Sophia thought excitedly.

The tape recorder was in near pristine condition. She could see that before being entombed behind the wall it had been well cared for. It was small; approximately seven inches square and had two control knobs; both the color of coffee after a goodly amount of cream had been added. The knob on the right was multi-featured and controlled the rewind, stop, play and record features of the unit. The knob on the left controlled the volume and had a range from "MIN" to "MAX". Just to the right of the volume control were three earphone type jacks. The first was labeled "E-PH" and was most likely for an earphone.

"I could probably plug in an external speaker in there." Sophia thought as she examined her find.

The second jack was labeled "REM" and meant nothing to her. Nothing like that had been discussed in her media class. She made a mental note to search out the jack's meaning.

"Or maybe this used to belong to Michael Stipes!" Sophia laughed out loud then hummed a few notes of "Stand"!

The last jack was labeled "MIC" and was obviously for the microphone. Sophia picked up the one that had fallen out when she had opened the case. She inserted its single prong into the jack, where it snapped into place. She had never seen a microphone like it before; it was as big as a television remote control and was the same coffee-colored tan as the knobs on the tape recorder. It also had a silver metal screen covering the top third. The one unusual thing Sophia noticed about the microphone was that it lacked any buttons or switches.

"I bet this is what turns it on and off." Sophia said to herself picking up the black cord. She plugged it into the "REM" jack. *"But I won't know until I get it powered up."*

Above and to the left of the audio and electrical jacks was a built-in speaker. It was white and about two inches square. Six of the eight screws that held the case together had the very beginnings of rust which were the only cosmetic defects Sophia could find on the front of the machine. On the back was the battery compartment whose door had some small scratches on it. When she looked closer at the scratches, she saw they were the letters "L K B". They were the only other defects she found on the old recorder.

"I wonder what that means." She thought.

Using both thumbs, Sophia began sliding the battery compartment's door open. It was slow going; it had been decades since the compartment had been last opened.

"I hope there are no batteries in here." Sophia thought. *"If there are, they would have leaked acid and ruined the whole thing."* The compartment popped open, it was empty and acid-free.

"Why is there a hole in your wall?" Dan Young asked from the doorway.

Sophia jumped; she had been so engrossed with inspecting the items from the cubbyhole she hadn't heard her father come into the room. She explained the incident with the box of books falling but omitted the part where she had kicked them.

"So, what's that in your lap?" He asked.

"It looks like an *old* tape recorder." Sophia said happily. "It's probably even older than you Dad; unlike most things!"

Although she had been put out with her father for the move and was still just a little mad about literally being sent to her room to finish unpacking; she could never stay mad at him for very long.

"And look what else I found." She said opening the box of old reel to reel tapes.

"Was there anything else?" He asked.

"Just these." Sophia opened the box of the film canisters. "There are just two of them."

"What are they?" Dan squatted down to get a better look at what she had found.

"Film; I think it's some old home movies." Sophia said.

Chuckling, he asked, "There's not a movie projector in there is there?"

"I don't know." She said. "Let me check."

Picking up the small but mighty L.E.D. flashlight, Sophia lay prone on the floor and pressed her face into the opening and pointed the light in the direction of where she had found the recorder. There was nothing but dust in the space that extended at least two feet beyond the edge of the opening. Turning the light to the other side of the cubbyhole, Sophia was rewarded with another dust-covered container; this one was much larger than the tape recorder.

"Oh wow! There *is* something else in here Dad." She exclaimed!

"What is it?" He asked.

"I'm not sure." Sophia said.

After a perfunctory tug, a bulky, dusty case of some type slid free, and Sophia set it on the floor amid the growing pile of grime-covered boxes.

"Bell and Howell?" She asked as she wiped some dust from the nameplate that was affixed to the case's side. "What is this?"

"My guess is that it's a movie projector." He said. "Here, let me see it."

There were two silver knobs on the front and after a couple of quick twists, Dan was able to remove one side of the case and confirm what he suspected. It was old, practically prehistoric Sophia would no doubt say, but the Bell and Howell projector, like the tape recorder, was in very good condition. The detachable power cord was limber, the arms that held the film reels, easily and smoothly rotated into position and both announced they were in their proper place with a loud click.

"Do you think it still works Dad?" Sophia asked.

"We'll know in just a minute." He answered.

Sophia watched her father expertly attach the take-up reel on the rear of the projector.

"Hand me one of those movies." He said.

Sophia handed him the "Easter 1954" reel and he threaded the old celluloid through the projector and attached the end to the take-up reel.

"I'll plug it in." Sophia said grabbing the cord, then rolled to her left and slid the prongs into the closest outlet.

"Here we go, Sophia!" He said. "Don't be surprised if the film breaks. I'm sure it's brittle if it's from nineteen fifty-four."

He turned the power switch to the "On" position, and the old projector rattled and clicked to life. Even though the lens was pointed at the wall, there was no image being projected.

"Well, at least we know it works." He said. "It probably just needs a new bulb."

"I don't think it needs a new bulb Dad.' Sophia said with a grin.

"You don't? Why not?" He asked.

She removed the lens cap and a blurry image flashed on the wall; it was a little girl hamming it up for the camera. After adjusting the focus, they could see she was blonde and looked to be about seven years old. She was wearing a frilly white dress, white gloves and a white, wide-brimmed hat. A few seconds into the film she picked up an Easter basket. When she would smile at the camera it was easy to see she was missing most of her front teeth.

"I wonder who she is." Sophia said.

"I guess you'll have to knock some more holes in the wall and see if you can find out." Dan said as he switched off the projector.

"Dad! It wasn't my fault!" Sophia protested.

"It was my toe's fault." She thought.

"I'm just teasing. Besides, it's kind of interesting what you found." He said. "Is there anything else in there?"

Sophia returned to her prone position and used the small LED flashlight to again investigate the cubbyhole and peered beyond where the old Bell and Howell projector had sat.

"Oh wow!" She said.

"What?" He asked.

"Hang on." She said, then contorted herself into the recently rediscovered space behind the wall in order to reach what she saw at the far end of the compartment.

"What is it?" He asked.

"Another box!" She said.

Unlike the projector, the latest find slid grittily and easily out of the cubbyhole's opening.

"I'm going to need to vacuum now." Sophia said as she brushed more dust and grit on to the floor.

The box was securely sealed with more of the tenacious brown packing tape. It took several hard tugs to finally get it to release its grip on the box. When it finally pulled free, it took a fair amount of the box's cardboard skin with it. Inside, wrapped in newsprint, was a Bell & Howell Filmo Double Run Eight movie camera.

"Whoa! It's a movie camera!" Sophia said excitedly. "I wonder if it works."

"Let me see it." Dan said.

Sophia handed the camera to her father who examined it from several different angles before flipping out a half-circle piece of metal from the right side of the camera that was stamped, "WIND FULLY AFTER EACH SHOT".

"It's spring-driven." He announced.

"What?" Sophia asked.

"No batteries." He said. "Here, watch this."

Dan began turning the half-circle counterclockwise. After several rotations he stopped, then depressed a small button below the lens and it rattled to life.

"Um, Dad?" Sophia asked. "Does it have any film in it?"

After a moment of study, Dan figured out how to open the camera.

"No, it's empty." He said showing her the space where the film was supposed to go.

Sophia picked up a random reel of tape from the box. She studied the writing on the masking tape that had been there for decades. It had a date and a small heart in fading red ink written on it.

"Hey." He said.

Looking up, Sophia asked, "What?"

"Here." He handed her a piece of paper.

"An address and phone number?" Sophia asked.

"An address and phone number." Her father confirmed.

"For what?" She quizzed.

"For an old lady who needs some help from someone like you." Dan said.

He was amused by his daughter's curiosity. Whenever something had intrigued her, she wrinkled her brow and the corners of her mouth pulled down into what could be mistaken for a frown. She wasn't frowning; this was just the mask she put on when she was truly interested in something and was thinking about it.

"Help doing what Dad?" Her curiosity had been piqued.

"Cleaning, most likely; she didn't really say." He said.

"And my name came up how?" She asked.

"It came up when this old lady was talking to me at the post office today just before I came home." He pointed at the piece of paper. "She was buying stamps and said she needed someone to help her at her house for a few hours this week."

"So, you volunteered me?" Sophia asked.

"Yup!" Dan Young said with a grin.

"She could be some sort of wacko. I mean we *are* living out in the middle of nowhere." Sophia said before adding with a grin. "I think I even heard banjos playing the other day!"

After he had finished laughing, Dan said, "I checked her out with the city carriers; Maude Adelaide is a bit eccentric, but she is a good person."

"Eccentric? What does that mean?" Sophia asked.

"It means she's loaded!" Dan said. "And she'll be paying whomever, fifty dollars a day and she would need whomever for at least two days, maybe more!"

"That's like…oh my gosh!" Sophia said drawing herself into a sitting position.

"Oh my gosh, like, for sure!" Dan said in his best imitation of his teenaged daughter's speech.

"Dad, I do not talk like that!" Sophia insisted with a giggle and a smile.

"I.K.R.? O.M.G. and L.O.L.!" He teased. "Like, I'm sorry for sure Soph-a-pillow!"

"Soph-a-pillow?" She looked at her father as if he had just lost his mind.

"Okay that one *was* pretty bad." He said. "But you are just sooo sweet!"

"If you don't get help here, Dad." Sophia began with a snort. "Get help somewhere."

He started to laugh, and his mirth drew in his daughter. For the next five minutes, they sat side by side as he recited verbatim Moon Unit Zappa's "Valley Girl" in pure eighties "Val-speak".

"Should I call her?" Sophia asked after he was done with his recitation.

"If you want the job, I think you'd better." Dan said.

~ ~ ~ ~ ~ ~ ~

Sophia called the mysterious Maude Adelaide, but there was no answer, so she left a message and her cell phone number. Fifteen minutes later while she was vacuuming up the grit and grime from her cubbyhole treasure, she received a text from the number she had called telling her to be at the address on the paper at eight o'clock the next morning if she didn't mind working on a Sunday.

"NO PROBLEM." Sophia replied. "SEE YOU IN THE MORNING."

"Now what?" She asked herself as she put the vacuum away in the laundry room. *"What to do, what to do?"*

A smile crept across her face as the answer to her question popped into her head. She quickly returned to her bedroom to the newly rediscovered tapes and the tape player. It didn't take her long to realize that the writing on the masking tape on the outside of the old reel to reel tapes contained the dates when the recordings were made. The dates began August 12, 1962 and ended July 31, 1969.

"Wow, seven years of someone's life." Sophia said to herself. *"Where should I begin?"*

On a whim, she picked up the tape labeled "8-27-66". It was the one with the faded red heart on it! She threaded the magnetic tape thru the player/recorder and around the take-up reel. Having the instruction manual was definitely a big help. Then, after plugging the unit into an outlet, she switched it on and waited for the recording to begin playing.

The speaker popped and crackled as the old tape made its journey through the old, but pristine machine. Sophia was pleased with her powers of deductive reasoning; the black cord was what controlled the tape recorder! When she flipped the switch from "ON" to "OFF", the tape and the recorder instantly stopped. She also knew the audiotape was old just like the film and she may get only one opportunity to hear what was recorded on it.

Using more of her media knowledge, she grabbed the laptop she had gotten for Christmas. She began rummaging through the nylon carrying bag and found the three-foot-long, braided audio cord that she had ordered from an online site with a gift card she had received for Christmas from her friend Audrey.

She turned the computer on, and after it had booted up, which took mere seconds thanks to a solid-state hard drive and thirty-two gigs of RAM, she clicked an icon on the laptop's screen labeled "Audio-Clone".

Audio-Clone was an audio recording program she had used to record music from the internet in nearly any format she wanted. When her parents heard what she was doing, they laughed and told her she was making a "mix tape". They laughed all the harder when she had asked what "mix tape" meant.

"If this works." Sophia thought. *"I can save all the recordings as digital files!"*

She inserted one of the male ends of the audio cable into her computer's microphone jack and the other end was inserted into the earphone jack of the old reel-to-reel tape recorder.

"Wait a second." She thought.

Digging through the many pockets of the laptop's carrying case, she found the "Y" shaped cable that had come with the long, braided audio cord and a set of small earbuds. Sophia unplugged the audio cord from the earphone jack and replaced it with the Y-shaped cable. She plugged her audio cord into one of the jacks on the Y-shaped cable and her earbuds into the other one.

"Now I can listen and record at the same time." She thought as she placed the small speakers into her ears. *"Here we go!"*

Sophia clicked the bright red virtual record button on the Audio-Clone program and moved the black cord's switch from "OFF" to "ON". The audio recording program instantly came alive as a female's voice began speaking from the old tape and the Audio-Clone screen turned into living Rorschach inkblots.

There was some popping and crackling on the tape as the unknown woman spoke, but surprisingly, the audio quality of a tape that was over fifty years old, was quite good.

"Well, today's the day! In just a few hours I will be married!" The woman said.

Sophia listened intently, but, if she were honest, she did feel a little bit guilty listening to someone else's recordings. The guilty feeling wasn't strong enough for her to stop listening however, so she kept the reels turning.

"I'm scared and nervous, but I am soooo happy!" The voice said. *"I think it's funny and just a little weird that it was on this exact date, four years ago that I met Jerry!"* The voice paused for a brief moment. *"Last night I couldn't sleep, and I did the math. I met Jerry one thousand four hundred sixty-one days ago which is thirty-five thousand, sixty-four hours or two million one hundred three thousand eight hundred forty minutes!"* The voice laughed then added, *"I am such a math nerd!"*

Sophia laughed at the admission. Like the woman on the tape, she was a bit of a math nerd too! She, unlike so many of her friends, found math a lot of fun!

"Okay...it's eight-thirty and I need to start getting ready! In just a few short hours I will cease being Laura Kay Butler and will become Laura Kay Collins!" The woman, Laura, said.

There was an audible pop as Laura switched off the recorder. Sophia pressed the Audio-Clone's virtual stop button as she flipped the black cord's switch back to the "OFF" position.

"Well, this is interesting!" Sophia said to herself. *"Too bad I have to go to bed."*

~ ~ ~ ~ ~ ~

After brushing her teeth and putting on her pajamas which were in actuality a pair of soft cotton shorts and an equally soft cotton tee shirt, Sophia slipped into bed. Before switching off the small lamp next to her bed, she looked at her laptop, the old reel-to-reel tape recorder and the old cigar box that contained the neatly labeled tapes.

"What am I going to hear?" Sophia asked herself. *"What is on those tapes?"*

Chapter 05

Maude Adelaide's house was completely on the other side of town, but as Sophia had observed, the town wasn't that big so walking there wasn't a real problem. She was going to ride her bicycle, but when she started to roll it out of the garage, she saw that the front tire was flat.

"Well, it's only flat on one side." Sophia thought as she parked it and began walking.

The dew was cold on her feet and for a moment she considered swapping her flip flops for the tennis shoes she had brought with her in her drawstring backpack, but after thinking about it she continued on; she didn't want to be late. As she walked, she again took in the town and had to admit, but only to herself, that it was what some would call quaint.

"Quaint?" She asked herself. *"Where did that word come from?"*

She became lost in her thoughts about the move and having to start over at a new school. The feelings of anger and despair begin to well up inside her. With a great deal of internal strength, she willed those feelings away.

"I am NOT going there today!" She said to herself.

Instead, she began thinking about all the items she had discovered in the cubbyhole and what she might find recorded on those tapes.

"I wonder why all that stuff had stayed hidden in the wall for so long?" She thought.

If she could ask C+C Music Factory that question, they would undoubtedly say, "Things that make you go, hmmm."

"You there, girl!" A voice called.

Sophia jumped as she was pulled from her thoughts and back to the street she had been walking. She had been "wool-gathering"; a term she had learned from her grandmother and hadn't noticed that the street had gone from tree-lined to tree overtaken.

"Hellooooo!" The voice said again, only this time with a shrill falsetto tone that reminded Sophia of Mrs. Doubtfire. "Oh, fish feathers, are you deaf?"

Sophia made a slow spin looking around for the person who had called to her. She couldn't locate the source of the voice, but from its strength, she knew the owner was close by.

"I *am* right over here!" The voice said.

Sophia saw a hand wave from some tall grass and, moving closer, she saw that an elderly woman was sitting on the ground next to a nearly obscured rusty mailbox.

"Are you okay?" She asked taking her cell phone from the front pocket of her jeans.

"Of course, I'm okay!" The woman snapped. "I just can't get up!"

"Why not?" Sophia asked.

"Gravity!" The lady enunciated each of the word's three syllables precisely. "Now, what are you going to do with that thing; change channels on a television or open a garage door?"

"It's a cell phone." Sophia said. "I'm going to…"

She stopped in mid-sentence; the small screen, which normally showed the time, date and a background picture that she changed at least once a week, was black.

"Oh man! I didn't charge it!" She thought.

"Well?" The old woman asked.

"The battery's dead." Sophia said.

She had spent so much time with the things she had found in the cubbyhole, she had completely forgotten to plug it in before going to bed. However, there was a charger in the drawstring backpack so she could charge it while she helped the old lady.

"Well, I guess you'll have to help me up yourself then won't you." The old woman said.

"Are you sure?" Sophia asked. "I mean you didn't hurt anything did you?"

The old woman laughed before saying, "I didn't hurt anything except maybe my pride. I dropped my newspaper and gravity took over when I went to pick it up. This heap of grass broke my fall. I just cain't get up."

The woman was small. With her direction, Sophia was able, without much effort at all, to help her to her feet.

"Are you sure you're okay?" Sophia asked.

"Right as rain; fine as frog hair!" The old woman said then asked abruptly, "Who are you anyway?"

Although not talking to strangers - *strange people* - had been drilled into her from an early age, Sophia felt revealing her name to this lady wouldn't be much of an issue. If picking up a newspaper had nearly incapacitated her, her threat level was pretty low.

"My name is Sophia Young." She said.

"Humph!" The old woman snorted. "I'm Maude Adelaide by the way, been expecting you."

"Oh, okay!" Sophia said.

Maude looked at Sophia and Sophia looked at Maude for several eternal seconds before Maude nodded down the overgrown drive that could easily be missed if you weren't looking for it.

"So, will the *young* help the old to her house?" She asked.

"Sure!" Sophia said and offered Maude her arm.

Together they picked their way down the path that had, once-upon-a-time, been a graveled driveway. Emerging from the emerald tunnel, Sophia was surprised by the house she saw. The yard was neatly trimmed; she could see the diagonal lines the wheels of a lawnmower had left in the grass. There were tidy flower beds arranged on either side of the steps that lead up to the front porch.

The colors were plentiful, and the fragrances were mixed and smelled wonderful! On the far ends of each of the neat flower beds were large lilac bushes! Their scent was Sophia's favorite as was their frosty purple color!

"There's a man coming later today to do something about that mess we just walked through." Maude said. "Myrtle never would let me tend to it properly before. She said since we don't have a car, keeping up a driveway is money wasted. I said that if you can't get to the street to go to the grocery store, all the money in the world wouldn't do you much good."

"Who's Myrtle?" Sophia asked while taking in the beautiful flowers.

"My twin sister." Maude said flatly.

Sophia turned away from the flowers.

"There are *two* of you?" Sophia asked without really thinking about what she was saying.

Chuckling, Maude said, "Yes, and I am the *nice* one!"

"I'm sorry. I didn't mean…" Sophia stammered hoping that she had not upset the old lady.

Maude Adelaide flapped her hands in a "Don't worry about it" type of motion and laughed.

"Where is your sister?" Sophia asked.

"She had to go in the nursing home for a bit." Maude said with no trace of being upset.

"Oh, my goodness, why?" Sophia asked.

She remembered some elderly relative who had had a stroke. After they were released from the hospital, they had to go to a nursing home to live.

"She took a fall and broke her hip last week. The old fool was trying to wash the windows and fell off a step ladder!" Maude said matter-of-factly as if it were an everyday occurrence. "I had to call the ambulance to come and get her and take her to the hospital. They could barely get down the drive, so I am having it cleaned up."

"That's too bad." Sophia said. "I hope she's doing alright."

"Myrtle is giving them what for over to the home." Maude said. "I'm sure they'll be glad when she leaves, no doubt about that!"

"Do you think she *will* be coming back here?" Sophia asked motioning to the house.

"A broke hip ain't going to slow Myrtle Adelaide down very much, even if she is a hundred and two!" Maude said. "She'll be up and at 'em in no time, mark my words! Fact 'tis, she is already using a walker to get around!"

"She's a hundred and two and broke her hip last week and she is already *walking?*" Sophia said.

"They had her up six hours after the surgery!" Maude said. "Darnedest thing I ever heard of!"

"Wait, wait, wait." Sophia said. "*You* are a hundred and two...too?"

"Last time I checked." Maude chuckled. "Fact 'tis, I will probably live forever."

"You will?" Sophia asked incredulously. "Why do you think that?"

"I looked it up...very few people die between the ages of a hundred and two and a hundred and three!" Maude said. "The odds are in my favor!"

Sophia stood looking at Maude gap mouthed. Her expression was not missed by the old woman who broke out into laughter which caused Sophia to laugh as well.

"When my Aunt Mae broke her hip, she didn't take her first step for nearly a month." Maude continued.

"A month, really?" Sophia asked.

"Yes." Maude said. "Then, just as she was getting back to her room at the hospital after the first time on her feet in weeks, she dropped dead."

"WHAT!?!" Sophia exclaimed.

"The doctor said it was some sort of blood clot. Said she had laid in bed too long before they got her up and around." Maude said. "I reckon that's why they get 'em up and around so quickly these days."

"I suppose so." Sophia agreed.

Their conversation ended and there was another awkward silence which went on just a little too long.

"I s'pect you want to know what I'm paying." Maude Adelaide finally said.

"Dad already told me." Sophia said, relieved Maude had started speaking again. "What I'd really like to know is what I'm going to be doing."

"Cleaning!" Maude said. "This house ain't been cleaned proper since…" Her voice trailed off

"Since when?" Sophia asked.

"If I recollect rightly, it was in nineteen sixty-three." Maude said.

"Whoa!" Sophia gasped.

In her mind's eye, she imagined the interior of the house to be like one of those hoarder's houses she had seen on television. The look of wide-eyed surprise on Sophia's face was not missed by Maude.

"Now don't go getting yourself all worked up, the house ain't *that* bad!" Maude said with a slight glint of mirth in her eyes that Sophia totally missed.

"I didn't mean…" Sophia started to say, but was interrupted by Maude's hand flapping, "Don't worry about it" motion.

"Besides, Myrtle had it cleaned last time so I s'pose it is my turn to do it. Let's go inside and get started." Maude said.

~ ~ ~ ~ ~ ~ ~

There were a couple dozen dusty, tape sealed boxes sitting on the living room floor that looked like they hadn't seen the light of day since, well, nineteen sixty-three. They reminded Sophia of the boxes she had found in the cubbyhole in her room. The rest of the living room was spotless.

"Maude was right." She thought. *"Not bad at all."*

"We're going to take out all the junk in those boxes and get rid of it." Maude said. "We'll put what needs saving back in 'em."

"Sounds good to me." Sophia said.

The first two boxes were easy, they contained tax records from the nineteen fifties and Maude saw no reason to keep them any longer.

"If the *Infernal* Revenue Service wants to audit us for nineteen and fifty-seven; more power to 'em!" Maude said with a wry smile.

"Don't you mean the *Internal* Revenue Service?" Sophia asked.

"No!" Maude said quickly. "I mean the *Infernal* Revenue Service."

She espoused the belief that the government wasted too much money and she wanted to provide them with as little of her hard-won earnings as possible.

As she was tossing the papers into a large, galvanized trash can, Sophia saw the income total for one of the sisters from nineteen fifty-seven; the amount was a staggering seventy-five thousand dollars!

"Whoa!" Sophia thought as she deposited the papers into the can. *"If that was back then, what is it now?"*

The other boxes were a different story; they contained photographs. The majority were in albums, but there were a fair number of loose pictures as well. Many were like those of her own family Sophia thought; old people holding babies, people sitting around a table loaded with food having to wait to eat while the picture was taken to memorialize the Easter, Thanksgiving, Christmas or other celebration's bountiful feast. Most of the people in them were wearing forced smiles and had the "Will you please take the picture already" look in their eyes.

Sophia picked up and looked at a picture of an elderly couple with three grown women standing with them. As she looked, she saw that one of them was a much younger version of Maude Adelaide who, like those in the larger group photo she had looked at, was wearing a forced smile.

One of the photo albums caught Sophia's eye after she had brushed off a coating of fine dust. She ran her hand across its white leather cover that was intricately embossed with an anchor wrapped by a chain and the letters "U.S.N." across its center.

"This is pretty!" She said admiring the fine craftsmanship of the tooled leather.

Maude snatched the album away. "I wondered where that got to." She said. "I ain't seen that in a month of Sundays!"

Sophia was taken aback by Maude's gruffness; there was no "please" or "thank you", just the lightning-fast snatch and grab of the old album. However, after watching how the old woman began to look through the album and smile; she realized the curtness was not personal, it was just her way.

After several minutes of looking at photos she hadn't seen in years; Maude noticed her young helper was staring.

"What? Ain't 'cha never seen someone looking at pictures before?" Maude asked.

Sophia giggled and smiled. "By the way you're smiling; I'd say they are pretty special pictures."

"Harrumph!" Maude snorted, then after a beat, she smiled and chuckled too. "I s'pose you're right about that Laura."

Giggling again Sophia corrected her. "My name is Sophia."

"Of course it is, that's what I said…Sophia." Maude spoke her name as precisely as she had the word gravity when they had first met by the mailbox.

~ ~ ~ ~ ~ ~ ~

"Someone must have had a good day!" Carol Young said when Sophia stepped through the front door.

She had verbalized what her husband was thinking, and Sophia *was* smiling! It was the first time either of them had seen her smile; really smile, since before they had made the move.

"It was really okay. The work wasn't that hard either." Sophia said.

Carol had been somewhat skeptical about letting Sophia go and spend time with a stranger but had kept those thoughts to herself. She knew if she had said anything, it would have only added fuel to the "I hate it here!" fire that Sophia seemed to stoke nearly every day.

"What is Maude Adelaide like?" Dan Young asked his daughter.

"Did you know she is a twin, and they are one hundred two years old?" Sophia asked.

"I did not!" Dan said. "I mean I knew there were two of them, but I had no idea how old they were. They sure get around pretty good."

"Maude does." Sophia said. "Myrtle broke her hip last week and is in the hospital. That's why Maude is cleaning house!"

"She's cleaning house because her sister broke her hip?" Carol asked.

"She's cleaning house because it's her turn to clean it." Sophia said.

"When did Myrtle clean it?" Dan asked.

"Maude said the last time it had been really cleaned was in nineteen sixty-three!" Sophia said.

"How bad is the house on the inside?" Dan asked.

Sophia laughed! "It's actually in better shape than ours!"

Dan and Carol laughed. They laughed less about what Sophia had said and more because she had laughed her old pre-move laugh; they had missed it.

"And she is a pretty neat old lady even if she does forget things." Sophia said.

"She forgets things?" Dan Young asked. "Like what?"

"Well, for starters, my name." Sophia said.

"She forgot your name?" Carol asked.

"Yeah, she kept calling me Laura." Sophia said. "I corrected her a few times, but I finally quit. It seemed like it was making her mad or something."

"You probably just reminded her of her granddaughter." Carol offered.

"She was never married Mom." Sophia said. "She was engaged, but that's all she told me."

"When are you going back?" Dan asked.

"Tomorrow. Maude wants me to help her go through some more boxes of junk with her." Sophia said. "Now, I want to go take a shower and get this dirt off me."

As she walked past her father, she held up her hands and pretended to wipe them down the front of his shirt.

"I wouldn't!" He warned with a grin.

"I might!" Sophia teased while wiggling her fingers at him.

With that, she headed to her bathroom to clean up. The shower felt wonderful as it washed away the dust and grime, she had acquired helping Maude clean. She followed her shampoo's directions and lathered, rinsed then repeated the process to make sure her hair was clean; moving the old boxes had stirred up a lot of dust.

~ ~ ~ ~ ~ ~

Supper was a treat; her mom fried three pounds of bacon which she combined with sliced, fresh tomatoes and lettuce; BLTs were always a big hit at the Young house. Sophia was even more pleased when she saw a brand-new jar of her favorite sandwich dressing sitting prominently in front of her plate!

"What's with the green label?" Sophia asked.

Her father tapped the label where it announced this version was made with olive oil.

"Healthier!" Dan said. "That means you can double up on it!"

"Does it taste the same?" Sophia asked skeptically as she spun the green lid off the jar and dipped the tip of her knife into the white sauce, dabbed a small amount onto her tongue and tasted it.

"Well?" Her dad asked. "Does it meet your impossibly high standards?"

"It will do." She said after a moment. "But with bacon, I bet that any health benefits are gone."

The sandwiches, all four of them, contained generous amounts of crispy, crunchy maple smoked bacony goodness, a thickly sliced tomato and copious amounts of the new olive oil infused sandwich spread.

Sophia left the lettuce off the sandwiches, it made everything slide around which usually ended up in a great sloppy mess that sometimes oozed down the front of her shirt. For dessert, there was a plate heaped with thick slices of watermelon.

"Where's the salt?" Sophia asked.

Dan Young slid the transparent acrylic tube, which had recently been filled with pink Himalayan salt, across the table to Sophia.

"You are going to have high blood pressure!" He said.

"You are the one who taught me to put salt on watermelon. You said it brings out the sweetness. My untimely hypertension will be on *your* hands!" Sophia said before taking a large bite out of the black diamond watermelon slice.

"Does that actually work?" He asked as he sprinkled some of the salt on Sophia's arm.

"What are you doing?" She asked.

"Trying to bring out *your* sweetness!" He teased.

Chapter 06

Helping Maude clean had worn Sophia completely out. After clearing the table of the supper dishes and loading the dishwasher, she went to her room making sure the pocket door was closed. It was her intention to digitalize more of the audiotape and didn't want to be disturbed. But first, she stretched out across the bed, her head at the foot and her feet on her pillows to take a quick cat nap. Instead, she fell into a deep, sound dreaming sleep.

~ ~ ~ ~ ~ ~

"Hello, Sophia!" A voice said from the shadows of an old, covered bridge.

After her eyes had adjusted, Sophia saw a balcony that overlooked a creek and standing near the balcony was a blonde-haired young woman who might have been fifteen years old; she might have been twenty years old; Sophia couldn't tell.

"Hello." Sophia said as she looked around at the dream world she was now in. "Who are you?"

"My name's not important right now." The young woman said.

"How do you know who I am?" Sophia asked.

The young woman's laugh was melodic; it reminded Sophia of the wind chimes her friend Audrey's mom had hanging on their patio back home.

"You're having a dream Sophia, so I know everything about you!" The young woman said.

"This dream seems so real." Sophia said.

"The best dreams always do!" The young woman said, then motioned toward the balcony. "This is one of my favorite spots!"

Sophia joined the young woman at the wooden overlook which jutted out from the bridge over the creek. The railing was course and weather worn and she felt the raised wood grain press into her forearms as she leaned on it. Standing there gave Sophia a wonderful view of the water that babbled and rippled in the rock-lined bed below. The trees on the opposite bank had the most intense shades of green she had ever seen; some were so dark they appeared nearly black. The sunbeams that found their way through the canopy of leaves were laser shots of white-gold light that looked like they would burn whatever they touched.

"I have never seen a covered bridge with a balcony before." Sophia said. "For that matter, I have never seen a covered bridge before. This is kind of cool!"

"It sure is!" The young woman said. "That's why I picked this place to get married!"

"I can see why; this is so pretty!" Sophia said.

Realizing what the young woman had said, Sophia spun away from the bridge's railing and felt a small sliver pierce her right arm halfway between her wrist and elbow. She winced at the splinter's sting but did nothing about it.

"Wait! _You_ are married? You don't look much older than me!" Sophia asked incredulously.

"Well, you are seeing my fifteen-year-old self. I chose this version of me so you could relate a little better." The young woman laughed her melodious laugh once again.

Sophia stepped away from the balcony's railing and looked at the blonde young woman. "What do you mean 'this version' of you?" Sophia asked.

Again, the young woman laughed. "You'll understand soon enough."

"I wish I understood now." Sophia said.

The young blonde-haired woman, who had the most intensely beautiful blue eyes Sophia had ever seen, stepped next to her. Sophia could smell a sweet floral scent; it was faint, but it smelled wonderful!

"You found some reel-to-reel tapes, didn't you?" She asked. "They were in that cubbyhole in the wall of your room."

"How do you know about...?" Sophia began but remembered this was a dream, albeit a very realistic one, so what the blonde woman knew came from Sophia's own thoughts and memories. "Yes. There was a box of them." She paused and thought before correcting herself. "Well, there was another box that had a couple of home movies in it."

"The tapes will help you." The blonde woman said.

"How will some tapes that are a hundred years old help me?" Sophia asked. "And why do you think I need help anyway?"

The blonde woman laughed heartily before responding. "They are more like sixty years old! Please don't make me any older than I already am! And once upon a time, I was 'The New Girl' at school too. In fact, I was 'The New Girl' my freshman year of high school at the same high school _you_ will be starting next week." She said.

"Dreams are strange sometimes." Sophia said.

"That they are Sophia." The blonde woman said. "That they are."

The young blonde woman was dressed in summer attire; her jean shorts were dark blue and were cuffed midway between her knees and hips. She had on a light blue three-button collarless short-sleeved tee-shirt and white tennis shoes. The shoes were spotless white Keds, and Sophia noticed she was not wearing any socks. Her hair was the color of ripe wheat and it had been put into a beautiful braid that ended just above her waist. And the young blonde woman seemed vaguely familiar to Sophia.

"You moved to a new school your freshman year of high school?" Sophia asked.

"Not just any high school. It is the same one you'll be going to next week!" The blonde woman said. "And thank you!"

"What?" Sophia asked.

"You were admiring my braid; thank you!" The blonde woman said. "It's really easy to do you know?"

"But how did…" Sophia began before remembering. "Dreams."

The young blonde woman laughed. "Yes, dreams! Now come with me, I want to show you something and I'll show you how to braid your hair like this if you want me to."

"Really?" Sophia said.

"Yes, really!" The blonde woman promised. "Now come on!"

They crossed the length of the bridge to its far end and scrambled down the mostly overgrown bank to the creek. Positioned almost under the bridge's floor was a large wooden platform that extended several feet out into the water.

"What is that?" Sophia asked when the wooden structure came into view.

"That is a fishing platform." The blonde woman said. "It's been down here since practically forever. That's where we are going!"

They continued their way down the embankment to the platform and the summer air cooled appreciably as they stepped into the shade underneath the bridge. The blonde woman had a broad smile on her face as she stood looking at the creek.

"This is one of my favorite places!" She said to Sophia. "I came here the first time in the summer of nineteen sixty-three!"

"But that was…" Sophia began.

Laughing, the blonde woman simply said, "You're dreaming Sophia. Time doesn't have to make sense in a dream!"

"Sorry." Sophia replied. "It's just…"

"It's weird!" The blonde woman said.

She crossed the width of the platform to retrieve two five-gallon buckets. She flipped them over, sat on one and motioned to Sophia.

"Come here Sophia, I'll show you how to braid your hair without anyone helping you." She said.

Sophia sat on the vacant, upended bucket that was just behind the blonde woman. It was metal and had a blue and white checkered pattern on it. Looking down she saw the words 'Hillyard' and 'St. Joseph, Missouri' written around its sides.

The blonde woman quickly removed the rubber bands at the end of her braid and ran her fingers through it. Her hair fell free and loose across her shoulders and back. Sophia watched and was envious; she wished her hair had the sunny hue that this young woman's hair had.

"Lemon juice and sunshine." The blonde woman said matter-a-factly as she continued to fluff out her hair.

"What?" Sophia asked.

"Lemon juice and sunshine." The blonde woman repeated.

"Lemon juice and sunshine?" Sophia asked.

Laughing, the young woman said, "You were wishing your hair was colored like mine. Lemon juice and sunshine helps with that, but I think your hair would turn red if you used it."

Sophia, laughing herself now, said, "Okay, but you knowing what I am thinking is kind of weird!"

"I'll try and not answer your questions before you ask them, but it is kind of hard so if I slip up, please forgive me." The blonde woman said.

"Will do!" Sophia said.

"I squeeze the juice from a whole lemon into a spray bottle, then I add a teaspoon of baby oil to it and top it off with water." The blonde woman offered.

"Baby oil?" Sophia asked.

"Baby oil keeps the lemon juice from drying out your hair and making it brittle." The blonde woman said. "And it smells good too! I call it 'Laura's Suntan Lotion for Blonde Hair'!"

Sophia thought for a moment before asking the blonde woman the question that had popped to the front of her mind.

"I knew nothing about using lemon juice and baby oil to lighten my hair." She said.

"Okay." The blonde woman said

"If this is my dream and you know what I know, how come I didn't know about that until you told me?" Sophia asked.

The blonde woman turned to Sophia, smiled her beautiful smile, wiggled her fingers like she was casting a spell and said, "Magic, I guess!"

Sophia laughed out loud. "Okay, magic it is!" She said. "But what is your name?"

The blonde woman looked at Sophia, her blue eyes seeming to stare right into her very soul. The look was so intense Sophia averted her gaze.

"I know you have lots of questions, but Sophia…" The blonde woman paused.

"Yes?" Sophia answered somewhat meekly.

"YOU already have the answers to those questions." She said.

"If I do, why don't I know what they are?" Sophia said.

The blonde woman laughed yet again. "Because you haven't thought about where those answers might be found! And I will tell you this, they are a lot closer than you realize!"

Sophia sat on the bucket thinking about where those answers might be found, but for the life of her she could not figure it out.

"Quit thinking so hard Sophia!" The blonde woman said, then asked, "Who is on that tape you listened to last night?"

"Uh…?" Sophia said. She could not remember any names that were on the tape. "I don't remember."

"Okay. What did I just call the suntan lotion for hair that I make?" The blonde woman asked.

"Laura's Suntan Lotion for… Are you Laura?" Sophia asked.

"Yes, I am Laura! Pleased to meet you!" Laura said. "I told you that you already had the answers!"

"Are you a ghost and are you haunting me?" Sophia asked seriously.

After Laura quit laughing, she said, "Let's get your hair fixed up"

Sophia moved her Hillyard bucket back a little and watched as Laura's hands moved effortlessly first dividing her hair into three equal parts then quickly weaving it into a braid.

"Did you see how easy that was?" Laura asked.

"Yes!" Sophia said. "Could you do it again and I'll do mine while I'm watching you."

Laura removed her braid again, then started over so Sophia could watch and follow along. Sophia's first several attempts were not that great. After the fifth attempt, Sophia's braid was much better than her first, but it still needed some work.

"Hey, let me do it for you this time." Laura said. They changed places and Laura quickly created a wonderful version of her own braid in Sophia's dark chestnut colored hair. "If you keep working at it, you will be able to do this and have the best braid you have ever seen!"

"How's it look?" Sophia asked.

"It looks great if I do say so myself!" Laura said with a giggle.

"I wish I could see…" Sophia stopped in mid-sentence as an idea popped into her head.

"You wish you could see what?" Laura asked.

"Hang on." Sophia said.

She took her cell phone from her back pocket. Even in this dream she had her cell phone with her.

"WHAT is that?" Laura asked.

"It's my phone." Sophia said.

"THAT'S a phone?" Laura asked. "You've got to be kidding me!"

Sophia looked at Laura and thought she was trying to be funny, then had a realization, "You really don't know what a cell phone is do you?"

"Never heard of it." Laura answered. "So, what are you going to do with that…phone?"

"Nothing. YOU, however, are going to take a picture of my braid." Sophia corrected.

"I thought you said that was a phone." Laura said. "So, it's a camera too?"

"Let me show you something." Sophia said, then gave the nineteen sixties Laura her first and most likely, only lesson regarding cell phones and their features.

"That is pretty neat!" Laura said.

She snapped several pictures of the braid she had woven into Sophia's hair.

"I have a question." Sophia said.

"What is it?" Laura asked.

"If you get lemon juice by squeezing lemons; where does baby oil come from?" Sophia asked mischievously.

Laura laughed heartily and shook her head back and forth and shrugged her shoulders as if to say she didn't know the answer to her question.

Once her laughter was under control, Laura said, "Please listen to the tapes. The dates that they were recorded is written on them so listen to them in order. They will help. Now, I have to go."

"Why?" Sophia asked.

Laughing, Laura said, "Because you are waking up!"

"I am?" Sophia said.

"Yes, you are!" Laura laughed. "Before I go, I want to ask you something."

"What?" Sophia asked.

"Are you feeling that you have lost your mind and are going crazy?" Laura asked. "Because of what's been going on this summer?"

"Yes!" Sophia confided. "I feel EXACTLY like that!"

"You know, sometimes you have to do something a little crazy to prove to yourself that you are actually sane." Laura said.

"What do you mean?" Sophia asked.

"You'll know when the time is right." Laura said.

~ ~ ~ ~ ~ ~

Sophia awoke with a jolt and her foot smacked her nightstand knocking her digital alarm clock onto the floor. The upside-down neon green numbers told her that it was ten twenty-three p.m. She had slept hard and vividly for just under three hours. Now, however, she was wide awake and remembered, amongst other things, that she hadn't brushed her teeth after supper.

"That dream was so real. Laura was so real!" She thought as she crossed the hall to her bathroom. "

As she was reaching for the lilac-colored, soft-bristled toothbrush that she had bought the day she had arrived in Podunksville, she looked in the mirror above the sink and screamed...really loud! In seconds, her mother and father were knocking on the bathroom door.

"Sophia!" Her mother asked as she tried to open the door. "Sophia, what's wrong?"

Fortunately, Sophia had other business to take care of besides brushing her teeth when she came into the bathroom, so she had pressed the small button lock next to the doorknob.

"Sorry, there was…" Sophia said trying to think of something that didn't sound too crazy. "…a spider in the sink."

She didn't lie to her parents, well, not too often anyway, but she couldn't tell them what had really made her scream.

"It sounded like you had seen a ghost or something." Carol Young said.

"Sorry, Mom." Sophia said.

"You do know you are bigger than a spider, don't you?" Dan Young asked with a laugh in his voice.

"I know Dad, but…uh…" Sophia stammered. "I just woke up."

"It's okay honey. You just scared us when you screamed." Carol said.

"Sorry, Mom. I just hate spiders." She wasn't lying; she *DID* hate spiders. "Goodnight." She said.

"Goodnight Soph." Dan said.

"Goodnight Honey," Carol said.

Sophia stood transfixed by what she was looking at in her mirror. It was her; she knew what she looked like, but there was a big change in her appearance and that change is what had startled her enough to scream.

Draped across her left shoulder was the most perfect braid she had ever seen. It was just like the blonde young woman's hair, Laura's hair, from her dream.

"How?" Sophia asked.

Her mirror twin said nothing; silence was her answer.

Sophia brushed her teeth, washed her hands and then went back into her bedroom. As she pulled her shirt off to get into her pajamas, she felt a sting on her right arm. Without needing to look, Sophia already knew what was there, but she looked anyway. Halfway between her elbow and wrist, sticking in her skin at a right angle was a piece of wood, a splinter.

"From the bridge." Sophia whispered. "Oh, wow oh wow oh wow!"

Chapter 07

During her walk back to Maude's house, Sophia had been just a little more than preoccupied with the happenings of the previous night.

"How did my hair get braided? Where did the splinter come from? Did I braid it in my sleep? Did I whack my arm on something and get the splinter from that?" She wondered to herself.

Before going back to sleep, Sophia had done an internet search on all the things she could think of regarding people's activities during their sleeping hours. She found literally thousands of articles about sleepwalking, including one about a girl who walked nine miles between her home and her uncle's house. There was another article about a man who mowed his yard while sleepwalking and he was totally nude when he did it! That article had made her laugh out loud even though she was still shaken up about her braided hair.

"I couldn't have done that braid; I don't know how to braid. Well, I didn't know how until Laura showed me how to do it and then actually did it for me before I woke up." Sophia thought. *"But Laura talked me through how to braid it. Maybe I saw a video on hair braiding and my subconscious mind took over and I did it in my sleep."*

She paused in her thoughts and concluded after a few more steps down the sidewalk that she had indeed "slept-braided".

Satisfied with her own counsel, Sophia continued her walk to the Adelaide house, but stopped again when she remembered the last part of her dream. With a little apprehension and a lot of nervous curiosity, Sophia took out her cell phone and hesitantly opened the folder labeled "Photos". Staring back at her were several pictures of her braid that had been taken outside.

"How did those pictures get on my phone?" She thought. *"They WERE taken outside during the day and it sure wasn't daylight when I was sleeping!"*

With a quick upward flick of her finger, on the first of the braid pictures, she found the "Details" heading that showed the date when the picture had been taken. This was followed by a series of numbers, the letters ".jpg", the words "internal storage/DCIM/Camera" and the size of the digital photo in both megabytes and pixels.

Had anyone been watching Sophia at that moment they would have seen her forehead wrinkle in a way that would have made one of the Star Trek Klingons proud! She swiped to the next braid photo and the one after that and the one after that. Each time the date said the same thing.

"How could I have pictures on my phone that were taken on June 17, 1963? The phone must have done one of its updates and messed up the date." She thought.

Looking around, she saw that she was close to the Adelaide's mailbox and the tuft of grass that had cushioned Maude when she had fallen. She pointed the phone's small camera lens at the mailbox and snapped a picture, then she opened the photo, swiped upward and saw the picture's date. It was many, many years after nineteen sixty-three.

"That is impossible!" Sophia thought. *"There's no way, no way at all."*

She felt mild nausea churn in her stomach. She also looked at the red spot on her arm where she had plucked out the splinter.

"What is going on?" She thought.

~ ~ ~ ~ ~ ~

Sophia had another weird feeling as she stepped clear of the Adelaide's overgrown lane; this one was a feeling of foreboding.

Sitting in front of the yard gate was a large dark green dumpster that appeared to have been delivered by an even larger truck based on the wide and somewhat deep tracks that were pressed into the soft dirt and gravel of the driveway.

"What has Dad gotten me into?" She asked herself as she climbed the steps to the front door.

"Where have you been?" Maude demanded when she opened the front door and found Sophia standing there with her hand poised to knock. "The day's half over!"

"Uh, it's eight-fifteen." Sophia said putting her hand down. "You told me to be here at eight-thirty."

"Of course, I did." Maude confirmed.

Cocking her thumb toward the driveway Sophia asked, "Did the man not come yesterday?"

"He did, but his help didn't." Maude said. "He'll be here tomorrow, or so he claims."

"Oh." Sophia said. "Okay."

"Well, what are you waiting for, there's work to be done." Maude said.

With that invitation, Sophia stepped inside, and she felt her stomach drop like it sometimes did when her father had topped a hill a little too fast while driving. Sitting in the middle of the living room were hundreds of boxes of all sizes literally stacked floor to ceiling.

"Where did all those come from?" Sophia asked.

"The backroom." Maude said flatly.

"Ugh!" Sophia groaned. "Where do we start?"

Chuckling, Maude said, "At the beginning; always at the beginning."

Sophia laughed in spite of herself and took off the baseball cap she was wearing.

~ ~ ~ ~ ~ ~

Before heading out to Maude Adelaide's house, Sophia had donned a baseball cap she had in her room. It was from the Warrensburg, Missouri High School baseball team, the Tigers! She didn't really have much of an interest in baseball, but a college friend of her father's, Chris somebody, had given it to her when they stopped for lunch on the day they had moved from Springfield to Podunksville. She thought her dad had said he was the head baseball coach at the high school there, but she didn't really remember.

The day they moved was a gigantic, teary blur in her memory. The cap, however, did allow her to hide her newly braided hair from her parents. She knew they would ask questions about it and she knew she did not have any answers for them, so for today at least, she was a Warrensburg Tiger!

Her mother had commented on the cap as Sophia was heading out the door. Thinking fast, Sophia said that her hair had gotten really dusty the previous day, so she was going to wear the cap to keep it cleaner. This was not a lie; her hair had been dirty as evidenced by the particles of grit left in the bathtub after she had showered. Her mother had bought the story hook, line and sinker.

~ ~ ~ ~ ~ ~

After entering the Adelaide's living room and seeing all the boxes, Sophia took the cap off. Maude began directing her to her tasks, but stopped in midsentence when she took a second to look at Sophia and asked, "What did you do to your hair?"

"It's braided." Sophia said simply. "I…uh…I got it done last night."

"Well, I s'pose it'll keep you cooler." Maude surmised.

The first two hours were easy; most of the boxes were summarily thrown away without needing to be gone through. Sophia enjoyed the loud dull thump some of the boxes made when she threw them into the empty metal dumpster. Helping Maude kept her mind occupied so she wasn't thinking about the dream.

"Dreams are strange sometimes." Sophia thought. *"Dreams are really strange sometimes."*

~ ~ ~ ~ ~ ~

During their first break, Sophia asked Maude a question. "You said something about someone named Charley yesterday; who was he?"

Maude looked at Sophia for a moment remembering that she had indeed spoken of Charley and she wondered why Sophia was interested. She decided to tell her what she wanted to know. It had been a very long time since she had spoken to anyone about Charley Reynolds.

Shuffling over to one of the end tables that stood guard on either side of the sofa, she retrieved the embossed white leather photo album that had caught Sophia's attention the day before. Maude opened it again and smiled.

"S'pose you are wondering why I am acting like a schoolgirl with her first crush, ain't you?" Maude asked.

"No! I…well…just a little." Sophia stammered.

"Come over here, I want to show you something." Maude said.

Sophia did as she was asked and was rewarded with a picture of a much younger Maude standing next to a handsome young man dressed in a spotless white Navy uniform.

"Charley was Charles Howard Reynolds!" Maude said fondly. "He was a good man who didn't deserve what he got."

"What do you mean?" Sophia asked.

"He died in World War Two." Maude paused and absently wiped away a single tear from the corner of her eye. "You asked about Charley. Are you still interested?"

"I am." Sophia said because she actually was interested.

"And don't think just because I'm talking, you'll be getting out of any work. You are going to earn your pay!" Maude said.

"No!" Sophia said emphatically. "Not at all."

To prove her point, she took a box from one of the stacks and began sorting through it.

"Charley was from the wrong side of the tracks." Maude said. "You know what that means don't you Laura?"

"He was poor?" Sophia asked even though she knew what the term meant.

She also knew better than to correct the name slip Maude had made. If she did, Maude would probably stop talking.

"As poor as a church mouse on a Saturday night as my daddy used to say. The Reynolds' didn't have a pot or a window either if you know what I mean!" Maude chuckled.

Sophia laughed. "I've heard that one!"

"Well, I'm getting ahead of myself; let me start at the beginning," Maude said.

She grew quiet as she collected her thoughts; she hadn't told any part of her story to anyone outside of her family before. Why was she telling Miss Sophia Young? She really did not know. Perhaps she was lonely, worried about Myrtle, getting senile or maybe a combination of all of the above; but whatever the reason, Maude Adelaide began telling her tale.

"Charley Reynolds and his brother started school with us when we were both in third grade if I remember correctly. Most times, at least when the weather was warm, he and his brother Alton didn't wear shoes. As I said, they were poor, and saving shoe leather was one way their family made their money go just a little bit farther. But let me tell you, they were both neat as pins and clean as whistles!

The first time I saw him I thought he was a good-looking boy, but my oldest sister Margaret didn't think much of them. She thought they were poor trash, and we should not associate with them." Maude said.

"Just because they were poor?" Sophia asked with widened eyes.

"Yes, just because they were poor and because we had more than most." Maude said. "I'm surprised Margaret never drowned when it rained either."

"Why?" Sophia was confused.

"Because Margaret's nose was always turned up in the air!" Maude said. "If it ever came a rainstorm she would have drowned for sure!"

"Oh!" Sophia laughed in spite of herself.

She hoped Maude wouldn't get mad because of it. She didn't. In fact, she laughed right along with her before she resumed her tale.

"And when her nose wasn't turned up, she used it to look down at people like Charley and Alton." Maude continued. "It was because of her, Margaret I mean, that Daddy kept Charley and me apart."

"That's just dumb!" Sophia said. "Just because you are poor doesn't mean you are a bad person."

Maude cackled with laughter. "Yes, you are quite right Laura."

"Can I ask you something, Maude?" Sophia asked.

"You just did, but I guess you can ask something else." Maude's eyes twinkled as she spoke.

"Who is Laura?" Sophia asked.

"Who?" Maude asked.

"Laura. You've called me that name several times." Sophia said.

Maude regarded the question for a moment before answering. "She was my great-niece; Margaret's granddaughter." Maude said. "She was the last person to help us clean house. She was about the age you are now." She paused before adding, "So sad what happened to her and her children."

"What did happen to her?" Sophia asked.

She could tell by the expression on Maude Adelaide's face that whatever had happened still bothered her.

"That story is for another time. I was talking about Charley." Maude said abruptly. "But just so you know, you and your folks are living in the house Laura and Jerry lived in right after they were married."

"We are? How do you know that?" Sophia asked.

"This town ain't very big. Folks know lots of things that go on around here. And when someone new moves in, well, that is a topic of discussion." Maude said.

"Did Laura have blonde hair and really pretty blue eyes?" Sophia asked.

"Yes, she did!" Maude said. "How did you know that?"

"This town ain't very big! Folks know lots of things that go on around here." Sophia teased.

Maude gave Sophia a surprised look, then a sly, knowing smile crept across her face.

"That's one for you Sophia!" Maude said.

"Was it a schoolgirl crush?" Sophia asked mischievously. "With you and Charley I mean?"

"Hush!" Maude said. Her tone was sharp, but she gave her admonition with a smile. "Or I won't tell you anything."

Sophia made a show of pretending to lock her mouth and then tossing away the make-believe key.

"Anyway, we went through school together, Charley and me, and when we got into high school, I found myself liking him. He really was a good-looking young man!" Maude said.

Chapter 08

"Hello Charley!" Maude said as she took her seat in American History class. "Did you study for today's test?"

"As best I could." Charley said. "Ma's been sick again and coughing and a hacking. It was hard to read with all that racket. I 'pert-near went out to the barn with a kerosene lantern to study."

"I'm sure she wasn't doing it on purpose." Maude said.

"No." Charley laughed. "I don't s'pose she was."

"Has she been to the doctor?" Maude asked with concern in her voice. "I hear pneumonia is going around."

"The doc come out 'tother day and listened to her." Charley said. "He said it was just a bad cold and she'd be right as rain in a couple of days."

Maude chuckled at her friend, not because she thought it was funny that his mother was sick, but because of some of the words he used. "'Tother" was one word that always made her smile. That "Charley-ism" was one of her favorites!

"That's good to hear Charley!" Maude said with a smile. "I'm glad she'll be feeling better soon."

"Thank you, Miss Maude." Charley said. His face flushed just a bit.

The bell rang and Mr. Hopkins took the roll. Once those present were accounted for, he handed out the unit test and quickly twenty-seven seniors were quietly penciling in the answers to questions regarding the American Revolution.

The only sounds that could be heard were the whispering scrapes of pencil lead on paper, the steady tick and tock of the ancient wall-mounted clock and the occasional cough or sniffle from one of the students. No one dared speak or even give the impression they were attempting to look at someone else's test; Paul Hopkins was a stern man who had no use for cheaters, and they all knew it. The story of what he had done to a student he <u>had</u> caught cheating the year before was legend.

~ ~ ~ ~ ~ ~

Amos Watson was an above average student and was well-liked by students and teachers alike. However, one fateful day, as the saying goes, Amos made an error in judgment that was akin to academic suicide.

Amos had spent entirely too much time studying Elizabeth Smoltz, who sang soprano in the school's mixed choir. Her voice was pitch-perfect and many at the school and the community as well thought she had an excellent chance at a singing career!

Amos knew she had an excellent chance at being his girlfriend if she would just go to the Prom with him, so he had redoubled his efforts in trying to win her over and completely forgot about Mr. Hopkins' history test.

"Why do I need to know about history anyway?" He had been heard saying right before class when he was reminded about the test. "It's over and done with and you can't change it even if you wanted to."

Ernest Hopper was seated next to Amos. Ern, as he was known, was a history genius. He could quote most of the Declaration of Independence from memory; he knew the significance of the year 1066 and could recite all the presidents of the United States from the most recent all the way back to George Washington.

Knowing this, Amos Watson didn't think it was that big a deal if he "proofread" Ern's answers. He wanted to compare Ern's answers to his own, just to see if they were both remembering what Mr. Hopkins had taught in the same way.

Paul Hopkins, however, thought otherwise when he saw Amos giving Ern's test numerous sideways glances then quickly scribbling something on his own test paper. Moving around the perimeter of the classroom, Mr. Hopkins took up a position where he could better watch Amos' activities.

When he had seen enough, he quietly positioned himself to the left of Amos' desk and cleared his throat with a loud "Ahem!" Amos looked up. Mr. Hopkins snatched the test from the desk. They looked at each other for an eternity. Then without looking away from Amos' upturned and noticeably paler face, Paul Hopkins shredded the paper, threw the tatters into the trash can and commanded that Amos make his way to the principal's office post-haste!

"The Shredding" as the incident became known, was the talk of the school. Amos Watson did pass history. However, for the rest of the year whenever there was a test, he took his at Mr. Hopkins' desk, well away from any other student.

As for the Prom, Amos asked Elizabeth Smoltz to go with him, but she promptly turned him down saying, "If you would cheat on a history test, who knows what you would do on a date!"

Elizabeth went on to study vocal music at Julliard and sang at Carnegie Hall on several occasions! She married a man from New York who was a virtuoso violinist in the New York Philharmonic, and they had three children.

Amos also went to college and became, of all things, a history teacher! He married a young woman he met there, and they raised four children: three girls and one boy! His son was named Paul!

~ ~ ~ ~ ~ ~

As they finished their test, each student would walk to Mr. Hopkins' desk and place it face down on the right-hand corner then quietly return to their seat where they would wait until all had finished or the class period ended.

Maude and Charley finished at the same time and spent the last twenty minutes reading the assignment for the next day's class. When the bell rang and as they were walking to their next class, Charley asked Maude a question.

"Did you know the answer to the extra credit question Maude?" Charley asked.

"Which one, there were two extra credit questions?" Maude asked.

"Who was the first person killed in the Revolutionary War?" Charley asked.

"It was Crispus Attucks." Maude said without a moment's hesitation.

Charley started laughing in great, whooping gales of laughter.

"What's so funny Charley?" Maude asked.

"I wrote in 'Crispy Attics'. Do you think I'll get any credit for that answer?" He asked still laughing.

Maude stopped walking and laughed out loud; so much so that several other students looked at her as well.

"I doubt it very much, Charley!" She said through bursts of giggles. "You know how Mr. Hopkins is, but I would give you ten points just for humor!"

~ ~ ~ ~ ~ ~

Did he get any credit for it?" Sophia asked.

Maude chuckled. "Yes, and he got a grin out of Mr. Hopkins too! That was a feat in and of itself because Mr. Hopkins was a serious man not prone to any sort of foolishness. I believe Charley Reynolds was the only student to get humor points from Paul Hopkins! In fact, he actually made Mr. Hopkins laugh out loud during class one time!"

"What did he do?" Sophia asked.

"We were studying the election process and Mr. Hopkins was talking about the Republicans and the Democrats. He asked if anyone knew what the symbol was for each of them.

Charley raised his hand and said, "The Republicans are elephants; I guess because they remember everything."

"What about the Democrats?" Mr. Hopkins asked.

"The Democrats are jackasses." Charley said.

"The silence in that room was deafening." Maude said. "We all knew Charley was going to be in big trouble for saying what he had said!"

"What happened to him?" Sophia asked.

"Nothing!" Maude said. "In fact, Mr. Hopkins doubled over laughing! When he had finally composed himself, he said, 'I have waited twenty-five years for someone to actually say that!' I am giving you twenty-five bonus points just because I haven't had a laugh that good in a long time!'

"Those twenty-five points bumped Charley from an A minus to a straight A when our report cards came out at the end of the quarter!" Maude said.

"That is too funny!" Sophia said. "Nothing like that ever happened in any of my classes."

"That's the only time it ever happened in any of mine." Maude said. "That was one of the funniest things that I ever witnessed in school!"

A pensive quiet then settled across Maude's living room; she was thinking of Charley Reynolds. Sophia began thinking of what her life used to be like before the move, about the dream she had had the night before, the splinter in her arm and of course, the braid in her hair. So much had happened and was happening; Sophia was having trouble comprehending it all. After several minutes Maude broke the peaceful silence.

"S'pect we ought to get back to going through these here boxes." She said.

"Yeah." Sophia agreed. "I think we should."

The rest of the day was quiet; Maude didn't have much to say other than what needed to be done with the contents of the numerous boxes. Sophia assumed that after talking about Charley Reynolds, Maude was revisiting some old memories and some old conversations.

~ ~ ~ ~ ~ ~

Sophia arrived back home a dusty, tired mess who headed to her private bath to clean up. The only part of her that wasn't dirty was her baseball cap. It had remained clean only because she had taken it off when she first got to Maude's house.

Her mother heard her come inside but only spoke; she was reading a magazine and didn't even look up. That was a relief to Sophia because she was carrying the baseball cap leaving her braid uncovered for all to see. Her father was busy mowing the backyard with the new riding mower and didn't see her arrive back at the house.

Sophia stripped off her dirty clothes in her pocket door protected hallway, then went into the bathroom and looked at herself in her mirror. Her face was dusty, her eyes were tired with just a hint of red in them and her hair was still braided.

"How?" She asked the mirror about the braid that had somehow come to be while she was dreaming.

Sophia took the braid out before she showered. She really liked how it looked and it had kept her cooler, but she just didn't want the questions her parents would undoubtedly ask about it. If she told them someone in a dream had braided her hair, they would probably have her locked up somewhere.

After showering and putting on clean clothes she looked at herself in the mirror again and noted that one of the benefits of having had her hair in a braid for nearly twenty-four hours was the wave and bounce it now contained.

"My hair looks really, really good!" She thought. *"Thank you, Laura!"*

When she arrived in the kitchen, her hair was still wet from another lather, rinse, repeat session in the shower and it was two shades darker because of the added moisture. Sophia paused to inhale the aromas in the kitchen.

"Something smells amazing!" She said.

"I would hope so." Her dad said. "In my experience, T-bones usually do!"

"Ooo, T-bones!" Sophia exclaimed!

The steak had been grilled perfectly medium-well just as Sophia liked it. The corn on the cob had also been grilled and was slathered with real butter! The house salad had "crunchies"; the name Sophia had given croutons when she was in pre-school! And the twice-baked potatoes were saturated with more of the real butter and copious amounts of sour cream!

"What's the occasion?" She asked suspiciously as she filled her plate. Suspicion was a good thing in Sophia's opinion, but a T-bone *was* a T-bone.

"I was hungry!" Carol Young said as she filled her own plate. "Besides, when we have steak, your father does the grilling, and I wasn't really feeling like cooking tonight!"

"Where are the corn pickers?" Sophia asked.

She knew "corn pickers" wasn't the actual name of the little yellow plastic corn shaped skewers, but that's what she had called them ever since, well, forever.

"They are in the silverware drawer where they always are." Her mom said.

After getting the perforated plastic box that contained the "corn pickers", Sophia gave a set to her dad and her mom before skewering a large ear of corn for herself. Then, just like her grandpa had shown her years ago, she slathered a slice of bread with more of the real butter that was sitting on the kitchen table. It had been out of the refrigerator for a while and had softened making it as easy to spread as the margarine they sometimes used.

She wrapped the butter covered slice of bread around the ear of corn, smearing the butter all over the already butter saturated cob ensuring complete coverage of every kernel!

"Did you know we went right by the town that is the home of sliced bread when we moved here?" Her father asked.

"We did?" Sophia asked.

"Yes." He said. "I think you were asleep, but we went right by Chillicothe, Missouri. That's the town where commercial sliced bread began."

"I will sleep better knowing that Dad." Sophia said dryly. "Pass the salt, please!"

"You are your grandpa's granddaughter." Her father said passing her the saltshaker. "No doubt about that!"

Once sufficiently salted, Sophia, using her "typewriter method" of corn-on-the-cob eating, began devouring the corn. Peeling two or three rows of kernels at a time, she ate her way across the cob from left to right. Once she reached the end, she rotated the corn, shifted her mouth back to the left end of the cob and repeated the process. The "typewriter method" was, for Sophia at least, a very efficient way to enjoy a summertime favorite and she never left a single kernel of corn on the cob.

"That, was gooder!" Sophia announced setting the kernel free corn cob to one side of her plate.

~ ~ ~ ~ ~ ~

Fully sated with steak, corn and the other food, Sophia and her mother cleaned up the supper dishes. The meal had been so filling, Sophia did not have any dessert which surprised her parents considering dessert had been strawberry shortcake.

"Are you not feeling well honey?" Carol Young asked.

"I am feeling...FULL!" Sophia laughed, patting her stomach. "And now, I am going to my room to digest!"

She had almost made it out of the dine-in kitchen when her father asked, "What? No hugs?"

"No Father." Sophia said in an exaggerated, overly dramatic tone that was edging on Shakespearian. "Alas, there are no hugs."

"Well then dear Daughter, mighten we shake hands?" Dan replied with equal overdramatization.

"Forsooth!" Sophia said.

"For what-th?" Dan asked. "Did you say you had a sore tooth?"

"Forsooth." Sophia repeated then added with a twangy inflection. "That right thar means...indeed!"

"Ah!" Her father said. "She is from the south of England!"

With that, Dan and Sophia began flapping their hands in the air at each other! Once done, Sophia did hug her mother and after a moment, she hugged her father as well before heading to her room.

"And that, ladies and gentlemen is the rare species of human known as Teenagercus Moodicus." Dan said after she had stepped into the hallway. "It is well-known for its ability to be grumpy one moment and goofy the next!"

"I heard that!" Sophia called from somewhere down the hall.

"You were supposed to!" Dan called back to her.

Sophia tried to comment back, but her response was interrupted by a rather large, yet satisfying burp.

"Sophia Elizabeth Young, that isn't very lady like!" Her mother scolded.

"In Japan, belching is considered a compliment." Sophia said with a laugh.

"Move to Japan then!" Carol Young said.

Sophia erupted with a second belch.

"That there is Japanese for Gracias, which means Merci Beaucoup!" She said.

Chapter 09

Her computer came to life quickly. However, the old reel-to-reel tape recorder was another story. When she flipped the switch on the black cord to "ON", nothing happened.

"What in the world?" Sophia thought.

She looked to see if the tan switch on the recorder was in the "PLAY" position; it was. She checked to see if the black "ON" and "OFF" cord had somehow come unplugged from its socket; it had not.

"What could it…" Sophia started to say before realizing what the problem was. "Well, DUH!" Reaching down under her desk, Sophia turned on the power strip. "If it had been a snake, it would have bitten me!" She said.

She picked up the tape labeled "08-12-62", loaded it into the old reel-to-reel recorder, activated Audio-Clone on her laptop and switched on the recorder. There were more pops and crackles as the tape wound its way through the player.

"Tell me more Laura." Sophia said.

~ ~ ~ ~ ~ ~

"Well, we are here in this little no-name town in the middle of nowhere Missouri in a house that is nothing like our home in Golf. It's just a house that I am being forced to live in, but I DO NOT have to like it ONE BIT!" Laura said choking back tears.

Laura went on to describe the house in some detail. It was a two-story Victorian with a round roofed turret and a wide, wraparound front porch whose roof was supported by eight large columns. Her father told her that the original columns had been made out of limestone but had been replaced with the current wooden ones. When she asked him how he knew that he had replied, "The aunts told me."

The house was nothing at all like the Cape Cod she had lived in just four weeks prior. Her bedroom was on the second floor and was fairly large. In one corner was a curved, double bookcase that was a part of the turret that could be seen from the street.

Laura really liked the room when they were considering the house and she asked if it could be her room. Her parents knew how upset she was about having to move, so they readily agreed hoping that it would help with the sadness she was going through, it was just a room after all.

The bookcase had a very unique feature, when outward pressure was applied equally on either side of the center of the middle shelf, the bookcase halves slid around inside the wall revealing a secret room housed in the turret itself. It was no more than ten feet in diameter and had a single octagonal shaped stained-glass window that filled the room with multi-colored light when the sun shone through it.

It also had two wall mounted light fixtures that looked like coach lamps which gave the space an eerie eighteenth century feel when the lights were turned on.

Laura said she hung the hammock she had used on several camping trips in the turret room and hid out from her parents and the world in general as she thought about the heartbreak that had beset her life.

The tape recording popped and crackled.

There were ruminations about the friends she had had to leave and the horror of having to start high school in a place where she knew no one at all.

The tape recording popped and crackled again.

"If there is anything good about moving here, and there isn't, but if there was, it would be this tape recorder Mom and Dad gave me for my birthday and the Turret Room.

At least I can actually say with my voice what I feel which is better than just writing those words in my diary. I wish I could have been with my friends on my birthday though, fifteen is a big deal! I mean I am starting high school in a couple of weeks."

Popping.

Crackling.

"Why did Dad have to get moved here to sell insurance? Why couldn't we have just stayed in Golf? I mean, I was going to be on the cheerleading squad! Mom called the local high school and I'll have to wait until next year because tryouts were before school got out in May, so there's no way I could get on the squad anyway. It is not fair!"

Laura dissolved into sobs.

Popping.

Crackling.

Laura told that after unpacking the boxes in her room and tossing the empties in the garage, she went for a walk. The town was little, but the houses were nice, and the people were friendly. As she walked, most of the people she encountered waved as they drove by in their cars.

In one case, when a carload of teenage boys went by, she was whistled at, which normally would have annoyed her, but in this instance, she was amused!

"At least someone appreciated me." She said.

Laura's good looks had been apparent since she was very young. She remembered countless times when people had gone on and on about how pretty she was to her parents. She, however, did not let the compliments go to her head like some girls might have done. In fact, the compliments made her just a bit uncomfortable; she was after all just a person, no better or no worse than anyone else.

Laura said her walk took her through most of the town; it wasn't really that big, and saw the local swimming pool that had a really steep slide that looked like it would cause you to skip across the surface of the pool like a flat rock when you hit the water. She thought it would be fun to go swimming, but she didn't know a single person and it would just be too awkward to go by herself.

"Maybe next summer." She thought. "Maybe never."

Laura turned and retraced her steps to the street where the majority of the town's businesses were located. Next to her father's insurance agency was the Payton & Son Hardware Store, it was running a special on, of all things, nails! The large sign in the window read; "One pound of any size nails – ONE DOLLAR!!!"

Laura giggled! "Big happenings at the old hardware store! The next thing you know, they will be having a Buy One, Get One sale on tape or something!"

Directly across from her father's office was a store that immediately caught her eye because of its name: The Ten Penny Emporium: Purveyors of Fine Collectables and Fascinating Oddities!

"Now THAT is the first thing in this little town that sounds interesting!" Laura thought.

She walked across the street without even considering going to the crosswalk. She had seen three cars driving down the street in the last five minutes and didn't think she would get run over. She was correct!

The Ten Penny did indeed contain collectibles and some really fascinating things she had never seen. Displayed in the large picture window was a desk of sorts. It had a writing area and drawers, but what made it interesting was that it was on tall legs that made the writing surface nearly four feet in the air. Next to it was an equally tall stool. As she looked at it, the image of Bob Cratchit came to mind. In fact, Laura said what she was thinking out loud and a lady passing by on the sidewalk chuckled! She went inside to take a closer look at the desk.

"That desk would be perfect in the Turret Room!" She thought. She looked at its price tag where she saw printed in neat handwriting $75.00. "Or maybe not!"

There was a wide assortment of the usual and the unusual ranging from antique apple peelers to a device that was listed as a zester, whatever that was. However, one thing that caught her eye was a rectangular framed needle point that read:
"Sometimes, you have to do something a little Crazy to prove that you are actually sane!"

~ ~ ~ ~ ~ ~

The recording ended and Sophia switched off the Audio-Clone, then reversed the old tape recorder from "PLAY" to "REW" and rewound the tape. After removing it from the tape player / recorder, she put it into a plain cardboard box she had labeled "RECORDED".

"One down." She said.

Before selecting a new tape to listen to, Sophia named this new digital audio file simply, "8-12-62".

"No need to get fancy," Sophia said to herself. *"It'll be easier to keep track of what I have done this way."*

Sophia made a quick trip to the kitchen for a cold drink, then returned to her room to continue listening to and preserving the cubbyhole tapes.

The next tape in the sequence was one labeled "8-13-62". She threaded it into the old reel-to-reel player, made sure the computer was ready, then switched everything on and began listening.

~ ~ ~ ~ ~ ~

"I took another walk around town today. There's not much here, Golf had so much more than this wide spot in the road of a town does, but I went to the library and I went back to The Ten Penny Emporium. There is so much interesting stuff in that place!

I looked at that framed needle point again; they wanted five dollars for it, so I used some birthday money and now 'Sometimes you have to do something a little crazy to prove that you are actually sane!' is hanging on the wall of the Turret Room!

I know Mom and Dad didn't move here just to mess up my life even if it seems like it. I was thinking about that last night as I was going to sleep, and I realized that I needed to get over being mad about having to move here. It's not like me being mad will cause us to move back to Golf. But the one thing that really bugs me is that I didn't have a say in it; I didn't have a choice. That's what bothers me the most."

Popping.
Crackling.

"I also found a book at the library today." Laura said. *"And it said something that got me thinking. Hang on."*

There was the sound of things being moved around and then the distinct sound of pages being flicked through.

"Okay, here it is. It says: 'Anger or hurt about the past is happening <u>now</u>. Your present experience in the now is what keeps the past alive. What is amazing about this is that it shows you that the way out of your suffering is always in the present. You can change your perspective by focusing on something different.'

"I am going to do this beginning right now. I'm tired of being mad." Laura said. *"I'm tired of feeling sad and I am going to get rid of these feelings."*

Popping.
Crackling.
Silence.

~ ~ ~ ~ ~ ~

"I think you are right Laura." Sophia said. "Being mad isn't going to change a thing except, like Dad said, maybe the lining of my stomach. But I wish I had had a choice." She paused, then added. "And I wish I could get rid of all the popping and crackling in these recordings."

With a flurry of mouse clicks and keyboard taps on her laptop, she researched the internet on how to rid an Audio-Clone file of annoying background noise.

"No way!" She said again to no one as she found the information she needed. "This will be easier to do than it is to remove backgrounds from pictures!"

In fact, with one of the many audio enhancement tools she found buried within the program, she was also able to enrich the sound quality of Laura's voice. When she was done, her voice was much stronger and clearer and didn't sound as distant as it first had!

With less than ten keystrokes, Sophia had an audio recording that was free of any background noise and she quickly cleaned up the first two recordings she had made.

She was ready to resume listening to more of the recordings, but when she glanced at the clock, she saw that it was ten-fifteen. She had gotten so engrossed with the boosting of the audio quality of her recordings, she lost track of time.

"I guess I'd better go to bed." She thought. *"Maude is going to work me pretty hard again tomorrow I bet."*

As she was getting into bed, her cell phone came to life with the clucking of a chicken. It was a sound file she had found somewhere that made her laugh every time she heard it. She made it the alert tone for when she received a text message and also used it as the tone for the phone's alarm clock.

"Who would be texting me at this time of night?" Sophia thought to herself. *"Probably Audrey or Laney."*

Her friend Leah had her own specific sound bite when she texted or called.

Looking at the phone's screen she saw that the text had not come from one of her friends, but from Maude Adelaide! After texting her about the cleaning job, Sophia had added the old woman's phone number to her list of contacts.

The text message was simple, direct and to the point just like the sender. It was also in all capitals: "DO NOT COME BACK UNTIL I CALL YOU LAURA! I HAVE TO GO CHECK ON MYRTLE. WOULD YOU BE AVAILABLE ON WEDNESDAY IF I NEED YOU?"

The phone clucked again as she was reading the message. "SOPHIA, I MEAN."

Laughing, Sophia texted back: "I CAN BE THERE WEDNESDAY. I HOPE MYRTLE IS OKAY."

"THAT WILL WORK FINE. THANK YOU." Came the reply moments later. "AND MYRTLE IS FINE TOO."

Sophia slid out of bed, went into the hall and slid open the pocket door. She looked into the living room, saw the lights were still on and could hear the television weatherman predicting tomorrow's temperature would be in the high nineties.

"Hey, you!" Her father said as she came into view. "I figured you'd be asleep by now."

"I was going to bed when I got a text. You'll never, in a million years, guess who it was from!" Sophia said.

"Leah?" Her mom asked referring to one of Sophia's best friends.

"Nope!" Sophia said. "Like I said, you will never guess."

"Some cute boy that you met walking to and from the Adelaide's house?" Her father teased.

"There are NO cute boys in this town as far as I have seen!" Sophia said. "If there are, they are probably busy with their banjo lessons!"

"Well, if they can play the banjo, they might be able to help you get some… *deliverance* and whisk you out of… What is it you call this town?" Dan Young said with bemusement covering his face.

"Podunksville!" Sophia said.

"Yes! Maybe some cute banjo-playing boy can carry you away to someplace far away from Podunksville!" Her dad teased.

"We can only hope!" Sophia said dryly.

"I can see it now, on the first day of school you will meet your true love… Melvin P. Snodgrass, a virtuoso of the banjo!" Dan said.

"The third." Sophia said with a flat tone in her voice.

"The third of what?" Carol Young asked.

"I want some cute banjo playing boy who has a fancy name. His name will have to be something like Melvin P. Snodgrass… THE THIRD!" Sophia said.

Carol and Dan Young both burst out laughing! After they were done Sophia returned to the original reason for their conversation.

"The text was from Maude Adelaide." Sophia said.

"Really?" The Youngs said in unison.

"Yes." Sophia said. "She doesn't want me to come tomorrow; she has to check on her sister or something. Besides, I think we are done with the major work. I think all we have left to do is sweeping, dusting and mopping."

"That's good!" Her father said.

"Actually, that will work out better for us." Her mother added.

"Why?" Sophia and Dan said at the same time.

"We need to go shopping for school supplies." Carol said. "We could do that tomorrow."

"That's right, they aren't charging tax on school supplies this week!" Dan added.

The realization that school was starting soon, mentally gut-punched Sophia hard. Working for Maude Adelaide and copying the reel-to-reel tapes was keeping her distracted. However, the bitterness of the move and having no choice in it returned in full force.

"I'm going to bed." Sophia said.

"Goodnight." Her parents said.

As tears trickled down her cheeks, Sophia exited the living room, closed the pocket door and walked down the short hallway to her room where she crawled into bed.

"School supplies." Sophia thought. *"For my first day at Podunksville High, home of the Fighting Possums."*

She switched off the lamp on her nightstand and waited for sleep to come and take her away if even for just a few hours.

Chapter 10

Eight o'clock arrived when her phone came alive with the clucking of a chicken. Sophia had slept a hard, refreshing dreamless sleep. She found a note on her bed from her mother. She must have been really sleeping hard because she never heard her come into her room.

"Dad is at work and I'm running some errands. We'll both be home around three. Maybe we can get the school supplies after that. There's breakfast in the refrigerator. - Mom"

She got up, went to the kitchen and opened the refrigerator and found a plate of scrambled eggs, some crispy bacon, a tub of strawberry flavored cream cheese and two enormous plain bagels that had already been sliced.

"Not too shabby even if the eggs are scrambled!" Sophia thought as she set the plate in the microwave and popped one of the bagels into the toaster.

The microwave beeped just as the toaster evicted the bagel. It flew out of the heated slot and landed in the open tub of cream cheese that was sitting on the counter. Its twin left its slot with lackluster force allowing it to only land unceremoniously atop the toaster.

Sophia placed both halves of the recently dispossessed bagel on the countertop, something her mother would have scolded her for, and slathered each with plentiful amounts of the strawberry cream cheese then placed them on the plate next to the eggs and bacon, poured herself a glass of milk and ate!

~ ~ ~ ~ ~ ~

The weather was perfect as she walked back to Coombs House Park and its ten million bricks. When she had discovered it, she had been in a really, really bad mood. However, as she retraced her path through town, she smiled thinking about the book that she had brought with her to read and about what Laura had said about changing your perspective to get over being angry.

"I know that it won't be easy, and it won't happen overnight." Sophia thought. *"But I am going to do it!"*

She continued her journey and was pleasantly surprised to see that Morton's was open for business. By the looks of all the cars, pickup trucks and one lone tractor parked on the street in front of the restaurant, it appeared that Marion was still busy with the biscuits and gravy crowd.

She continued walking and found herself on the tree-lined street where she had met Sandi and her friends playing kickball. She secretly hoped the little girl would be outside and that she would tell her again that she wasn't, "… 'posed to talk to strange people.'" The little girl had brightened her otherwise dreary day when she had made the comment. Unfortunately, the street was quiet.

With only her flip flops' soft "thwap, thwap, thwap" and the copy of the book as her company, Sophia finally arrived at Coombs House Park where the wrought iron gate screeched hello as she opened it just enough to enter the amazing red brick structure.

"Ten million bricks!" Sophia thought as she again looked around the entrance to the park. *"Wow!"*

Aside from the many benches and, of course, the red granite boulder fountain, Sophia found a trumpet vine-covered, red brick grotto containing a picnic table and chairs. There was a noticeable temperature change when she entered the covered area and sat down to the sound of the water coursing down the red granite boulder into the pool surrounding it, the birds chirping their summer songs and the sweet smell of grass and the trumpet vine.

"This is nice!" She thought as she opened the book and read the opening words: "An attic is an interesting place to visit; it holds treasures and secrets. Sometimes the secrets are the treasures."

Although she had slept well, Sophia's eyes grew heavy.

"But first, a quick cat nap. Then I'll start reading." Sophia thought, then leaned back in the chair and closed her eyes.

~ ~ ~ ~ ~ ~

Laura was standing at the railing of the covered bridge's balcony. She looked the same as she had in the first dream, except for her clothes. Her tee-shirt was a pale-yellow and her shorts were white denim. The only thing that was the same was her shoes; Sophia saw that she was wearing the spotless white tennis shoes.

"Hi, Sophia!" Laura said cheerfully.

"Hi!" Sophia replied, then crossed the bridge's wood plank floor to the balcony.

"Are you listening to my tapes?" Laura asked.

"Yes." Sophia replied thinking how weirdly normal this conversation had begun. It was like she and Laura were old friends.

"What am I doing?" Laura asked.

"Uh…" Sophia began. "Standing on a bridge."

Laura began laughing hard; so much so she had to put her head down on her arms that were resting on the balcony's railing. When her laughter had subsided, Laura spoke again. "I meant, what am I doing on the tapes!"

Sophia felt her face flush slightly. "Oh."

Laura looked at Sophia for a too-long moment before smiling and asking again, "What am I doing Sophia?"

"Well, I listened to one where you had just moved into the house with the turret room." Sophia said. "But before that, I listened to a different one."

"Which one was that?" Laura asked.

"Well, uh…" Sophia did not want to tell her.

Laura burst out with another gale of her melodious laughter. "Oh! Is it the tape I made on my wedding day where I talk about being nervous about the wedding night?"

"That's the one." Sophia confessed.

Smiling, Laura said, "No need to be embarrassed Sophia, I don't go into intimate details!"

"I know. It's just…" Sophia began.

"Don't worry about it, okay?" Laura said.

"Okay, I sort of picked that tape at random, but now I am going back and starting at the beginning like you said." Sophia said with noticeable relief in her voice.

"Good!" Laura said.

They stood at the balcony's railing just looking at the creek, the trees and the beautiful scenery surrounding the bridge.

"School will be starting soon Sophia." Laura said breaking the silence.

"In six days." Sophia said as the gloomy feelings she had regarding the move swam quickly to the forefront of her mind.

Laura put her hand on Sophia's arm. Her touch, Sophia noticed, was warm and soft. "I'm glad you're listening to the older tapes first."

Sophia didn't respond, her thoughts were of the move, her old friends and her old life.

"Once upon a time and not that many years ago, I was where you are right now Sophia." Laura said.

"It's not fair." Sophia whispered as she felt tears in her eyes and her throat tighten as the pain of the move, the sense of loss and the fear of the unknown well up inside her.

"No." Laura said. "No, it's not. It wasn't when I moved. But..."

Sophia stood, quietly watching the water in the creek head downstream to who knew where. She waited for Laura to finish her thought and when Laura's pause had gone on longer than Sophia thought it should, she finally asked, "But what?"

"But it wasn't nearly as bad as I had made it out to be either." Laura said with a smile. "In fact, the first day of my freshman year of high school changed my life!"

"It did?" Sophia asked. "How?"

Laura laughed. "I guess you'll need to listen to those tapes and read that book to find out, now won't you!"

"Fine!" Sophia said with a laugh of her own.

An ant crawled across the raised grain of the bridge's railing. It was large, black and Sophia knew its pinch would get your attention if it clamped down on your skin.

"Maude said something had happened to you and your children, but didn't say what it was." Sophia said as she watched the ant disappear over the edge of the railing.

"Aunt Maude is tight lipped about a lot of things." Laura said.

There was a pregnant pause in the conversation, then Sophia asked, "What happened?"

Laura's sunny smile disappeared just as fast as the ant had disappeared over the bridge railing.

"I knew you would ask about that eventually." Laura said as her smile returned. "Listen to the tapes, the oldest ones first, then read your book!" She paused for just a second before continuing. "I need to be getting back. But..."

"But?" Sophia asked.

"But before I go remember this: *What you focus on is what will grow inside you. If you focus on sadness, then sadness will become your reality.*" Laura said.

"I know." Sophia said.

"Be like that camera you call a phone and change your focus Sophia!" Laura said. "At some point you just have to let go of what you thought should be happening and live in what is_ happening!"

The dream world dissolved into nothingness.

~ ~ ~ ~ ~ ~

"Jeezly crow!" Sophia said using the term she had read in Stephen King's "The Stand", a book of his that she actually liked. "I was asleep for THREE hours!" She picked up her still unread book and headed home. "I guess you and the attic will be keeping your secrets just a bit longer; I've got some tapes to listen to."

As she stood to leave, the book slipped from her hand and fell on the red bricked ground with an audible "Thwomp!" When she picked it up, the book was open to a full-page color photo of a blonde-haired young woman sitting next to an evergreen tree wearing a blue and white cheerleading uniform. Her legs were stretched out in front of her in the grass with her feet crossed at the ankles; her white socks contrasted with her bronzed skin and she was holding a football in her hands and a set of pom-poms were lying on the ground next to her. At the bottom of the photo was the caption: "LAURA BUTLER – SOPHOMORE - VARSITY CHEERLEADER".

"Whoa!" Sophia said. "Laura you are gorgeous!"

Chapter 11

Her laptop was still connected to the old reel-to-reel tape recorder and the last tape she had listened to was still wound through the mechanism. Sophia switched the old recorder on and turned the multi-feature knob to "REWIND". The tape quickly retraced its steps across the recording/playing heads and wrapped itself back around its reel.

While the tape was rewinding, Sophia looked through the tapes in the old White Owl cigar box. When getting ready for her walk to The Coombs House Park, she had knocked it over and the tapes had been ejected all over the floor. She had quickly picked them up and tossed them back into the box. It was for that reason that the tapes were not in any particular order, so she had to sort them out according to the dates written on the old yellow masking tape labels.

The tape finished rewinding and there was the rapid thwap, thwap, thwap as the end of the tape left the mechanism and began slapping it with each rotation of the rewinding reel.

"Oh man!" Sophia said and turned the multi-function knob to "STOP", the rapid thwap, thwap, thwap ended and Sophia finished sorting the tapes.

~ ~ ~ ~ ~ ~

She went to the kitchen, grabbed a bottle of water and was going to rummage through the refrigerator for something to snack on, but her mother spoke, and Sophia jumped and screamed. Carol Young laughed as Sophia spun around to face her.

"Hi honey, I'm home!" Carol laughed. "Aren't you glad to see me?"

Sophia, with her hand on her chest, resembled Fred Sanford right before announcing to his dearly departed Elizabeth that he was coming home.

"When did you get home?" She asked.

"About five minutes ago. You were in your room doing something with that stuff you found in the wall. I didn't want to bother you." Carol said. "Time flies when you're having fun, I guess! So, what have you been up to today since you had the day off?"

Sophia told of her trip back to the Coombs House Park and her walk around town.

"They really used ten million bricks to build a park?" Carol asked, obviously surprised.

"That's what the sign said." Sophia said. "You would have to see it to believe it."

"Well, when your father gets home, we might stop by when we go out tonight!" Carol said.

"Where are you two going?" Sophia asked.

"All *three* of us are going out!" Carol said.

"Where?" Sophia asked.

She doubted there was anything in the greater Podunksville metro area that would be remotely interesting. However, she did like the idea of not staying at the house for another night.

"I'm not going to tell you, it's a surprise!" Carol said with a knowing smile. "I think you'll like it!"

"Humph!" Sophia snorted. "I'm sure it will be *ever* so much fun."

Carol laughed at Sophia's guarded statement. "You'll see!"

Sophia went back to her room and moped.

"Oh good, another choice made FOR me and I didn't have any say in it at all. I need to do something that is MY choice." She thought.

~ ~ ~ ~ ~ ~

When he had taken their new minivan to get it licensed, Dan Young had surprised everyone when he paid for personalized license plates. The one who was most surprised was Carol, she laughed at the vanity plates that read "SCR-MOM".

"Dan, Sophia hasn't played soccer since the third grade." Carol reminded him when she had seen the plates.

"I know." He said.

"Soooo?" She asked pointing to the plate on the rear of the van.

"Because it is funny!" He said smiling.

A then twelve-year-old Sophia came outside to look at their newest form of transportation. After walking around the van, she asked, "Why do you want to scare Mom?"

Dan and Carol doubled over with laughter!

The memory made Sophia smile, but now, almost three years later she was in the SCR-MOM van with her parents leaving the house *they* called home, but she swore she never would.

"Home is where the heart is, and my heart is NOT here!" She thought.

Their trip took them through the little town where her father was the new postmaster, her mother was the postmaster's wife and Sophia was…

"Who am I?" Sophia asked herself. Without much thought at all she answered herself, *"Oh yeah, I am the new girl, the postmaster's daughter, the girl with no choice."* She audibly "Harrumphed" from the middle row of seats.

"What did you say Sophia?" Her mother asked.

"I didn't say anything Mom." Sophia said.

"Oh, okay. I thought you said something." Carol said.

"I coughed." Sophia said.

"Hey, can you show us that park you told me about?" Carol asked.

"Sure." Sophia said.

After driving a few blocks and making a series of right and left turns, the Young family pulled up in front of the Coombs House Park and Sophia's parents marvelled at the red bricks.

"Didn't you say they used ten million bricks to build this place?" Carol asked.

"That's what the sign by the gate says." Sophia said.

"I guess we could count them, but that might take a year or twelve!" Dan said.

Then he and Carol got out to investigate the unique park. They asked Sophia if she was coming with them, but she opted to stay in the van because she had already been to the park.

As her parents walked up to the bronze plaque to read what she had already told them, then opened and stepped through the wrought iron gate into the park. Sophia began to sulk just a bit.

"They decide everything for me, make me move away from everyone and everything I know and now they come here. I can't even have a spot to call my own." She thought. *"The next chance I have to make a choice, a real choice, I am making it! I don't care what it is! It WILL be MY choice and I will own it! And then I will start changing my focus, but not until!"*

She had gone to sleep the night before thinking about what she had heard on Laura's tape recording. It *did* make sense, but she was still angry.

With her parents inside the park looking around, Sophia sent Audrey a lengthy text detailing how awful things had become. She hated texting Audrey, Leah and Laney, what she really wanted was to spend some time with her best friends, but that was impossible, so texting and the occasional phone call had to suffice.

"HEY! CAN WE TEXT LATER? I HAVE SOMETHING GOING ON." Audrey's text read a few minutes later.

"SURE. LATER." Sophia replied with a sigh.

"Even Audrey doesn't have time for me anymore." She thought.

Tears started to well up in her eyes and the large lump that she had felt so many times this summer began to swell in her throat. The front doors opened, and Sophia was yanked away from her thoughts as her parents slid back into their seats.

"That is an interesting place Sophia!" Carol said. "Thanks for telling us about it!"

"Where are we going?" Sophia asked changing the subject totally. "You said something about getting school supplies."

"We'll do that tomorrow Soph." Carol Young said. "The tax-free school supplies lasts until Saturday, so we have a few more days."

"Where are we going *tonight*?" Sophia asked.

"It's a surprise!" Dan said.

"I hope it's not like the surprise when you told me we were moving." Sophia thought. *"Hey Sophia, your dad got a new job and in three weeks we're moving two hundred fifty miles away from everything and everyone you have ever known and as an added bonus, you get to give up your cheerleading spot that you worked your tail off to earn and you also have no say what-so-ever in this decision. SURPRISE!"*

"Oh joy." Sophia said then put her earbuds in and began listening to some music as they passed the city limit sign and an old barn.

~ ~ ~ ~ ~ ~

"Sophia!" Her mother said distantly from the other side of "Sunflower", a violin cover of the Post Malone song done by a young Russian girl named Karolina Protsenko. "Sophia, are you awake?"

"Yeah." Sophia said foggily. She sat up, turned off her music app and looked out the van's windows. "Where are we?"

The van was parked in a grassy field and over the tops of all the vehicles parked there she could see the large, round, neon light festooned skeleton of a Ferris wheel!

"It's the Podunksville County Fair where you can get a foot-long corn dog, cotton candy and throw darts to win a prize, sometimes all at the same place! Yuck, yuck, yuck!" Her dad teased.

Sophia tried not to laugh which was hard as she had just woken up from a cat nap.

"You're going to laugh Sophia!" Her father said, grinning at her.

"No, I'm not!" Sophia said consciously squeezing her lips closed.

"Your lips are quivering!" He said. "You're going to lose it!"

"Am not!" Sophia said.

"You have Jell-O lips!" Her father teased.

Sophia felt her lips quivering from the effort of trying not to laugh. For a brief moment she thought she would be able to suppress it, but Dan Young knew his daughter almost as well as she knew herself. He knew her weaknesses when it came to making her laugh.

~ ~ ~ ~ ~ ~

When she was just five months old, he discovered one of her "giggle triggers" while he and Sophia spent the day together, just the two of them.

She had just woken up from a nap and was cooing contentedly while trying to eat her toes even though she smelled like something that could be anything but contented.

After cleaning her up and changing her into a football themed onesie that someone had given them at a baby shower months before Sophia was born, Dan took her arms and moved them above her head and said, "TOUCHDOWN!"

Sophia had giggled a husky little baby laugh!

Dan laughed and moved her arms above her head again and repeated. "TOUCHDOWN!"

Sophia's wonderful laugh returned, but this time it was joined by a joyful laugh from her father!

They played TOUCHDOWN! for several minutes, each time Sophia and Dan laughed heartily! Then Sophia started getting fussy and Dan realized it was lunchtime and gave her a bottle.

She had just finished drinking her lunch when Carol got home from the trip that had given them some one-on-one, father-daughter time.

"Hey watch this!" Dan said to his wife.

He went to Sophia who had the "drunken baby" look of an infant who was fully gorged and took her arms, moved them above her head and said, "TOUCHDOWN!" Sophia promptly spewed most of her lunch all over her father and her football themed onesie.

"Neat trick, Dan!" Carol said through snorts of laughter. "I'll get another outfit while you two get cleaned up!"

When she was a toddler, Dan found that wiggling his nose and eyebrows had a similar effect as TOUCHDOWN! and he could do it from a safe distance in case she evacuated her lunch again!

~ ~ ~ ~ ~ ~

He began wiggling his nose and eyebrows and Sophia exploded into laughter!

"You are such a dork, Dad!" She said.

The Podunksville County Fair, as Dan Young had called it, was a lot of fun! Sophia and her dad had quite the competition at the dart throwing/balloon popping booth. When all was said and done, and the "done" part arrived when the twenty-dollar bill Dan had laid on the countertop when they first stepped up to the booth had completely disappeared, Sophia had popped two more balloons than her father.

For her efforts, Sophia had won a huge stuffed velociraptor whom she toyed with the idea of naming Cuddles! For his second-place finish, Dan won a slightly smaller but cuter, according to him anyway, stuffed badger whom he did name Earl!

The only person that was not happy with the wins was the man who operated the booth. When Sophia suggested they continue playing, the booth operator abruptly announced that he was going on break and the booth was now closed.

By Dan's reckoning and after a quick internet search, their wins had cost at least sixty dollars if you paid retail. While walking to the food trailer advertised as "Frank's Corn Dogs – Purveyors of Hot Diggity Dogs", Dan explained that they would not be going back to the balloon popping booth because they had done so well.

"We really cut into his profits Soph." Dan said motioning to their winnings. "If we went back, I bet he would tell us to leave."

"That's okay Dad, one velociraptor and one badger are more than enough for one night! By the way, why did you name your badger Earl?" Sophia asked.

"Because he looks like an Earl!" He said.

"Oh, well okay then." Sophia said. "That totally explains it."

The Youngs ate corn dogs slathered with copious amounts of yellow mustard, looked at the various booths that sold things only found at fairs and, of course, rode the rides! Sophia asked that they save her favorite ride for the very last.

They walked the midway three or four times with the carnival barkers trying to entice them into their games of chance with various claims that their game was the easiest to win and only a fool would pass up on the chance.

"But a fool and his money are soon parted." Dan said to one particularly aggressive barker.

His comment had elicited a momentary stunned look that was followed by a wide, mostly toothless grin and a cigarette smoker's hacking laugh!

"You have a good evening sir!" The barker said bowing his head slightly before continuing with his phlegm laden laugh.

After a few seconds of ragged coughing and laughing, the barker hocked a large yellow-brown wad of something and spit it on the ground next to the "Whack-a-mole" styled game booth he was running.

"Well, *that* was ever so lovely." Carol Young said with sarcasm as they continued on down the midway.

Fortunately, she had worked as an EMT during college so bodily fluids and the like had no real effect on her. Cut or mangled fingers however, well she could do without those.

"Mother!" Sophia said. "I highly suspect he was noble born and is only here so he can learn to relate to us commoners just a bit better."

"Do you really think so?" Carol asked.

"Cross my heart and hope to spit!" Sophia said as she mimicked spitting on the ground.

Like her mother, Sophia had no aversion to such things. She had several friends who were boys, and they were, at times, gross. Of course, her girlfriends could be pretty gross too when you got right down to it.

On their way out of the festivities as they were heading to the minivan, Dan, Carol and Sophia rode the Tilt-a-Whirl with Earl the Badger and Cuddles the Velociraptor! It was Sophia's most favorite ride!

"Shall we give it a spin?" Dan asked pointing to the ticket booth.

"Don't you mean, shall we give it a whirl?" Carol added.

"We shall!" Sophia said.

Since the first time she had ridden it when she was barely four years old, Sophia had loved the spinning, swirling ride! And like the first time she had ridden it, Sophia had laughed and laughed and laughed as the car they were sitting in spun as it swirled around, up and down the undulating track!

Dan and Carol really enjoyed hearing her laugh, since the move it had been mostly non-existent.

"That ride always makes me laugh!" Sophia said after exiting the ride with tears of mirth trickling down her face.

"I wafted too!" A little voice said from behind her.

Sophia looked around and saw the voice's owner, it was Eva, the little girl from The Coombs House Park. She was with her mother, a boy who looked to be about ten and a man, most likely their father. He smiled then continued on toward the carnival with the boy right behind him.

"Little Miss Allbody!" Sophia thought.

"Does it make your tummy tickle?" Sophia asked the little girl who was holding her mother's hand.

"Yeah!" Eva said. "I gets flutterbys in my tummy!"

"Flutterbys?" Sophia mouthed to the little girl's mother.

Eva's mother mouthed back, "Butterflies."

"Oh yeah, flutterbys!" Sophia said. "I get those!"

"I gets 'em whens I go down an ask-u-later too!" Eva informed. Sophia looked at Eva's mother inquiringly.

Eva's mother stifled a giggle and mouthed, "Escalator."

"Oh, an escalator." Sophia said. "Those are fun!"

"No, they is scary!" Eva said in a serious voice.

Sophia didn't know how to respond to Eva's statement and the look on her face must have betrayed her because Eva's mother spoke, "That's why we take the elevator when we can, right Eva?"

"Right Momma." Eva said. "Can we go tatch a duckie?"

"Sure!" Eva's mother said.

"I losted my duckie." Eva said to Sophia with her toddler tale of woe. "Buts Mama and Daddy said I cans get a 'nudder one!"

"You can never have too many rubber ducks!" Eva's mother said. "Thank goodness the duck catching game here at the fair is still open!"

"Hey Eva!" Sophia said spontaneously. "Who loves you?"

As she had done in the park by the granite rock fountain, Eva squatted down and put her hands on the ground before launching herself upward as high as she could and shouted, "Allbody does!" Everyone laughed at the little girl's jubilant answer!

"Let's go catch that duck Eva." Her mother said. "Then we can catch Mikey and Lo-Lo."

"Mikey's my big brudder and Lo-Lo is my big sister! They's at the carn-i-bell." Eva announced. "And dat's Tori!" Eva pointed at the boy walking with her father. "He's my little big brudder."

"I hope you all have fun!" Sophia said.

"We will!" Eva said. "Bye durl! See you ats the park!"

"See you later alligator!" Sophia said.

"I's nots a al-gu-lator; I's a duckie!" Eva insisted.

Everyone laughed again, then Eva and her mother headed toward the midway and Sophia and her family headed to their van. As they were walking across the field that was doubling as a parking lot, Sophia spied a spot of bright yellow lying next to a tuft of grass.

"Hey, look at this!" Sophia said. "I think I found Eva's duck!"

She spun around looking for the little girl and her family, but they had been consumed by the fair going crowd.

"Maybe you'll see her again at the park." Carol said. "And you can give it back to her then."

"Good idea, Mom!" Sophia said.

~ ~ ~ ~ ~ ~

The ride back was longer than she had realized. On the way to the fair, she had absorbed herself in the music she streamed through her phone and had fallen asleep. However, her phone's battery was now nearly dead, the small battery icon read nine percent and she had forgotten her charging cable. She shut down all the apps except for the most important ones. Unfortunately, her music streaming app did not fall into the important category when it came to saving power, and she regretfully turned it off.

During the ride through the countryside, she saw the bright stars that twinkled and sparkled. *"Lucy in the sky with diamonds!"* She thought as she whisper-sang the old Beatles tune in her head. Then her mind drifted and she felt her eyelids start to grow heavy again.

She would have drifted off to sleep again if her nearly dead cell phone hadn't alerted her to a text message with a loud "Tah-Dah!" instead of the chicken clucking. The text came from Leah Sterling, her first best friend since the first day of kindergarten!

She unlocked her phone and with a couple of taps on the home screen of her cell phone, the text messaging app opened, and she saw the words, "I won!!!"

Sophia laughed as she thought about her friend!

~ ~ ~ ~ ~ ~

Sophia and Leah met the first day of kindergarten. She was wearing the white blouse and tartan patterned "skort" her father had picked out for her when they had gone shopping for new school clothes in the weeks before classes had actually started. He also got her a pair of black and white saddle oxfords to go with her first "first day of school" outfit.

Leah was dressed in a light blue romper with Winnie the Pooh's smiling face looking out at everyone. Her left tennis shoe was emblazoned with Piglet. Her favorite character, Eeyore, was on the right shoe and Kanga and Roo were on her socks.

The rest of the Hundred Acre Woods gang could be found on her brand-new backpack which she showed to anyone who displayed the slightest interest in it, or the A.A. Milne characters emblazoned upon it.

"You look like Jasmine from Aladdin!" Leah said when she saw Sophia.

"You have Pooh on your shirt!" Sophia observed after seeing Leah's outfit.

Had anyone been paying attention, they would have heard a stifled chuckle from their parents and their new teacher who were standing just inside the door of the classroom. Also, if anyone else had looked closely at Leah or Sophia's parents they would have seen more than one tear in their eyes.

As with many young children, Sophia and Leah became best friends rather quickly. The promise to be such took place during their first recess while they swung side by side trying to touch the clouds with their feet right after they found out they shared the same middle name and that they lived only a few houses from each other. Leah and her parents had moved into the neighborhood the week before school had started.

"Do you want to be my best friend?" Leah asked Sophia.

"Sure!" Sophia answered. "Do you want to be mine?"

"Yes!" Leah said with a wide smile.

With that simple proclamation, they were officially Best Friends!

From kindergarten through fourth grade, Leah and Sophia were in the same classroom and on more than one occasion got into trouble for talking or passing notes back and forth when they should have been listening, but it was never anything too terribly awful.

There were sleepovers at each other's houses, birthday parties, skating parties, trips to the mall and going to the movies!

However, things began to change when they started middle school. Leah's interests began to shift from the tomboyish activities she had shared with Sophia to a more feminine focus. She entered her very first pageant her first year of middle school. She also continued her writing.

~ ~ ~ ~ ~ ~

Since the second grade, Leah had attended the Young Writer's Conference which was held on the Missouri State University campus. Groups of young writers were given the opportunity to meet published authors who had read and critiqued their stories.

One author in particular had taken an interest in Leah. He had not only given her copies of his books but had made her a character in what was then his newest fiction novel. She didn't know what he had done until the book had been published and she read it!

~ ~ ~ ~ ~ ~

"You are doing what?" Sophia asked just to make sure she had heard Leah correctly.

"I am entering a pageant!" Leah repeated.

Sophia had to admit that Leah was very pretty; she had the most gorgeous almond shaped blue-green eyes! They both had been born with brunette hair, although since the beginning of first grade Leah's had begun to lighten and it was now more of a strawberry blonde whereas Sophia's had taken on a darker chestnut color.

They both wore the same size clothes too, which they swapped routinely, but Leah had something else that just made her shine! Sophia couldn't put her finger on it, but whatever it was, Leah had it!

"A beauty pageant?" Sophia asked. "Why?"

"Not a beauty pageant." Leah corrected. "It's just a pageant, but I can get money for college if I do really well! This one has a FIVE HUNDRED DOLLAR scholarship if you win!"

They talked about the pros and cons of pageants. Sophia thought they were kind of silly while Leah thought they were a means to an end. For a girl just entering sixth grade, Leah was wise beyond her years.

The following weekend, Sophia accompanied Leah and her mother on a shopping excursion to find "The Pageant Dress". One dress in particular was too over the top for Sophia's taste. Leah didn't care for it either, but her mother thought it was perfect and made Leah try it on.

"It comes with a tiara!" Leah's mom enthused.

When Leah stepped out of the dressing room wearing the dress, heels and of course, the tiara, she said, "Tah-dah." in a flat, non-enthusiastic monotone. It was because of that; Leah's ring tone was "Tah-Dah"!

"What do you think?" Leah asked a bit self-consciously hoping against all hope that Sophia would hate it as much as she did.

"You look like a princess!" Gushed Leah's mom.

"Mom!" Leah said before looking back at Sophia.

"Well..." Sophia began.

"Yes?" Leah asked.

"You're not quite a princess. I think you are..." Sophia said.

"What Sophia?" Leah demanded. When Sophia didn't answer fast enough, she added, "Sophia Elizabeth Young, YOU drive me crazy!!!"

"I think you are... a Pretend-cess!" Sophia finally said, coining what would forever be her nickname for her best friend. Then she burst into laughter!

Leah and her mother looked at Sophia as they thought about her pronouncement. After several long seconds they finally joined Sophia in her laughter and a new nickname was born! The dress and tiara stayed at the store.

~ ~ ~ ~ ~ ~

"What's so funny Sophia?" Her mother asked from the front seat.

"Apparently." Sophia said. "The Pretend-cess won one of her pageants, but all her text said was, 'I won!!!' I think this one had a cash prize of maybe two thousand dollars. They went to St. Louis for it."

"Why don't you call her and find out what happened?" Carol suggested.

"I will." Sophia said.

However, her phone chose that exact moment to signal its short-term demise with the sound effect of Pac-Man dying. She had found the ring tone on some third-party app site and set it as the death knell tone for when her phone's power finally gave out.

"Or not." Dan added with a chuckle.

Carol looked back at her daughter, she was concerned that a text message from and talking about Leah would send Sophia into another grumpy funk. However, Sophia seemed upbeat and even asked that they listen to one of her father's oldies station on the satellite radio system since her phone was dead and she couldn't use her music app.

"Music from the eighties is NOT old!" Dan teased.

"You're right Dad." Sophia countered. "It's not."

"It isn't?" He asked wondering where this was headed.

"Nope!" She said. "But the people who listen to it ARE!"

Sophia started laughing again and that made Carol happy.

"What are you going to do tomorrow?" Carol asked.

"Finally read that book I got at the library!" Sophia said. "Or help Maude if she needs me."

"Hmmm?" Dan said. "I figured you would have devoured that a long time ago."

"Nope, but I think tomorrow I shall dine. What are you two going to do?" Sophia asked.

"I am going to do something wild!" Dan said.

"What?" Sophia asked.

"I am going to…" He began. "Go to work and sort mail!"

"Step back from the edge Dad." Sophia said. "You're starting to worry me."

Chapter 12

The clucking chicken alarm tone woke Sophia at precisely seven o'clock. When she had set it, she had wondered about her sanity with it still being summer and that she wasn't going to help Maude Adelaide at her house, but then remembered what Laura had told her.

"Sometimes you have to do something a little crazy to prove that you are actually sane!"

After a quick shower, she didn't take one after getting home from the fair because she was tired and just didn't want to. She ate a bowl of some sugar frosted something or other and two hardboiled eggs. She put on her favorite pair of running shorts and her black Darci Lynne and Friends tee shirt that featured the young singing ventriloquist and her puppets, Petunia the Rabbit and Oscar the Motown Singing Mouse!

"Darci makes the best faces!" Sophia thought as she looked at the shirt. *"And she sings better with her mouth closed than most people do with their mouths open!"*

Ever since she had seen a home video of Darci at a school talent show and then on America's Got Talent, Sophia, like so many others, had become diehard fans and had cheered her on as she progressed to the finals before finally and rightfully winning Season Twelve!

Sophia had gotten the shirt when she got to see Darci's live show at The Midland Theater, an old, ornate and fully restored theater in Kansas City. Her parents would have liked to have stayed closer to home to see the show, but the single night show in Springfield at the Gillioz Theater had sold out before they could buy tickets. However, they were able to find three tickets for the Kansas City show the very next night.

"That poor man!" Sophia giggled as she pulled the shirt over her head and remembered the show.

~~~~~~

After intermission, Darci came back on stage in a cute, little black dress carrying her ornery old lady puppet, Edna Doorknocker, who immediately began flirting with a man in the front row.

Sophia, her parents and the rest of the audience laughed when Edna gasped and said, "Oh my goodness! I see a something I like!" in reference to him.

They laughed even harder when he checked to see if it was him she was talking to and Edna said, "He looked around, but it's YOU!" She emphasized "YOU" by pointing her cane at him!

Darci said the man was much too young for her, but Edna countered with, "He's breathing ain't he!"

After some friendly banter, the man was invited on stage so Edna could sing to him. What took a lot of people by surprise was what the man had done as he sat on the stool next to Edna and Darci. He smiled at Edna then turned to the audience, kissed the tip of his index finger and touched Edna on the tip of her nose!

The crowd loved it and Darci, not to be upstaged, had Edna say, "Oh no he didn't!"

The man said something that caused Darci to smile, but he didn't have a microphone so the audience couldn't hear what he had said.

Edna then sang "A Natural Woman" to him just as she had done to Simon Cowell on AGT! Unlike Simon though, the man's face did not turn red while Edna crooned!

Sophia thought Darci's "little black dress" was absolutely perfect and spent most of the long ride back home trying to convince her parents that she needed one.

It was a discussion she was still having, but now that she was going to be a freshman in high school, she thought her chances would improve. In fact, she felt her chances were nearly one hundred percent because she had seen her mother looking at black dresses on the internet the week before and her birthday *was* coming up, so…

~ ~ ~ ~ ~ ~

Sophia found her flip flops, one of her drawstring backpacks and a fleece blanket that was adorned with the Missouri State University logo.

She wanted to attend Missouri State someday, more so now that she was two hundred fifty miles away, where she would study…something. She wasn't sure what she wanted to be when she grew up, but she knew she wanted to be a Missouri State Bear!

She put her copy of the book in her bag, but she had removed the dust jacket. If the book's cover got dirty, the dust jacket would cover it.

She added two peanut butter and jelly sandwiches, six hardboiled eggs and an insulated thermos of ice-cold milk in the bag as well and headed to the door, but she paused, then returned to her room and fired up her laptop.

She wasn't going to record any of the old reel to reel tapes, at least not right then. Instead, she opened a search browser and typed in "Covered Bridges in Missouri". After just a few milliseconds, her search produced the result she was certain she would find.

"Bingo!" She said to herself as she clicked the small map showing the location of her query. *"And it looks like it's only a few miles away!"*

As she cut across the lawn toward the garage, she realized she had made a mistake due to the heavy dew that coated every single blade of grass. She returned to her room and replaced the flip flops with her tennis shoes then headed out the door a second time. She used the sidewalk on this restart of her journey and walked to the garage to retrieve her bicycle, a burgundy Schwinn three speed.

~ ~ ~ ~ ~ ~

After her failed attempt to ride it to the Adelaide's house due to a flat tire, she had asked her dad to fix it for her. He had refused, but he did show *her* how to fix it and use the nifty – his words, not hers – little air compressor he had in the garage to air it up once the inner tube had been patched.

"Soph, I could do it for you, but in a year, you will be sixteen and probably driving. I need to start showing you how to do things like change a flat and even change the oil, but for now I'll show you how to patch a bicycle tire." Her dad had said.

She had agreed and listened and done as he said as he talked her through the steps of taking the wheel off the bike, the tire off the rim, removing the inner tube, then finding and patching the hole with a "vulcanizing" tire patch.

She had been intrigued when he set it ablaze. She watched the fire cross the diamond shaped patch; the smell reminded her of the "snakes" fireworks she had as a child on the Fourth of July.

Once the patch had cooled, she replaced the tube in the tire and the tire on the rim, then aired it up and put it back on her bicycle. The total repair took maybe twenty minutes.

"It's a little different with a car tire, Sophia." Dan had said. "You need to take the flat to a shop to get that fixed, but you still need to know what the process is."

"That was really cool Dad!" She had said.

"Here in a couple of weeks, I'm going to replace the brake pads on the van, and I want you to watch that too. Besides, to do the brake pads you have to take the tire off just like you do when you have a flat, so you can help me."

"It's a date!" Sophia said.

~ ~ ~ ~ ~ ~

The morning air was almost chilly and gave a hint of what early autumn would be like in this part of the Show Me state. Sophia had considered going back to her room for a light jacket or her fleece hoodie but decided against it; after two false starts she wanted to get to the Coombs House Park and start reading the book. Besides, she knew the morning's cool temperature would not last long; the forecast was for a high nearing one hundred degrees.

The park gate screamed its rusty "I need oiled" hello, as Sophia opened it and wheeled her bike on to the red brick path. The fountain that normally babbled a watery greeting was silent, which was slightly concerning to her.

"I wonder what's up with that." She thought looking at the dry red granite boulder.

As if answering her silent question, the fountain gurgled and belched then a large spray of water shot skyward as it sprang to life. Within a matter of minutes, the red granite boulder was glistening in the morning sunshine.

She looked at the bench where she had first met little Miss Eva Allbody and decided it might be too cool for her liking this early in the morning; it faced west and was completely shaded in the small grotto of red brick.

On the opposite side of the red granite bolder fountain, she saw a trumpet vine covered niche that housed a wooden bench that was longer than she was tall that faced east and was bathed in the sun's morning glow. She looked at the bench and hoped it was as warm as it looked.

Sophia stashed her drawstring backpack under the bench after retrieving the Missouri State blanket, her book and one of the hardboiled eggs. She stretched her small frame across the bench and wrapped the blanket around her bare legs. Even though the sun was shining on the bench, it had not warmed up nearly as much as she had hoped.

She started to open the book, but paused when she noticed a sparrow fly down to a puddle next to the boulder fountain.

"I'm going to call you Jack. As in Jack T. Sparrow!" Sophia said to the bird. "The T is for 'The' by the way!"

The bird looked at her then hopped to the edge of the puddle, dipped its bill into the water, tipped its head back and took a drink!

"I guess you are thirsty!" Sophia said as she watched Jack T. Sparrow take several more drinks and then take a bath before he fluffed out his feathers and took flight to parts unknown. Sophia watched the bird disappear into the clear morning sky.

She opened her book and again read the opening sentence: "An attic is an interesting place to visit; it holds treasures and secrets. Sometimes the secrets *are* the treasures."

"Cubbyholes are pretty cool too!" Sophia thought with a small giggle.

On impulse, she riffled the pages of the book with her thumb until she randomly stopped on a page and began reading.

~ ~ ~ ~ ~ ~

"Does everyone have eggs?" Laura asked.
All the girls nodded that they did.
"Oh!" Allison Taylor said. "Here's some for you two."
She handed Meg and Laura a dozen eggs each.
The eight girls all began to nervously giggle, then they broke from the shadows of the bleachers and crossed the parking lot to where Eddy Best's car sat unattended.
After five minutes of "egg-orating" as the girls had called their endeavor, they stepped back to admire their handy work.
"I think that's going to cause him some real "egg-citment" when he sees it." Laura said.
The girls all laughed.
"I think it looks "egg-ceptional." Meg chimed in with a pun of her own.
"He's getting "egg-xactly" what he deserves." Allison said.

~ ~ ~ ~ ~ ~

Sophia chuckled as she read about the egging of a car; it brought back a memory of something she and Leah had done the summer they turned eleven. It was a week before they started the fifth grade.

"Wow!" Sophia thought. *"That was four years ago!"*

~ ~ ~ ~ ~ ~

"What's in there?" Sophia asked, pointing at an old looking building across Leah's grandparent's large gravel drive.
"That is the chicken coop, but I think it's more like a chicken condo!" Leah said. "You want to go inside?"
"Sure!" Sophia said.
The girls entered and were greeted with a cacophony of chickens alerting each other that there were strangers in their home. The large multi-colored rooster "cock-a-doodle-dooed" once, then returned to whatever it is roosters do.
"It smells in here." Sophia said while crinkling up her nose.

"You get used to it." Leah said. "Now come on, let's get some eggs."

"Where are they?" Sophia asked, somewhat puzzled.

"Right here!" Leah said as she thrust her hand under a large chicken that was sitting in a wooden box with straw spilling out of its top.

The hen "ba-ba-bocked" its surprise and flapped her wings in protest, but this wasn't Leah's first-time getting eggs and was well out of striking distance of the flailing chicken.

Sophia, on the other hand, was not so lucky. The hen she tried to relieve of its egg was in its box next to the aforementioned "cock-a-doodle-dooing" multi-colored rooster. When the hen "ba-ba-bocked" its displeasure, the rooster crowed, Sophia screamed, the hens erupted into a loud cacophony of angst and the rooster began flogging her with its wings. Leah sat down hard on the floor laughing hysterically!

It was the laughing Sophia remembered later that got to her. She was scared of the chickens and all Leah did was laugh; her best friend since forever did nothing but laugh! And that is what caused her to throw the brown, freshly laid egg.

Normally, Sophia was not very accurate when it came to things like throwing, but every once in a while, like when the moon was in conjunction with Mars and Jupiter, she could hit what she was aiming at. Much to the chagrin of Leah, the day she took Sophia to the chicken coop was one such day. The egg splattered evenly across the side of Leah's laughing face which instantly contorted into a mask of outrage and revulsion.

"Sophia!" Leah screamed. "Why did you do that?"

It was Sophia's turn to laugh. She couldn't help it; the sight of egg yolk dripping down the side of her best friend's face was just too funny! Like Leah had done moments before, Sophia sat down hard on the floor and began laughing; she laughed and laughed and laughed! In fact, she was so into her laughing that she didn't notice that Leah had gotten up and accosted another hen for her egg.

"Sophia." Leah said.

Sophia giggled a nearly inaudible, "Yeah?"

Leah summarily smashed an egg on top of Sophia's head which wiped the smile from her face and the laughter from her lips.

"Wha...why...Oooo!" Sophia stammered with a voice that was nearly a growl.

Leah busied herself with trying to squeegee the eggshell fragments and yolk from her hair with her fingers. Sophia busied herself with gathering three more brown eggs. Her anger at being slimed by Leah must have been noticed by the hens because not one of them "ba-ba-bocked" in protest.

Leah had removed most of the egg and its shell fragments from her hair and the side of her face, but her efforts were futile because Sophia smashed three more eggs on the back of her head and neck where the shell fragments, yolk and albumin ran down the back of her shirt.

It was most likely Leah's screams at being triple egged that alerted her parents and grandparents, but they were in the backyard and a fair distance from the chicken house. In the time it took them to get to the girls, an all-out egg war had erupted, and the girls were egg and straw covered messes.

Leah's parents were angry when they saw what had happened. However, Lloyd and Lois Sterling, Leah's grandparents, doubled over with laughter when they saw what had been going on. They had to remind Nancy and Ron about an incident regarding eggs when they were dating in high school.

"Do you remember anything about a few dozen eggs, a teacher's house and the police?" Lloyd said when Ron and Nancy began to scold the girls.

Leah's parents quieted down then snorted at the memory.

"Fine!" Nancy said to her father-in-law. "But you two have a mess to clean up!"

"And it has to pass Grandpa's and Grandma's inspection, or you'll clean it again!" Ron added.

The girls didn't speak to each other for the first several minutes of their cleaning; both were silently blaming each other for the trouble they were in. They were also blaming each other for the egg smelling stickiness that had run, dripped and basically coated their upper bodies and legs.

"This is so gross!" Sophia finally said. "It feels like my skin is tearing when I bend my knees."

"Mine too." Leah agreed.

Sophia looked at her best friend and smiled. Leah returned the gesture and in seconds the smiles had turned into giggles then outright laughter. It didn't take very long to sweep up the mess they had made, and they were still giggling when they headed to Leah's grandparent's house.

"Hold it!" Ron said as they were ready to mount the steps and go inside.

"Dad!" Leah implored. "We're gross and need to wash up."

"I know." He said. "And I'm going to help you."

The blast of cold water hit Leah first and she screamed. Sophia was hit seconds later with the same ear-splitting result. The girls made a dash toward a large lilac bush but were halted by Leah's mother and a second cold water firing garden hose.

After nearly five minutes of being drenched, Ron and Nancy decided the girls had been sufficiently de-egged so they were handed towels and directed to the basement bathroom where they could shower.

Fortunately for both girls, they had been to a sleepover at their friend Audrey's house the night before and both had their "sleepover bags" with them. They were able to wear their pajamas while their egg covered clothes were run through Lois' washer and dryer.

~ ~ ~ ~ ~ ~

Sophia laughed at the memory, but felt a familiar and rather large lump in her throat and the beginnings of tears in the corners of her eyes. After a couple of deep, calming breaths, she was able to quell the emotion that had risen so quickly inside her.

"No!" She said out loud to the book and the gurgling fountain. "No more!"

After two or three more steadying breaths, Sophia opened the book to its first page and began reading the book in earnest.

Chapter 13

Sophia learned how Laura had met Jerry and how that first meeting had made such a figurative and literal impact on them both.

She learned how L. Frank Baum had contributed to their first kiss! Butterflies – *flutterbys* - took flight in the pit of Sophia's stomach as she imagined the moment when their lips met for the first time at Laura's Halloween party!

She learned how nice and thoughtful Jerry was the first Christmas they were dating, even though they couldn't officially date. It sounded to Sophia that the luck of a four-leaf clover wasn't needed when it came to Laura meeting Jerry. It sounded to her that fate was the main player and fate, like attics and cubbyholes, can be a very good thing!

She learned that there are other options when you and your girlfriend or boyfriend cannot go to Prom because you are both freshmen.

Sophia opened up her favorite music app on her phone and listened to Elvis' version of *Can't Help Falling in Love* after reading the passage about the "Freshman Prom" that had been held in the hayloft of an old barn.

She learned that a sprained ankle is an unusual yet wonderful way to find out that the boy you really care about admits that he loves you and is not afraid to cry in front of you when he tells you! Sophia also learned that you could get your hair washed while lying on a sofa when you are laid up with a sprained ankle too!

"That would be amazing!" Sophia thought.

She learned that spontaneity can be fun even if it means you jump into a creek with all your clothes on when visiting a covered bridge!

"They really went to a covered bridge?" Sophia asked herself. *"I wonder if the bridge I found on the internet is the covered bridge from my dream."*

She learned that boys can be jerks, but she also learned that Laura was a forgiving person even after Jerry and his friends had ruined a backyard sleepover she and her friends were having.

"Jerry, don't do stuff like that. I expect better than that from you." Laura had said to Jerry.

As she read that particular passage, Sophia could feel the disappointment Laura felt for Jerry and the remorse he had felt for what he had done.

"I'm kind of glad she didn't talk to him for a few days." Sophia thought. *"I bet it made him really think about what he had done and what he had to potentially lose by being a jerk."*

She knew that Laura had been a cheerleader, she had found her photo when she dropped the book the last time, she came to the Coombs House Park. Reading about her initial entrance at the first pep assembly at the beginning of her Sophomore year of high school made Sophia smile. Knowing that Laura had been able to secure a spot on the cheerleading squad her Sophomore year gave Sophia a little more hope.

"I worked so hard to make the squad! I will make it next year even if it is cheering for The Mighty Possums." That last thought made Sophia laugh and smile!

She learned there are self-centered people in this world as well. They will do anything, anything at all, to show they are the best even when they are far from it. Tears formed in Sophia's eyes and ran down her cheeks as she read about Laura's concussion and other injuries from the attack by Bill Morris.

And she learned again that Jerry was a true gentleman who loved Laura with all his heart when he once again washed her hair while she was on her sofa recovering from the repercussions of what Bill Morris had done. He proved it further when he agreed, albeit begrudgingly, not to retaliate for what Bill Morris had done to Laura during the unofficial basketball championships.

She learned that the wider world can, at times, be an evil place. Sophia felt more tears slide down her cheeks as she read about how Jerry and Laura lived through the assassination of John Fitzgerald Kennedy.

She learned that an unexpected snowstorm could make you realize once again that your boyfriend is as much of a gentleman as you had thought and hoped he was, when you were stranded with him in a little motel miles and miles from home.

"I cannot imagine having to call my parents and ask them if it would be okay to spend the night in a motel with my boyfriend." Sophia thought.

She also learned that you should pay attention to your surroundings before laying a lip lock onto your boyfriend because your parents just might be sitting on the sofa just a few feet away when you do it!

"Hi Durl!" A little voice said.

Sophia jumped when Eva spoke and drew her out of the story and back into the present. The tiny girl was standing a few feet away, grinning and was wearing a Paw Patrol tee shirt emblazoned with a husky named Everest.

"Hi there! Sophia said putting the book into her backpack. "How are you?"

"Good!" The little girl said, grinning.

"Eva, don't bother...." Eva's mother began but stopped when she saw Sophia. "Oh, hello! Did you enjoy the fair?"

"Hi!" Sophia said. "Yes, I did!"

"I'm doeing fountain climbing!" Eva announced while her fingers danced around each other. "Buts I can't gets too wet."

"Fountain climbing?" Sophia asked.

"Yes! I walks around the fountain likes I'm climbed it!" Eva said.

She scampered to the low red brick wall that surrounded the large red granite boulder and tentatively dipped her right index finger into the pool to test the waters so to speak.

"That's a big rock isn't it?" Sophia asked from her spot on the bench.

"It's big-normous!" Eva said.

Sophia, still smiling, fought the urge to laugh. Little Miss Allbody was so cute, and her statements were so naturally funny it was hard not to giggle when she was around.

"Do you think you could lift that big red rock Eva?" Sophia asked.

The little girl slowly turned her head and faced Sophia. She had an "Are you kidding me?!" look on her face. When she spoke, Eva enunciated each word slowly and almost as precisely as Maude Adelaide had pronounced the word gravity the day they had first met.

"That wock is too hebby for me and you!" Eva said plainly.

"You know, you are right!" Sophia said.

"I knows I is! That's the biggest rock ever!" Eva said. "Momma, can I go fountain climbing again?"

"Okay, but this is the last time." Eva's mother said. "We have to stop by and see Marion on our way home, remember?"

"Can we get ice cream?" Eva asked hopefully.

"Of course!" Eva's mother said.

"Marion has the bestest ice cream!" Eva said to Sophia.

"I know!" Sophia said. "I love her strawberry milk shakes!"

"Strawberry is gooder!" Eva announced.

Eva's mom laughed. "If you want ice cream, you need to finish fountain climbing."

"Okay!" The little girl said.

As Eva began her trip around the red granite boulder fountain, Sophia opened her drawstring backpack and removed the little yellow rubber duck that she had found at the fair. When Eva was on the other side of the boulder, Sophia quickly left the bench, placed the duck in the water and returned to her seat and waited to see Eva's reaction.

"I found that at the fair last night." Sophia said quietly. "I think it might be the one she lost."

"It could be." Eva's mother said.

Eva was humming a tune that somewhat resembled the theme song of Barney and Friends as she came around to Sophia's side of the fountain. When she spied the little yellow rubber duck bobbing in the water, her humming stopped and she squealed, "DUUCKIE!" Eva plunged her hands into the fountain and snatched the toy from the water.

Sophia watched the scene from her spot on the bench. Eva's mother made eye contact with her and mouthed, "Thank you!"

Sophia mouthed back, "You're welcome!"

Little Eva was joyous with the little yellow duck! She held a complete conversation with her newly found toy and provided the voices for both. The one she created for the duck was high pitched and contained numerous quacks!

"Hey, Eva?" Her mother asked. "Do you think Duckie wants to get some ice cream?"

Duckie's high-pitched, quacky voice assured her that ice cream would be a good idea!

"Well, let's get going then. I know Marion will be happy to meet Duckie!" Eva's mom said.

"Okay!" Eva said. She turned to Sophia and spoke. "What's your name?"

"Sophia." Sophia said.

"Bye, Sofa!" The little girl said.

"Sofa. She sounds just like Caiter-tot." Sophia thought.

"See you later Miss Eva! Have fun with Duckie!" Sophia said.

"I will!" Eva said. "I gots more duckies at home!"

"Do you have a flock of duckies?" Sophia asked.

"No! I has a _box_ of duckies!' Eva corrected emphatically.

That last declaration, "…a box of duckies!" caused Sophia to giggle out loud. She didn't want to hurt Eva's feelings; she didn't want her to think she was laughing at her. Sophia's concerns were for naught.

"We's going to get ice cream!" Eva said. "Bye Durl! I meaneded Sofa!"

"Who loves you Eva?" Sophia asked.

Eva put her hands on her little hips and said, "Allbody does, don't you 'member?"

"I do now, Eva." Sophia said.

Little Eva Allbody scampered to the gate with her mother; it announced their departure with a high-pitched squeal reminiscent of multiple fingernails scraping down an old chalk board.

Sophia sat quietly for a moment listening to the sounds of the morning. She heard birds, perhaps the siblings or cousins of the recently bathed Jack T. Sparrow. She heard an occasional car making its way down the street that ran on the other side of the brick wall. She heard the distant voices of some children. Maybe they were the voices of Sandi and her friends starting another game of kickball.

Sophia sighed. It wasn't a sad or morose sigh; it was just a sigh. After another moment of listening to the greater world, she looked at her cell phone, saw it was nine o'clock, then took out the book and began reading again.

~ ~ ~ ~ ~ ~

Sophia learned Laura, the girl of Jerry's dreams and the girl *in* Sophia's dreams, was a force to be reckoned with when it came to going to Prom their Sophomore year.

"A loophole is a loophole!" Sophia thought as she read about Laura's simple, yet brilliant plan of having her friend Amy Ford ask Jerry to the Prom and Amy's boyfriend Will Shelton asking Laura!

Sophia learned that some people just don't get it, in this case, it was Bill Morris, again.

"What a complete and total jerk!" She thought as she read about the events that took place at the Prom.

She also learned Laura was a "spitfire" as she read about how she had taken care of Bill. The line, "What stopped him was a well-placed knee…" caused Sophia to smile, but the line that said, "He knee-ed to know…" made her laugh out loud!

"Served him right." Sophia thought.

She learned that the cost of having a vehicle to call your own, sometimes came with a heavy price. Sophia teared up as she read that Jerry's grandfather left him his old pickup truck after he had died. The tears continued when she read about Laura's grandmother Margaret leaving her a Rambler convertible when she died just a few weeks later.

Two thoughts immediately popped into Sophia's mind. First, all her grandparents had passed by the time she was thirteen so having any of them leave her a car was something that would not happen. Second, and more importantly, was that maybe, just maybe Maude Adelaide's sister Margaret may have changed her haughty ways before she had passed away.

"I know Maude said Margaret was not the nicest person, but maybe she had changed. She did leave Laura her car after all." Sophia thought. *"I'll ask Maude about it the next time I'm at her house…maybe."*

Sophia learned and again laughed out loud as she read about the last time the Adelaide sister's house had been cleaned. Like Maude had said, it was in nineteen sixty-three and that cleaning had been prompted by Myrtle, instead of Maude and Laura had been the hired help.

"I guess they take turns cleaning every fifty or sixty years!" Sophia thought!

She learned how Jerry had lost a bet to Laura about who would win the annual boy's and girls' Fourth of July ball game and what Laura had done to him. She also learned how a rattlesnake had lost to Laura as well.

"I think I would have passed out right there." Sophia thought. *"Or maybe wet myself."*

Sophia paused in her reading and digested what she had learned so far. While she digested the book, she retrieved another hard-boiled egg and began digesting that as well. She nearly choked on her snack when she read the next section.

"They went skinny dipping!?!" Sophia said rather loudly while coughing.

Her shocked and giggling outburst caused a squirrel to poke its head out of a knot hole in one of the trees over-looking the fountain and chitter at her for disturbing its peace. The little red coated tree rat: a term her father sometimes used to describe squirrels, gave one last irritated and indignant "chert" then disappeared back inside the tree.

The squirrel's scolding and her choking on the hard-boiled egg broke Sophia's concentration, so she put the book down, stood up and walked, first around the red granite boulder – fountain climbing – looking at the multi-colored, wet stone from various angles. A quick gust of wind threw one of the fountain's belches from atop the large stone onto the top of Sophia's head. It wasn't much water, but it got her attention and made her giggle just a little!

The fountain was at the main gate of the Coombs House Park, but Sophia could see there was much more than the fountain, trees and shaded benches. Walking beyond Little Miss Eva Allbody's "favoritest" spot in the whole world, Sophia saw that the red brick paved ground formed an ambling path around the lot.

Sophia strolled and took in the flowers, trees, bushes and some cast concrete sculptures of some of the world's most famous statues. There was the Venus De Milo surrounded by some sort of red flowers. However, someone had made a sign from a pizza box and propped it against Ms. De Milo's exposed abdomen with two upward pointing arrows and the words, "Can't you see I'm cold!".

Sophia snatched the sign from the statue and tore it in half before unceremoniously shoving the remains in a nearby trashcan then continued her walk through the park.

"I don't know why I haven't taken the time to look at more than just the boulder fountain; this place is really nice even if there are nit-wits who make signs!" Sophia thought.

She came across a bench made entirely out of the red bricks.

"I bet that's comfortable. Not!" She thought as she looked at the seating space.

Behind the brick bench was a second statue with its own water effect. It wasn't a fountain like the one at the entrance; this was a statue of a mermaid sitting on a rock. The bronze plaque attached to the fountain base said: "The Little Mermaid (Danish: den Lille Havfrue) a bronze statue by Edvard Eriksen. The original is in Copenhagen, Denmark. This replica was purchased for $5,000.00 in 1950 and placed in the Coombs House Park by the Coombs family in honor of their children and grandchildren. It is for the enjoyment of the community!"

Water flowed out of the top of the red granite boulder between the mermaid's hand and leg just an inch or two above the rock's surface before cascading across the top and down its sides. The catch basin was made from the same red bricks as most everything in the park was made, but Sophia could see that they were just a decorative outer layer and simply surrounded a water tank. The fountain at the entrance was constructed in a similar way and both tank's interiors were painted a light, whitish blue like a swimming pool.

Sophia reached into her pocket and found a single coin, a nickel, closed her eyes and wished, *"I want to make some choices of my own; I wish I could do that."*

She flipped the coin with her thumb, just like her grandpa had taught her, high into the air where it flipped end over end before plunging with an audible "ploop" into the fountain's water.

As she continued her stroll, she noticed more benches, some made entirely of red brick, some made of black painted cast iron with oak seats and backs. There were little niches that held some of the benches, the shade of the many trees held the others. The Coombs House Park was peaceful, and Sophia liked the way it made her feel!

She came upon a third water pool at the back of the park. The round pool was surrounded by red bricks like the boulder fountain and the Little Mermaid fountain, but this one contained a model of a covered bridge. Someone had painstakingly created a miniature landscape of not just a bridge, but of the area around it and the water in the creek underneath it flowed!

"That is…" Sophia began. "THE bridge I dreamed about!"

Like the other fountains, the bridge fountain, if you could call it a fountain, had a bronze plaque attached to it that said the model of the Little Grand Creek Covered Bridge was built and donated to the Coombs House Park as a part of an Eagle Scout project. It had been dedicated, August 18, 1964.

"Okay." Sophia said to no one. "I am going to see that bridge right now!"

She quickly returned to the boulder fountain, gathered up her things and put them in her backpack before wheeling her three speed out through the oil deprived gate. It was ten o'clock.

Chapter 14

For what turned out to be her last Christmas in Springfield, Sophia's parents had given her a cell phone holder that mounted on her bike's handle bars, a set of wireless Bluetooth ear buds and of course her laptop.

Her father had mounted the cell phone holder on her bike's handle bars and as she straddled the Schwinn, she placed her smartphone into the cradle. She had already done an internet search for all the covered bridges in Missouri and had pinpointed the Little Grand Creek Covered Bridge on a GPS mapping app.

"Three miles to the bridge." Sophia thought looking at her phone's screen.

She found the tiny ear buds in her backpack, removed one of them from the case which doubled as its charging base and inserted it into her ear. She repeated the process for the other ear bud then put the case back into the backpack. She knew that a small L.E.D. light on both of the ear buds would alternate from red to blue then back to red indicating they were on, functioning properly and awaiting to pair with her phone.

A nasally voice advised the ear buds had successfully linked to the mapping app with a simple, "Connected."

"Thank you, Meagan!" Sophia said to the electronic voice.

Meagan advised, "Fifteen minutes to your destination."

"Please don't try and kill me again." She said before starting her journey to the Little Grand Creek Covered Bridge and remembering with amusement the trip where Meagan became Meagan and had, according to family lore, tried to kill the entire Young family.

~ ~ ~ ~ ~ ~

Shortly after she received her smartphone, Sophia and her family made the hour or so trip from Springfield to Silver Dollar City; the amusement park that helped make Branson, Missouri famous. During the trip, her dad asked her to try out the mapping app on her new phone. After setting it up and connecting it to their minivan's stereo system via an audio cord and the stereo's auxiliary port, the Young's heard the app's voice for the first time.

"In three hundred feet, turn right." The voice said.

Dan Young flicked the turn signal's lever up. He turned down a street that connected Highway seventy-six, Branson's version of the Las Vegas strip, to another street that was supposed to get them off the beaten path and to Silver Dollar City quickly.

"Look out!" Carol Young shouted.

A four-wheel drive pickup truck with a large metal pipe grill guard that appeared as big as their van, suddenly filled their windshield.

"Recalculating." The app's voice said.

"CRAP!" Dan Young said.

The ball cap wearing driver of the four-wheel drive pickup made a well-known gesture with his left hand and turned his truck to the right, away from their van.

Dan saw the entrance of an alley between two buildings and whipped the van to the right and off the street.

"In seventy-five feet, make a U-turn." The app said in its nasally, valley girl sounding voice.

"Thanks Meagan!" Dan said. "I'll get right on that as soon as I get my heart started again!"

The van was totally quiet for several seconds before Carol, then Sophia and finally Dan began laughing. It seemed stress had the same effect on all the members of the Young family.

"Dad?" Sophia asked once her giggles had subsided. "Who is Meagan?"

After they turned around and resumed their tourist clogged trip down Highway seventy-six, Dan and Carol told the story of a girl they knew from high school named Meagan.

"She sounded like…" Dan began. "…like THAT!" He pointed at the screen on Sophia's phone. "But at least she didn't try to kill us!"

From that point, whenever the Young family travelled and they needed directional assistance, someone would say, "Let's ask Meagan and hope she doesn't try to kill us."

~ ~ ~ ~ ~ ~

The bike ride to the Little Grand Creek Covered Bridge was pleasant, well, as pleasant as a bike ride in Missouri in the last half of August can be. The projected high temperature was going to be met, if not exceeded, and the chilly morning air was just a memory.

The last time the burgundy Schwinn had been ridden was two days before it had been loaded into the U-Haul truck that brought all their worldly possessions to Podunksville. As she rode, she began thinking about that last bike ride in Springfield.

~ ~ ~ ~ ~ ~

Sophia had left her house with no particular destination in mind just before her life irrevocably changed. She was upset about having to move and could do nothing; not one single thing, about it. The choice had been made for her. So, she cruised her neighborhood with tears slowly running down her cheeks, remembering.

Many of the houses she passed were the homes of friends. Laney Williams lived in the Cape Cod that had an actual in-ground pool in the backyard at the end of the block. Laney, Leah, Audrey, Sophia and most all of the kids in the neighborhood had spent many summer afternoons splashing in that pool.

There had been a large neighborhood get together and cook out at the Williams' home two nights before where everyone on the block congregated around the pool munching on hamburgers, hotdogs and a host of other picnic type food. Although no one would come right out and say it, it was a farewell and good luck party for Sophia and her family.

Dave VandeKamp and his sisters lived in the ranch style with the three-car garage. Sophia had thought it weird that someone with two cars would have a three-car garage. However, once she had seen all three doors open, she understood.

Dave's father, also named Dave, used the garage furthest from the house for his woodworking shop. Sophia knew he did small wood carvings; Little Dave had brought one to Show and Tell when they were in the third grade. It was a realistic statue that looked surprisingly like the comedian Robin Williams swinging a tire iron at what looked like a red and white striped croquet ball that was sitting on a can of pork and beans! She assumed that the pork and bean can was a subtle reference to their last name.

Audrey Noble lived in the brick house at the other end of the block. They were the same age and had been best friends since first grade. In the sixth grade when middle school began, she and Audrey had found new interests much like she and Leah had.

Audrey, by her own admission, had become a complete and total band geek when she discovered the tenor saxophone. Sophia had gravitated toward more tech related things and Leah focused on her pageants. They were all still the best of friends; they just didn't do the same things or have the same interests as they once did.

Those first weeks of sixth grade were warm and dry which allowed Audrey to practice her saxophone outside. Sophia, her parents and most of the other residents of their once quiet suburban street were tolerant of Audrey's musical learning curve. However, only Meg Noble, Audrey's mother, was the one who was most thankful that Audrey could be outside learning scales that initially sounded like someone strangling a goose!

Sophia remembered how good Audrey's playing had become and in a fairly short amount of time. The first time there were tryouts for the ten saxophone chairs in the band, Audrey impressed everyone by securing First Chair! It was the chair she still held, and based on the last time Sophia had heard her play; Audrey would probably be in that chair until she graduated high school!

Sophia was a little jealous of Audrey; not because of her saxophone playing ability, but because of her amazing complexion. Sophia's own complexion was nothing to be ashamed of; there was the occasional pimple, but those flair ups were few and far between and were easily concealed.

Audrey, however, was truly blessed in the skin department. When 'Aunty Acne' had begun paying visits to Sophia and her friends, Audrey's porcelain skin remained unblemished.

"She should be a model." Sophia and her friends had said on more than one occasion. When they mentioned it to Audrey, she laughed it off as if it were the most ridiculous thing she had ever heard. That's what made Audrey truly an attractive person; she had no idea how outwardly pretty she actually was. All who knew her readily agreed that by the time she was a senior in high school, outwardly Audrey would be stunningly beautiful which would finally match the striking inner beauty she already had!

Sophia remembered one Saturday night in particular. After several hours in Laney's pool, she, Audrey, Leah and Laney had a sleepover in her downstairs family room. She remembered Laney bemoaning the fact that she was getting a zit on her chin and there was the "Welcome Back" dance in six days.

Laney was upset with the prospect of having something resembling a little red Volkswagen coming around a corner on her chin; a phrase she had borrowed from a very old episode of Saturday Night Live they had watched on Netflix.

Audrey perked up and asked if anyone had an aspirin. One of the girls dug through the little clutch purse that doubled as their cell phone's carrying case and handed her a small drab brown travel packet of aspirin. Audrey ripped open the packet and dumped one of the little white tablets into an unused snack bowl, crushed it into a fine powder with the blunt end of a knife, added a few drops of water to it and made a paste.

"Put this on your zit." Audrey advised. "It will dry it out overnight."

Someone said, "Audrey the skin doctor." Everyone, Audrey included, laughed!

"I want to be a dermatologist, I think." Audrey said. "I love watching those pimple popping videos on the internet."

Her confession was met with a rousing chorus of, "Yuck!" and "You are gross!" and "Disgusting!"

Audrey said, "Yeah, it's kind of weird, I know. Anyway, I read about that aspirin paste in some magazine."

"You're not going to try and pop it when I'm asleep are you?" Laney asked.

"Uh, no!" Audrey said emphatically. "That <u>would</u> be gross!"

The paste was applied and covered with a small round Band-Aid. The next morning everyone was awakened by Laney's shrieks of, "The zit is almost gone! Audrey you are a genius!"

Sophia would miss Audrey and the times they had shared just as much as she would miss her friends Laney and Leah. There were sleepovers, birthday parties, going to the Battlefield Mall and those other extraordinarily ordinary things you do with the friends you've known your whole life.

Sighing heavily, Sophia rode slowly back to her house, parked the Schwinn in the garage, went to her room and collapsed onto her bed sobbing.

~ ~ ~ ~ ~ ~

The large, choking knot that used to visit just before the tears came, but had been held in check, returned with a gut-wrenching vengeance as she remembered that last bike ride. Sophia tried to quell the tears, but they rolled down her cheeks and gave her vision the same effect a summer downpour gave a car's windshield before the wipers were turned on.

Through the tears she saw the old barn she had seen when she and her parents were heading to the fair. Sophia rode into the barn's gateway, laid the Schwinn onto its side, stepped inside, sat down next to one of the supports and cried with great hitching sobs.

She cried about having to move. She cried about the loss of her friends. She cried about the loss of her spot on the cheerleading squad. She cried about having to be "the new girl" when school started. But most of all, she cried about not having a choice about any of it; that's what bothered her the most, not having a choice!

~ ~ ~ ~ ~ ~

She didn't know how long she sat inside the barn, but finally the tears subsided, and she stepped outside, picked up the Schwinn, and resumed her ride to the old, covered bridge.

"Ten minutes to your destination." Meagan advised.

"Shut up Meagan!" Sophia said to the mapping app and began pedaling down the road.

The rest of her trip was emotionally uneventful. Her sniffles subsided, the tears on her cheeks were gone, the resentment and hurt of having been uprooted lessened and Meagan did not try to kill her!

Thinking that last thought actually brought a smile to her face.

The black asphalt switched over to a brown hard packed chip and seal surface not too far from the barn. After a few more minutes Sophia came to a sign that said, "LITTLE GRAND CREEK COVERED BRIDGE – ONE MILE". Underneath the sign was an arrow pointing to the right along with the words: "DEAD END".

She turned off the chip and seal and began riding down the gravel and dirt road in one of the well-worn ruts that an untold number of tires had created over the years. They were smooth and easier to navigate than either the asphalt or chip and seal had been.

Sophia had to grab the rear tire's brake lever and squeeze it hard when a small cotton tailed rabbit ran across the road in front of her. She braked, the Schwinn's rear wheel locked up and she skidded to a stop.

"Be careful Mr. Bunny Rabbit, you don't want to get run over." Sophia said.

The rabbit was unphased. It looked at Sophia, wiggled its nose and bounded across the road and disappeared into a patch of tall grass.

"Recalculating." Meagan advised.

"So am I." Sophia said and switched the mapping app off, removed the ear buds, put them back in their case and into her backpack.

In the distance, she could see the roof of some sort of a building. If it weren't the bridge, she would reactivate the mapping app. However, further consultation with the homicidal Meagan was not needed. After five more minutes of easy, rabbit free pedaling, Sophia coasted down a small hill to the Little Grand Creek Covered bridge. Its roof was white, and its walls were "barn red".

She remembered reading somewhere that farmers used to seal their barns with linseed oil and add rust to it because it killed fungi and moss. It also turned the mixture red. When actual paint became more readily available, many farmers used the same shade of red as a nod to tradition.

Sophia noticed the temperature had gotten warmer since she began her ride. She glanced at the weather app on her phone and saw that it was eighty-five degrees. She also saw that it was eleven forty-five; she had spent more time crying in that barn than she had realized.

The rough wooden planks of the bridge's floor made a "ker-tikity" sound as the Schwinn's tires rolled across them. When she saw the bridge's balcony that overlooked the creek, she stopped.

"It's real! This place is really real!" She thought.

She made a U-turn and doubled back to the bridge's entrance where she grabbed her cell phone and laid her bike off to the side of the road in some tall grass to conceal it just in case someone drove by and wanted to make it their own.

She walked to the balcony and tentatively touched the railings rough surface. She half expected Laura to speak to her from the interior shadows of the bridge as she had done when they met in the first dream. She glanced over her shoulder checking to see if Laura was there; for all Sophia knew, she was asleep on the bench in the Coombs House Park, and this was another hyper-realistic dream. However, Laura was nowhere to be found and Sophia had never felt more awake than she was at that moment.

The world around her was alive with color, sound, texture and smell! The trees' leaves and the grass and weeds that covered the ground were shades of dark, dark green. A lone airplane droned above it all on its way to somewhere. Birds sang and the wind whispered its secrets as it snuck by Sophia's ears. On that same whispering breeze Sophia smelled fresh cut grass, or maybe it was hay from some farmer's field, and there was the familiar pungent musky scent of trumpet vine! Underlying all of it was the sweet smell of the creek!

The bridge's railing was rough, and weather worn; Sophia made sure not to rub her arm across its surface, she didn't want another splinter. She peered down at the water hoping to see a fish or something else swim by and she was not disappointed. Cruising through the crystal-clear water was the largest goldfish she had ever seen.

"I didn't think goldfish could get that big!" She thought.

She pulled her cell phone from her pocket, leaned over the edge of the balcony and snapped a quick picture, then opened the phone's photo gallery and looked at what she had just taken.

The fish, in all its orange gold glory, was on the left side of the photo. When she zoomed in, she could make out individual scales on the fish's side! Her phone's camera took great pictures that were one hundred eight megapixels in size which made zooming in without losing clarity extremely easy.

On the right side of the picture on the other side of the creek was a wooden object that was mostly hidden underneath the bridge. She leaned over the railing to get a better look and saw a wooden platform about ten feet square with two buckets sitting on it. To see it fully, you would have to lean so far out from the balcony's railing you would be to the point of falling off and in the water.

"Oh! My! Gosh!" Sophia thought. *"The fishing platform from the dream is really down there too!"*

In her excitement, she fumbled her phone and watched in horror as it tumbled onto the balcony railing, took one bounce then fell over the edge and plummeted end over end into the Little Grand Creek. There was an audible "Ker-ploosh!" as it broke the water's surface and sank.

Had anyone been there to see Sophia, they would have seen her standing at the balcony looking down the fifty or so feet to the creek with her mouth formed into a perfect "O" of terror and the color draining from her face. They would have then seen her bolt to the far end of the bridge and scurry down the creek bank to the fishing platform.

"Oh man, oh man, oh man!" She said over and over as she ran the length of the bridge and half ran, half slid down the embankment. "If that phone is dead, so am I!"

She bounded onto the fishing platform stopping just long enough to kick off her tennis shoes next to one of the upended buckets. Then in one smooth fluid movement, dove into the creek and swam under the balcony where she looked down into the water and saw her purple cased phone.

"Okay." She thought. *"There it is!"*

She took a deep breath and dove. The creek was incredibly clean and clear which made it easy to see the bottom, but it was hard to judge how deep the water actually was. On her first attempt, she was able to almost touch the phone case, but her lungs started to burn. She surfaced and the tears began.

"If that phone is ruined..." She thought. *"No! It'll be okay, it has a waterproof case."*

Sophia took two deep breaths then held a third and dove to the rocky bottom. The water was at least twenty feet deep, but she held her breath, snagged her phone, planted her feet on the creek's rocky bottom, kicked hard and surfaced. Water and a wave of relief of having her cell phone back in her hands washed over her as she swam back to the fishing platform, put the phone on its deck and pulled herself back onto its warm surface.

Not only had the creek been deeper than she realized, but it was a lot colder than she would have guessed being the twenty-second day of August. She picked up her phone hoping and praying that it was still working.

"Please work! Please work! Please work!" She thought.

As if in answer to her pleading, the phone rang or more correctly, clucked! Sophia laughed out loud as she answered the call and was thrilled to tell the caller that she was not in the market for vinyl siding or triple pane windows before telling them to have a good day and hanging up! It was eleven fifty-five and all was mostly right in her world again.

"Thank you, Dad!" Sophia thought. *"For getting me this case when you got me this phone. I never thought I would really need something waterproof."*

She tucked the phone into one of her tennis shoes and checked to see if anyone was around. She knew there wasn't, but she checked all the same.

"I'm gonna dry off you three." Sophia said to her Darci and Friends tee shirt as she peeled it off. "Sorry about getting you wet in the first place, but I had to get my phone. I hope you understand."

As she had observed from the balcony, someone would have to practically be hanging off the side of the bridge to actually see anyone down on the fishing platform, so she felt safe taking her shirt off. Besides, the sports bra she was wearing covered a lot more skin than many of the bikinis she had seen on her last shopping trip with her mom to the Battlefield Mall.

She wrung a surprisingly large amount of water from Darci Lynne, Petunia and Oscar. She moved the two upended buckets together and laid the shirt across them to dry in the hot August sun. She considered taking off her shorts, wringing them out and letting them dry alongside her shirt, but didn't.

"They are Quik-Dri shorts." She thought.

A large splash erupted from the creek behind her, and Sophia spun around trying to see if someone was watching her and had thrown something into the water to get her attention. Although something had seen her in her current state of mild undress, it was all the way across the creek and was most likely the cause of the splash and large circular ripples coursing across the creek's surface.

She wasn't sure what it was at first, but the creature; she could tell it was some sort of animal, flipped and dove under the water causing its large flat tail to slap the water's surface causing a second loud splash.

"A beaver?" Sophia wondered.

She picked up her cell phone and set the camera to record video and stepped to the edge of the fishing platform to wait. In less than a minute, the creature broke the surface again, swam around for a few seconds then dove back under the water. The slap of its tail hitting the water sounded like a gun shot.

"I got it!" Sophia said. "I bet it was chasing that big goldfish or something!"

Her hands were still wet from wringing the water from her tee shirt and she was excited to not only have her phone back undamaged and functioning, but because she had just taken a video of a beaver in the wild!

As she flipped the phone from vertical to horizontal to view the video full screen and maybe screenshot some still pictures from it, the phone slipped from her grasp, fell to the platform's deck and, as it had done on the balcony's railing, bounced once and plunged over the edge into the water with an audible "Ker-ploosh!".

"Are you kidding me?" Sophia said as she watched her phone sink to the bottom of the creek again.

Chapter 15

Sophia stood on the platform looking down at her phone that was once again lying on the rocky bottom of the Little Grand Creek. A random thought popped into her head; it came from one of the last passages she had read in her book.

"That happened right here on this fishing platform." Sophia thought. *"And no one is here but me."*

The butterflies – *flutterbys* – took flight in her stomach. They had always done that when she was thinking about doing something she might get in trouble for or that was risky in some way.

Sophia was a very rational and logical person. Her father had once commented on her sensibility to think things through before acting on them by calling her "Polly Pragmatic". She liked that name so much, she used it for the name of the internal voice, her conscience, that she argued with when she was trying to decide on a course of action.

"That is the dumbest idea you have *ever* had!" Her inner, logical Polly Pragmatic voice said.

"I could just…" Sophia's thought trailed off.

"No, you could "just" not!" The internal voice said. "You'll get caught and be totally humiliated."

"No one is around." Sophia countered. *"No one will see me."*

"Someone could be around." Her Polly voice said.

Sophia slowly made a complete three hundred sixty-degree turn looking high and low; and she saw no one. The fact was, she hadn't seen anyone since she left town on her bicycle.

"There is no one here but me." She said to her conscience.

"Someone will show up and see you!" Pragmatic Polly said. "You are making a bad choice."

"You know what." Sophia said to herself. *"This whole summer has been nothing but having choices made for me! I have had no say whatsoever in anything other than what I want to eat, and I wasted that choice by having pineapple on a pizza!*

I was forced to leave my home, my friends and everything else I have ever known! And I had to give up my spot on the cheerleading squad too! If I want to do this, then…" She paused in her thoughts.

"Then what?" Her Polly voice asked.

"I made a wish at that fountain this morning to be able to makes some choices for myself!" Sophia said to herself with a force and a confidence she never knew she had. *"I am choosing to do this!"*

"No Sophia, don't! This is a mistake!" Polly said.

"It may be a mistake! It may be a _big_ mistake, but you know what, it is _my_ mistake! It is a mistake _I_ am choosing to make!" Sophia said.

She peeled off her soaked sports bra and wrung the water out of it and laid it across her shirt to dry.

"You are topless Sophia! If someone saw you, they could…" Polly's voice trailed off.

"They could what?" Sophia asked. "See my boobs?"

"YES! They could see your boobs!" The Polly voice said.

"Good!" Sophia thought.

"Good?" Polly asked.

"Yes! Good!" Sophia thought.

"Why is having someone see your boobs a good thing?" Polly asked.

"Because I have really nice boobs that's why!" Sophia laughed at this as a light breeze blew across her wet skin and goose flesh erupted all over her body. "They are Goldilocks and the Three Bears boobs!"

"What are you talking about Sophia?" Polly Pragmatic asked. "Goldilocks and the Three Bears boobs?"

"They aren't too big. They aren't too small. They are just right!" Sophia said to herself using the description she had come up with one night when she and her friends were together.

Logical Polly Pragmatic groaned inside her head.

Sophia looked at her chest and remembered the sign she had taken from the Venus De Milo statue in the Coombs House Park just before riding her bike out here to the bridge.

"Maybe the Venus De Milo had just retrieved her phone too!" Sophia thought before laughing out loud.

She slid her thumbs under the waistband of her Quik-Dri running shorts, pushed them down around her ankles, stepped out of them, picked them up and wrung what little water was left clinging to them onto the platform and tossed them on top of her drying shirt and sports bra.

Her Polly voice spoke up, "Sophia, what are you doing?"

"What I am doing is getting my phone." Sophia thought. "Again!"

"And the only way you can get it is by taking off all your clothes?" Polly asked.

Sophia looked down at herself; the only thing left on her body was a pair of old white low-rise bikini briefs that were totally soaked and were basically see-through.

"Yes!" Sophia thought.

"WHAT!?!" Her Polly's alarmed voice asked.

"I am making <u>choices</u>!" Sophia thought.

"Don't do it Sophia!" Polly Pragmatic warned.

"Why not!" She thought.

"You aren't leaving anything to the imagination!" Polly said.

Sophia gripped the bikinis on either side of the waistband, shoved them down her legs and around her ankles, stepped out of them and yelled, "NO IMAGINATION REQUIRED!"

She looked at her underwear lying on the fishing platform's deck for a moment, then picked them up, tied them into a ball and threw them as hard and as far as she could into the creek letting the current carry them away.

"Why are you doing this?" Polly asked.

"Because sometimes you have to do something a little crazy to prove that you are actually sane!" Sophia thought. *"Laura told me that I would know when the time was right to do it too! And now, <u>is</u> that time!"*

"Sophia, you are completely naked, and you are outside in plain view!" Polly said.

"Why yes, yes I am! And no one is telling me I have nice boobs either. It must be because I am the <u>only one</u> out here!" Sophia thought. *"So, I guess I need to say it; 'Sophia you have really nice boobs!'"*

"You are making a terrible mistake!" Polly Pragmatic said.

"But I <u>do</u> have nice boobs!" Sophia thought. *"Not too big, not too small; they are just right! Goldilocks would be proud!"*

"I mean about taking off all your clothes!" Pragmatic Polly said. "You literally just took your underwear off and threw them into the creek!"

"They were old and needed to be pitched anyway." Sophia said to herself.

"You are making a terrible mistake by running around out here totally naked!" Pragmatic Polly said.

"I know. Look what I've done to him." She pointed at her shirt; Oscar the Motown Mouse was staring at her with a surprised, open-mouthed look on his face. *"Sorry Oscar, but the underwear had to go!"*

"You are crazy!" Her logical Polly voice said.

"You might be right." Sophia said to herself. *"But I am doing this because I need to get my phone, and more importantly, I am doing this because I <u>choose</u> too!"*

Sophia took three quick steps and dove back into the Little Grand Creek's cold, clear water. She angled her body down and touched the rocky creek bottom, then let her momentum carry her back to the surface before swimming back to the edge of the platform where she dove down and retrieved her phone for the second time. When she resurfaced, she placed the phone on the fishing platform's deck and pulled herself up and out of the water.

"Okay, you've skinny dipped." The Polly voice said. "Are you happy now?"

"Yes!" Sophia said to herself. *"I am very happy! That felt really good, just like the first time! But you know what is different from the first time I skinny dipped and today?"*

"What?" Polly Pragmatic asked.

"This time the sun is out, and I am not worried about someone seeing me!" Sophia said to her conscience. *"Because there is <u>no one</u> out here <u>to</u> see me!"*

"Put your clothes on, Sophia!" Polly said.

Sophia ignored the Pragmatic Polly part of herself. Instead, she went over to where her clothes lay, picked up her running shorts and pulled out two elastic hair ties and put her hair into a ponytail.

"Get dressed!" Her rational voice commanded again.

"No!" Sophia said to herself.

She jumped back into the Little Grand and swam several laps from the platform to the opposite bank and back again enjoying how the water felt as it flowed unimpeded across her body.

"What are you going to do Sophia if someone comes along?" Her logical voice asked.

"If someone comes along?" She thought. *"I guess they would get to see ALL of me especially if they were standing on the platform and wouldn't leave or give me my clothes."*

"What if they *took* your clothes and left?" Polly Pragmatic asked. "What would you do then?"

"I guess I would..." She hadn't considered something like that as a possibility.

"You guess you would.... what?" Her Polly voice asked.

"If they took all my clothes, I guess I would wait until it got totally dark and sneak back home." She thought.

"It is several miles back to the house! How would you get all the way there without being seen?" Polly Pragmatic reminded her. "How would you get to your room without your parents seeing you?"

"That is just paranoid." Sophia thought. *"That is not going to happen!"*

"It could happen." Polly Pragmatic said. "What would you do if "The New Girl" was found wandering around totally naked and that got out to everyone at the high school? What then?"

"I'm not sure what I would do, but…" Sophia said.

"But what?" Her Polly voice asked.

"But I bet I would be <u>very</u> popular with the boys!" Sophia laughed.

Her Pragmatic Polly voice groaned.

~ ~ ~ ~ ~ ~

Sophia continued to swim, enjoying the feeling of freedom and liberation that skinny dipping gave her. After nearly thirty minutes in the water, she climbed back onto the platform, wrung out as much of the water from her ponytail as she could, and checked her phone to make sure it was still working; it was.

"You need to get dressed Sophia!" Her Polly Pragmatic voice said.

"No." She said to herself. *"I'm going to dry off first."*

"PUT ON YOUR CLOTHES!" Her practical side commanded.

"NO!" Sophia yelled back to herself. *"No, I won't! There were no tire tracks on that old gravel road. I saw that when I was riding my bike out here. I'm the first person to come to this bridge in a long time!"*

"You are going to get caught!" Practical, Pragmatic Polly said flatly. "Then you are going to be terribly, terribly humiliated."

"I wish I had my backpack." She thought. *"That fleece blanket is in there and so are those sandwiches. I am kind of hungry."*

She looked at the creek, which was more like a small river, and considered swimming across and climbing up to where her bike and backpack were laying in the tall grass, but the opposite bank was rocky and looked a lot steeper than the bank she had scurried down to retrieve her phone. It was twelve-forty-five.

"I'll take the bridge." She thought.

~ ~ ~ ~ ~ ~

When she had done her internet search, she read that The Little Grand Creek Covered Bridge was over two hundred fifty feet long. It is the longest covered bridge in the state of Missouri and the only covered bridge with a balcony! With the fifty or so feet of embankment that lead up to the road, getting her backpack would take a round trip of at least six hundred feet; six hundred feet totally and completely out in plain sight wearing nothing at all.

"That's more than a tenth of a mile." Polly Pragmatic calculated. "A tenth of a mile where you <u>will</u> be seen totally and completely naked!"

"Let's find out." Sophia thought and she crossed the platform heading toward the embankment.

"Do you want to be seen?" Polly asked. "Do you want to get caught?"

"I'm not going to be seen because there is no one out here to see me. But if they do see me, I have really nice boobs! We've already discussed that, remember?" She removed the hair ties and her wet hair fell down her back.

"What are you doing Sophia?" Her inner, logical voice asked.

"I'm letting my hair down so it will dry and I'm getting my backpack. And look at this!" Sophia moved her hair, so it covered her chest. *"Now you can't see my boobs, so it is all good!"*

"They can still see everything else!" Polly Pragmatic said.

Sophia laughed and flipped her hair to her back and stepped off the platform onto the grass covered embankment and headed up to the road.

"If you are going to really do this Sophia, and you shouldn't!" Her inner, logical voice advised. "You should run! For Pete's sake, you are completely naked!"

"Yes, I am, but just so you know, I prefer the term "nude"; it sounds so much more sophisticated." Sophia thought.

"Why are you doing this?" The Polly voice asked.

Sophia paused, looked down at herself and thought, *"I am doing this because I can, because I want to, because I <u>choose</u> to and because it feels good! I don't care if someone sees me either. You only live once!"*

She walked up the embankment, stepped onto the gravel road and looked both ways to check for traffic.

"I thought you didn't care if someone saw you." Polly said.

"Old habits die hard!" Sophia thought as she walked across the bridge toward her bike and her backpack.

"What if a car comes down the road?" Her inner, logical voice asked. "What would you do?"

She giggled at the thought of someone out for a leisurely drive seeing her standing on the bridge wearing nothing but a smile.

"Princess wave!" Sophia thought as she held her hand in the air and rotated it at the wrist like she was a member of the Royal Family.

"Run Sophia!" Her logical voice implored.

"I'll walk, thank you." She said to herself.

The day had turned hot. When she had first gotten to the bridge it was eighty-five degrees according to her cell phone's weather app and that wasn't cool by any means. After her phone's second plunge in the creek, she had checked to see if it was still functioning, and the weather app said it was ninety-four degrees which had surpassed the predicted high by one degree. As she crossed the bridge, a hot breeze blew across her body and felt wonderful as it dried her skin and hair!

"Hurry up!" Pragmatic Polly implored. "Get your backpack, get back to the platform and get your clothes on!"

She answered her inner, logical voice's command to run with another firm, *"NO!"*

The inner Sophia, the rational Sophia, Miss Polly Pragmatic, was stunned by her own actions and thoughts. She was strolling across the old, covered bridge completely nude without a care in the world!

"Why are you doing this?" Her inner, logical voice asked again.

"I told you; because I can!" Sophia answered. *"I am doing this because I want to, because I* choose *to! I have never done anything so…so…"*

"So completely insane? So totally stupid? So entirely senseless?" Her Polly voice asked.

"I had to move here, to…to…Podunksville, away from everything and everyone I have ever known! I had no choice! I had no say! But doing this IS my choice even if it is an odd one.

I chose *to take off my clothes! I* chose *to go skinny dipping! And I am* choosing *to walk around in plain sight risking being seen. This is something I have control over! I like how actually making a choice makes me feel and I like how not having any clothes on feels too!"* Sophia said to herself feeling tears begin to form in the corners of her eyes. She took a deep breath; she didn't want a repeat of the barn meltdown.

"Sophia…" Polly began.

"In five days, FIVE DAYS, I will be "The New Girl" at a school where I won't know anyone! I had no choice *in that either! And I had to give up being on the cheerleading squad; I definitely had no choice in that! If I were still back home, you know what I would have done last week?"*

"Sophia." Polly said.

"I would have been at cheer camp at Missouri State with my friends and with a couple of hundred other cheer teams from all over the state! But instead, I got to watch PAINT DRY on the front porch of the house where I have to live now! I had NO CHOICE AT ALL in any of it! But I do have a choice in this!

If someone sees me, so what. The human body is not dirty; <u>my</u> body is not dirty! In Europe at the swimming pools and beaches, the girls and women wear nothing but their swimsuit bottoms. I don't know why people here are so hung up with boobs!" Sophia thought.

"People can see more than just your boobs Sophia." Her Polly voice said calmly. "You have *everything* on display!"

"And what's on display looks darn good too!" Sophia thought. *"I have a great looking body and I'm getting an awesome tan! If I was already in high school and had a boyfriend who I trusted, I just might bring him out here and go skinny dipping with him!"*

"And you might end up a little pregnant too!" Pragmatic Polly said.

"The first time I have sex." Sophia thought. *"Will be on my wedding night and my husband, whoever that will be, is going to get to enjoy ALL of me and I'll get to enjoy ALL of him, but not until then!"*

She stood at the balcony, leaned on the railing and gazed at the water below taking several deep breaths in an attempt to calm herself down.

Polly Pragmatic went silent.

After several minutes, she walked to her bike and retrieved her backpack, then walked back across the bridge and started to go down the bank to the fishing platform. However, she stopped and crossed the road to read a small sign she hadn't noticed when she had first bounded down the bank to get her phone.

The sign said: "LITTLE GRAND CEMETERY – 5 MILES". There was an arrow pointing down the road away from the bridge. Underneath the arrow was another sign that read, "DEAD END".

"I'm sure it is." She thought.

When she was back on the fishing platform, she looked at her cell phone again; she had taken thirty minutes to get the backpack and return. Her body was completely dry, and her hair was just damp.

"That wasn't so bad, was it?" She asked the Polly part of herself.

Her Polly Pragmatic voice said, "You have gone totally insane!"

"Have I?" She asked.

"Yes!" Her inner, logical voice said. "You have gone crazy! You just walked a tenth of a mile totally nude Sophia; *A TENTH OF A MILE*! Not only that, but you were standing in plain view for half an hour!"

She looked at herself again and saw her tan lines. Since school had gotten out for the summer and before she moved, she and her friends had spent several hours every day at Laney's backyard pool swimming and laying out. She had never paid any attention to how tan she had gotten, but now she could easily see where her swimsuit had been.

"I wonder." Sophia thought.

She dug through the backpack and found the bottle of suntan lotion she was almost certain was there. Then she began covering herself with the coconut scented oil. There were places on her body that had never needed suntan lotion before.

"What are you doing?" Polly Pragmatic asked.

"I am getting rid of my tan lines!" Sophia said to herself. *"No one is out here to see me, so why not!"*

Sophia got one of her peanut butter sandwiches from the backpack, took a bite and walked back up the embankment to the road and walked slowly back to the balcony. She stood looking at the creek while she ate the rest of her sandwich, then, after several minutes, she went to her bike, turned around to go back to the platform but stopped.

"You only live once! Sophia thought and turned and started walking down the road toward town.

"What are you doing?" Polly asked.

"I am walking to where this gravel road starts." Sophia thought.

"It is one mile back to the paved road Sophia!" Polly said incredulously. "You don't even have on shoes and you are totally naked!"

"I am wearing suntan lotion!" Sophia said to herself.

"Sophia, it is one mile to the paved road which means it's two miles back to the bridge where your clothes are!" Pragmatic Polly said. "That is two miles, Sophia, TWO MILES of you outside walking down a road with absolutely nothing on!"

"Then I had better get going so I can get back!" Sophia said to herself.

~ ~ ~ ~ ~ ~

"Hey Polly?" She asked herself. *"Two miles totally and completely nude and no one, not one single person saw me because there is no one out here but me!"*

Her inner, logical voice did not respond.

It was five minutes after two when she took the fleece blanket from the backpack and spread it out on the fishing platform. The walk to and from the paved road had been enjoyable and she was seen by no one other than birds, bugs and a lone jet that was tracking its way across the sky. She looked at her backpack and thought about her copy of the book.

"I want to read more of the story, but…" She thought.

"You want to put on your clothes!" Polly was back with exasperation in her voice.

"No, I don't." She responded to herself. *"I like this! It feels good!"*

"But…" The inner, logical voice protested.

"But nothing!" She dove back into the cold creek for another ten minutes of swimming!

~ ~ ~ ~ ~ ~

Refreshed and invigorated, but done swimming, Sophia climbed back onto the platform, wrung out her hair and sat down on the blanket.

"Are you going to put on your clothes *now*?" The inner, logical voice asked.

"I can't." She said. *"I'm all wet; I need to dry off. I'll get dressed right before I head back to the house, but not until then."*

"You are going to get caught." Polly said.

"If I do, I do." She supposed. *"What's the worst thing that could happen if someone sees me?"*

"They could call the police." Rational Polly said.

"And?" She thought.

"And they would take you home and tell your parents you were skinny dipping!" Polly said.

"I'm sure I'd get a lecture about being modest and that 'nice' girls don't run around outside naked. It's not like they can make me quit anything because of it; I already had to quit the cheerleading squad.

Who knows, maybe they would be so upset and embarrassed that we would move back home. If that were the case, I would walk down the middle of Podunksville's Main Street princess waving to everyone!" She thought. *"It's not like I'm out here smoking weed or drinking or having sex!"*

"What *are* you doing Sophia?" Polly Pragmatic asked.

"I am making choices and I'm getting an awesome suntan!" Sophia said to herself.

She picked up her cell phone; it was two thirty-five p.m., and the weather app said the temperature was ninety-six degrees. There had been some clouds earlier in the morning, but now the sky was a beautiful, cloud free cobalt blue and a hot breeze was blowing!

She picked up the bottle of suntan lotion and read the label that proclaimed this brand contained something called "Tan Booster Ten", a substance that would help your skin achieve a golden glow ten times faster than other brands and it helped protect the user from sunburn.

Sophia had never gotten a sunburn in her life; it had something to do with her great, great grandparents on her mother's side having been Greek, or so she was told. She was blessed with Mediterranean skin.

Any time she was in the sun, her skin would redden, but by the next morning the area that had been red would be a warm, brown tan. In her nearly fifteen years of life, she had never known the pain of a sunburn and in her current state of undress, that was a good trait to have.

She applied more of the Tan Booster Ten and remembered a comment Audrey Noble had made about her tanning ability.

"Geeze, Sophia!" Audrey, the aspiring dermatologist had said. *"All you have to do is think about going out in the sun and your skin turns brown! If I think about going out in the sun without sun block or suntan lotion on, I turn into the guest of honor at a lobster boil!"*

"Would any of your friends have gone skinny dipping with you?" Her Polly voice asked.

"They might!" Sophia thought and smiled as she remembered her first foray into the realm of skinny dipping.

Chapter 16

At their last sleepover, Leah, Laney, Audrey and Sophia played Truth or Dare after consuming mass quantities of chips, pizza and sodas. Before Truthing or Daring, Audrey, always the lady, had challenged them to a belching contest. The rules were simple, they each had to chug a sixteen-ounce glass of warm soda as quickly as they could and then wait for the warm carbonation to kick in.

Sophia's dad was recruited as judge for the event, and he determined two things after listening to their carbonated endeavors.

First, Leah was declared the overall winner for her rendition of "Mary Had A Little Lamb". Second, it was his learned opinion that all four of them were gross human beings and as such conferred upon each of them the honorary rank of "Belchers – Third Class"! When asked why they were not "Belchers – First Class", Dan Young chugged a glass of soda and nearly rattled the windows with his deeply base belch.

"That, is a first-class belch!" He said. "When you can meet it or beat it, come talk to me!"

All four girls high fived him before kicking him out of the family room! After he left and went to bed, the four talked and watched several back-to-back episodes of a show called "The Worst Witch", before turning their attention to Truth or Dare.

They had adapted the game and used two dice that were four-sided and shaped like blunt tipped pyramids to decide who had to tell the truth or take a dare. The first die rolled decided if it was a truth or a dare; odd numbers were for telling the truth and even numbers were for dares. The second die rolled chose the truth teller or the dare taker.

The player's numbers were assigned by a random roll of a die as well; Audrey rolled a one, Laney rolled a two, Sophia rolled a three and Leah rolled a four. One rule they had added was this: If the second die came up with the number of the player who rolled it, then that person decided who had to tell the truth or take a dare; they called it a "Roller's Choice".

They had each written ten truth questions and had contributed ten dares on halves of three by five index cards that were designed to be as embarrassing as possible. They were separated into the truth and dare piles and were shuffled twice by each player.

When it was Leah's turn to roll, her first die came up three; a truth card. She rolled the second die, and it was Laney who had to truthfully answer: Tell something you have done and now you regret doing it.

"Well, I went for a swim in our pool one day when everyone was at the mall and I had on a really skimpy bikini. Big mistake!" Laney said.

"And you regret it, why?" Audrey asked.

"Yeah, if you were by yourself, why do you regret it?" Leah pressed.

"Someone saw me." Laney said.

"Who?" Leah asked.

"My brother's friend, Chuck. He came over to our house looking for Bryan." Laney said.

"And?" Leah asked again. "Lots of people have seen you in a bikini when we go to the public pool."

"Okay, here's what happened." Laney said. "Everyone had gone to the mall and weren't going to be home for, like, three or four hours, so I decided to go swimming. I had ordered a new bikini online and it had come in the mail earlier that day, so I put it on and swam in that."

"And your brother's friend Chuck saw you?" Sophia asked.

"Yes." Laney said.

"I call foul!" Leah said. "Laney, the dare is 'Tell something you have done and now you regret doing it'. You said you went swimming and were seen wearing a bikini. Big deal."

"Hang on." Laney said reaching for her phone. "I have a picture of me in that bikini." She scrolled through the cell phone's photo gallery. "Look."

She laid her phone on the table and the three others looked at the picture that was displayed.

"Wowzah!" Sophia said. "You almost have that bikini on Laney!"

"It barely covers your…uh…essentials!" Audrey said. "But what you do have on is cute! How much was it?"

"It was, like, forty-five dollars from Bikini World's online site." Laney said. "And it was on sale too."

"You paid forty-five dollars for two dollars' worth of material." Sophia said pointing at the picture on the phone.

"If that much." Laney said. "Flip to the next picture. I used my self-timer to take a picture of the back."

They flipped to the next picture and Sophia, Leah and Audrey all gasped at the same time.

"Almost all of your back is completely uncovered!" Audrey said. "I mean the top is only just a string and one that's pretty thin too!"

"And the bottoms…" Sophia said. "You can see most of your…"

"Assets!" Leah finished.

The room erupted into laughter!

"I didn't read the description before I ordered it." Laney said pointing to the photo. "I didn't know they were thong bikini bottoms."

"I take back my foul." Leah said. "Does your mom know you have that bikini, if you can even call it a bikini?"

"No!" Laney said. "And if you tell her I will kill you!"

Audrey started giggling!

"What?" Laney said.

"Did it come with a free tube of toothpaste and a toothbrush?" Audrey asked.

"What are you talking about Audrey?" Laney asked.

"They should have sent you a tube of toothpaste and a toothbrush so you could brush your teeth then use that bikini to floss with!" Audrey said pointing to the picture.

After their laughter had died down again, they continued talking.

"Can't your neighbors see your pool from their house?" Sophia asked. "I remember last year, right before you all shut the pool down, that kid who was visiting your neighbors kept looking out the window at us."

"That's why Dad put up that taller wooden fence before we opened the pool this year." Laney said. "That kid was creepy!"

"So, how did Chuck see you?" Leah asked.

"So, I got out of the pool next to the diving board and was going to get my towel; it was on the patio table, you know *completely* on the other side of the pool right next to the gate that he came through." Laney said.

"What did you do?" Leah asked.

"I said 'Hi.'" Laney said.

"You just stood there with him looking at you in *that*?" Leah asked pointing at the picture on the phone.

"I didn't have much of a choice. And just so you all know; I didn't turn around either." Laney said.

"Did he suggest 'The Big Monkey Ooo-wah-doo!'?" Audrey asked then giggled as did Leah and Sophia. Her phrase "The Big Monkey Ooo-wah-doo" and its meaning always made them laugh.

"You are disgusting Audrey!" Laney said.

"So, what did he do?" Leah asked. "Stare and drool with his tongue hanging out?"

"No, his face turned totally red, and he kept looking around and not at me." Laney said.

"Oh, he looked at you!" Audrey said. "Why else would his face be red?"

"Why was he there?" Sophia asked.

"He wanted to know if Bryan was home. When I told him he wasn't, he said something pretty funny as he was leaving!" Laney said.

"What did he say?" Audrey asked.

"He said, 'Oh…okay…uh…well…uh…nice seeing you.' Then his face got even redder when he realized what he had said, and he left." Laney said.

"I bet he's telling all his friends that he saw Bryan's little sister practically naked!" Leah teased.

"He'd better not! If he did and Bryan found out, Chuck would be toast." Laney said. "That's the cool thing of having a big brother who loves his little sister; he's six-five and is going to play football at Ohio State!"

Audrey started laughing and got out her phone.

"What's so funny?" Laney asked.

Audrey was busily scrolling through the pictures on her phone. When she found what she was looking for, she handed her phone to Laney and said, "Amateur!"

Laney looked at the picture.

"WHAT is this Audrey!" She exclaimed.

"What is what?" Audrey asked with an overly innocent tone.

"This!" Laney said setting the phone on the table where the others could see the picture.

It showed Audrey sitting on a pool deck with a diving board in the background with her knees bent and her ankles crossed in front of her. Her arms were resting on her knees, her elbows slightly bent, and her hands were folded on top of each other on her knees. Lying next to her was a towel; it was the only piece of cloth in the picture.

"Oh that." Audrey said. "What about it?"

"You are totally naked Audrey!" Laney said. "I mean look at you!"

"WOWZAH!" Sophia said. "I mean, like, WOW – double – owzah!"

"Laney regrets wearing that string bikini and being seen by her brother's friend, but you don't regret…THAT!?" Leah asked.

Audrey slumped down and slid out of her chair from laughing so hard.

"Audrey!" Laney said. "This isn't funny! That picture is, like, pornography! If someone saw it…"

Audrey got her laughter under control and got back into her chair.

"Look at the next picture." She said.

Laney, who was giving Audrey a hard look, flicked her finger across the screen and the next photo slid into view. It was almost the same picture, except in this one Audrey's arms were not flexed as much as they were in the first one.

"All is not what it seems." Audrey said with a laugh. "Mom nearly had a fit when I showed her the first one. She wanted to know who had taken it."

"Who did take that picture, the first one I mean?" Sophia asked.

"I did!" Audrey said. "I used my cell phone and the self-timer."

"What did your dad say?" Leah asked.

Audrey picked up her phone and flipped back to the first picture. "He laughed!"

"He laughed?" Leah asked.

"Yup!" Audrey said. "Unlike any of you or Mom, he saw this."

She pointed to the left side of the picture where you could see the single pink line of the string of her bikini top.

"He said, 'Nice try!'. Then went back to doing whatever he was doing." She said.

"Why did you do that Audrey?" Leah asked.

"I was bored." She said. "It was funny!"

Laney picked up the dice and tossed them to Audrey.

"Your turn, porno girl!" She said.

Audrey caught the dice and said, "Be right back. Too much soda."

When she returned, she tossed the first die onto the table. After it bounced several times, it landed on the number two; a dare roll. She rolled the second die which bounced several times before it fell on the floor next to her seat. Audrey picked it up and said it had come up on the number one, which was her number and she got to choose who had to take the dare.

"Who is it?" Leah asked.

"Eeney, meaney, miney moo. It's gonna be one of you!" Audrey said in the old rhyming chant they had learned as kids and as she was pointing at Laney, Leah and Sophia in turn trying to decide who was going to be dared. "It could be Leah or Laney Sue. It could be me, but it's YOU!"

Audrey pointed at Sophia!

"Oh, oh!" Sophia said.

Audrey took the next card from the dare pile, read it to herself then asked, "What time is it?"

Leah looked at the clock. "It is one forty-five."

"What is the dare?" Laney asked.

The room was silent in anticipation for the reading of the dare card.

"The dare is…" Audrey paused for dramatic effect. "You have to go skinny dipping." She said and laid the card on the table.

"Oh joy." Sophia said flatly.

"Let's sneak out and go to Laney's pool!" Audrey proposed.

"Her house is like a block away!" Sophia said.

"It's not 'like a block away'!" Laney began. "It IS a block away and it's on the other side of the street too!"

"I don't know, that means we could be seen going over there." Leah said. "I mean if someone were coming down the street…"

"She has to do this." Audrey said. "Or she'll have to do *this*!"

She picked up the Truth or Dare "penalty" envelope which contained the consequence for not taking a dare. They had each written a penalty the month before at the sleepover for Audrey's birthday and sealed them in envelopes. They decided that whenever they played Truth or Dare, one of the envelopes would be selected randomly in case a dare was not done.

~ ~ ~ ~ ~ ~

Although Audrey's actual birthday was June twenty-third, they had held the party on Friday the nineteenth at Leah's, continued it at Laney's pool on Saturday afternoon and it finished up with a sleepover that night at Sophia's.

Audrey was the oldest of the four by just a few weeks. Laney's birthday was July seventh, Leah's was July tenth and Sophia's, the baby of the group, was August twenty-fifth.

Although Audrey, Laney and Leah could have started kindergarten the year before Sophia, their parents had waited an additional year; they felt the extra time would only help the girls, and it did. Instead of being the youngest in their class, the four were now the oldest.

~ ~ ~ ~ ~ ~

"A dare has been made." Audrey said. "If that dare is not done, Sophia will <u>have</u> to do what's in here. And we all know what that penalty could be, don't we?"

They all knew what they had individually put in their sealed envelope and by the looks on their faces, they thought sneaking out and walking to Laney's house for a midnight swim was no big deal in comparison.

"We all have our swimsuits. I mean we did go swimming this afternoon." Audrey reminded them. "We could sneak back to Laney's, Sophia could skinny dip and then we could go swimming for a while, then sneak back here. No one would ever know we were gone."

"If we got caught…" Leah started to say.

"We would be in so much trouble." Sophia said.

"We should make it worth our trouble and do something really risky!" Audrey proposed.

"Like what?" Laney asked.

Audrey picked up one of the pyramid shaped die and said, "An even number means we all go to Laney's in our swimsuits, an odd number means we all go to Laney's in our swimsuits, but Sophia…"

"But Sophia…what?" Sophia asked.

"But Sophia walks to Laney's…wearing NOTHING AT ALL!" Audrey said.

"No, no, no!" Sophia said. "Doing it that way means I am the only one taking a risk."

"I like that!" Leah said.

"Me too!" Laney agreed.

"No argument here!" Audrey said.

"I'm sure you all *do* like doing it that way!" Sophia said.

"Do you have a better idea?" Audrey asked.

"Yes!" Sophia said. "An even number means we all walk to Laney's in our swimsuits, then I have to do the skinny-dipping dare. An odd number means we ALL walk to Laney's wearing NOTHING and I go skinny dipping! How's that for taking a risk?"

"Who rolls to decide?" Laney asked.

"Sophia does; it's her dare!" Audrey said and tossed a single die to Sophia. "Our fate and modesty are in your hands."

Sophia looked at the die, looked at her friends and swallowed hard. "Here goes."

She tossed the die high into the air and the four watched as it fell onto the table where it bounced, rebounded, spun and finally stopped next to Audrey's empty soda glass.

"What is it?" Leah and Laney said at the same time.

"It's a two." Audrey said looking at the die. "It looks like we will all be sneaking over to Laney's pool wearing our swimsuits!"

"What if someone sees us." Laney asked.

"That's what makes it fun!" Audrey said.

"Yeah, it's like playing the lottery and not getting caught means you win!" Sophia added.

She tried to sound confident when she made her statement, but her stomach was suddenly tightening up with the thought of actually sneaking out of her house with her friends.

"If I get caught, I am so dead!" Sophia thought.

"Besides, it's almost two o'clock in the morning. No one but us will be outside. If we don't do this, we <u>all</u> now have to do that." Audrey said pointing to the penalty envelope. "Because everyone was added to the dare with that last roll. And I know what I wrote for a penalty and I don't want to have to do *that*!"

"But..." Laney said.

"But what? Is Chuck hanging around your house or something?" Sophia asked with a grin.

"If he is, are you going to wear your *string* bikini?" Audrey asked.

"Funny. Not." Laney said. "But if he was there and I had it on, Sophia would be the one he was staring at because she won't be wearing anything at all!"

That got a laugh from everyone!

Sophia went to the bathroom right off the family room and put on her swimsuit; it was a bikini with a strapless aqua blue top and white bottoms. Compared to the one Laney was wearing in the picture on her phone; Sophia's bikini looked positively Victorian!

Leah changed next. Her bikini was all white with a strapless top and high cut French bikini briefs. That style made Leah look like she had very long legs, even though she was just five foot tall.

Laney slipped on her emerald green swimsuit next. Her bikini had a strapless top as well that was tied in the back with a bow. Her bottoms were secured with bows at each hip.

The first time she had worn it to a public swimming pool, a boy they knew had tried to untie the bows of her bikini bottoms when he snuck up behind her. Laney felt his hands on her hips, and she had elbowed him in the solar plexus like her former Marine hand-to-hand combat instructor father had taught her. Then, as the boy was bent over trying to get his breath, she spun around and drove her elbow into the base of his skull causing him to fall onto the concrete on his face and broke his nose.

A lifeguard witnessed what he had tried to do and banned him from the pool for the rest of the summer. When Laney had told her brother what had happened, Brian had found the young man and strongly advised him to never come around his sister again!

Audrey was the last of the group to change. Her bikini was cotton candy pink, which surprised her friends the first time they saw her wear it. Audrey was extremely pretty, but she was not usually a pink wearing girly-girl. She was very much a very pretty tomboy.

Her bikini's top was strapless and was basically two cups held together by a single piece of string that wrapped around and fastened in the back. The bottoms were similar to Laney's and were secured with bows at each hip. Although Audrey's bikini was not quite as skimpy as Laney's mostly string, string bikini, it came in a close second.

Once they had all changed, the four of them, three of whom would be going to Kickapoo High School and one who would be going to a high school in a little town she would call Podunksville, quietly slipped outside.

Chapter 17

"So far, so good." Leah said.

"We just stepped outside!" Laney said.

"It's a start." Leah said.

"Hush!" Audrey said.

The foursome crept around to the front of the house.

"We have to cross the street, so let's do it here because the streetlight is out." Sophia said. "Okay?"

"On three!" Laney said.

"One!" Sophia said.

"Two!" Audrey added.

"Three!" Leah said.

They scurried across the dimly lit street to the vacant house with the for-sale sign planted in the front yard, then hurried down the sidewalk using the shadows of the trees and parked cars for cover. They weren't worried about being seen in their bikinis, they did wear them to the public pool and at Table Rock Lake whenever they went to Branson. Their stealth on this occasion was so they wouldn't be seen out on the street at two o'clock in the morning.

"I never realized how far it was from your house to mine Soph." Laney said after they had gotten three houses down the street. "And I never knew how many little rocks were on this sidewalk. I wish I had put on my shoes."

"Me too." Sophia said.

"We can go back." Leah said.

"I'm not doing what's in the penalty envelope." Sophia said. "No way!"

"Car!" Audrey said.

They crouched beside a minivan as the car drove by; they were not seen.

"Oh my gosh!" Laney said peering down the street at the car that had just passed them.

"What?" Audrey asked.

Laney started laughing. "I think that was Chuck's car!"

"Does he have some sort of radar that knows when you or any of your friends are in their bikinis, Laney?" Leah asked.

"He must!" Laney said and all four started to laugh.

"Is anyone at your house?" Sophia asked. "I thought you said everyone else was gone and that's why you were staying with me tonight."

"No one is home. And just so you all know; Chuck doesn't live very far from here. He drives down this street all the time." Laney said. "I bet he was just going home."

Leah started laughing.

"What is so funny?" Sophia hissed, trying to keep everything as quiet as she could.

Once she had gotten herself under control, Leah said, "What if Chuck was sneaking over to your house Laney, because he knows you are supposed to be out of town, and he is swimming when we get there!"

"Do you think Chuck has a Speedo?" Audrey asked.

The group dissolved into hushed giggles at the thought. They kept laughing, albeit quietly, until the porch light on the house across from them came on and a man in a white shirt and white pants stepped outside.

"That's Mr. Livingston, he works at a bakery. At least that's what my dad said. They just moved in a few weeks ago." Sophia whispered. "I bet he's going to work."

Ed Livingston, a rotund man of about sixty, crossed his yard, stepped into the street and headed to his car which was parked directly in front of the minivan the girls were using for cover.

"Go to the back of the van!" Audrey whispered urgently. "He's coming this way!"

The four girls scurried behind the van to their new hiding spot which got them out of Mr. Livingston's sight line, but it put them directly underneath a fully functioning streetlight. Had someone been driving up the street from behind them, they would have seen four bikini clad teenaged girls crouching behind a minivan entirely illuminated by one of Springfield's brand new, super bright L.E.D. streetlights.

Ed Livingston worked at the Colonial Bakery on West Kearney Street and ironically enough, he had been born in Chillicothe, Missouri! He was in charge of the large mixers that got the water, flour, salt, yeast and other additives ready to go into the loaf pans. He liked to say that he made a lot of dough at his job!

He would also tell you that the dough making process could not be rushed. After being in the bread business for nearly forty years, he had one speed which could best be described as plodding.

He ambled across the street to his car, walked around to the passenger side, pulled out his keys, opened the door and set his lunch box on the floorboard. On his way back to the driver's side he stopped, put his keys back in his pocket and looked at the right rear tire, mumbled something about needing new tires before winter, then lumbered his way around to the driver's door.

"Oh, come on!" Audrey hissed. "Snails go faster than you do."

She had crept back around to the van's right front corner when Mr. Livingston had finally gotten back to the driver's door.

Mr. Livingston pulled out the wad of keys from his white baker's pants again and fumbled with them for what seemed like an eternity until he found the one that unlocked his car. He slid it into the lock, opened the door and slid in behind the wheel where he adjusted the rear-view mirror, put on his seatbelt and finally started his old, yet reliable Buick, put it into gear and drove down the street.

Leah, Sophia and Laney crept up behind Audrey just as another car was coming up the street behind them. Had Mr. Livingston taken any more time to get going, they would have easily been seen.

"Let's go!" Laney said. "That last car was for sure Chuck!"

Leah giggled. "He wants to *see* Brian's little sister again!"

"No, he wants to see Sophia!" Laney said with a giggle. "When she's skinny dipping!"

"If he comes back, I'll push you into the backseat of his car!" Sophia said.

"You wouldn't dare!" Laney said.

"I might!" Sophia said.

The quartet dissolved into another quiet fit of laughter as they crept down the sidewalk and made it to the pool without any more trouble or traffic.

Once there, Laney considered turning on the pool and patio lights, but she didn't want to attract any attention if they had a night owl neighbor, so she left them off.

"Sophia!" Audrey said. "I believe it is dare time!"

"Yeah, yeah." Sophia said. She mounted the diving board and took off her bikini top. "What, no admiration for my Goldilocks and the three Bears boobs?"

"Your what?" Leah asked.

"My Goldilocks and The Three Bears boobs." Sophia repeated.

"I know I am going to regret this, but I'll ask: What are you talking about Soph?" Laney asked.

"I have Goldilocks and the Three Bears boobs." Sophia said. "They aren't too big, they aren't too small, they are just right!"

After the groans and laughter from her friends had subsided, Sophia took off her bikini bottoms and tossed her swimsuit onto the pool's deck. Then she bounced twice on the diving board and dove into the pool with a near perfect dive that barely rippled the pool's surface.

When she had surfaced and swam to the pool's edge she said, "Okay, the dare is done. Toss me my swimsuit."

Audrey snatched Sophia's bikini from where it lay on the pool deck. "I'll hang on to this for you for a little while, thank you very much!"

Sophia gasped! "Audrey! Give me back my swimsuit!"

"No." Audrey said.

"Why not?" Sophia asked.

"Do you remember the last week of school?" Audrey asked while grinning her most mischievous grin! "Specifically, the last Wednesday of school when a certain someone, who just went skinny dipping and is now completely and totally naked, filled our lockers with shaving cream."

"Audrey! Give me back my swimsuit!" Sophia hissed.

"I know I do, and I am sure Laney and Leah do too." Audrey continued totally ignoring Sophia. "Right ladies?"

Laney and Leah put on grins of their own and started laughing.

"I do!" Laney said.

"Me too!" Leah said.

Sophia remembered all too well their last week of school and what she had done to her friends. She had been perusing the internet and came across a practical joke website where she learned what fun could be had if you froze a can of shaving cream, then cut off its bottom and put the frozen contents into a zippable sandwich bag and left it in a school locker. She had had triple the amount of fun by leaving a frozen gift in each of her friend's lockers.

"It was a joke." Sophia said. "I didn't know it would expand *that* much."

"It practically filled our lockers!" Leah said. "I mean it was dripping on to the floor."

"I said I was sorry, and I helped clean it up." Sophia said.

"I'll be right back." Audrey said and quickly crossed the pool's deck and exited through the side gate with Sophia's swimsuit in hand.

"Audrey!" Sophia said as loud as she dared. "Bring back my swimsuit!"

"I guess she didn't hear you." Laney said.

"Hear what?" Leah asked with a giggle.

Audrey reappeared moments later, grinning. Sophia's bikini was nowhere to be seen.

"Where *is* my swimsuit Audrey?!" Sophia demanded.

"Well, the last time I saw it, it was lying in the middle of the street directly underneath one of those very new and very bright streetlights! If you want it back, you will have to walk out into the middle of the street and get it!" Audrey said. "If anyone were driving down the street or happened to be up and looking out the window, well, they would get a very different view of Sophia Elizabeth Young! Too bad you don't have some of that shaving cream to cover up…uh…your essentials!"

"Laney, can you at least get me a towel?" Sophia asked.

Laney grinned and crossed her arms across her chest. "Sorry, the towels are inside, the house is locked, and the alarm is set. If I try and turn it off after midnight, it notifies my dad and the police."

"Isn't *that* convenient." Sophia said knowing full well Laney could come and go as she pleased.

"Leah?" Sophia began.

"My backpack was *totally* covered in shaving cream!" Leah said mimicking Laney's pose.

Sophia put her head down on the edge of the pool's deck and giggled. She knew she was going to have to get her swimsuit and she knew she would be totally naked when she did. She also knew that had Audrey done the shaving cream prank to her and then had to do the skinny-dipping dare, she would have done the exact same thing to her if she had thought of it.

When she had confessed to the shaving cream prank, Laney, Leah and Audrey had sworn they would get even somehow. When they hadn't done anything within a week or so after school had gotten out for the summer, Sophia had kind of forgotten about it and their vow of revenge.

"Why didn't I hold on to my bikini when I jumped in the pool? And why did I try and prank those three? They don't forget anything." Sophia thought.

"Fine, I *will* go get my bikini and I will look good doing it too! Goldilocks will be ever so proud of me!" Sophia said.

She swam to the opposite end of the pool, climbed the three steps, and headed toward the side gate dripping water, with her three friends following her; all four were giggling!

There was a large tree next to the sidewalk in Laney's front yard that provided shadowy coverage. From her vantage point she could easily see her bikini lying in the circle of light directly underneath the bright L.E.D. streetlight across the street. Audrey had positioned it, so it looked like someone had been lying down and their body had disappeared leaving only the swimsuit on the pavement.

"Okay, joke's over. Will one of you *please* get my swimsuit?" Sophia asked in a last-ditch attempt to avoid having to go out into the middle of the incredibly well-lit street wearing nothing but her skin.

Laney, Leah and Audrey looked at her, crossed their arms over their chests and in one voice said, "No!"

"Please!" Sophia begged. "What if Chuck drives by again."

"He'll forget all about my mostly string bikini!" Laney said.

"Leah?" Sophia said with pleading eyes.

"My backpack still smells like shaving cream!" Leah said.

Sophia didn't even bother asking Audrey; she knew what her answer would be!

"If you want your swimsuit shaving cream girl." Audrey said. "Go get it!"

"For the record, it was shaving *gel!*" Sophia said.

This brought on a new wave of fresh giggles! As Sophia started to leave the cover of the large tree's shadows, a car rounded the corner up the block and headed toward them at a high rate of speed.

"Oh, crud monkeys!" Laney said. "That *is* Chuck!"

The four crouched down behind the tree as the old Impala sped past. The turbulent flow of air that its passing created, tumbled and tossed Sophia's bikini further down the street where the top and bottoms landed in the middle of the intersection that had not one, but two of the new L.E.D. streetlights illuminating it!

"Bummer about your bikini." Audrey said once the old Impala had passed. "Now you will be really lit up when you have to get it."

"Thanks Chuck." Sophia said sarcastically as the car disappeared down the street. She turned to her friends and asked, "What are the chances one of you would go get my swimsuit now?"

"None!" Laney said.

"Zilch!" Leah said.

"Nadda!" Audrey added.

"You know I hate all three of you, right?" Sophia asked.

"We know." Audrey said flatly.

"Yup, we are dead to you." Leah said.

"Now, I just have *two* best friends." Laney said.

Snorts of quiet laughter filled the air!

Sophia checked for traffic again and seeing none said, "Why not!"

She walked nonchalantly to the middle of the street, turned to her friends, waved and strolled down the middle of the street to where her bikini was lying. She picked it up and strolled back down the middle of the street before crossing over to the tree where her friends were hiding and watching.

"I cannot believe you walked, like, a block down the middle of the street with nothing at all on, picked up your bikini and then walked all the way back here!" Audrey said once Sophia had rejoined the group. "Why didn't you put it on after you picked it up?"

"If you got it, flaunt it!" Sophia said. "And just so you all know; we are even in the practical joke department!"

The four friends giggled quietly and headed back to Laney's pool where they swam for another two hours. Sophia surprised everyone and didn't put her bikini on even when they headed back to her house at four o'clock to sneak back inside.

After they had gotten dressed, they all crawled into their sleeping bags. In the quiet of the Young's family room, Laney asked, "Want to open the penalty envelope and see what we would have had to do if one of us had backed out of doing the dare?"

"Shouldn't we save that for the next game?" Leah asked.

"We would still have the three other envelopes." Sophia said.

Audrey jumped up and snatched the envelope from the table, grinned and asked, "All in favor of opening the envelope say 'Aye', all opposed say 'Nay'!"

"Aye!" Laney said.

"Aye!" Leah said.

"Aye!" Sophia said.

"Aye!" Audrey said.

She tore the envelope open and read what was written on the card.

"Well?" Laney said. "What does it say?"

"It says…" Audrey began. "You have to go skinny dipping!"

They all burst out laughing!

~ ~ ~ ~ ~ ~

"Would any of your friends have gone skinny dipping with you?" Her Polly voice asked again, drawing Sophia away from her memory of the events at her last sleepover.

"*Actually, they did. When we got back to the pool and I didn't put mine back on, the three of them decided to skinny dip too.*" Sophia thought. "*My friends are kind of free spirits!*"

"And you're not a free spirit?" Her rational voice asked.

"*I guess maybe that sleepover was when I started becoming more of a free spirit!*" Sophia said to herself. "*It was the first time I had ever skinny dipped, and it was the first time I had walked around outside totally nude! And...*"

"And what?" Polly asked.

"*And even though I was terrified someone would see me. I mean Chuck was driving around.*" Sophia thought. "*I kind of liked doing it too!*"

"You *liked* having to go out in the middle of a street under those bright streetlights wearing nothing?" Polly asked.

"*I was terrified, but I liked the thrill of it. I mean I could have been seen, but I wasn't.*" Sophia thought.

"What do you say about *today*?" Polly asked. "You've done more than just gone out to the middle of the street to get your bikini."

Sophia thought about the question and realized she would probably look back on this day as the day she went against everything her inner self said not to do. It was the day when she threw caution, and her bikini briefs to the wind.

If someone would have asked her last week or even yesterday if she would ever consider stripping off her clothes to spend several hours on a hot summer afternoon skinny dipping and taking a long walk where anyone who came along could see her when she was wearing nothing but suntan lotion, she would have said a resounding, emphatic "No!"

When she was with her friends back home and had skinny dipped after retrieving her bikini, it was after two o'clock in the morning and no one was awake, but now she was sitting outside in broad daylight covered head to toe with suntan lotion and nothing else.

She would remember today as the day where she started to let go of what she thought should happen and instead started living in what was happening. It was the day she stopped hiding and cowering behind the great "What if!" It was the day she got to make a *choice* and she had already decided to come back to the covered bridge and go skinny dipping again before school started if she could. She might even come out here even after school started. It stayed warm into late September and sometimes even into October, so she had opportunities!

"I would say I really enjoyed doing what I have done today!"
Sophia said to herself. *"And the day is not over!"*

Sophia stretched out on the fleece blanket on her back, picked up her book and reread the passage where Laura had tricked Jerry into skinny dipping! Her eyes started to grow heavy, so she closed the book, stretched her arms above her head and dozed in the hot summer sun.

~ ~ ~ ~ ~ ~

She awoke with a start when the siding and window people texted her offering an amazing deal that she had to act on in the next hour.

"Take a hint!" She thought.

She blocked the number, deleted the text, then checked to see how long she had slept. Her cell phone's clock showed it was three o'clock; she had napped for maybe thirty minutes.

"What if some man had come along while you were asleep and found you that way?" Her inner, logical voice asked. "He could have taken advantage of you! He could have had his way with you!"

"But no one did come along, did they?" Sophia asked herself. *"And no one had their way with me either, did they? And for the record, the term 'had their way' is old and outdated."*

"Is there another term you prefer?" Her Polly voice asked.

"Yes!" Sophia thought.

"What is it?" Polly asked.

"What if some man had come along and did The Big Monkey Ooo-wah-doo with me!" Sophia thought with a laugh!

Polly Pragmatic wasn't through with her questioning. "What would you do if Brent Edwards showed up and saw you right now?"

"You're really pulling out all the stops aren't you Polly." Sophia thought.

Brent Edwards was a boy she had known since first grade. Sometime towards the end of their sixth-grade year, she had developed a crush on him. If she were honest, she would say she still had a crush on him; she thought he was really cute!

"What I would do is point to my face and say, 'My eyes are up here Brent! They are not on my chest or below my waist!'" Sophia giggled!

Her inner, logical voice had nothing more to say on the subject.

Sophia laid in the hot sun enjoying how it felt and as she did, she had a random thought, one that was completely radical and a lot riskier than sneaking out at two o'clock in the morning or walking down the block to retrieve her bikini or even walking out to the end of the gravel road had been.

"Hey Polly?" Sophia said to that rational part of her being. *"Let's go for another walk!"*

"Get dressed, please!" The Polly voice begged.

"Okay, I will put something on." Sophia said.

"Finally!" Polly Pragmatic said.

Sophia applied another coat of suntan lotion. *"There, I'm ready to go!"*

"SOPHIA!!" The rational part of herself shouted as she walked up the embankment to the road.

"Are you going back to the bridge?" Polly asked.

"Nope!" Sophia answered.

Instead, she walked across the gravel road and reread the sign that said, "LITTLE GRAND CEMETERY – 5 MILES", then turned left and headed down the road.

"Why did the nude girl cross the road?" Sophia asked herself.

Polly Pragmatic answered, "Because she has lost her mind?"

"No!" Sophia thought. *"Because she chose to! I'm going to check out that cemetery!"*

"That cemetery is FIVE miles away!" Said her pragmatic self. "Do you realize that when you get back here you will have walked TEN miles totally and completely naked?"

"More like twelve. Remember, I walked out to the paved road and back earlier. That was a round trip of two miles." Sophia thought. *"That's what makes it fun!"*

"Fun? Walking around totally naked is what you think of as FUN?" Pragmatic Polly asked.

"Doing something like this is FUN because it is a choice!" Sophia said. *"It's like playing the lottery and not getting caught doing it is winning! Besides, this is a dead-end road; there won't be any traffic, so I win!"*

"You hope." Her Pragmatic Polly side said.

"I know!" Sophia responded.

Chapter 18

Sophia walked, and just took in the nature all around her. There were huge old oaks, walnuts, elms and many other kinds of trees she could not name, growing on either side of the dusty gravel road. There were wildflowers as well in all sorts of colors. She thought about picking some but decided not to just in case there was poison ivy.

"That would be fun to explain to Mom and Dad." She thought.

Pragmatic Polly spoke up. "Hey Mom, I need to go to the doctor because I spent the day outside wearing nothing but a smile. I picked you some flowers and now I have poison ivy everywhere …and I do mean EVERYWHERE!"

"Shut up!" Sophia giggled as she continued walking and getting lost in her surroundings.

A weed her father called Foxtail was standing straight and tall in the center of the road which told Sophia it had been quite a while since anyone had driven out this way. She brushed against it as she walked by and it tickled her leg.

"I wonder how far I have walked?" Sophia thought.

She turned and looked back the way she had come and could not see any part of the bridge. She unlocked her phone and opened the mapping app. When she had turned it on for the trip to the bridge and it had kept running in the background. With a couple of clicks it told her what she wanted to know.

"I have walked three and seven tenths miles?" She thought. *"No way!"*

"And you are totally naked and out in plain view!" Polly chimed in.

"Excuse me, I am <u>nude</u>, not naked!" Sophia said to her conscience. *"We discussed that, remember?"*

Pragmatic Polly "Harrumphed!".

A short time later Sophia noticed a path going back into the trees on the right side of the gravel road and she decided to investigate. The path, that was paved with smooth stone, ran parallel to the road for several hundred feet. Every now and then she could catch glimpses of the gravel through the dense trees.

"The Grove." She thought. *"That's what this place should be called."*

The path began descending down a steep incline that turned into a staircase of sorts whose steps were wide, smooth and easily navigated. As she descended, Sophia could feel herself leaving the heat and humidity that was trapped under the green canopy of trees.

At the bottom, she found herself in a mostly circular space that was at least two hundred feet in diameter. The walls were rocky outcroppings fifty or sixty feet high. Half of its floor was flat, smooth and level; the other half was a large, clear crescent shaped pool that was kept full by a waterfall that poured down from the top of the rocky outcropping to her far right. The space reminded her of Marvel Cave at Silver Dollar City, except this cave was open at the top.

"A sinkhole maybe?" Sophia thought as she removed the elastic hair ties from her ponytail and let her hair fall free.

She sat her phone on a rock at the pool's edge and stepped into the cool water. She dove just under the surface and opened her eyes and what she saw amazed her! The left half of the pool, the part farthest away from the waterfall, was DEEP and dark and appeared to actually be a cave.

"I won't be diving down there." She said to herself after surfacing. *"That's a good way to become a memory."*

Sophia swam back to the shallow part of the pool and got out to look around; she was finding the sinkhole to be very interesting. She walked to the far side of the former cave and saw that someone had made a fire ring out of several good-sized rocks. There was a stack of ten or twelve decent sized logs stacked close to the fire ring along with some smaller kindling. She also saw that someone had made a fire at some point, but the ashes that were there had been there for quite some time. No one had been down to the floor of the sinkhole in quite a while and that suited her just fine!

"I wish I had known about this place when we first moved here." Sophia thought. *"I would have lived out here this summer! This place is amazing! I will definitely be coming back!"*

With that internal pronouncement, Sophia retrieved her phone, climbed out of the sinkhole and returned to the world of heat and humidity.

~ ~ ~ ~ ~ ~

A few minutes after resuming her walk on the gravel road, she saw the gateway that had "Little Grand Creek Cemetery" written above it in wrought iron. However, when she got to the gate, she did not enter.

"Oh!" Pragmatic Polly said. "So now after running all over the country without any clothes on, you are afraid the dead will be upset?"

"No." Sophia said. *"Look how tall the grass is. I don't want to get any chigger bites."*

She stood by the gate and looked at the closest headstones. Many were hard to see because the grass needed to be cut, but it was a lovely cemetery despite that. One headstone caught her attention; it was down on the other side of a small rise and was the color of a polished apple.

"That's pretty!" She thought.

After looking at the cemetery and surrounding countryside for a few minutes, Sophia headed back toward the bridge enjoying the hot summer air and the choices she had made!

She paid another visit to the sinkhole. This time she took a cold shower in the waterfall and discovered a large space behind it! The water, as it coursed over her skin, felt good and Sophia felt good about herself even if her way of expressing it was…a bit different.

~ ~ ~ ~ ~ ~

A little over an hour later she was nearly back to the bridge and she stopped and looked down at herself. There was a sheen to her skin, partially from the humidity in the air and partially from the perspiration from her walk. There was also a noticeable darker shade to her skin as well.

"I am getting <u>tan</u>!" She said to herself. *"I mean <u>really</u> tan!"*

Up ahead, she noticed a wide spot next to the road that was gravel free. It reminded her of a buffalo wallow that was described in one of the books by Laura Ingalls Wilder. When she got to it, she saw the dirt was a fine powder that was several inches deep and the wallow, if that is what it really was, was at least fifteen feet in diameter.

"Why not!" Sophia said making another choice for herself.

She laid on her back and made a "dirt angel" by moving her arms up and down and her legs back and forth in the dirt just like she did when she made snow angels in the winter! She got up carefully, trying not to smudge her body's outline and looked at her creation.

She laughed! *"I know what I am going to do now!"*

She moved over a few feet and laid down in the soft, powdery brown dirt again and made a second dirt angel, but for this one she laid on her stomach.

The second dirt angel was quite detailed and the phrase "No imagination required!" popped into her head. Seeing the detail gave her an idea for the next time she came out to the bridge.

Pragmatic Polly, her rational self, said, "You have lost your mind!"

"You may be right, but I am having fun!" She said back to herself. *"And what I am doing is <u>my</u> choice!"*

When she got back to the fishing platform, she checked her phone and saw that it was nearly four-thirty p.m. She had spent the better part of the day fully unclothed enjoying the sun!

On a whim, and there had already been many whims, she used the camera's self-timer and one of the buckets to take a picture of herself; this one was a full-length body photo.

"Now you are taking nude photos of yourself?" Polly Pragmatic asked.

"Another first!" Sophia said to herself. *"I just want to see how I look covered in dirt."*

"You look naked with dirt all over yourself." Polly observed.

"Hush." Sophia thought and looked at the picture, smiled then reset the camera and took a picture of her back.

"Are you going to send those to Brent?" Her Polly voice asked.

"I don't have his phone number." Sophia thought. *"Besides, I am not into sexting or whatever sending naked pictures of yourself to someone is called!"*

"But you are into running around naked?" Pragmatic Polly asked.

"Yes, because it feels amazing!" She said. *"I guess I should tell the girls that daring me to go skinny dipping has caused me to become a nudist!"*

There had been a few times during the day when she had looked at herself and realized she wasn't wearing anything. She had become so absorbed in her surroundings; she had forgotten her clothes were lying across the buckets on the fishing platform. Sophia laughed at her thoughts then climbed back up the embankment and walked back down the road to where she had made the dirt angels. She snapped a picture of both of her creations.

"If someone sees those, it will really make them wonder!" She thought.

"What would they wonder?" The Polly voice asked.

"They would wonder what hottie with the body made them!" Sophia thought.

She went back to the platform, sat her phone on one of the buckets, backed up to the far edge and took another running dive back into the Little Grand Creek!

She did not dive as deep as she had when she went to retrieve her phone. This dive was shallow, maybe only three feet below the surface. It allowed her to quickly surface and look back at where her body had passed through the water. She laughed when she saw the streak of the gravel road dirt!

She swam for thirty minutes and when she was done, she climbed back onto the platform, wrung out her hair then set up her phone's camera and took another full-length picture of herself.

"WHAT ARE YOU DOING?" Polly Pragmatic demanded.

"I'm taking a picture." Sophia responded.

"At least in the dirt covered picture you couldn't see everything clearly, but now…" Polly said.

She studied the photo and smiled! *"I have a cute bellybutton!"*

"Are you going to have those published in the yearbook?" Pragmatic Polly asked in a sarcastic tone. "Your popularity would be epic!"

"Uh, NO!" Sophia said.

"Delete them!" Her rational voice said. "If they accidently got sent to someone…"

"Deleting them now!" Sophia said to herself and with three quick taps on her phone's screen, they, along with the ones of her covered in dirt were gone.

"What about the picture of the dirt angel?" Polly asked.

"What about it?" Sophia said.

"That one shows *everything* in perfect detail." Pragmatic Polly said.

"Everything, except for my face." Sophia thought. *"No one would know it was me that made them. I'm keeping that one!"*

"At least get dressed." Her Pragmatic Polly voice said.

"No!" Sophia said.

She dropped her phone back on the bucket and did a cannonball back into the creek. She swam to the far bank and back to the platform and climbed out. She ran back up the embankment back to the "dirt angels" and rolled in the dirt without disturbing them before running back to the platform and diving in the creek!

"NOW, I'll put on my clothes!" She said to herself after rinsing off for the second time.

Her Polly voice groaned.

She got dressed, but not entirely; her bikini briefs were, after all, floating downstream somewhere. She put on her shirt, running shorts and tennis shoes for her trip back to the house, however, she stowed her sports bra in the backpack.

"I'm going commando!" The thought made her giggle!

She paused at the bridge's balcony to look at the water again when her phone came to life with a text message notification from Maude Adelaide.

The text said, "DON'T COME TOMORROW. NOT SURE IF I TOLD YOU THAT OR NOT. I WILL LET YOU KNOW WHEN YOU NEED TO COME NEXT."

Sophia grinned! She had another totally free day!

"What are you doing tomorrow Sophia?" Pragmatic Polly asked.

She laughed! *"The same thing I did today except I will get here earlier and stay later!"*

"Didn't you take enough chances today?" Her rational voice asked.

"Not even close!" Sophia said to herself.

"You have lost your mind!" The Polly voice said.

"Maybe so, but at the very least I'll have a killer tan!" Sophia said to herself. *"My tan lines will be gone if I come out here again tomorrow."*

She got her Schwinn out of the grass to begin her ride back to town but didn't get on.

"You need to get home." Her Polly voice said.

"Yes, I do, but…" She answered.

"But what?" Polly asked.

"But…I am making another choice and taking another chance today!" Sophia thought.

"What are you going to do?" Polly asked.

"This!" Sophia thought.

She engaged the kickstand and quickly took off her shirt and shorts and stuffed them in the backpack.

"I'll put them on when I get to the end of this gravel road." She said to Polly.

Miss Polly Pragmatic groaned at her decision. "Now it's nude bike riding?"

"Sometimes you have to do something a little crazy to prove that you are sane!" She thought as she began the bike ride back toward town.

~ ~ ~ ~ ~ ~

When she got back to where the gravel met the chip and sealed road, she used the kickstand to prop up her bike and put on her clothes. This was a fortunate choice because, as she slid her arms through the sleeves' openings and her head through the neck hole of her shirt, a winged bug of some sort began flying around her head and face. Just as her hand connected with the bug, a white pickup truck turned onto the gravel and pulled up next to her and stopped. She had been so focused on the bug; she hadn't heard it coming down the road.

"Everything okay?" The man behind the wheel asked. "It looked like you were dancing quite a jig!"

"I'm fine. I am just out for a bike ride. I was trying to swat a bee or something that was flying around my face." Sophia said.

"If you had been one minute faster, you would have seen me dancing wearing just my shoes!" Sophia thought.

"I thought you didn't care if anyone saw you." Polly Pragmatic observed.

"Shut it!" Sophia thought.

"By the looks of your hair, you look like you went swimming too." The man said.

He was older, probably in his early seventies. On the driver's door of the truck was a magnetic sign that said: "LARRY THE LAWN GUY" which had a phone number underneath a picture of a man pushing a lawn mower.

"If you only knew!" Sophia thought with an internal giggle.

"Well." Sophia said sheepishly. "I accidently did go swimming."

Larry gave her a quizzical look. "How can you accidently go swimming?" it seemed to say.

"I was taking a picture and I sort of dropped my phone in the creek, so I had to go get it." Sophia said. "I am sure glad the creek's water is so clear."

"But your clothes are dry Sophia!" Polly said. "How will you explain that if he asks?"

"I'll tell him I had my swimsuit in my backpack." She thought.

"How convenient." Polly replied.

"You didn't ruin it, did you?" He asked. "My niece dropped her phone in a sink full of dish water and that's all she wrote!"

"No, it's fine." Sophia said. "I have a waterproof case, so it didn't get hurt."

"Well, that's good." Larry remarked. "I bet the water was cold, wadden' it?"

Sophia laughed. "It wasn't warm!"

"That creek is spring fed you know. There's a natural spring upstream from the bridge…oh…a mile or two. The water that comes out of there is fifty-six degrees year-round!" Larry said.

"Really?" Sophia said.

"Yes! It's cold in the summer and they say it's kind of warm in the winter, but I wouldn't want to jump in New Year's Day to find out!" Larry laughed.

"It *was* cold today, but at least there was that platform down below where I dried off in the sun." Sophia said.

"Oh yeah!" Larry agreed. "I forgot about that fishing platform."

"So, do very many people go out to the bridge?" Sophia asked.

"Sophia the detective quizzes an unsuspecting local." She thought trying not to giggle.

"No young lady, they don't." Larry said. "Well, except for the historical bridge folks that is. They come out here every now and again and spruce things up, but that's about it. I bet you are the first person to go out there since I was out there last month to go mow the cemetery that's five or six miles past the bridge. Did you know there was a cemetery out there?"

"I saw the sign for it." Sophia said.

"I'm headed there right now. Been meaning to get out there, but I took a little vacation to see an old friend!" Larry said. "I bet the cemetery sure needs a trim by now."

"After a month, I bet it does!" Sophia agreed knowing full well that it did.

"Well, just thought I'd stop and see if you were okay." He said.

"Thank you for stopping!" Sophia said. "I appreciate it!"

"You're welcome young lady, any time!" He put his truck in gear and headed down the gravel road.

While waving her hands in the air trying to dispatch the bug, she had knocked the Schwinn into the road's ditch. It took her a little bit to get it out because the ditch was deep and full of that same fine powdery dirt that she had rolled in earlier. After she had wrestled her bike back onto the road, she got on it and began her trip back to town.

She was pleased to know her new favorite spot was one where not a lot of people visited. And now there was an additional new place to visit which would require some additional swimming and she just might do that in her favorite swimsuit!

"Larry the Lawn Guy could have caught you." Pragmatic Polly said from inside Sophia's head.

"He could have, but he didn't!" She answered. *"And if he had, at his age seeing me with nothing on but a smile, well, he might have had a heart attack!"*

"If he sees your dirt angels, he will know it was you who made them you know." Polly added.

"If Larry the Lawn Guy would happen to stop on the other side of the bridge and look down, he will get to see two very detailed dirt angels that were definitely made by a girl!" Sophia thought. *"I can't do anything about that now. If he finds them, he finds them, but if he does, I hope that he appreciates the detail of my work!"*

Pragmatic Polly did not say anything.

Chapter 19

"Why is your hair wet?" Carol asked when Sophia came through the back door at a quarter till six.

"You wouldn't believe me if I told you." Sophia said.

"Try me!" Carol said.

"So, I went back to the Coombs House Park this morning at like ten o'clock and I saw Little Miss Eva Allbody." Sophia said.

"Who?" Her mom asked.

"Eva, the little girl I talked to at the fair last night who was going to catch a duck." Sophia said. "I saw her and her mom at the park at the big fountain and I gave her that duck I found when we were walking back to the van!"

"So, you fell in the fountain at ten this morning and your hair is still wet?" Her mother began.

"No!" Sophia said. "I left the park and went out to the Little Grand Creek covered bridge and spent the day there and I saw the coolest thing!"

"What was that?" Carol Young asked her daughter.

"This." Sophia pulled out her cell phone and opened its photo gallery. "That is the biggest goldfish I have ever seen! I didn't know they could get that big!"

Carol looked at the picture and said, "That's a carp!"

"A what?" Sophia asked.

"A carp." Carol repeated. "It's just a big goldfish! Grandpa Mort showed me them when we would go fishing when I was younger than you."

"*You* went fishing?" Sophia asked in total and complete amazement. Sometimes people you thought you knew extremely well, including your parents, could surprise you.

"Yes, Sophia. I have gone fishing. I have even baited my own hook!" Carol said. "So how did you get wet? You haven't told me that yet."

"I got wet because of that fish." Sophia said. "After I took the picture, I sort of dropped my phone in the creek."

"You dropped your phone in the creek?" Carol said. "If it's broken…"

Sophia couldn't help herself and she burst out laughing.

"It's not funny Sophia!" Carol said. "That's an expensive phone and if it gets broken you won't get another one until you can buy it yourself!"

"Mom?" Sophia said.

"What?" Carol said tersely.

"If it was broken, I couldn't have shown you the fish picture." Sophia said.

Carol looked at Sophia with a hard look on her face as she processed what had just been said. Her terse look broke as she started to laugh at her "If it's broken..." statement. "Sorry honey, it's just..."

"It's okay, Mom." Sophia said. "I was scared that it was ruined from the water too, but thanks to Dad it wasn't."

"What do you mean?" Carol asked.

"When you got me the phone, Dad got one of those Life-Guard phone cases. It protects it from drops of up to, like, fifty feet, has a nearly indestructible screen protector built into it and it is completely waterproof down to over one hundred feet." Sophia said.

Carol confessed. "I forgot all about that."

"Me too." Sophia said.

"So, I guess you got wet when you jumped in the creek to save your phone." Carol asked.

"Yup!" Sophia said. "And I jumped in a second time too."

"Why?" Carol asked.

"Weeell, I sort of dropped my phone in the creek a second time." Sophia said as she continued with more of her confession.

Carol Young very nearly doubled over with laughter when Sophia told her about her second trip into the creek.

"Your father has always said we should have named you Grace!" Carol said.

Sophia had heard this before, usually after she had hurt herself in some minor way or, worse yet, when she had merely fallen off her shoes.

"Thanks Mom, I appreciate your concern and support." Sophia said dryly.

"I do what I can!" Carol said. "I do what I can!"

"Oh, look at this!" She opened the video app on her phone and played her footage of the beaver slapping its tail on the water's surface as it dove out of sight.

"It sounds like you had an interesting day Sophia!" Carol said.

Sophia laughed; the sound escaped before she could stifle it. *"You have no idea how right you are, Mom!"* She thought. *"No idea at all!"*

Carol Young hugged Sophia in a tight embrace then kissed her cheek!

"Supper will be ready in about a half hour." She said. "Why don't you go and shower. You smell like creek water."

"Okay Mom!" Sophia said and headed to her room.

"Sophia?" Carol asked. "Why are your clothes dry, but your hair isn't?"

Sophia was thankful that her back was to her mother. Had Carol Young seen her daughter's face, she would have seen a look of panic.

"She would know I didn't have my swimsuit with me." Sophia thought.

"Sophia?" Carol repeated.

She turned around and said, "Mom, I rode my bike. They dried out on the way home. It is just a little hot out there."

"Ah!" Carol said. "That's right."

"You got away with that one." Polly said.

"Shut it!" Sophia said to her conscience and headed to her bathroom.

~ ~ ~ ~ ~ ~

For the third time that day Sophia took off her clothes. It didn't take as long as it had out at the creek as she was only wearing her shirt and shorts. She remembered to take her sports bra out of the drawstring backpack and toss it in her laundry hamper.

"I don't want to have to explain why that was in my backpack." She thought.

Before stepping into the shower, she looked at herself in the long mirror that hung on the back of the bathroom door. What she saw, she already knew from the pictures she had taken on the platform; the formerly untanned areas of her body now had a reddish color to them and in a few hours those red areas would be tan, and her tan lines would be less defined.

"I CANNOT wait to go back there!" She said to her mirror image. "But tomorrow I will get there earlier and stay longer!"

~ ~ ~ ~ ~ ~

Dan entered the kitchen surprising Carol.

"I didn't hear you get home." She said.

"I rang twice! I always do!" He said with a grin. "And I am doubly blessed to come home to two of the most beautiful women ever!"

"What does he want, Mom?" Sophia teased as she walked into the dining room with her hair wrapped in a fluffy towel and a big smile on her face!

"I don't know, but I bet we find out soon." Carol answered with a wry smile of her own.

"What I want is a hug and a kiss from my favorite wife and my favorite daughter!" He said.

"Why?" Sophia asked. "Wouldn't your second-favorite wife and second-favorite daughter do that for you?"

"No!" Dan said. "That's why I want you two to do it!"

Sophia and her mother burst out laughing then they double teamed Dan. Carol kissed him on his left cheek and Sophia kissed his right!

"You are in a good mood!" Carol said. "You both are!"

"I'll be glad to have that training out of the way that's all." Dan said.

"What training is that Dad?" Sophia asked.

"Being a Postmaster for Dummies." Dan said with a grin.

"You will do well then!" Sophia said. "Didn't you say it's going to be in Columbia?"

"Yes, and it's tomorrow. Your mom and I will be leaving before six in the morning." Dan said.

"Are people even awake at that hour of the day?" Sophia asked with a grin.

"Just the ambitious ones!" Dan said returning the grin. "And you look like the cat who caught the canary! What have you been up to?" Dan asked.

"Well, if you really want to know, I spent six or seven hours today outside completely and totally nude! I went skinny dipping for the second time in my life, but for the first time in broad daylight! I love how the water feels!

Just so you know, the first time I went skinny dipping was when Leah, Laney, Audrey and I had that sleepover right before we moved. Yeah, we snuck out of the house at two o'clock in the morning and went to Laney's to swim in her pool.

I got a dare, so I had to go skinny dipping. Big mistake! Audrey grabbed my bikini and laid it in the middle of the street right under a streetlight and I had to go and get it! Then we all went back to the pool and skinny dipped for another two hours!

I walked TWELVE miles today wearing nothing but suntan lotion and a smile!

I showered in a waterfall that was wonderfully cold!

I made a very detailed 'dirt angel'!

I laid out in the sun and I am getting a killer tan that you would not believe!

Speaking of that, thank you for getting me that Tan Booster Ten suntan lotion for me when school got out, it is the awesome sauce!

Are you shocked?

Are you mortified?

Are you ashamed?

Are you worried that you didn't raise me correctly?

Are you wondering if what I did today was due to poor potty training?

Are you wondering <u>why</u> I would do such a thing?

Well, it's not your fault, but it kind of is too. You see, you have not given me the ability to make any significant choices about much of anything this summer. I have been uprooted and moved away from everyone and everything I have ever known, and I do not like it one bit!

Because of your job change Dad, I had to give up my spot on the varsity cheerleading squad that I have been working for since before I started middle school. I know you took the job because it pays more and will help us a lot in the money department but come on! I had made the squad as A FRESHMAN! Only one other girl had done that and that was back when Brad Pitt was a junior at Kickapoo High!

And Mom, you are even picking out that little black dress for me. You have really great taste, but I think I can pick out a dress that I am going to be wearing!

The only choice I did get to make this summer was the last time I was with Audrey, Leah and Laney that I just told you about. I'm glad I did that. I think that choice helped me do what I did today.

Because of those things, I chose to take off my clothes today! I did enjoy how the sun and the water, and the breeze felt on my skin, but the best part was how I felt being able to make a choice about <u>something</u> this summer!

There is a big positive from today's adventures in nudity; I like how I look! And just so you both know, I look AMAZING! I guess all those years of gymnastics and tumbling and cheerleading have paid off! I am kind of like the Tan Booster Ten suntan lotion; I <u>am</u> the awesome sauce! And if either of you ever says the word Goldilocks, I will most likely fall to the ground and laugh until I pass out!

By the way, I don't have to help Maude Adelaide tomorrow, but I may, accidently on purpose, forget to tell you that because I am going to go back to the bridge tomorrow. When I get there, I will be taking off my clothes again, but not just for six or seven hours. No, I am going out there and will be au natural for probably twelve or thirteen hours considering you two will be gone all day!

I am going to lay out coated in Tan Booster Ten suntan lotion.
I am NOT going to have any tan lines!
I am going to read my book and listen to Laura's tapes.
I am taking another walk that will be at least ten miles long!
I am going back to that waterfall and let it pour all over me!
I am going swimming!

I am going to find the spring that feeds the creek! I'm not sure where it is, but I will find it and I will be totally nude when I do. You know why? Because I can!

But don't worry Mom and Dad, I am not drinking or doing drugs or attempting to make you grandparents before I finish my freshman year of high school. I don't know anyone in this town so "hooking up"; I think that's what it's called, would be just a bit difficult.

What I did today and what I am going to do tomorrow was because I could and because I can. It's my choice. I like not wearing clothes! If someone sees me, well, I hope they like what they see! Because I know I like what I see!" Sophia thought.

"I just had a really good day!" Sophia said. "What about you Mom?"

"I'll be glad to go to a mall and do some shopping!" Carol said. "Too bad you have to help Ms. Adelaide, Sophia."

"Yes, it is, but there will be other trips. And I don't have to get up before the chickens." Sophia said.

"Day Two of the Suntan Lotion Only Festival starts in just twelve hours! If Mom finds a little black dress and gets it for me, so be it. I will gladly give up making that choice so I can go back out to the bridge!" Sophia thought.

"The early bird catches the worm Sophia!" Dan said.

"But he's too tired to do anything with it because he had to get up before the sun was awake!" Sophia said.

Dan laughed then added, "Just so you both know, there is a slight, slight, slight chance that we may have to stay in Columbia overnight if all the training doesn't get done."

"Slight?" Carol asked.

"Slight." Dan replied with a grin.

"How slight?" Carol teased.

"Slightly slight." Dan said.

"If that happened, would you be okay staying here by yourself Soph?" Carol asked.

"Oh, I wouldn't be by myself Mom." Sophia said with a straight face. "I would be having a PAR-TAY!!! Tomorrow isn't Saturday but it is summer so a party can happen anytime!"

"Shall I reserve one or two kegs of beer for you?" Dan asked.

"Just one Dad, it's a small party!" Sophia said.

"I'll know if we have to stay over by five p.m. So, if we are staying, I'll call the liquor store and have them deliver it by eight p.m. Is that okay?" Dan grinned at Sophia.

"Could you make it seven instead?" Sophia asked. "I want to be partying down hard by eight!"

"Anything for you Sophia-love!" Dan said. "Seven it is!"

"The beer will be cold won't it?" She asked.

"Of course! No underaged daughter of mine will be having a kegger with warm beer! What kind of a father do you think I am?" He said. "You will be "the new girl" at school and we want you to make a memorable first impression!"

"I would have made a memorable first impression if anyone had seen me today!" Sophia thought.

"You two are not right!" Carol said.

Dan and Sophia broke into laughter! Carol soon joined them and really enjoyed seeing Sophia smile and hearing her laugh!

"I don't know what you did to have such a good day today Sophia, but whatever it is, you need to keep doing it!" Carol said.

"Woo-hoo! I just got permission for Day Two of Sophia's Adventures in Nudity!" She thought.

"What *did* you do today anyway, Sophia?" Dan asked. "You never really said."

"I went out to an old, covered bridge in the middle of nowhere and sort of dropped my phone into the creek." She said.

"What?" Dan said with just a little bit of alarm in his voice.

"Relax Dad!" Sophia said. "That waterproof case you got me was a very good investment."

"Ah, I forgot about that." Dan said. "So, it worked?"

"Yup!" Sophia said. "Twice!"

She told about her phone's second plunge to the bottom the Little Grand Creek and like her mother, her father commented that she should have been named Grace.

"Did you do anything else besides wash your phone?" He asked.

"Oh yes! After I dropped my phone in the creek, I took off all my clothes, jumped in and got it then spent the rest of the day skinny dipping. I also decided to walk about twelve-miles wearing nothing but a smile and suntan lotion!" Sophia said truthfully and with a straight face.

Dan laughed out loud! "I hope you didn't get a sunburn!"

"I don't sunburn, Dad." Sophia said. "It's my Mediterranean genes you know!"

"Stop it you two." Carol said. "It's time to eat!"

Chapter 20

Sophia went out to the garage after supper after watching two episodes of a really good political drama with her parents. They were addicted to the show and were just a little disappointed that only three seasons had been filmed before the show was cancelled.

She found the wire basket and the panniers that she had removed from her bicycle at least three summers ago and reattached them with some zip ties she found on her father's work bench. Before going back inside, she located the one other item she was going to take with her on her trip back to the covered bridge.

"Tomorrow I can add another 'ist' to my resume!" She thought. *"Today I became a nude-ist, tomorrow I will be an art-ist!"*

As she came into the kitchen through the laundry room, her mom reminded her to get her clean clothes that were folded and sitting in a basket on the laundry folding table. Sophia did an about face, grabbed the basket of clothes and made a mental note to come back and get the basket of towels and wash cloths for her bathroom that were also folded up and sitting in a basket.

"Thank you!" Carol said as Sophia passed through their living room on the way to her room. "Don't forget your towels."

"I won't." Sophia said, but ultimately, she did.

She unloaded the basket and reloaded her dresser. She started giggling when she put away her underwear knowing she now had one less pair to worry about, then she yawned!

The bike ride to and from the bridge, the skinny dipping, the twelve miles of walking to and from the chip and sealed road and to the cemetery and back, the waterfall; just being outside all day, had tired her out.

"A day of many firsts!" Sophia thought. *"And now a night of firsts!"*

She had spent a large part of her day not wearing anything at all, and now she would spend the entire night the same way! It was nine-thirty when she peeled off her clothes for the fourth time, took another look at herself in the mirror and smiled at what she saw! She plugged in her phone, making sure she had set her alarm for six a.m. then crawled into bed!

"Because I can and because I choose to!" Sophia said to herself as she slipped off to sleep.

~ ~ ~ ~ ~ ~

"Sophia? Sophia, wake up." A voice said rousing her from sleep.

"Wha..." Sophia said groggily.

"Wake up, Sophia. We need to talk." The voice said, but without any real urgency.

Sophia rubbed the sleep from her eyes and saw Laura sitting on the edge of her bed.

"Am I dreaming or am I awake?" She asked.

"It's the same as the other times where we've talked Sophia." Laura said.

"I need to go to the bathroom." Sophia said.

"Go!" Laura said. "I'll wait."

Sophia threw off the covers and got out of bed before remembering that she wasn't wearing anything.

"Oh, sorry." She said to Laura.

Laura shrugged and laughed. "I am pretty sure I know what the female body looks like!"

Sophia laughed! "I guess you do!"

Sophia was comfortable not wearing clothes, more so since spending the day at the bridge. All through middle school she and the other girls had to change in an open locker room when dressing out for P.E. class. Some of the girls were uncomfortable and tended to slip into the shower stalls to change, but Sophia, Laney, Leah and Audrey were not; they didn't care.

The only reason she and the girls had used the bathroom to change into the swimsuits the night of the truth or dare skinny dipping was because her father had been known to come in and check on them. Had they been changing; it would have been very awkward for everyone.

Sophia crossed the hall to her bathroom and returned a short time later looking both relieved and concerned.

"Are you okay?" Laura asked.

"Yes, but..." Sophia's voice trailed off.

"But what?" Laura asked.

"If you are dreaming and go to the bathroom..." Sophia started to say.

Laura laughed heartily. "You did not wet the bed Sophia! You're fine!"

Relieved, in more ways than one, Sophia sat on the bed next to Laura.

"What's up?" Sophia asked.

"Can I tell you something?" Laura asked.

"Sure!" Sophia said.

"What you did today, I did myself once upon a time!" Laura said. "I did it several times actually. Well, everything except for the twelve-mile walk."

"You did?" Sophia asked sounding surprised. "Why?"

"For the same reasons as you. I wanted to do something I had complete control over even if it was kind of risky." Laura said. "And I wanted to work on my tan!"

"I'm going to do it again tomorrow!" Sophia said.

"That sounds fun!" Laura said. "How's the tape project going?"

"It's going," Sophia said. "But it's going slow."

"I thought so." Laura said.

"I'm sorry." Sophia said. "It takes a long time to listen and record them."

"Ah!" Laura said. "About that. If you look in the instructions for that... whatever you call it, you'll see there is a really fast way to copy the tapes."

"Really?" Sophia asked.

"Really!" Laura confirmed.

Sophia went to her desk where the laptop was still connected to the old reel-to-reel tape recorder / player. She powered up the computer and found the "Fast Recording" instructions for the Audio-Clone program and quickly made the changes to the program's settings that would allow her to rapidly digitalize the old tapes. She moved the recorder's multi-function knob to the "REW" setting and returned the current tape to its starting point.

"I hope this works." Sophia said.

"It will." Laura said.

Sophia switched the Audio-Clone program on and pressed the virtual "RECORD" button. She moved the multi-function knob to "FF" and watched the tape spin and listened to the fast, high-pitched sounds coming from the recorder's small square speaker. In less than a minute the tape finished its trip through the recorder's mechanism and Sophia turned off the recorder and rewound the tape.

"Let's see if it worked." She said, then opened the recently created digital file on the laptop, renamed it to match the date that someone – Laura – had written on a piece of masking tape and attached to the tape's reel.

"Here we go." She said.

After a few pops and crackles, Laura's voice came through clearly and plainly.

"Do I really sound like that? Laura asked.

"You do!" Sophia confirmed.

Laura laughed her sweet laugh and said, "You need to listen to those tapes Sophia. And finish reading that book too."

"I will finish the book tomorrow or the day after." She paused. "And I will listen to most of the tapes over the next couple of days! Now that I know how to quickly copy them, I can put them on my MP3 player and listen to them whenever I want even if I'm riding my bike or..."

"Or roaming around outside by the covered bridge wearing just suntan lotion?" Laura asked with a knowing smile.

"Especially then!" Sophia said.

"One more thing before I go." Laura said. "Do you remember when I braided your hair?"

"How could I forget about that?" Sophia exclaimed. "I mean, you braided it in a dream, but when I woke up my hair WAS braided for real! That kind of freaked me out!"

Laura laughed again. "Just so you won't get freaked out, in the morning, the tapes will be on your player."

"Really?" Sophia asked. "How?"

"Magic!" Laura answered with another of her wonderful laughs. "But you're going to have to take all the pops and crackles out of them!"

"Can I ask you something Laura?" Sophia asked.

"Sure!" Laura said.

Sophia sat on her bed again and grew quiet.

"Umm..." She began.

"Yes?" Laura said.

"Does skinny dipping and running around outside in the nude make me weird or something worse?" Sophia asked.

Laura smiled. "No Sophia, you are not weird or something worse! You are just getting comfortable with your body. A lot of girls your age really have a hard time with how they think they look and couldn't, not in a million years, have gone skinny dipping." Laura said. "And they would have never considered walking twelve miles wearing nothing at all where someone might see them! I know I couldn't have done that!" Laura paused then added, "I will give you one piece of advice though."

"What?" Sophia asked.

"Don't tell anyone that you are doing it" Laura said. "Keep that YOUR secret. People who are not as confident as you would try to make more out of it than what it really is. By the way, it takes a LOT of confidence to do what you did and are going to do."

"I like how not wearing clothes feels, Laura!" Sophia said. "I mean I was totally comfortable."

"You look totally comfortable right now." Laura observed. "I only felt that comfortable after I was married and..."

"And?" Sophia asked.

Laura giggled! "After I was married, I was comfortable like you are now, A LOT! Usually after the supper dishes were done things got...uh...well...comfortable!" Laura paused, smiled then continued. "I remember one night not very long after we got married, Jerry and I were sitting on the couch watching television and he got feeling frisky! I grabbed his hands and said, 'Jerry, my parents!' He took my left hand and pointed to my wedding ring and said, 'What about your parents?'" Laura said.

"What did you say Laura?" Sophia asked.

Laura laughed! "I didn't say much and before long, we both got ... um...comfortable! For all I know, that was the night we became parents!"

"I won't know anything about The Big Monkey Ooo-wah-doo until I am married." Sophia confessed.

"The what?" Laura asked.

"The Big Monkey Ooo-wah-doo!" Sophia said. "It's something my friend Audrey came up for...you know."

Laura grinned and whispered, "S-E-X?"

Sophia grinned back and whispered back, "Y-E-S! But I won't be doing that until I am married."

"Good!" Laura said. "I waited until I was married, and I am so glad I did. It made it so much more special. But I will tell you, there were a few times I was tempted."

"Really?" Sophia said.

"Oh yeah! In fact, on one of the tapes I'm putting on your...what did you call it?" Laura said.

"It's an MP3 player." Sophia said.

"One of the tapes I'm putting on your MP3 player kind of talks about one of the times I would have done The Big Monkey Ooo-Wah-Doo! Jerry never knew and I never told him, but the thought did cross my mind and had he asked I would have said yes."

"Really?" Sophia asked.

"There's nothing wrong with being tempted you know. But you can run into problems when you act on those temptations. The only things that stopped me was that I didn't want to get pregnant in high school and that Jerry and I had promised each other that we would wait until we were married. We did do some serious kissing, but that was about it." Laura said. "I guess before we were married, Jerry and I did The Little Monkey Ooo-wah-don't!"

Sophia laughed. "I hope I can find my Jerry someday."

"You will Sophia!" Laura said. "And whoever he is will show up at just the right time too!"

"I hope so." Sophia said. "Because this summer has really..."

She felt tears begin to well up in the corners of her eyes and the all too familiar lump began to grow in her throat.

Laura hugged her and asked, "Sucked big green weenies?"

The tears in her eyes and the lump in her throat vanished and were replaced with a laugh.

"Exactly!" Sophia said. "This summer has really sucked big green weenies!"

"You think about that a lot, don't you?" Laura asked.

"Yeah." Sophia confided. "I do. It's just so unfair! I mean..."

"When you keep thinking about those things and how unfair they were, you keep them alive and that keeps you stuck." Laura said. "If you want to move forward Sophia, you have to let that stuff go. Thinking about the would have, could have, should have changes nothing except, well, maybe the lining of your stomach."

"Have you been talking to my dad?" Sophia asked. "He said the exact same thing."

"Believe it or not Sophia." Laura said. "Your father is right."

"Not when you're almost fifteen he isn't!" Sophia said straight-faced, then she and Laura started laughing.

They laughed in the same way she and Audrey and Leah and Laney had laughed when they were together at a sleepover. When the giggles subsided, they grew quiet for a moment before Laura broke the silence.

"Do you have everything ready for tomorrow?" She asked.

"I have my outfit already picked out!" Sophia said with a giggle!

Laura laughed! "Really? What does it look like?"

Sophia stood and spun in a circle. "It's an old one I've had for a long time, but it fits like a glove!"

"It does look like it is skin-tight!" Laura said.

"Do you think Brent Edwards would like to see it?" Sophia asked channeling Polly Pragmatic.

"I think if you showed up wearing just _that_ outfit, Brent Edwards, or any other guy for that matter, would drool all over themselves, their eyes would pop out of their sockets and then they would faint!" Laura said. "What's that word you said when your friend showed you the picture of herself in that skimpy bikini?"

Sophia thought for a moment then laughed and said, "Wowzah!"

"Yes!" Laura said. "Brent Edwards would say, 'Wowzah!' if you showed up wearing just _that_ outfit!"

"I am getting an awesome tan!" Sophia said.

"And by the looks of things, your tan lines will be totally gone very soon." Laura said.

"I'm hoping they will be gone by tomorrow." Sophia said.

"Hey, do you have a calendar and a pencil?" Laura asked. "I want to show you something."

Sophia handed her the calendar and a pen that were lying on her desk. Laura began circling dates as she flipped through its pages before handing it back.

"No one will be at the bridge at all tomorrow except for you, so you can do whatever you want wearing whatever you want." Laura said. "In fact, no one will be out there for quite a while. You could go out there on any of those days and finish off that killer tan."

Sophia looked at the calendar. "So, any of the dates that are circled means no one will be out there?"

"Yes!" Laura said.

"How do you know?" Sophia asked.

"Inside information!" Laura said with a knowing smile.

"Oh, okay. Thanks!" Sophia said.

"By the way," Laura said. "It's okay to go into the cemetery too."

"Are you sure?" Sophia asked.

"I'm sure. The people that are there won't care." Laura said.

Sophia "harrumphed" dramatically.

"What's wrong?" Laura asked.

"They won't care about this?" Sophia said making exaggerated arm motions up and down her body. "They are dead to me!"

Laura slid off the bed and onto the floor in convulsions of laughter! "You are too funny Sophia!"

"I know you have to be going soon, but before you do I have a question." Sophia said.

"What is your question?" Laura asked.

"Why did you circle August twenty-seventh with a heart?" Sophia asked.

Laura smiled! "Because that's the day I met Jerry and it's our wedding date too!"

"And if I had finished reading the book and listening to the tapes, I would have known that, right?" Sophia asked.

"Yes!" Laura said. *"Now I need to go. I'll see you later!"*

Chapter 21

Sharp needles of light pierced the darkness that was Sophia's world of sleep and she instantly regretted putting two more bulbs into her ceiling fan.

"Sophia?" Her mother said from the doorway of her bedroom. "Soph, are you awake?"

"I am now!" Sophia responded grumpily.

She had pulled her quilt over her head when the lights came on. It wasn't only because the light hurt her eyes; she didn't want her mother to see that she wasn't wearing any clothes.

"And just so you know Mom, you can burn out someone's retinas by turning on their bedroom lights when they aren't ready for them to come on! I could be blind now!"

Carol laughed! "Well, while your father and I are out today, we'll pick up a white cane for you!"

Sophia giggled! "That's love right there!"

"It's five forty-five and we are getting ready to leave for Columbia. We won't be home until after seven tonight unless we have to stay over. I am taking a bag just in case." She said. "Are you sure you will be okay if we have to spend the night?"

Sophia lowered the quilt to where she could squint at her mother.

"I'll be fine Mom. I have a kegger to host, remember?" She said.

"How could I forget that! I love you Sophia!" Carol blew her a kiss.

"Love you too, Mom!" Sophia said.

Carol left and Sophia turned off her phone's alarm and waited and listened for SCR-MOM to pull out of the driveway. When she finally heard it, she got out of bed and peeked out the window just in time to see the van's taillights head down the street.

She crossed the hall to her bathroom and took a shower. When she got out and had dried off, she looked at herself in the mirror. The areas of her body that were reddened from her time in the sun had begun their transformation to what would be a golden tan!

"I look good!" She said. "After today the tan lines will be gone!"

She picked up her phone and called her mother.

"Anything wrong Sophia?" Carol Young asked after only one ring.

"Where are you?" Sophia asked.

She was trying to sound like she had just woken up and was groggy with sleep. She hated lying to her parents, but she needed to know they were for sure on their way to Columbia and the house was totally hers.

Carol laughed. "Sophia, Dad and I are in the van heading to his training class. Don't you remember me talking to you before we left?"

"Oh." Sophia said. "I thought that was a dream."

Carol laughed again. "We'll be home after dark."

"I remember that now." Sophia said. "Sorry."

"Did I tell you we left some money in the kitchen for you?" Carol asked.

"No." Sophia said. "Why?"

"We left you some money so you could order pizza or something." Carol said.

"Oh, okay. Thanks!" Sophia said.

"While I am out today, I will pick up your school supplies for you too." Carol said.

"That's okay." Sophia thought. *"Otherwise, I would be going with them and not to the bridge. How hard is it to get a few notebooks and a binder or two?"*

"Thanks Mom." Sophia said.

"We'll call you later, okay?" Carol said.

"Okay, bye!" Sophia said.

"Bye Sophia!" Carol said then ended the call.

Satisfied she was totally alone; she didn't bother getting dressed and walked into the kitchen to fix some breakfast. Lying on the kitchen counter next to the coffee maker were two twenty-dollar bills! She started singing part of the old Pink Floyd song, "Money", picked up the cash and went back to her room.

She saw her MP3 player lying on top of her now closed laptop and picked it up, turned it on and scrolled to the screen that would show what files had been loaded onto it. The player's file directory showed several new files that were labeled with dates from the nineteen sixties.

"Way to go Laura!" She said.

~ ~ ~ ~ ~ ~

Sophia had begun planning what she was going to take on her trip back to the bridge as she was riding her bicycle home the evening before and had gathered up the items she was taking after supper. She checked the weather forecast on her phone and saw that the predicted high was supposed to be ninety-eight degrees.

"It's going to be HOT!" She thought. *"But the creek water will be cold!"*

However, the current six a.m. temperature was a chilly sixty-three. With that in mind, she decided to wear her grey sweatpants and grey sweatshirt but realized she might die of heat stroke if she wore them on her ride back, so she threw a pair of shorts and a tee shirt into the drawstring backpack for the return leg of her journey.

Sophia packed her backpack with the other items she was taking with her: the fleece blanket, a bath towel she could use to dry her hair, the bottle of Tan Booster Ten suntan lotion, hair ties and some other odds and ends she thought she might use.

She went back into the kitchen and made herself some sandwiches, grabbed some bottled water and put that into a soft side lunch box and added some reusable ice packs to keep everything cold. She took everything to her room and added it to the items already there.

Pragmatic Polly chimed in. "What if someone is out at the bridge when you are?"

"Laura said I would be alone, so I'm not worried about it." Sophia said.

"That was just a dream Sophia, only a dream." Her Polly voice said.

"And that dream loaded my MP3 player with all those audio files and marked up my calendar too." Sophia countered. *"And now, sunrise!"*

She made her way to the laundry room, opened the back door and walked out into the backyard.

"The whole neighborhood can see you Sophia!" Pragmatic Polly said. "Why didn't you put on your sweats?"

"Because I didn't want to." She thought.

Sophia walked to the back part of the yard where there was a small depression. Her dad said it looked like there had been a tree there at some point.

She watched the sun come up over the horizon, then strolled across the yard and went back inside to her room where she pulled on her sweatpants and sweatshirt; she loved this particular set of sweats; they were micro-fiber lined and oh so soft!

"Today is going to be a great day!" She thought.

"Today is going to be a disaster!" Pragmatic Polly said before going silent for the rest of the day.

~ ~ ~ ~ ~ ~

Sophia set the backpack into the bike's newly reattached basket and added a few more bottles of water. She placed a plastic tub that had begun life as an ice cream container and the one other item she had searched for, and finally found in the garage the night before, into one of the panniers and her soft side lunch bag into the other.   Finally, she snapped her fully charged phone into the holder on her bike's handle bars; it was six forty-three a.m.

"It's a new day for more firsts!" She thought.

The ride to the bridge was chilly. At six-fifty a.m. she had made it to where the black asphalt turned into brown chip and seal and not too far from there the gravel road. She made the right turn just like Larry the Lawn Guy had done, then looked down at the tracks that his truck had made in the dust. There were two sets: one coming and one going. Occasionally, she saw part of her bike's tire tracks that she had made the day before.

"Larry the Lawn Guy was the last person to come out here. Sophia thought. *"And now it's just me! It's all mine!"*

~ ~ ~ ~ ~ ~

After removing the backpack from the basket, her cell phone from its holder and the soft side lunch bag from the pannier, Sophia laid the Schwinn in the tall grass nearly in the same spot she had laid it the previous day.

"I'll get the rest of it later." She thought.

She walked to the balcony and inhaled deeply; the air was crisp, cool and not so much smelled, but tasted clean and sweet. She smiled again and headed across the bridge and down the creek's bank stepping onto the fishing platform at exactly seven o'clock.

The lower half of her sweatpants were wet from the dew and that dampness made her shiver just a little. She kicked off her shoes, walked to the edge of the platform and dipped her toes into the creek.

"Oh boy! That's cold!" She said as she shivered.

She waited for Pragmatic Polly to tell her what she was doing was stupid and she should just go home, but Polly was silent.

Sophia stood looking at the creek watching the water flow to parts unknown before finally setting the lunch bag next to and the backpack on one of the upended buckets where she opened it. She took out the fleece blanket and spread it on the platform in the same place it had laid the day before. She took out the bath towel that she had rolled up into something that looked like a cloth log and tossed it on the blanket, then dug through and found the bottle of Tan Booster Ten suntan lotion and tossed it on the blanket too.

When she was getting ready for the day, she had decided to wear just the sweatshirt and the sweatpants, no bra and no bikini briefs either. Sophia pulled her sweatshirt over her head and dropped it next to the buckets. The chill in the air was immediately evident and she was reminded of the Venus De Milo statue in the Coombs House Park.

Sophia untied the sweatpants' drawstring and released the tension that held them around her waist; a slight wiggle of her hips caused them to drop around her ankles and she stepped out of them and flicked them with her foot onto the sweatshirt.

"I am almost ready for the day!" She thought. *"But, man, the air is chilly, and that water is going to be COLD!"*

She knelt down and dug into the backpack. It took her a couple of tries, but she finally located the elastic hair ties and pulled her hair back into a simple ponytail. After a tightening tug, she stood and looked at her phone. The weather app said the temperature was now sixty-six degrees at ten minutes after seven.

"Polly Pragmatic may be right. I may be crazy!" She thought and laid her phone on her sweats then looked at the creek. *"Here we go!"*

Sophia ran across the fishing platform and launched herself into the creek in the same arching dive she had done when she was covered in the gravel road's brown dirt. The creek water shocked her! She had known it was cold, her toes had told her that, but she hadn't realized just how cold the creek really was until her entire body was submerged in it.

"COLD! COLD! COLD! Oh, this is SO cold!" She gasped when she surfaced.

She wanted to go back to the platform and wrap up in the fleece blanket, but if she did, she would have to get back in the water at some point and get used to it all over again. Instead, she swam with her teeth chattering to the middle of the creek and floated, letting the current carry her downstream while she got used to the chilly spring fed water.

After drifting twenty-five or so yards, she kicked with her legs and stroked with her arms and swam back underneath the bridge to where her phone had taken its first plunge.

"Okay." Sophia said to herself. *"This is getting better, not as cold. Either that, or hypothermia has set in!"*

She took in a big gulp of air, did a kind of a flip and dove down to the creek's rocky bottom then returned to the surface. She floated in the creek again catching her breath before she dove again. When she had surfaced the second time, she swam to the opposite bank as fast as she could, then swam with the same intensity back across to the platform. She made at least ten of those speed laps back and forth across the creek before finally climbing up on the platform breathing hard and fast.

"Okay, that was cold, but it was fun!" She thought.

She looked at the platform and again contemplated wrapping the blanket around herself, but she resisted the urge. Instead, she stepped into the cold dew-covered grass and climbed the embankment to the road and stood in the chilly morning air, enjoying the sun's rays on her skin.

She stretched with her arms above her head wiggling her fingers in the air and went up on her tip toes extending and stretching the muscles in her calves, thighs, abdomen and chest. She felt her back crackle and pop.

"I sound like Laura's tapes!" She said to herself.

Sophia walked back to the spot where she had made her "dirt angels" and was pleased to see they were still intact and still showed all of their intricate detail. She also noticed that the dust had hardened overnight, probably from the dew, and that made Sophia smile!

"Time to do some art!" She thought.

She went back to her bike and retrieved the other items she had brought with her.

When she returned to her dirt angels, she began her artistic endeavors and mixed part of the five pounds of Plaster of Paris in the old ice cream container with the extra bottled water she had brought along. She carefully poured the mixture into her second dirt angel that she had created the day before, then mixed up another batch to complete the project. As she had noticed, the dew had hardened the dirt making her casting project extremely easy to do.

"When that is dry," She thought. *"I am taking it to The Grove! But now..."*

Sophia returned to the fishing platform and grabbed one of the five-gallon buckets and filled it with creek water. She struggled as she carried it up to the road and back to the spot where her plaster casting was drying. On the opposite side of the dirt patch, well away from her dirt angels, Sophia broke up the crust of the dirt the dew had formed and poured the water onto the ground.

"I made my first dirt angel yesterday!" She thought. *"Today, I'll make my first 'mud angel'!"*

She stepped into the cold mud and removed the hair ties, put them on her wrists then laid down on her back.

"A mud bath is supposed to be good for the skin!" She thought. *"Maybe I'll text Audrey and ask her about it later."*

She attempted a mud angel, but the mud was too soupy and her "angelic impression" filled in as soon as she stood up to look at it.

"Oh well." She thought. *"Maybe I'll try again later after the sun has dried this up a little. But now I need to wash off."*

It took several minutes to rinse all the mud off; the hardest part was getting her hair clean. She had to dive and dive again, rapidly shaking her head from side to side and run her fingers through it underwater to get all the mud out.

"I wish that waterfall was closer." She thought.

Once she had rinsed off, Sophia retrieved the bucket from the road and returned it to the platform, then collapsed onto the fleece blanket on her back and used the towel roll for a pillow.

"Note to self, don't get mud in your hair!" Sophia thought, then picked up her phone and saw that it was seven forty-five a.m., the temperature had risen to sixty-eight degrees and no one had called or texted her.

"Now what?" She asked herself. *"Oh, Audrey!"*

Sophia clicked on Audrey's picture and tapped out: "AUDREY. DUMB QUESTION. ARE MUD BATHS GOOD FOR YOUR SKIN?".

Within thirty seconds the phone clucked telling her that she had received a text.

"THEY ARE AWESOME FOR YOUR SKIN, IF IT'S THE RIGHT KIND OF MUD." Audrey's text said. "MUD FROM PLACES THAT HAVE VOLCANOS AND HOT SPRINGS ARE THE BEST. WHY?"

"Good to know!" Sophia thought.

She texted back, "NO REASON. JUST CURIOUS. I'LL TALK TO YOU ABOUT IT LATER."

"WHY ARE YOU UP SO EARLY ANYWAY?" Audrey asked.

"JUST WOKE UP EARLY I GUESS." Sophia responded.

"AND YOU STARTED THINKING ABOUT MUD BATHS?" Audrey asked.

"YUP!" Sophia texted back.

"YOU ALWAYS WERE AN ODD ONE!" Audrey said.

"AND YOU ARE MY FRIEND. SAYS A LOT ABOUT YOU!" Sophia said.

"MISS YOU BEST FRIEND!" Audrey said.

"MISS YOU EVEN MORE!" Sophia responded.

"CAN'T WAIT TO SEE YOU AGAIN!" Audrey texted.

"DON'T KNOW WHEN THAT WILL BE, BUT WHENEVER IT IS, I HAVE A LOT TO TELL YOU!" Sophia texted. "AND I HAVE AN ADDITION FOR THE NEXT TIME WE PLAY TRUTH OR DARE!"

"SHARE!" Audrey texted.

"I WILL WHEN I SEE YOU NEXT TIME." Sophia texted.

"OKAY! LOL!!!" Audrey texted. "CAN'T WAIT TO PLAY AGAIN!"

"ME EITHER!" Sophia texted.

"LOL!!! TTYL!" Audrey texted.

"TTYL!" Sophia replied.

"Now, let's go find that spring." Sophia thought.

She remembered Larry the Lawn Guy saying The Little Grand Creek was spring fed and the spring was upstream from the bridge. She sat up and put her hair back into a ponytail and rummaged in the backpack searching for one particular item.

After emptying the bag out on the blanket, she finally found her set of swim goggles. Sophia had no problem opening her eyes underwater, she had mastered that ability during her first session of swimming lessons when she was three. However, she liked using the goggles because they allowed her to swim for longer periods of time underwater. There was something about being able to see that allowed her to hold her breath and stay down longer.

Lying amid the jumble of stuff that the backpack had vomited onto the blanket was her MP3 player, the case containing her blue tooth earbuds, a fully charged battery pack that could recharge her phone three times and a black data sync cord that she hadn't seen in months.

"Well nuts!" She thought when she saw the cable. *"If I had known that was in the backpack, I wouldn't have bought another one."*

She wished the MP3 player were waterproof or had a waterproof case like her phone, but as she picked up her earbuds, she had a thought, an epiphany of sorts.

"My phone is waterproof because of the case. The earbuds are waterproof because they were made that way." She thought. *"If I moved Laura's tapes to my phone, I could listen to them when I am laying out in the sun, when I am riding my bike or even when I was swimming underwater!"*

Sophia connected her phone to the MP3 player and after a couple of taps on the phone's screen, she began moving the audio files. The phone's screen said it would take two hours and twenty-two minutes to complete the process, so she also connected the battery pack to her phone.

"I guess I'll go find the spring this afternoon." She thought. *"Now, I think I'll take a nap and wait for the plaster to dry, then I'll take my masterpiece to The Grove, but first…".*

Sophia grabbed the bottle of Tan Booster Ten suntan lotion and covered herself in the coconut scented lotion and laid back on her fleece blanket to take a nap; five forty-five had come early and she was still a bit sleepy.

~ ~ ~ ~ ~ ~

The annoyingly cute chicken clucking startled Sophia to consciousness. When she had fallen asleep, she had gone deeply into a dreamless slumber. When her phone had alerted her to an incoming text message, she had physically jumped before picking up her phone to read the message.

"MADE IT TO COLUMBIA. DAD IS AT HIS TRAINING. I AM GOING TO THE MALL. – MOM".

"COOL!" Was Sophia's reply.

"YOU'RE AWAKE?" Carol texted.

"YES, BUT I AM STUMBLING AROUND RUNNING INTO THINGS BECAUSE YOU BLINDED ME THIS MORNING!" Sophia's text said.

"I DIDN'T REALIZE YOUR PHONE HAD BRAILE ON IT!" Carol said.

"THERE'S AN APP FOR THAT!" Sophia replied.

She laid the phone and MP3 player on the platform to continue the file transfer and tossed the goggles down beside them. She grabbed a small white bottle she had dropped into the backpack as she was leaving to come out to the bridge, climbed the embankment and headed out for the cemetery.

However, as she stepped into the roadway, she had a thought and went to her bicycle to get the two last items she had placed in one of the panniers, then returned to the platform.

She totally emptied out the backpack before putting the bath towel, a bottle of water, the goggles, the two items from the pannier, her charging phone and the MP3 player in it, then climbed the embankment and walked to the wallow to see if her casting was ready.

The instructions on the bag said to let the plaster dry at least thirty minutes and it had been nearly an hour and a half since she had filled her dirt angel impression. She pressed lightly in the center of the casting and the plaster was firm. She pressed harder and was unable to make an indentation.

"It's done!" She thought.

Sophia knelt down and dug around the edges of the casting; it took very little effort to pop it loose from the ground. When she raised it up, she held a five-inch thick, life-size plaster image of her torso that started at her collar bones and ended two inches below her navel.

"Wowzah!" Sophia thought as she looked at her plaster image; the detail was incredible!

She had left the ice cream container that she had mixed the plaster in, lying in the grass next to the patch of dirt. She propped the casting up on it while she rinsed the dirt from her three-dimensional plaster clone with a bottle of water, she had brought with her. After rinsing away the dirt she noticed her plaster twin also had a nice brown tan.

"Maybe the dirt has Tan Booster Ten in it!" Sophia thought as she carefully wrapped the casting in the bath towel, placed it in the backpack and began her walk down the road to The Grove.

~ ~ ~ ~ ~ ~

The path through the trees that led to the sinkhole was beginning to heat up and the humidity painted a sheen on her skin. As she descended, the temperature cooled rapidly and when she reached its floor, the air was almost chilly.

"When it's really hot outside, this will feel great!" Sophia thought. *"And I bet it will feel warm in the winter too."*

She took the plaster casting to the fire ring and gently laid it facedown across two logs where she carefully unwrapped it and exposed its back. She found a small piece of burnt wood about the size of a pencil and used it to write the following:

~ Choices ~
"Sometimes you have to do something

a little crazy to prove that you are sane!"
~ Sophia Elizabeth Young ~

"Putting my entire name on this is probably a dumb thing to do, but sometimes you have to do something a little crazy! You only live once!" She thought. *"Besides, I'm going to leave it down here and by the looks of things, whoever set up this fire ring did it a long time ago. If someone does find it, I hope they enjoy looking at it!"*

Sophia took the other two items she had retrieved from her bicycle's panniers; the first was a quart can of clear acrylic varnish, the second was a two-inch foam brush. After shaking the can for a full minute, she popped it open and began covering the plaster, being careful not to smudge what she had written. When the first coat was applied to her satisfaction, she picked up the bath towel, left the sinkhole and headed to the cemetery.

"I'll come back and finish that later." She thought looking at the back of "Choices".

Chapter 22

Larry the Lawn Guy had done a great job cutting the cemetery's grass and cleaning up a majority of the trimmings. The headstones that had been mostly obscured by the tall grass, were now easily read. Sophia stepped through the gate half expecting …well…she didn't know what to expect.

"No one out there will care…" Laura's voice said from inside her head.

The only thing that did happen when she entered, was a rabbit bounded out from behind a headstone and exited the gate before stopping in the middle of the road.

"Do I look that bad?" Sophia called after the rabbit!

She looked down at herself; most of her skin was a golden brown and the areas that weren't, would be by the end of the day.

"Hey, rabbit?" She called through the gate. "I look amazing!"

The rabbit offered no opinion other than a wiggling of its nose, then hopped away.

Sophia strolled across the grass, reading names and dates on various headstones. Some were upright and made of granite or other stone; others were bronze plates mounted on stone and laid flat against the ground. The oldest grave she found belonged to someone named Mayme Louise Rush, who had died at the age of one hundred ten years, six months and seventeen days. Her year of birth was eighteen nineteen; she had died in nineteen twenty-nine.

"Wow!" Sophia said in a hushed voice. "Over one hundred ten years old!"

On the far side of the cemetery and down a small rise was the highly polished, apple colored stone that had caught her attention the day before. She approached and saw the name "COLLINS" etched onto its surface and below this was the name MEGAN ANNE (GORDAN). Next to her name was GERALD (JERRY) ANDREW. Next to his name was another woman's name, LAURA KAY (BUTLER). Below Laura's name were two additional names, STEPHANIE KAY & STEPHEN ANDREW. There were two photos that had been printed onto oval shaped metal plates and attached to the stone.

Sophia felt her mouth fall open with surprise and she dropped to her knees in front of the memorial.

"Laura!" She said.

The first photo was of a man, a woman and a young dark-haired girl who looked familiar to Sophia, but she could not remember where she had seen her. The second photo was of the same man who was considerably younger. To his left was Laura and two small children.

Sophia spread out the bath towel and stretched out on her stomach where she could look at the picture. She stared at it for a long time studying Laura, Stephanie, Stephen and Jerry. She wondered what had happened to them. Maude Adelaide had said it was something awful but had said no more. Laura, Stephen and Stephanie shared the same date of death – August 2, 1969.

"What happened to you Laura?" Sophia whispered. "What happened to you and your babies in nineteen sixty-nine?"

~ ~ ~ ~ ~ ~

"Hey Sophia! You are asleep in the sun." A familiar voice said.

Sophia opened her eyes and looked into Laura's smiling face; she was sitting in the grass next to the headstone, her headstone, and she was wearing the same outfit she had been wearing the last time they had spoken.

"I was asleep in the sun." Sophia said dryly.

A large obnoxious bug, maybe a cousin to the one who had besieged her right before she had met Larry the Lawn Guy, began buzzing around her face. She rolled away from its attack and down the slight hill to get away from it.

Laura laughed!

Sophia crawled back on to her towel and Laura asked, "Aren't you afraid of getting a sunburn? I mean the sun is shining on places that should not be sunburned?"

"I have never had a sunburn in my life Laura." Sophia said. "I turn kind of red, but there's no pain. Then by the next day, I'm tan!"

"You are lucky." Laura said, paused, then added. "I wasn't so lucky one time."

"What happened?!" Sophia asked.

"If you want to know what happened to me, read that book and listen to the tapes. They will be ready when you get back to the fishing platform." Laura said.

"Do you always just pop in and out of people's dreams just because you can?" Sophia asked.

"I only pop into the dreams of the people I need to talk to, to help." Laura said. "And you need some help dealing with your move here. I wish someone had done that for me when I was in your shoes."

Sophia grinned!

"I know, I know. You aren't wearing any shoes or anything else for that matter!" Laura said.

"I forgot you know what I'm going to say." Sophia said. "So, I need help?"

"We all need help from time to time." Laura said.

"Do I need to quit coming out here and quit taking off my clothes?" Sophia asked.

"No." Laura said. "As long as you are between here and the bridge on the dates I circled, you will be fine. Besides, your tan is nearly complete. There aren't any lines anywhere on your back now!"

"Good!" Sophia said.

"I have a feeling you will be out here a lot!" Laura said.

Sophia, who was now sitting, plucked a long piece of grass that Larry the Lawn Guy had missed, then she looked at Laura.

"What happened to you and your kids?" She asked. "I mean..." Sophia pointed to the headstone.

Laura smiled sweetly and said, "In due time, Sophia. In due time. But now, I have a question for you."

"What?" Sophia asked.

"When you are out at the bridge or out here." Laura said. "You seem to fall asleep a lot. Why is that?"

"I'm tired I guess." Sophia said.

"Tired?" Laura asked. "Or are you hiding?"

"Hiding?" Sophia asked. "What would I be hiding from?"

"Maybe you are hiding from having to deal with the move here?" Laura asked. "I know I did when I had to move. In my old house there is that hidden room behind the curved bookcase; the one in the turret. I think you heard about that on one of the tapes I made."

"Yes! I would love to see it!" Sophia said. "That would be so cool to have something like that in my room!"

"But instead, you only have a cubbyhole!" Laura said with a laugh.

Sophia laughed too! "Well, there is that!"

"When we were looking at the house, the real estate lady showed it to me when Mom and Dad were looking at the closet in what would become their bedroom. It was cedar lined and they were excited about that." Laura said. "She saw me looking in what would be my room and she said, 'Let me show you something.' She went to the bookcase, slid open both halves and showed me the space behind it. 'I think your parents might like to see this!' The real estate lady said.

'They might like it, but I know I love it!' I said. 'Can I be the one to show them?'

'Sure! And speaking of your parents, I better get back to them in case they have any more questions.' She said.

When she left, I opened the turret room, stepped inside and shut the bookcase behind me. It was such a neat place! I used to go in there and...well...hide from the world when I got homesick. I made a promise to keep it hidden for as long as I could. Mom and Dad didn't know about the turret room for over a year."

"How did they find out about it?" Sophia asked.

"Someone who knew the previous owner told Dad about it." Laura said.

"I wish I had a place like that." Sophia said.

"You DO have a place like that!" Laura exclaimed.

"I do?" Sophia asked.

"Yes!" Laura said. "You do!"

"Where is it?" Sophia asked.

"You're there right now! You're there when you are at the bridge! You're there when you are at The Grove and down in the sinkhole!" Laura started laughing. "Your hiding place is a lot bigger than the Turret Room!"

"Oh, man!" Sophia said.

"I have to be getting back Sophia. I just wanted to check on you and let you know that what you want to know is close by." Laura said.

"The tapes?" Sophia asked.

"Yes!" Laura said as she stood up.

"The book?" Sophia asked.

"Yes!" Laura said.

Laura started walking down the small hill Sophia had rolled down to escape the bug. She simply faded away just before she reached the cemetery's fence.

~ ~ ~ ~ ~ ~

Larry the Lawn Guy's clippings had stuck to her skin when she had rolled off her towel to get away from the obnoxious insect. Now, she was covered front and back with pieces of dried out, itchy grass.

"Time for a shower." Sophia thought and she picked up her towel and headed back to the sinkhole.

The Grove was just a ten-minute walk from the cemetery and when she got there, she made her way down the stone path to the stairs into the sinkhole where she grabbed the little white bottle of body wash and shampoo. After her impromptu head to toe mud bath earlier in the morning and now that she had grass clippings stuck to her, she waded to the waterfall and spent several minutes lathering, rinsing and repeating in the waterfall's shower of cold water.

"The next time I come out here I am going to bring a water bottle so I can have some of this to drink when I am at the fishing platform!" Sophia thought as she tilted her head back and filled her mouth with the waterfall's sweet water!

After she dried off, Sophia draped her towel across a large rock then went over to where "Choices" lay and lightly touched the first coat of the acrylic. She was surprised to feel that it was not the least bit sticky. She carefully turned the casting over, opened the can, and using the foam brush, she began covering the front and sides with its first coat of the clear acrylic.

As she applied it, she saw how it accentuated the brown tone the dust from the gravel road had given the plaster. She also noted the similarity her casting had to the torso of the Venus De Milo statue in the Coombs House Park.

Although the Venus De Milo's abs had been sculpted with hammer and chisel, Sophia's abs had been sculpted by doing a hundred sit-ups and fifty crunches before bed almost every night. She was amazed at how the plaster had perfectly captured her "innie" bellybutton as well as the rest of her.

Once the acrylic was on, Sophia returned to the water while it dried. She swam the length of the crescent shaped pool several times as fast as she could. Then she retrieved her goggles and went to the deep end of the pool.

She remembered seeing a television show about free divers who would go hundreds of feet down on a single breath. One of the things they did to get ready is hyperventilate.

After breathing fast and deep for a full minute, Sophia held her last breath and dove down to look at the underwater cave's opening. The water was crystal clear, and she could see the cave continued down a very long way before the light faded and the cave became a large maw of darkness.

She surfaced, then swam to the waterfall to investigate the large space behind it. She had noticed the space the first time she had stepped into the waterfall's cold cascade, but she had not taken the time to really look at it.

Just behind the waterfall was a ledge that angled down slightly. It was a little more than bellybutton high and Sophia had to jump and push herself up with her arms to get out of the water. The space was at least ten feet tall, at least six feet deep and more than twice that in length. What was amazing was how dry it was, considering a waterfall was pouring into the pool just a few feet away. The other thing that caught her attention was how beautifully distorted the light was as it passed through the waterfall.

"I am putting "Choices" in here!" Sophia said to herself. *"This will be my art gallery! No one but me will know it is back here!"*

~ ~ ~ ~ ~ ~

She walked back to the bridge and thought about Laura and what she would discover once she finished listening to the tapes and reading the book. It was one-thirty when she got back to the platform and she tossed her backpack onto the fleece blanket then looked at her phone. The file transfer from the MP3 player to her phone was complete and its battery was at one hundred percent charge.

She reloaded the backpack with the things she had dumped out when she was looking for her goggles and had a thought.

"Why not!" She thought. *"Laura did show me how to do it and my hair is mostly dry!"*

Sophia sat down on one of the buckets and began braiding her hair. She had to stop and rework some of the steps, but she finally finished the braid. Once done, she used the self-timer on her phone's camera and one of the buckets to take a picture of her back and the braid. She also waited for a scolding from the Polly Pragmatic side of herself, but the scolding never came.

"The braid looks great!" She thought. *"And Laura was right; the tan lines on my back are gone! One more day in the sun and I won't have any tan lines at all!"*

She deleted the picture, placed the earbuds in her ears and clipped the earbud case to her phone's wrist strap, then cinched it around her wrist.

An automated voice announced, "Pairing", then a few seconds later she heard, "Connected."

Sophia slipped her goggles on her face making sure its strap covered the ear buds to keep them from falling out when she was swimming. She knew the ear bud's audio quality was exceptionally good, at least it had been the last time she had used them. However, she hadn't been swimming or gone under-water with them in her ears.

"Here goes." She thought before taking a deep breath and submerging.

Her phone's touch screen worked perfectly! She was able to access the file list, but before getting down to the business of listening to Laura's tapes, she chose to first listen to a rendition of Queen's "Bohemian Rhapsody" that was sung by a thirteen-year-old girl from Norway named Angelina Jordan. Both Leah and Audrey had seen her on an America's Got Talent Champions show and sent the link to her, but Sophia had not yet listened to it.

"Let's see if this works." Sophia thought.

She surfaced just long enough to fill her lungs again, hit play on her phone, then sank to the creek's rocky bottom. The girl's voice had such a haunting beauty to it! Angelina's highs, lows; her whole range was pitch perfect!

As the song ended, Sophia pushed with her feet and ascended. Her head broke the surface, and she took in a deep breath of air as the last note faded.

"Oh!" Sophia gasped. "That was beautiful!"

Knowing that the ear buds worked, she started swimming upstream to find the spring that fed the Little Grand Creek and as she did, she began listening to the recordings Laura had put on her MP3 player and that she had transferred to her phone.

"What am I going to learn?" Sophia thought.

Chapter 23

Popping.

Crackling.

"Okay." Laura said. "I did something today kind of...of..."

Popping.

Crackling.

"I did something today that I never ever thought I would do."
Laura said. "Today, I went...skinny dipping!"

Popping.

Crackling.

"Jerry took me out to the old, covered bridge last week after my
ankle had healed and I was able to ride my bike without too much
problem. That was when I jumped in the creek with my clothes on! I
think Jerry thought I had lost my mind when I did that!"

Popping.

Crackling.

"If he knew what I did today, he would say I was crazy!"

Popping.

Crackling.

"So, I rode my bike out to the bridge again today, in fact, I just got
back a little bit ago. I'm glad Mom and Dad aren't home. I don't know
how I could explain why my hair is wet and my clothes are dry."

Popping.

Crackling.

"Anyway, I went down to the fishing platform and thought about
jumping in again, but I didn't want to get my clothes wet."

Popping.

Crackling.

"I looked around and didn't see anyone. In fact, I hadn't seen
anyone since I left town so, I took off my shirt and shorts. Well, I took off
my shoes too, but anyway, right as I was getting ready to jump in, I said
to myself, 'Why not! There's no one around to see me.', so I took off
everything else and I jumped in the creek."

Popping.

Crackling.

"The water was crystal clear and cold! But you know what? I
liked it! I liked it A LOT! I have never done anything like that before and
I don't know why I did it today, but it felt wonderful!"

Popping.

Crackling.

"After swimming for, I don't know, two hours..."

Popping.

Crackling.

"Oh My Gosh, I was outside without any clothes on for TWO HOURS! TWO ENTIRE HOURS!"

Popping.

Crackling.

"When I was done swimming, I laid out on the platform to dry off. The sun felt incredible! Then I did something totally crazy! I don't know what possessed me to do it, but I went up and stood at the bridge's balcony! I stood there watching the water and I was totally naked when I did it! Crazy huh?"

Popping.

Crackling.

"I'm glad you can see a lot of the road coming to the bridge because as I was standing there, I first heard, then saw a car coming and I panicked! I ran across the bridge as fast as I could and got back down to the fishing platform. I could hear the car getting closer and I didn't want anyone to know I was there, but I didn't have time to put my clothes on, so I shoved them and my shoes under one of the buckets that are down there, and I dove in the water and swam under the bridge. There was a big bunch of tall cat tails and I was able to hide behind them and not be seen."

Popping.

Crackling.

"The car stopped on the bridge and I heard someone get out and slam their door. I can tell you; I was really scared that whoever it was would come down to the platform and see me."

Popping.

Crackling.

"Diary...they DID come down to the platform! It was Mr. Nelson, the high school principal, and he sat down on the bucket that had all my clothes under it!

He lit a cigarette and sat there just looking at the water. I think he sat there for ten minutes, maybe longer. I'm glad he never looked under the bridge, he might have seen me, and I don't know what I would have done then! After he finished smoking, he got up and went back to his car and drove away."

Popping.

Crackling.

"As soon as I heard him leave, I got back up on the platform and got dressed as fast as I could! Then I ran up to the bridge, got on my bike and headed home. I'm glad I laid it in the grass, it was pretty much out of sight, otherwise he might have seen it."

Popping.

Crackling.

"When I got back to the paved road, I heard his car. He must have gone out to the cemetery Jerry told me was out there and turned around. Anyway, when he caught up to me, he stopped and asked if I wanted a ride. He said my bike would fit in the trunk of his car. I told him no, I just was out for a ride and was going home."

Popping.

Crackling.

"Then he said, 'Well, nice seeing you!' and drove off."

Popping.

Crackling.

"After he left, I just started laughing! I'm sure he would never have guessed that his newest cheerleader had just spent over two hours swimming and laying out in the sun totally naked!"

Popping.

Crackling.

"But you know what, even though I almost got caught, I am going back out there and do it again sometime! I liked how it felt swimming like that!"

Popping.

Crackling.

"There is one problem though; wearing a bra is going to be fun for the next few days. I don't think I will be riding my bike for a few days either! I got a sunburn on areas that should not be sunburned!" Laura giggled a pained giggle.

Popping.

Crackling.

"It was worth it though! Next time I will take suntan lotion or go in the evening, but right now, I am going to get in the bathtub and pour apple cider vinegar all over myself, it really takes the sting out of a sunburn."

Popping.

Crackling.

Silence.

~ ~ ~ ~ ~ ~

Although she could not really relate to the pain of a sunburn due to her non-sun burning, easily tanning Mediterranean heritage skin, Sophia felt sorry for Laura.

"I wonder if Laura had to go commando for a few days! I'll ask her the next time I see her." She thought, right before bursting out in laughter.

Sophia had swum slowly while she listened to Laura's recording. When it ended, she looked around and saw she was maybe four hundred yards from the bridge and her phone showed she had been in the water for fifteen minutes.

"I wonder how far it actually is to the spring?" Sophia thought.

She swam to the creek bank, climbed out, raised her goggles to her forehead and opened the phone's mapping application. The Little Grand Covered Bridge was easy to see on the app's satellite picture; the white roof really stood out against the greens of the grass and trees. However, there was no sign of anything indicating a natural spring until she clicked the app's "Points of Interest" tab. When she did that, two blue inverted teardrop shaped markers instantly appeared; one pointed to the covered bridge and the other showed the location of the Little Grand Spring! In between those two points and just a little bit above the covered bridge was a green marker that blinked on and off showing her location.

With her finger, she drew a line between the bridge's marker and the spring's marker. The app calculated the distance between them at one mile!

"Wait a minute." Sophia thought. *"That can't be right."*

She cleared the screen, then carefully traced the creek and all its meanderings from the bridge to where the spring was supposed to be. The app estimated that distance at three miles!

"Jeezly crow!" Sophia thought. *"Three miles through water!"*

The creek bank where she stood was covered with small, mostly rounded stones, sand and dirt. It formed a path three or four feet wide, but if you stepped off it on the creek side, you would drop several feet before hitting the Little Grand's clear, cold water.

Upstream from where she was standing, Sophia could see a large flat rock with water flowing around it that made small whitecaps on its outer edges. The sun poured through an opening in the canopy of trees illuminating its flat top.

She thought about jumping back in the water and swimming to it but decided to walk the path instead. A bug landed on her hip and she swatted it with a loud, stinging slap. When she looked at the place she had hit, there was a faint outline of her fingers. She rubbed the spot and continued up the path until she was directly across from the rock.

"Time to get wet again." She said to no one, as she adjusted the goggles and jumped back into the water letting her weight and gravity carry her to the bottom.

When her feet impacted, she bent her knees and pushed herself back to the surface and swam to the rock that protruded above the creek's surface by just a few inches. She pulled herself out of the water, sat down, took off the goggles, removed the ear buds and put them back in their case.

"Now, I'm going to lay here in the sun for a little while." Sophia thought.

She laid back on the rock, listening as the birds chirped their songs and as she floated between consciousness and sleep on the sun warmed stone, until her cell phone's chicken clucking ring tone got her attention.

"Hello?" She said.

"Hi Honey!" Carol Young said. "Are you up and dressed for your day?"

Sophia glanced down the length of her five-foot one-inch body, smiled and said, "Yes, and I am wearing an outfit that fits perfectly! I used to not like it very much, but I am really, really liking it now! It's my new favorite!"

"What outfit is it?" Carol asked.

Sophia giggled internally before saying, "It's that tan one! I've had it for a while now!"

"That's good! I'm glad you like what you have on." Carol paused then said, "Sophia, I know I told you we would be back around seven tonight, but it's going to be later than that."

"How much later?" Sophia asked.

"Your dad thinks eleven at the earliest. Will you be okay?" Carol asked.

"I'll be fine Mom!" Sophia said. "I'm fifteen, not five."

"I know how old you are! I'm pretty sure I was there when you were born!" Carol said with a laugh, then asked, "What are you doing today anyway?"

Sophia glanced at her body again and said, "Oh, I don't know Mom. I may go roll around in some mud and then go skinny dipping!"

Carol laughed! "If you did that, you would get that outfit you like so much all dirty!"

"I wouldn't be wearing an outfit to skinny dip in Mom, I think that's the point of doing it." Sophia said.

"Don't get sunburned while you are out skinny dipping!" Carol advised with a chuckle.

"I don't sunburn." Sophia said. "It's my Mediterranean skin, remember?"

"Bye Sophia!" Carol hung up laughing.

"They won't be back until eleven tonight which means I can stay out here a lot later than I had planned! This is going to be the best day ever!" She thought.

She laid back on the rock and thought about what Laura had said about *her* adventures in skinny dipping. She laughed remembering the scared tone in Laura's voice when she was telling about almost being seen by her high school principal.

"That would have been very awkward!" Sophia thought. *"Very, very awkward! I wonder if that's why she told me the dates when no one else would be out here. I bet it was."*

When she was ready to continue her journey, she adjusted the goggles then slid into the water and continued her way up the creek in search of the spring. Sometimes she swam on top of the water, sometimes beneath it and sometimes she walked alongside it. She made sure not to brush up against any of the plants that grew next to the rocky pathway. She had seen at least one poison ivy plant and wanted no part of that!

After several minutes of walking, she heard a rushing, roaring sound and noticed the creek's channel had tapered considerably. The creek's banks were now solid rock and formed a canyon of sorts that was maybe fifty feet wide, that caused the current to move drastically faster.

"The Narrows!" Sophia thought as she stood looking at the creek's tapered channel. *"That's what I am calling this place!"*

Above The Narrows, the water had backed up and formed a large, deep pool. If her information was correct, the Little Grand Creek bridge was over two hundred fifty feet long and this pool was at least twice that long and twice that wide.

"This is awesome!" She thought. *"I wish Laney, Leah and Audrey were here to see this!*

Sophia walked the rocky path around the edge of The Narrows' pool, slipped into the water and let the current pull her downstream. When she entered the channel and looked underwater, she could see that it was deep, but the churning water made it hard to estimate just how deep. She did notice, however, that the channel was at least a hundred feet long and there were no rocks or logs that could be hit as you swam through.

"This is fun!" She thought as the current propelled her downstream; she thought of it as kind of a water Tilt-O-Whirl!

Once through, she swam to the bank, exited the water and ran up the rocky path back to the pool and dove in again. She rode the current through The Narrows five or six times.

"Making choices like this is fun!" She thought.

Chapter 24

On the far upstream side of The Narrows and the pool it created, the Little Grand Creek continued for several hundred yards before it made a left-hand turn. After swimming around this bend, Sophia saw a large rocky outcropping on the right side that overhung a part of the creek that had widened into another pool. It was at least twice as big as The Narrows' pool, its surface roiled and was noticeably bluer in color.

"The spring!" Sophia said.

There was another flat-topped rock peeking above the water near the creek's left bank. It wasn't big enough to lay out on, but it was large enough that four or five people could sit on it. She laid her phone and ear buds on the rock then swam toward the churning, cold spring.

"What was it that Larry the Lawn guy said, water from the spring was something like fifty-six degrees? I think he was wrong; this feels a lot colder than that!" Sophia thought.

The water made her knees ache and her teeth chatter. She wanted to get out and warm up, but the spring is what she had come to see and see it she would. So, she treaded the chilly water and got used to the much colder temperature.

"Spring water is supposed to taste really good." She said to herself.

She lowered her head, took a drink and was rewarded with a delicious, sweet taste. After quenching her thirst, she decided to see how far she could dive into the blue pool.

She took a deep breath and submerged just under the surface. The water was a lot deeper than the other parts of the creek she had seen, but it wasn't so deep that she couldn't see the bottom.

"It looks about as deep as it was down to the cave opening in the sinkhole." Sophia thought.

She surfaced and began breathing rapidly. After a full minute of hyperventilating, she took a large lung full of air and dove down to where the spring was erupting from the rocks. Its force was enough to push her away when she got within five feet of its underwater opening.

"Wow! That's a lot of water coming out of there!" She thought as she surfaced.

She made several laps across the spring both on top of the water and underneath it. Then she swam back to the flat rock where she had left her phone and ear buds. As she was retrieving them and getting ready to go back to the bridge, she saw two figures moving through the trees toward her on the spring side of the pool.

One appeared to be an adult and was wearing a bright red shirt which was what had caught her attention. The other was a child and she could see he or she had a on a bright blue ball cap.

"Oh crud!" Sophia said.

She grabbed her phone and ear buds from the rock, dove and swam as fast and as hard as she could toward the rocky overhang. There was a small ledge just above the water's surface that she could pull herself onto and stand out of sight. It wasn't nearly as big as her Art Gallery behind the waterfall, but it was big enough to conceal her from the two people who were headed her way.

"She was right here! I seed her!" A little boy's voice said. "There was a mermaid swimming in the water!"

"You saw a mermaid swimming in the spring?" The older voice asked.

Sophia held her breath and listened, they were just a few feet directly above her.

"I did!" The little boy said. "It was the mermaid from the park!"

"Where was she?" The older one asked.

A rock plunged into the spring's pool no more than ten feet from where Sophia stood.

"She was right there!" The little boy said.

"Well, seeing a mermaid is pretty cool!" The older one said.

"She had dark hair that was really long, and she was pretty too!" The little boy said.

"I bet she was!" The older one said.

"Are there mermaids in high school?" The little boy asked earnestly.

"I don't know buddy. I don't start high school until next week." The older one said. "I'll let you know if I see one."

"He's not a man!" Sophia thought. *"He's starting high school just like me!"*

"And she didn't have a shirt on or nothing!" The little boy said. "Just like the one in the park!"

The older one laughed. "Now, I wish I <u>had</u> seen her!"

"Wouldn't that have been a great way to meet a new classmate." Sophia thought. *'Hi, I'm Sophia! I'm the postmaster's daughter and The New Girl!*

By the way, my eyes are up here, not on my chest or below my waist!

That's better! Thank you sooo much!'"

"We need to get going." The older one said. "We have one more thing to do, then I'm helping Steve tonight."

"What about the mermaid?" The little boy asked.

"Well, I read somewhere that if you see a mermaid, especially a pretty mermaid with long dark hair swimming in this spring, you will have good luck and…" The older one paused.

"And what?" The little boy asked.

"And you do have good luck because we are going to Morton's and get ice cream once we are done out here!" The older one said.

The little boy cheered! "Thank you, mermaid!"

"You are welcome! I am so glad I could help!" Sophia thought and successfully suppressed a laugh.

"Come on, buddy." The older one said.

Sophia wasn't going to take any chances on being seen again especially by someone who she might be going to school with next week, so she stayed under the overhang for several minutes to make sure they were gone.

Her phone clucked and she was thankful that she was alone. Looking at it, she saw she had a text from her mom. When she opened it, there was a picture of a very smart looking dress – a little black dress!

The message read: "I HOPE YOU LIKE IT! THE SKIRT IS KIND OF SHORT. IT WILL PROBABLY COME TO JUST ABOVE YOUR KNEES. WILL THAT SHOW TOO MUCH?"

Sophia laughed out loud then replied: "THE TAN OUTFIT I HAVE ON RIGHT NOW SHOWS MORE SKIN THAN THAT ONE WILL! THAT DRESS IS CUTE! THANK YOU!"

Carol replied: "YOU'RE WELCOME! HAPPY BIRTHDAY A COUPLE OF DAYS EARLY!"

Her stomach growled. She looked at her phone again and saw it was two forty-five and the temperature had hit ninety-nine degrees.

"I need to get back to the bridge." She said to herself.

Sophia jumped from the ledge above the spring's pool and plunged into the blue water; she was again shocked by its fifty-six-degree coldness that caused goose flesh to instantly form all over her body. Then she headed downstream where she paused and made five trips through The Narrows.

She loved the feeling of being pulled through the water by the cold current; it gave her a wonderful fluttery - flutterbys - feeling in the pit of her stomach! After her last trip through, Sophia inserted her ear buds, secured them with the goggles' strap then pressed play on the file labelled "August 30, 1963" and listened as she floated and swam back toward the bridge.

~ ~ ~ ~ ~ ~

Popping.

Crackling.

"I made the biggest mistake of my life yesterday!" Laura said seriously.

Popping.

Crackling.

"Mom and Dad had gone to Kirksville, wherever that is, and didn't get home until after eleven which I am grateful for. I finally got home from school at nine-thirty last night!" Laura said.

Popping.

Crackling.

Laura sighed. "Where to start?"

Popping.

Crackling.

"Okay. Here's what happened. Yesterday was really hot. In fact, they let school out at noon because none of the schools are air conditioned and the old ceiling fans only stirred the hot air in the classrooms. I'm really glad they did too because it gave everyone an extra half day for the Labor Day weekend. Why they didn't start school after Labor Day is anyone's guess, but they didn't."

Popping.

Crackling.

"Jerry and his parents left for the lake as soon as he got home, the lucky duck! Anyway, after school got out, I went home and changed clothes. I put on an old pair of shorts, an old tee shirt and my old pair of Keds, that's it, no underwear. I went back to the covered bridge to skinny dip because it's fun and because it was so hot!

I would have gone to the swimming pool to swim, not skinny dip, but it closed once school started. What I really should have done is stayed home because it was so hot, but I didn't. I walked out there."

Popping.

Crackling.

"I got to the bridge at around two o'clock and went down to the fishing platform. It was actually cooler down there, probably because it's right next to the water. I did remember to bring suntan lotion and a towel, and I made sure everything was lotioned too! I wasn't going to smell like a pickle like I did after I went skinny dipping three weeks ago and got sunburned!" Laura said with a laugh."

Popping.

Crackling.

"I swam for over an hour and the water felt really good! I found out today the temperature reached one hundred three yesterday, so I guess after walking the three or four miles out there that's why the water felt so good!

Jerry told me the last time we were out there about a natural spring that supposedly ran into the creek and it wasn't too far from the bridge. When he told me about it, he showed me a path that ran alongside the creek and he said you could walk there."

Popping.

Crackling.

"I got out of the water. I don't know why I didn't put my clothes back on right then other than it was really hot and humid and not wearing anything felt really good! And I guess I liked the thrill of possibly being seen by someone even though if someone had seen me, I would have been totally embarrassed and humiliated. Sometimes taking a risk is kind of fun even if that risk could get you into trouble."

Popping.

Crackling.

"I hope saying it was a thrill to possibly get caught running around naked doesn't make me sound crazy. But I have to tell you, the possibility of being caught outside totally naked...I don't know...it...it just was kind of fun! It's hard to explain."

Popping.

Crackling.

"For whatever reason, I decided I was going to walk to the spring, so I put my clothes under one of the buckets on the fishing platform!

Diary, I have never done ANYTHING like that before in my life! Like I said, it felt really good not having anything on and it felt good to be able to make a choice to do that even if that choice was a little off-the - wall.

I do like it when I do get to make a choice and I do like that after I moved here, I met Jerry, he is the best thing to happen to me ever, but I still have lots of things decided for me."

Popping.

Crackling.

"Anyway, I started walking up the path to see if I could find the spring. I will tell you that, at first, it felt weird being outside walking around with nothing on, but after a few minutes, I kind of forgot about it. Weird huh?"

Popping.

Crackling.

"The path was really pretty and kind of rocky. I almost went back and got my shoes, but I didn't! The path was almost like someone maintained it or something, but with all the trees and grass and stuff it was even more humid and like I said, it was really hot!

The sweat was dripping and running down my chest and my arms and my legs. My hair was soaking wet, so I jumped back in the creek and started swimming just to keep cool.

I don't think Jerry really knows how far it is to the spring, but his idea of '...not too far...' and how far it really was, are two entirely different things! I went to Morton's today and I asked Fran if she knew how far it was between the bridge and the spring and she said it was something like three miles!

Not too far my foot, Jerry Collins!" Laura laughed.

Popping.

Crackling.

"I finally made it to the spring. It took me something like two hours to get there, but of course I did stop several times to swim and cool off. But it was worth the wait; the spring is beautiful!!! The water is actually blue, and it is COLD!"

Popping.

Crackling.

"After I swam in the spring's pool for a while, and it was hard because the water is so cold, I headed back to the bridge.

Oh! There's this place right before you get to the spring where the creek gets really narrow. The water goes through there really fast too! When I was heading back to the bridge, I swam through there several times and it was a LOT of fun!

When I finally got back to the bridge, that's when things got really bad."

Popping.

Crackling.

"I had been walking on the path for quite a while and I was hot, so instead of getting dressed, I jumped back into the water and cooled off before I decided to head home.

I mean I had been out there running around since two o'clock and it was almost seven, so I had been skinny dipping and everything for about five hours.

By the way, my tan is looking really good now, but I would just as soon not have gotten the all-over tan if I had known what was going to happen next."

Popping.

Crackling.

"When I got back on the platform, I went to get my clothes from underneath the bucket, and everything, my shirt, shorts and shoes; everything was gone!"

Popping.

Crackling.

"I found a note that said, 'Whoever you are, we hope you have fun getting home! We took your clothes! If you want them back, they will be hanging from the flagpole in front of the high school!'"

Popping.

Crackling.

"I did not know what I was going to do, Diary. I mean I was completely naked several miles from home and no one knew I was there and even if they did, I couldn't call them. I mean, can you imagine if I could have called Jerry and asked him to come and get me. What would I have said to him when he got there? 'Hey Jerry, like my new swimsuit?'

So, I started to think how I was going to get home and not be seen. It didn't get dark until almost nine which meant I had at least two hours before I could really do anything. So, I started walking back toward the spring on the path. I figured I wouldn't be seen going that way and it was headed in the right direction.

When I was at the spring the first time, I could see the highway that goes back into town. I had to look just right through the trees, but I could see the road and the bridge, not the covered bridge but a regular bridge, that crossed the creek a mile or so outside of town. It's not that far from Jerry's aunt and uncle's farm.

When I got back to the spring, it was still hot, so I swam until it did get dark and tried to figure out a way to get out of the mess I was in. I mean, how would it look for the newest varsity cheerleader to be seen walking around town wearing nothing at all!"

Popping.

Crackling.

"I started walking up the creek away from the spring and I made it to the little bridge but hadn't gotten under it when a car went by. It was dark enough that I don't think they saw me, it didn't slow down or anything, but I stayed under the bridge for a few minutes until it got even darker."

Popping.

Crackling.

"I finally made it home at nine-thirty, but let me tell you, it was hard getting here. I was almost seen at least ten times. The closest I came to getting caught was when someone's dog started barking when I was sneaking down an alley behind their house. When the dog barked, someone turned on a light and came outside. I got really good at hiding behind trees and bushes!

When I finally made it home, the back door was locked! I mean I had finally made it back to the house and I didn't have a key. I would have had a key, but I left it on my desk when I changed clothes after school. So, I had to go to the FRONT of the house, you know, right in plain view of the whole neighborhood and get the spare key we have hidden there. I'm really glad the front porch lights weren't on."

Popping.

Crackling.

"When I finally got inside the phone started ringing, it was Mom. She wanted to let me know they would be home later than they thought, which was a relief. I was worried they would be home when I got there, and I didn't want to have to explain why I was coming in the front door totally naked!

So, I got dressed and took my bike for a ride. Yes, I went to the high school and saw that my shirt, shorts, shoes and even my towel were at the top of the flagpole. A whole bunch of people were there looking at them, laughing and making their guesses as who the clothes belonged to.

I went over and saw some of the football boys. They were telling how they went out to the covered bridge and found my clothes. I laughed right along with everyone else. There was no way I was going to let anyone know those were my clothes and I was the one who had been skinny dipping!

After a while, everyone started leaving, so I got on my bike and rode away like I was going home, but I doubled back and got my stuff."

Popping.

Crackling.

"You know, even though I had to sneak back home through town completely naked, I still plan on going back to the covered bridge and go skinny dipping again! Next time though, I will hide my clothes better. There is a place under the bridge that would work for that. I saw it when Mr. Nelson almost caught me."

Popping.

Crackling.

Silence.

~ ~ ~ ~ ~ ~

When Sophia was back at the bridge, she pulled herself up onto the platform and the buckets were exactly where she had left them. After hearing what had happened to Laura, she flipped the buckets over and all of her belongings were there.

She quickly arranged the blanket on the platform's deck, retrieved the towel roll and her food, then set her phone's alarm. She was tired from her trip to the spring, six miles round trip mostly in water, and knew she might doze off and she still had more tapes to listen to.

She devoured one of her sandwiches without really tasting it. She ate a second sandwich, this time she chewed slower and actually tasted what she was eating.

The bottled water she had brought from home wasn't cold, it was at best lukewarm and wasn't nearly as sweet tasting as the spring's water had been, but it was good enough to wash down the peanut butter and jelly sandwiches.

After eating, she took out the suntan lotion and began reapplying it. She noticed that her tan lines were the same as gone!

"My tan lines match my modesty!" Sophia thought. *"Of which I apparently have none! Isn't that right Pragmatic Polly?"*

Her conscience remained silent.

Sophia again wondered if running around nude for the better part of the last day or so made her weird. She decided that it might be a little odd, but she *was* getting a nice tan and she was really liking how she looked!

"Laura had the same thoughts." Sophia thought. *"And it is kind of a different way to rebel, but there's really nothing wrong with it especially when you are the only one who knows about it."*

Once her body was sufficiently lotioned, she took out a small spray bottle that contained "Laura's Suntan Lotion for Blonde Hair". It was the formula Laura had told her about in the braiding dream. Sophia took her hair out of its braid and liberally coated it with the mixture of lemon juice, baby oil and water.

"This should bring out the auburn in my hair just a little." Sophia said to herself.

She laid down on the fleece blanket with the towel roll as her pillow. She splayed her hair out behind her so it would get maximum exposure to the sun. Then, she stretched her arms above her head and closed her eyes. However, her phone announced an incoming call; it was her mother.

"This is she!" Sophia said.

When she was three and waiting for her mother to pick her up at dance class, she had heard a woman say that particular phrase and she immediately began saying it whenever she could. It drove Carol Young crazy and every now and then Sophia used it…just because.

"Stop it!" Carol Young said.

Sophia laughed! "Mom, that dress looks great, thank you!"

"I'm glad you like it Soph." Carol Young said. "I found it at the mall, and it was on sale!"

"How much was it?" Sophia asked.

"It was ninety-five dollars, but…" Carol said before being cut off.

"Ninety-five dollars?!" Sophia said. "Mom, it's a cute dress but it's not ninety-five dollars cute! You don't need to be spending that much on one dress! That could buy four or five pairs of jeans!"

"That's why you are my favorite daughter Sophia, always practical." Carol said. "I didn't pay anywhere close to ninety-five dollars for it."

"How much *did* you pay Mom?" Sophia asked.

"It's a birthday present! I'm not telling you what it cost." Carol said.

"Mom!" Sophia said.

"I paid…." Carol paused for dramatic effect. "Eighteen dollars and sixty-seven cents after tax!"

"Whoa!" Sophia said. "You go Mom!"

"I love a good bargain!" Carol said. "It is a size four. Will that fit?"

"I am a size four, Mom!" Sophia said. "That will fit perfectly!"

"Sophia…" Carol said.

She heard something in her mother's voice that concerned her.

"Is something the matter Mom?" Sophia asked.

"Sophia, would you be okay staying by yourself tonight?" Carol asked.

"Well, Dad did say that could happen." Sophia said.

"Yes, he did." Carol said. "When I talked to your father, he said he wanted to get everything here taken care of tomorrow and get it finished."

"When will you be home?" Sophia asked.

"Your dad said noon at the very latest." Carol said.

"Woo-hoo! Party time!" Sophia teased. "Have Dad tell the liquor store I want the beer no later than seven tonight! I'm going to have me a kegger!"

Carol laughed out loud! "I'll text him, but forty dollars isn't enough money for bail, so you better be careful!"

"Oh, I forgot you only left me forty bucks. Cancel the keg, it looks like I'll be having root beer, pizza and watching television all alone instead." Sophia said.

"Are you sure you'll be okay?' Carol asked.

"I am old enough to stay by myself for one night. I have done it before." She said.

"Okay, Sophia." Carol said. "So, what are you doing right now?"

"I am at the covered bridge." Sophia said.

"What are you doing out there?" Carol asked.

"Well, mom, I came out here early this morning right after you left, stripped off my clothes and have spent the whole day completely nude just like I did yesterday afternoon! And my entire body is tan!" Sophia thought.

"I have been skinny dipping and rolling in the mud!" Sophia said.

"Oh!" Carol laughed. "You did say that was on your agenda today!"

"Yes, and a boy saw me swimming and thought I was a mermaid!" Sophia said truthfully. "But the water was kind of cold so now I am just laying out in plain view getting a suntan!"

"Sophia Elizabeth Young, you are terrible!" Carol said through snorts of laughter. "And you have your father's sense of humor too!"

"The thing is Mom; I am telling the truth." Sophia thought.

"Hey Mom, the football team just showed up, so I have to go, okay?" Sophia teased. "They want to skinny dip with me and..."

Carol laughed. "And what?"

"Well, they want to skinny dip with me, but I'm the only girl. Does that mean I'm popular?" Sophia asked.

"You don't need *that* kind of popularity Sophia!" Carol laughed.

Sophia held the phone away from her mouth and yelled, "Hey guys, my mom said I can't be popular, so you need to leave!" Carol was laughing hard when Sophia put the phone back up to her ear. "I told them Mom, but I don't think they liked it!"

"Bye, Sophia. We will see you tomorrow!" Carol laughed.

"Bye Mom!" Sophia giggled and ended the call.

She did an internet search for the times of sunrise and sunset for the month of August. After some quick math, she smiled broadly!

"At least thirteen hours without clothes today and seven yesterday plus all night last night which was nine hours; I have spent twenty-nine of the last forty-eight hours au natural!" Sophia thought. *"I like making choices!"*

She laid back, fluffed her hair out behind her again and closed her eyes.

~ ~ ~ ~ ~ ~

When she awoke, she was in the same position she had been in when she had closed her eyes.

"I guess I needed that nap." She paused, then thought, *"I wonder."*

She took a picture of herself. This one, however, was not a full-length body shot. Instead, it was a "head and hair shot"; she wanted to see if "Laura's Suntan Lotion for Blonde Hair" had lightened her hair like the Tan Booster Ten suntan lotion had darkened her skin. She was not disappointed.

"Wow!" She said. "That stuff really works!"

Sophia giggled at the idea that had popped into her head and she quickly texted her mother: "I HEARD LEMON JUICE, BABY OIL, WATER AND SUNSHINE WILL LIGHTEN BLONDE HAIR. LOOK WHAT IT DID TO MY HAIR." She attached the photo and hit send.

"Three, two, one." Sophia said and pointed at her phone.

It came to life with a response from her mother: "WOW!!! YOUR HAIR IS A LOT LIGHTER! WE WON'T RECOGNIZE YOU WHEN WE GET HOME TOMORROW!"

"You wouldn't recognize me right now, Mom!" Sophia thought.

"THE FOOTBALL TEAM LOVES IT!" Sophia texted back. "THEY NEVER LEFT. I THINK I WILL BE THE MOST POPULAR GIRL IN HIGH SCHOOL!"

"LOL!" Was her mother's response. "I GUESS THE BABY OIL KEEPS YOUR HAIR FROM DRYING OUT AND GETTING BRITTLE?"

"YUP!" Sophia replied.

"I DIDN'T KNOW I WAS GOING TO HAVE A RED HEAD!" Carol texted. "IT LOOKS GOOD HONEY!"

She had seen on the weather app that the predicted high temperature had been met and exceeded. It was an even one hundred degrees. She got up, grabbed her goggles and took a running dive into the Little Grand Creek. She swam back and forth, making five complete laps before swimming to the center of its channel and letting herself drift with the current downstream, thinking about everything and nothing.

After floating for ten or fifteen minutes, Sophia looked around and realized she could not see the bridge, but she could hear water roaring and the current had begun to pick up speed. Downstream she could see a large concrete structure jutting from the water.

"A dam?" She thought.

She angled toward the bank and got out. There was a rocky path like the one she had followed to the spring, so she walked to the dam. It was at least twenty feet tall, and the water roared as it flowed over it and crashed below. Sophia thought about taking the plunge, but quickly decided not to. She was here alone and had read that water going over a dam can sometimes cause an undertow that could pull you under and drown you. Besides that, she didn't know how deep the water was at the bottom and didn't want to go over and break her neck.

"Going over might be fun, but…uh…no!" She thought.

When Sophia was walking back to where she had gotten out of the creek, she saw an old log that was nearly as long as she was tall, lying on the bank.

"This could be interesting!" She thought.

She pushed the log with her foot, and it rolled into the water. She jumped in beside it and steered it to the main channel then swam back to the creek bank and followed its progress as she walked the path back to the dam.

"I wonder if the log will get caught in the undertow or if it will make it and go on downstream?" She thought.

The log topped the dam and plunged into the churning water where it disappeared. Sophia saw it pop up once then get pulled under and disappear altogether.

"Good call, Sophia. Today is not a good day to drown." She said to herself as she made her way back to the platform.

Chapter 25

Sophia unwrapped her last sandwich, took a bite and a single drop of water struck her nose. She absently wiped it away with the back of her hand, swallowed and took a second bite. Another drop hit her leg, so still munching, she looked up into the sky and saw a large bank of dark and ominous looking clouds moving in from the west.

"Oooh! It's going to rain!" She thought with excitement!

Rainstorms had always fascinated her, so she rewrapped her sandwich, put it away and started to climb up the bank. After looking at the sky again, she went back, grabbed her phone, and shoved her backpack with the book, shorts and tee shirt in it under one of the buckets. Then she climbed up to the road and started walking towards the cemetery.

"It is going to storm and I'm going to get wet!" The thought made her smile!

~ ~ ~ ~ ~ ~

When she got to the entrance of the cemetery, she was dripping wet and her hair clung to her neck and back, but the moisture was not from rain, it had only occasionally sprinkled while she walked. The moisture coating her body was from the humidity in the air.

When she stepped through the cemetery's gate there was a blinding flash of lightning and a tremendous clap of thunder that exploded all around her.

"I thought you said no one would care if I came out here like this, Laura!" Sophia said as rain began to pour down in great torrents.

She tilted her head back and closed her eyes enjoying the feeling of the warm rain pelting her skin and running down her body.

A lightning bolt struck a tree several hundred yards down the road from where she stood, and the air was filled with white-blue light and another deafening explosion of thunder.

"I need to get under some cover." She thought and began running back the way she had come.

The torrential rain had flooded the ruts made by untold car tires over the years. It turned the dust into slick mud which caused her to slip and fall into the brown slurry. Coated from chin to foot in brown mud and water, she stood and began running again, no worse for the wear, to The Grove.

As she entered the circular space and crossed to the pool, she noticed the floor of the sinkhole was dry, her muddy footprints were the only imperfection to the otherwise clean stone floor.

"Time to take a shower!" She thought and waded to the waterfall.

Once the mud was off, she climbed into the Art Gallery, looked at her plaster casting, then sat down and put in her ear buds. The next recording on the file list Laura had added was titled "11-22-1963".

"What are you up to Laura?" Sophia thought and hit play.

~ ~ ~ ~ ~ ~

Popping.

Crackling.

"Today was the worst day ever!" Laura said quietly.

Popping.

Crackling.

"But I have the best boyfriend ever." She continued.

Popping.

Crackling.

Laura sighed heavily.

"When we were in history class today, Mr. Nelson made an announcement for everyone to meet in the auditorium."

Laura's breathing was ragged and there were several stifled sobs before she continued.

"When we got there, Mr. Nelson told us that…"

Popping.

Crackling.

"President Kennedy was killed today!"

The sobs came in earnest and continued for a full minute.

"Sorry. It's just so unfair. Why would someone do that? Why would someone just shoot someone else?"

Popping.

Crackling.

"Anyway, Mr. Nelson said we could go home if we wanted. If we didn't, they had set up some televisions so we could watch the news. Jerry and I stayed. We did have a minor run in with Bill Morris, but all he did was some name calling. He is such a jerk!

Tonight, Mom and Dad invited Jerry and his parents over for dinner and we watched the news. They just left a few minutes ago. Hang on a second."

Popping.

Crackling.

"I had to get a tissue. After we ate, we watched television for a while and then Jerry and I went outside, and I cried some more."

Popping.

Crackling.

"Jerry just held me. He's good about that, he just knows when I need that. Okay, today I think anyone would have known that, but... He just knows."

Popping.

Crackling.

"I am so glad I met him after we moved here. He really took the bitterness away. I mean look what he did when I sprained my ankle! He waited on me hand and foot; no pun intended. He washed my hair for me! If that's not love, I don't know what is! And I can tell you this, I do love him, and he loves me!"

Popping.

Crackling.

"I know we are still in high school and we are just Sophomores, but I am going to marry Jerry Collins someday!"

Popping.

Crackling.

Silence.

~ ~ ~ ~ ~ ~

"Laura, you are so lucky!" Sophia thought. "Jerry sounds like a great boyfriend. Maybe someday I can find someone like him."

She looked at the audio list and played the one labeled 01-04-1964.

~ ~ ~ ~ ~ ~

Popping.

Crackling.

"I am so cold right now! I don't think I will ever be warm again! And it is all Jerry's fault too!" Laura giggled.

Popping.

Crackling.

"We hung out at my house today. Mom and Dad had gone to dad's office to start working on a bunch of insurance claims from the snowstorm on New Year's Day. We got A LOT of snow! And with the wind, some of the drifts are really deep."

Popping.

Crackling.

"We started playing Monopoly and Jerry started saying how bad he was going to beat me! If you know me, you know I am competitive, so I told him that I would be winning!"

Popping.

Crackling.

"We made a bet, and the loser would have to do whatever totally stupid thing the winner came up with after the game was over. If I hadn't landed on Boardwalk and his hotel, I might have won."

Popping.

Crackling.

"Anyway, after we had put the game away, Jerry reminded me that I had lost the bet and he had the perfect stupid thing for me to do. I can tell you; I was a bit nervous because of the big goofy grin he had on his face."

Popping.

Crackling.

"The stupid thing I had to do is the reason I will never be warm again! Jerry said I had to make a snow angel. That wasn't so bad until he said I had to do it wearing my swimsuit. He is pure evil!" Laura laughed.

Popping.

Crackling.

"So, I went and put on my bikini and then Jerry and I went out onto the back porch and I looked at the thermometer. It was fourteen degrees, and the wind was blowing! I tried my puppy dog look and asked if I really had to go outside. You know what he did...he opened the back-porch's door, grinned and pointed outside! He can be a jerk at times!"

Popping.

Crackling.

"We went out in the backyard and I made a snow angel in snow that was probably two feet deep! When I was making it, Jerry came over and piled snow on top of me! He buried me in it, I was totally covered! And all he did was laugh!"

Popping.

Crackling.

"He will pay for that! I don't know when and I don't know where, but Jerry Collins will be getting his sometime, I guarantee it!"

Popping.

Crackling.

"We went back inside, and Jerry laughed the whole time. I have to admit, I thought it was pretty funny, but I won't be telling him that. I took a long, HOT shower and put on the warmest clothes I could find. I even put on THREE pairs of socks because my feet were so cold."

Popping.

Crackling.

"When I came back downstairs, Jerry had made hot chocolate, popped some popcorn and had started a fire in the fireplace. Then he wrapped a big quilt around me, and we snuggled on the couch! Even if he is pure evil, and a jerk and is going to pay, he's still pretty okay!"

Popping.

Crackling.

Silence.

~ ~ ~ ~ ~ ~

Sophia left The Art Gallery giving her plaster clone a final appraising look before walking through the waterfall and wading to the edge of the pool. The storm had lessened, and she headed back to the bridge.

She got back to the fishing platform at seven-thirty. The once torrential rain had lessened to just sporadic sprinkles that ended altogether by a quarter of eight.

When she started packing up, she groaned out loud. Although she had put the backpack with the book and the clothes she was going to wear back to the house under one of the buckets, she had not thought to do the same thing with the fleece blanket, towel, her sweatshirt, sweatpants or shoes.

Sophia emptied out her shoes on to the platform; they were literally full of rainwater. She then had a thought that even her irrational, non-Polly Pragmatic side had considered absolutely crazy the day before.

"It's getting dark. And no one comes out here anymore. At least that's what Larry the Lawn Guy said yesterday, and Laura has today circled on the calendar!" She thought. *"I'm not getting dressed until I get back to the chip and sealed road just like yesterday!"*

She wrung as much water out of the towel, the sweats and the fleece blanket as she could, then rolled everything up together. She grabbed the backpack with the still dry book, shorts and tee shirt in it and climbed the bank to the road and crossed the bridge.

She put the backpack in one pannier and the wet blanket roll in the other, snapped her phone into its holder then made the mile-long bike ride to where the gravel road met the chip and sealed road, but continued on without getting dressed.

"Why not!' She thought. *"Sometimes you have to do something a little crazy to prove that you are actually sane!"*

She got to the old barn several minutes later with the butterflies – flutterbys – of taking such a risk tickling her stomach. She pulled in and slipped on the tee shirt and shorts she had brought for the ride back to the house just as a car drove by. She laughed when she saw it. Her stomach rumbled. She looked at her phone; it was eight-fifteen.

"I wonder how late the pizza place delivers." She asked herself.

A quick internet search told her that Show Me Pizza delivered until ten p.m. When she placed her order; they said it would be delivered in twenty-five minutes and it would be free if it wasn't in her hands by eight-forty.

"I can just make it." She thought and mounted the Schwinn and started toward town.

Chapter 26

Sophia closed the garage door and looked at her phone; it was eight thirty-five p.m.

"Five minutes to spare." She said to herself. *"But..."*

The "but" happened three minutes after leaving the old barn when a second round of torrential rain broke loose. There was no lightning or thunder, just a heavy drenching downpour that soaked her to the skin in mere seconds with more of the shower water warm rain. Her problem, the "but", was that the clothes she had brought for the ride back to the house were white cotton and had become, for all intents and purposes, completely see-through.

"Definitely no imagination required!" Sophia thought as she looked down at herself.

She didn't want to go dripping into the house and have that mess to clean up, so she kicked off her shoes and peeled off her wet clothes then looked out the garage's side door window to the backdoor of the house. The rain was still pouring. Although it wasn't totally dark, it was dark enough for her to get to the backdoor without being seen, so she scampered across the green space.

Dan Young made a decision after buying the house. He said he did not want to carry a "wad of keys" in his pockets, so he installed programmable, keyless door locks on all the doors and set them with the same five-digit code. It made unlocking and entering the house and garage very easy as long as you remembered the code.

He had also put one of the locks on the door that led into the back half of the garage, but when Sophia had tried the code that worked on all the other doors, that one remained locked.

When she got to the backdoor, Sophia pressed eight, one, eight, six and four, turned the knob, pushed on the door and...nothing. On a few occasions, like after painting the front porch, the backdoor would stick shut, just because. Tonight, while Sophia was standing outside completely nude with a pizza delivery imminent, the door decided to be obstinate yet again.

"Oh, come on!" Sophia hissed as she jiggled the doorknob. "Open!"

She entered the code again, but the door would not budge. She contemplated going back to the garage and putting on her thoroughly drenched clothes, but the pizza would literally be arriving any minute and she had to get inside to get the money to pay for it.

"I asked to be able to make some choices and now I have to decide: Do I use the front door and risk being seen or do I put on my clothes that are basically see through and risk being seen?" She thought about her dilemma for a moment then laughed. *"Sometimes you have to do something a little crazy! This could get interesting for me and the pizza guy if I can't get inside before he gets here."*

From somewhere in the back of her mind she thought she heard Pragmatic Polly chuckle!

Sophia crept to the corner of the porch and stood behind the large bush that was planted there. From behind her there came a loud crash. When she turned to see what had caused it, she saw that one of the garage's down spouts had fallen to the ground.

"Dad can fix that later." She thought, then returned her attention to the front of the house.

A car, with a lighted "SHOW ME PIZZA" sign on its roof came down the street and slowed as it passed the house. She could see that it was an old Monte Carlo like the one her dad had driven when he was a teenager. He kept a picture of his jet black "Monty" in a frame on his desk. Unlike her father's car, the one with the pizza sign on its roof was a dark blue and had shiny mag wheels. It sped up and continued down the street.

"They didn't see the house number, but they will be turning around and coming back!" Sophia said to herself. *"I hope the pizza guy is cute!"*

The rain increased and Sophia took a deep breath, broke cover, crossed the front yard and ran up the porch steps and was instantly bathed in the brand new, extra bright, extra illuminating L.E.D. lights her dad had installed the week before.

"Definitely no imagination required now!" Sophia thought.

She entered the door lock code but missed one of the numbers and had to clear it and try again. From up the street she saw the glow of a car's headlights.

"Oh, crud monkeys!" Sophia thought.

"I don't care if someone sees me either. You only live once!" Polly Pragmatic mimicked in a sarcastic tone. "Isn't that what you said out at the bridge?"

"Shut up!" Sophia said to her conscience.

"What's the matter? You *do* have Goldilocks boobs; not too big, not too small, they are just right!" Polly Pragmatic laughed!

"It's going to take more than pizza for me to show them off to the pizza delivery guy." She thought.

"You just spent the last two days running around all over the countryside wearing nothing at all!" Polly said. "What would the pizza guy have to do to get to meet Goldilocks and her two boobs?"

"Pizza, breadsticks AND a wedding ring! I do have my standards!" Sophia thought.

She punched in the code again, twisted the doorknob and the front door swung inward. She stepped inside as the Monte Carlo with the "Show Me Pizza" sign on its roof was just two houses away.

She ran to her bathroom, grabbed a towel and wiped as much of the rainwater from her body and hair as she could. Then she crossed the hallway to her bedroom, pulled on a pair of black running shorts and slid on a black tee shirt that said in large letters, "Kickapoo High School Varsity Cheerleader ~ Home of the Chiefs!" The shirt had arrived the day after her parents told her about their impending move. Today was the first time she had ever worn it. She slid one of the twenties her parents had left her from under her laptop and headed to the living room just as the doorbell rang.

"Made it, but just barely." She thought.

She peeked through the front door's peep hole and saw a young man in a red "Show Me Pizza" shirt wearing a rain poncho and holding a pizza box. With the distorted view the peep hole gave plus the poncho's hood, it was hard to see what he looked like.

"Hey Polly. If I was still trying to open the door when he got here, would I have had to give him a tip?" Sophia wondered.

"You have lost your mind!" Polly said from somewhere inside Sophia's head.

"Probably." Sophia thought, then opened the door.

"Hi!" She said.

"Hi!" The pizza guy said. "Are you the B.O.M?"

"I like to think so!" Sophia said with a big grin. "But I ordered a beef, onion and mushroom pizza."

Pizza Guy laughed, lowered the hood of his rain poncho and blushed.

"Oh my gosh he has the bluest eyes I have ever seen!" Sophia thought as the flutterbys took flight in her stomach! *"And blonde hair! Podunksville may not be so bad after all!"*

"That was good!" He looked down at the receipt in his hand and said, "It is…uh…seven dollars."

"He might have seen you." Polly chimed in.

"If he had seen me, his mouth would be hanging open because of my amazing tan and my Goldilocks and the Three Bears boobs!" She thought. *"They're not too big. They're not too small. They are just right! Remember?"*

"Why did he blush?" Polly asked.

"Because I am the awesome sauce!" Sophia thought.

"Here you go!" Sophia said.

She handed him the Jackson and leaned coquettishly on the door frame. He handed her the pizza, took the money and his eyes quickly darted from her face to her legs, then returned to her face.

"If you would have been here a minute or two sooner, you would have seen more than my legs!" Sophia thought.

"Thanks!" Pizza Guy's face reddened just a bit.

"Have you been busy tonight?" Sophia asked.

"You are the first delivery we've had tonight; it must be the rain." He said. "Thanks for turning on the porch lights. Did you see us drive by or something?'

"Actually, the lights came on when I ran up to the front door totally nude trying like crazy to get it open." Sophia thought.

"I just turned them on because I knew you would be here soon." Sophia lied.

"You know, we missed the house number the first time we drove by. We were late, so this is going to be free." He said trying to give the twenty back.

"You missed the house number because Dad hasn't put it back on since he painted the porch." Sophia pointed to the large black numbers that were lying on the floor next to the front door. "You made it on time, or would have, if the numbers had been where they are supposed to be."

Back home, Laney's older brother Bryan had delivered pizza for a place that guaranteed on time delivery. He was late once and had been fired. Even if the pizza had been late, she was more than willing to pay for it. Had he been just a little earlier, it would have been very awkward for both of them.

"Excuse me! My eyes are up here! They aren't on my chest or below my waist! Thank you sooo much!" Sophia heard herself saying in the scenario playing in her head.

"Oh yeah, no house numbers. Thanks!" He said giving her two fives and three ones back in change. His face remained flushed.

Sophia took the two fives.

"That's yours." She said.

She thought a three-dollar tip for a seven-dollar pizza was a pretty good tip!

"Thank you!" He said flashing her a grateful smile.

"Oooh! Cute smile! There is still some hope for this little no-name town." Sophia thought.

"So, I just moved here. Are you in high school?" Sophia asked.

"I will be a freshman this year!" He said.

"Me too!" Sophia said. "But you're driving?"

"No, I'm riding with my friend." He said. "I help him sometimes and we split the tips."

"That's pretty cool, but don't spend that all in one place." Sophia motioned to the three ones he held in his hands.

Pizza Guy laughed. "A hundred thousand more of these and that Lamborghini will be mine!"

Sophia laughed again and thought, *"And a sense of humor for the cute, blue eyed, blonde haired Podunksville Possum!"*

"Enjoy the pizza...Sophia Young!" He said.

"How did you know my name?" Sophia asked, a bit surprised.

"I'm psychic!" He said with a big smile. "Either that, or it's because your name is printed on the receipt."

"Oh, duh!" Sophia said. She felt her face flush which was something she rarely did. "My blonde must be showing just a bit."

"Hey now!" Pizza Guy said. "Careful with the blonde comments!"

"Ooops!" Sophia said. "I didn't mean..." She felt her face turn warm again.

He laughed. "It's okay! Have a good night Sophia!" He said before starting back to the car.

"You too!" She watched him until he opened the Monte Carlo's door then she shut the front door.

"Oh, my goodness was he cute!" Sophia said to the living room. "Those blue eyes...WOWZAH!"

~ ~ ~ ~ ~ ~

Sophia took her pizza to the kitchen, put it in the oven's warming drawer and pressed the pizza icon. It automatically set the temperature to one hundred fifty degrees, which was hot enough to keep the pizza warm but not enough to burn it.

"Before I eat, I need to get my stuff from the garage and wash it." She said to the empty kitchen.

She went to the laundry room and looked outside just as the sky opened up and the deluge commenced again. She tried opening the backdoor knowing full well it was stuck, but on her first try, it swung open easily.

"I hate you!" Sophia said to the door then she took off her shirt and shorts and said, "Because I choose too!"

The rain was falling straight down like a curtain of water that made it hard to see the garage. She smiled as an idea formed.

"Please keep raining like this for at least ten more minutes." She said to the sky. *"I want to…no…I am choosing to do something else totally crazy!"*

Sophia sprinted across the yard to the garage, rummaged through her backpack and grabbed one specific item before stepping outside into the torrent.

With the amount of rain that was coming down, Sophia couldn't see the front of the house, much less the street, and knew no one could see her either. However, she could see the downspout that was lying in the grass next to the garage's side door. The garage's gutters were pouring unimpeded onto the ground.

"Because I choose too!" Sophia thought again.

She walked to the downspout, loving how the pelting rain felt on her back, chest and legs, to where the rain from the gutters gushed onto the ground. She stepped into the deluge with the bottle of body wash that doubled as shampoo and took a shower!

She went through three complete lather, rinse and repeat cycles before she stepped back into the garage to retrieve her clothes and the fleece blanket. The rainstorm surged again, pounding on the garage roof.

"Wow!" She said. "It is really pouring!"

She could barely see the house but dashed back across the yard and tossed the clothes and blanket on the floor next to the washing machine, then went back outside to the garage and stood under the pouring downspout and washed her hair for the fourth time.

"Because I choose too!" She thought again, then raised her arms above her head and turned her face up into the gushing warm rainwater!

~ ~ ~ ~ ~ ~

Sitting neatly on the laundry room's folding table was the basket of towels that she had forgotten to put in her bathroom the night before. Sophia grabbed the one on top, unfolded it, dried herself off then wiped up the water that she had dripped onto the vinyl flooring. She grabbed a second towel and rapidly dried her hair before tossing both towels, her clothes, blanket and the towel roll that had gotten soaked at the fishing platform along with some laundry soap into the washing machine and hit start.

Underneath the table was "the rag bag"; she grabbed several old washcloths and stuffed them inside her shoes to dry them out, then went to her bathroom and brushed out her towel tangled hair. As she brushed, she looked at herself in the mirror above her sink and smiled as she appraised her image.

"My tan lines are gone!" She thought.

After brushing her hair, she returned to the kitchen and took the pizza from the warming drawer and put a couple of slices on a plate, poured herself a large glass of cold milk and went to the living room to watch one of her favorite shows! She also plugged in her phone; the battery was at thirty-one percent, and the fast charger would top it off in less than an hour.

"Taking a shower under a downspout in your yard was really pretty stupid." Polly Pragmatic said.

"Yeah, it was a dumb thing to do." Sophia agreed. *"But it felt really good! The water was actually warm!"*

"If the rain had stopped, everyone in the neighborhood could have seen you." Polly added.

Sophia laughed! *"And they wouldn't have had to give me a wedding ring either!"*

~ ~ ~ ~ ~ ~

When the washer signaled her laundry was done, she turned off the television, put the uneaten pizza in the refrigerator, went to the laundry room and tossed her clothes into the dryer.

It was nine-twenty p.m. and she headed to her room where she set her cell phone's alarm for five a.m.; she wanted to watch the sunrise from the fishing platform. She was getting ready to send a quick text to her parents telling them, "Good Night!" and climb into bed when her phone rang; it was her mother.

"Hi Mom!" Sophia said.

"Hi Sophie!" Carol said. "What are you up to?"

"Well Mom, I am sitting on my bed totally naked just like I spent the last thirteen or fourteen hours out at the covered bridge. I ordered pizza and as the delivery guy was heading up the street, I was standing at the front door totally nude trying to get inside.

Oh, by the way, Dad's new lights, you know the ones on the motion detector, yeah, they work really well!

Then I took a shower outside by the garage in the rain; I washed my hair four times standing outside in our yard completely naked...er...nude!

And for the record, I will be sleeping in the nude from here on out; I love how not wearing clothes feels!" Sophia thought.

"Getting ready to go to bed." Sophia said.

"It's kind of early isn't it?" Carol asked.

"Yeah, I'm kind of tired." Sophia said. "We ran out of beer at the party, so everyone left."

Carol Young laughed!

"Do you think I'll have a hangover Mom?" Sophia teased. "The room is really spinning!"

"Stop it!" Carol laughed, then her voice took on a more serious tone. "Are you sure you'll be okay staying there alone tonight? Carol asked.

"Mom, I will be fine." Sophia said.

"Are you sure?" Carol asked. "I know that you aren't happy about the move and…"

"I'm fine Mom, really." Sophia said. "Actually, I am kind of liking being here alone. It's giving me a chance to think about a lot of things. I miss my friends, sure, but I need to get over that, you know?"

"That's good to hear honey!" Carol said. "That's really good to hear!"

"So, when did you say you will be back?" Sophia asked.

"No later than noon tomorrow." Carol said.

"Okay." Sophia said.

"How are you doing money wise?" Carol asked.

"I spent ten bucks on pizza tonight." Sophia said. "I'll be fine. If things get tight, I saw we had some hot dogs in the refrigerator. I can always fix them, some pork and beans and of course, Dad's Weenie Water Gravy!"

~ ~ ~ ~ ~ ~

When Sophia was seven years old, she had been in a Brownie troop of the Girl Scouts. After getting home from a troop meeting, it was just her and her dad, both were hungry, so they scoured the kitchen looking for something to eat. The only acceptable items they could agree on were hotdogs and pork and beans.

After boiling the hotdogs and heating up the pork and beans, Dan had tried something different. He wanted gravy, so he added some flour to some of the hotdog water, whisked it briskly with a fork and began simmering it while constantly stirring the mix in the saucepan waiting for it to thicken. Once it had reached an acceptable consistency, he ladled some of it over a piece of bread he had torn apart and put into a cereal bowl. They sampled his unique creation and deemed it absolutely awful before pouring it into the garbage disposal.

Dan's Weenie Water Gravy was the code phrase they used when they wanted to go out and eat.

~ ~ ~ ~ ~ ~

"Wait... What?" Carol asked.

"I said I'll make some Weenie Water Gravy!" Sophia repeated while trying not to laugh.

"Oh my!" Carol said. "I'll let you go now. You know you can call me if you want to talk."

"Actually, there is something I do want to talk to you about if you have time." Sophia said.

Carol had been hoping Sophia would want to talk about …well…anything for some time now. Since the move, Sophia had been distant, and her moods shifted between sullen and a total jerk; sometimes the shift occurred midsentence.

"What is it Sophia?" Carol asked.

"Well, I will be starting a new school in a new town next week." Sophia said.

"Yes, you will." Carol said.

"And I'll be "the new girl". Sophia said.

"I cannot believe I keep saying that about myself." She thought.

"Yes, you will." Carol said.

There was a long pregnant pause before Sophia blurted, "Mom, I want to cut my hair!"

"You do?" Carol asked. "You have been growing it out since you were in the fourth grade. I mean it's down to your waist."

"New town! New school! New girl! New hair! New me!" Sophia said. "And my hair is *past* my waist Mom. It's below my butt!"

"Do you have a style in mind?" Carol asked.

"Yes!" Sophia said. "I want it how Calysta Bevier had her hair when she got the Golden Buzzer on America's Got Talent."

"When who, got what, where?" Carol asked.

"I'll send you a picture...hang on." Sophia said.

"I am having an AGT kind of day! First the Darci Lynne tee shirt, then the Angelina Jordan song and now, Caly Bevier!" Sophia thought.

The connection went quiet while Sophia found the picture she was looking for and Carol was quietly celebrating this change in her daughter! She had been worried about Sophia.

She was afraid she might do something really crazy like run away and hitchhike back to Springfield to see her friends. She had discussed her concerns with Dan who reminded her that even though Sophia was angry about having had to move, she was also very level-headed. Carol had agreed, but she still called Sophia's friend's parents and asked them to pay attention to what Audrey, Laney and Leah were saying when it came to Sophia.

Carol's phone chimed; Sophia's text had arrived.

"I just sent it to you Mom." Sophia said.

"Just got it." Carol said. "Opening it now."

"Do you like it?" Sophia asked.

"Oh my, Sophia! That is short!" Carol said. "Are you sure this is what you want?"

"Absolutely!" Sophia said. "And I want to donate the hair they cut off to one of those places that makes wigs for cancer patients too!"

"Well, it is short, but it is a cute style. I think it would look good on you, but..." Carol said.

"Here it comes." Sophia thought. *"The choice will be made for me and I'll be stuck with it."*

"But what, Mom?" Sophia asked.

"But you will lose all those gorgeous auburn highlights you made with that stuff you put in your hair today!" Carol said. "Are you sure about this?"

"Absolutely, Mom!" Sophia said.

"Well, it is your hair!" Carol said. "And you are fifteen, so it's your decision."

Sophia was relieved, she had been wanting to have this conversation for a few weeks now but was afraid the choice would not be hers to make when it came down to it.

"It will be easy to take care of too!" Sophia added. "And if I don't like it, I can always just shave my head and be bald!"

"You might look cute bald too!" Carol said once she had finished laughing. "But you will look cute with that style in the picture you sent me. How about we make a trip to the salon and get your hair done? I'll make the appointment. The lady who runs the salon lives just down the street. Her mother works with your dad at the post office."

"That would be awesome Mom!" Sophia said. "Then I can still go to that book signing on Sunday. I bet there will be some kids from school there and I can make my appearance as the totally cute new girl with the short hair!"

"Sophia, you are something else!" Carol laughed.

Sophia feigned a yawn. She had an idea and she wanted to get started on it.

"I'll let you go." Carol said. "You sound tired."

"I am. Bye Mom!" Sophia said this time yawning for real.

"Bye Sophia, see you tomorrow!" Carol said and hung up.

It was nine-thirty-five p.m. and Sophia bolted from her bed and began gathering supplies for what was probably her craziest, most risky choice yet! The flutterbys had taken wing yet again!

"I cannot believe I am going to do this." She said and headed to the garage.

Chapter 27

Sophia found one of her dad's larger "dry bags" in their camping supplies. Before the move, she and her parents had gone on several days long canoe trips where they carried all their gear with them and camped alongside the river they were traveling. The dry bags protected the camping gear if their canoe flipped or if it rained. There was nothing worse than a totally soaked sleeping bag when you were out in the middle of nature alongside a river.

She found her easy-up tent; it was small and folded up into a bag about the size of a football. She looked at her sleeping mat that self-inflated when unrolled; it made a very comfortable place to sit or sleep, however, she put it back on the shelf and took one of their low-profile camp cots instead. She liked the cot because you did not have to lie directly on the ground.

She also took a small heater head and a completely full propane canister! Even though the days were reaching the upper nineties or beyond, the night-time temperatures had been a bit chilly, so a heater might come in handy especially where she was planning on spending the night.

She crossed to the garage's side door and looked outside again. The rain had left a fresh, clean scent in the air. However, there was another smell in the garage. It was the smell of cut wood and its fragrance was the strongest when she was next to the unlockable door that led to the other half of the garage.

"I wonder what Dad has been doing in there." She thought.

"I bet he hasn't been running around without any clothes on." Polly Pragmatic said.

"I'm sure he hasn't." Sophia thought. *"I bet he's building the screen frames for the front porch in there."*

She then thought about what she was going to be doing tonight. *"I have lost my mind! This is crazier than laying out on the fishing platform or taking ten-mile-long walks!"*

"THEN GO INSIDE AND GO TO BED!" Pragmatic Polly commanded.

"Nope!" Sophia said to her conscience and crossed the yard to the backdoor and saw that it had closed when she went to the garage. *"Oh man! I hope it opens."*

It didn't, and Sophia was forced to go to the front door again and be illuminated in all her tan and Goldilocks glory by the porch's L.E.D. lights.

"At least there's not a pizza delivery guy coming down the street." She said to herself.

"And it's not raining now either." Pragmatic Polly observed. "I bet the neighbors across the street are getting quite a view of "the postmaster's daughter"!

Once inside, Sophia peeked through the curtains at the houses across the street. There were no lights on in the front rooms, so she felt safe.

"No one saw me." Sophia said to the living room.

"You <u>hope</u> no one saw you." Polly said. "Remember, this is a small town where people see things then make phone calls."

"Well, if they did see me, I hope they liked what they saw, and I hope they are telling all their friends! I look amazing, and based on Pizza Guy checking me out, I must have nice legs too!" Sophia said to herself.

She packed food for what she was calling her "Grand Adventure in Nudity"! She also made a large thermos of hot tea and took a couple of bottles of water for good measure. The drawstring backpack and lunchbox fit easily into the dry bag on top of the camping gear she had brought in from the garage.

"This is going to be fun!" Sophia thought.

"This is going to be a disaster." Polly said.

Sophia made a quick sweep of her room looking for any additional items she might need. She looked at the calendar on her desk to confirm what she already knew; Laura had circled all but one of the days for the next three weeks as days when no one would be at the bridge.

"Oh, I'll definitely need those." She said and picked up another portable battery pack and her small but mighty L.E.D. flashlight; both were fully charged!

The clock in her room said it was nine-fifty p.m. She crossed the hall to her bathroom and got what toiletries she would need. She then put on her white sweatshirt and white sweatpants; they were micro-fiber fleece lined and very soft just like her grey set.

"I'll be riding my bike in the dark." She thought. *"I want to be seen."*

"You should be seen in your bed asleep." Polly interjected.

"Shut it!" Sophia said to her conscience as she gathered up what she was taking with her and headed to the garage.

With the help of a couple of bungee cords and the panniers, Sophia was able to secure the dry bag that held her camping gear, food and everything else she was taking to the bridge. Her fully charged phone said it was ten p.m.

"Here we go!" She said.

~ ~ ~ ~ ~ ~

The ride back to the bridge was uneventful. The roads were wet from the earlier rainstorms, but the clouds were breaking up, and a couple of times Sophia saw the moon peeking down at her.

As she rode through town, she started thinking again about how much time she had spent wearing no clothes the past couple of days and how much more time she would be spending wearing nothing at all before her parents got home.

"Sometimes you have to do something a little crazy to prove that you are actually sane!" Sophia thought. *"And because I choose to!"*

When she passed the last house of Podunksville and before she got to the old barn, she pulled to the side of the road, put the bicycle's kickstand down, got off and made another choice.

"If I'm going to do this, I am going to do this!" She said to herself and took off her sweatshirt.

Her phone erupted with the chicken clucking sound at that moment and when she looked at the screen, she saw it was her mother calling. She answered using the speaker phone.

"Hello." She said.

"It's coming off!" Carol said.

Sophia looked at her phone to make sure she hadn't accidently turned on the video calling feature. Although she knew her mom had seen her without clothes on probably more times than she had seen herself without clothes on, she didn't want to have to explain why she was outside alongside a road with her shirt off.

"What did you say?" Sophia asked.

"It's coming off! I called the lady down the street about getting your hair cut, she can do it tomorrow!" Carol said.

"Cool! Thanks Mom!" Sophia said as she stuffed her shirt into the dry bag. "What time?" She asked.

"Twelve-thirty." Her mom said. "We will be getting back at noon, so that will work just fine."

Sophia kicked off her tennis shoes and released the drawstring of her sweatpants, letting them pool around her ankles. She stepped out of them and the August night breeze caressed her skin.

"I told her kind of what you wanted, and she said she could get it done in an hour or so! And because you are donating your hair for the cancer patient wigs, the hair cut is FREE!" Carol said.

"Cool beans!" Sophia said and she picked up her sweatpants and put them in the dry bag as well.

"That is causing one problem though." Carol said.

"What's that Mom?" Sophia asked.

Carol laughed! "Now your dad has to get you something else! He was paying for the haircut as a part of your birthday present!"

Sophia laughed. "If you hadn't told me, I wouldn't have known!" She said enjoying the warm night air.

"Yes, Polly, I am taking a huge risk of being seen, but at this time of night I think I am pretty safe. Besides, I really like not wearing clothes!" She thought. *"I think I might have a problem when school starts."*

"Winter should be fun too." Polly said in a dry sarcastic tone.

"You know what Miss Practical Polly Pragmatic, when there's snow on the ground I am going out to the bridge, take off my clothes and make a snow angel just like Laura did!" Sophia thought.

"You might get frostbite too!" Her inner voice said. "On areas that should not be exposed to snow!"

Sophia laughed at her inner dialogue! She sometimes wondered if anyone else argued with themselves as much as she argued with the Polly Pragmatic side of herself.

In the distance, she saw headlights coming toward her. She grabbed her phone, laid her bike in the grass and stepped across onto the road bank where there was a good-sized tree and slipped behind it, so she was out of sight when the car passed by.

"That could have been awkward." She said watching the car pass by.

"What could have been awkward?" Carol asked.

"Uh, it could have been awkward if you had said the haircut was part of my birthday present and then the lady cutting my hair said it was free." Sophia said thinking quickly.

Carol laughed. "Yes, it could have! He told me he has something in mind that he knows you will like!" She said.

"Hey Mom, I need..." She feigned another yawn. "...to go."

"Okay honey!" Carol said. "Talk to you later!"

"See you tomorrow Mom!" Sophia said.

She hung up and, thankfully, was still standing behind the tree when a pickup truck drove by with its radio on, its windows were down and Joe Diffie was wailing, "There's something women like about a pickup man!"

"Yee-haw!" She thought. *"You go have yourself a real good time! Yuck, yuck, yuck!"*

"And you put your clothes on!" Polly Pragmatic said.

"No, I'm going to risk it. If I am seen, then I am seen." She thought. *"And I look good, so what they see will be something to remember!"*

"Now you sound conceited." Polly said.

"That did sound conceited didn't it." Sophia thought.

"Yes!" Polly said. "It did."

"Sorry about that." Sophia thought, then added. *"It must be because of my amazing Goldilocks boobs and awesome sauce tan!"*

"If you don't care about being seen, why were you in such a hurry to get in the front door tonight when the pizza guy was just two doors down and why did you jump behind that tree when that car and truck came by?" Polly asked. "Where was that princess wave?"

It was Sophia's turn to go silent.

"Me thinks your silence speaks volumes." Polly said.

"Maybe just a little." Sophia admitted as she slipped on her shoes, got back on her bike and headed to The Grove!

~ ~ ~ ~ ~ ~

Her tent went up without difficulty and the stakes that secured it to the ground weren't needed because there wouldn't be any wind down in the sinkhole to blow it over. Even if there was, she couldn't have pounded them into the solid stone floor of the sinkhole anyway. Next, Sophia set up the camp cot inside the tent; she also put the heater and the rest of her gear inside, then set about building a fire.

"This just might work!" She said to no one.

She gathered up some of the dry kindling and arranged it in a teepee shape inside the fire ring then mounted the stone steps and climbed out of the sinkhole and into The Grove. She found some dry grass which really didn't surprise her. Even though it had rained really hard earlier, The Grove's leaves were dense and were a natural umbrella.

When she was back at the fire ring, she used the propane heater to light her campfire. The fire popped and crackled to life as the grass, smaller sticks and twigs began to burn. She began adding bigger pieces of wood to the flames and once those had caught, she added one of the logs, kicked off her shoes, pulled the camp cot out of the tent and sat down.

"This feels nice!" Sophia said looking at her phone.

The phone's clock said it was ten forty-five p.m. The weather app said the temperature was eighty-two degrees, but the temperature in the sinkhole was much cooler. Sophia's face said she was happy!

She added a second large piece of wood to the fire, it caught quickly and before long she had to move closer to the tent; even there the heat was noticeable.

"What should I do while I am out here?" Sophia wondered aloud. "Besides listen to Laura's recordings and read my book?"

Polly Pragmatic started to speak, but Sophia stopped that part of herself.

"I am not getting dressed! I am not packing up! I am not going back to the house! I am staying here, and I will not be wearing anything at all!" She said to herself. *"Tomorrow, I will be laying out in the sun! I will be finishing up Laura's tapes and the book! I will swim! I will walk to the cemetery! I may even roll in the mud again! And I will not doubt these choices, they are mine and I own them!"*

The fire popped and crackled. Polly Pragmatic was silent.

"And now, I will be taking a walk back to the bridge. I've sunbathed, now I'm going to moon bathe!" Sophia said. *"Because I choose too."*

~ ~ ~ ~ ~ ~

When she got to the fishing platform, she saw the moon and how it shown on the creek's water. She raised her phone and snapped a picture that showed the moon's light reflecting off the surface of the creek and just off center was a portion of the bridge in full silhouette.

"I'm going to print this one!" She thought.

Sophia climbed back up the embankment and walked to the bridge's balcony. She tightened her phone's strap around her wrist as she walked, she didn't want to drop it in the creek again, especially at night. She watched the moon lit water and listened to an owl off in the distance adding its voice to the other night-time sounds. There were frogs and crickets in full voice and somewhere in the distance she heard a dog bark.

"There aren't wolves in Missouri are there?" She asked herself.

"Look it up." Polly suggested.

"Good idea Polly!" Sophia thought. *"When you aren't bugging me about putting on clothes, you sometimes have pretty good ideas."*

She called up her phone's internet app and typed in, "Are there wolves in Missouri?" and hit send.

"Good news Polly." She said to herself. *There aren't any."*

"I shall sleep better knowing that." Polly said.

"I wonder." Sophia thought and then typed, "Is talking to and answering yourself a sign of being crazy?" and hit enter.

Instantaneously she had over forty-five million results. All the ones she read said that those who talked to and answered themselves were not mentally ill, but instead were highly self-reliant, highly proficient and could figure out what they needed.

"More good news Polly!" Sophia said to herself. *"We're not crazy!"*

"Well, I'm not!" Polly said. "But I'm not so sure about you!"

"You are right about that!" Sophia said.

"I am right about what?" Polly asked.

"I am crazy!" Sophia said. *"I'm going for a walk!"*

Chapter 28

When she got to where the gravel road met the chip and seal, Sophia saw a vehicle headed down the road towards her. By the sound of the engine, it was moving fast.

"What is it with cars tonight?" Sophia thought.

She didn't have a lot of time to get out of sight, so she slid down into the ditch where her bike had fallen when she was fighting off the head buzzing bug. Instead of being full of dry powdery dirt, the ditch was full of a slurry of mud and water that came up to her waist.

"I didn't think I'd be taking a mud bath tonight." Sophia thought.

She tossed her phone, earbuds and flashlight into the grass and crouched down to wait until the car passed.

"When I get back to the sinkhole, I will be taking another shower in the waterfall." She said to herself.

"If you get back." Polly said. "Because if they see you…"

"Yeah, I know. They will have their way with me. When school gets out next summer, Mom and Dad will have a grandchild, and for my sixteenth birthday I will have a three-month-old spit up all over me and my first set of wheels will be a baby stroller. It will be glorious." Sophia thought sarcastically.

The car pulled onto the gravel and stopped less than fifteen feet from her. The headlights were extremely bright, they were probably halogen or L.E.D. and they were pointed toward her hiding spot. She ducked down even lower, and the watery mud came up to just under her collar bones. The engine was turned off and the headlights went out, but the parking lights stayed on and someone opened the driver's door and got out. She could hear rock and roll music playing from the car's radio.

"You're right Bobby boy!" A male voice said. "Rock and roll never forgets!"

Sophia heard the distinct sound of a zipper being unfastened, then she heard water or some variation of it, hitting the ground.

"Is he…" Sophia thought. *"Oh gross!"*

"Steve, I have to get home before midnight!" A second male voice from inside the car said. "Hurry up!"

"I gotta go man!" The driver, Steve, said. "Hang on!"

On top of the car, a light came on and began flashing. Sophia could see the words "Show Me Pizza!!!".

"Hang on a second and quit flashing that light!" Steve said. "If that gets broken, I have to pay for it!"

"If I'm late I am so grounded." The passenger said. "I have stuff to do tomorrow."

The passenger got out of the car and stood in front of it less than fifteen feet from the tall grass that was concealing the muddy water filled ditch where Sophia was crouched.

"That's Pizza Guy!" Sophia thought.

"We've got plenty of time." Steve said doing up his fly and lighting a cigarette. "Tell me about that girl we delivered the pizza to tonight. You said she was cute, but that's all you said."

"She was *totally* cute!" Pizza Guy said. "She looked like she had just gotten out of the shower because her hair was wet and kind of messy like she had just dried it with a towel or something. And man, it was long! It was down past her waist!"

"I thought you didn't like long hair." Steve said.

"I don't, but hers…" Pizza Guy said. "Hers was really nice, for long hair I mean."

"How was her face?" Steve asked.

"I said she was totally cute! And her eyes were… They were brown, but they were greenish too, you know?" Pizza Guy said.

"How old?" Steve asked. "You said she wasn't very tall. She's not like twelve, is she? Because if she is, she is *jailbait!*"

"Dude! No! She asked if I was in high school and when I said I was going to be a freshman…." Pizza Guy said, paused, then added. "When I said I was going to be a freshman, she said she was too! She is my age and going to be in my class!"

"Did you notice anything else about her?" Steve asked cupping his hands in front of his chest.

"One million points from Steve for being a letch." Sophia thought stifling a laugh in spite of the predicament she was in.

"Apparently, Steve likes Goldilocks." Polly said.

"Okay, no points for talking about my amazing Goldilocks boobs, but he is still a letch." Sophia thought. *"Pizza Guy, the ball is in your court. What you say next will determine if I speak to you again."*

"Steve!" Pizza Guy said. "No!"

Sophia watched Pizza Guy's face turn a moderate shade of crimson that started at his shirt collar and continued up his face into his hairline. Even in the dim light of the car's parking lights it was obvious that he was embarrassed.

"And one hundred million points for Pizza Guy for not being a letch!" She thought. *"We are still on speaking terms."*

"Didn't you say she was wearing shorts?" Steve asked.

"She was! Dude! She had nice legs; they were really tan!" Pizza Guy said. "And I think she was a cheerleader too."

"Why?" Steve asked.

"Her shirt had some high school's name on it, and it said 'Cheerleader'." Pizza Guy said.

"So, do you think your new cheerleader girlfriend has an *all-over* tan; if you know what I mean?" Steve asked lewdly. "All those cheerleader girls go to tanning places you know."

"Okay, two million points from Steve the Letch." Sophia thought. *"And just so you know Steve-a-rino, this cheerleader, well…I guess it is former cheerleader now, goes to the fishing platform, takes off her clothes and takes long walks in the sun to get her tan! Sometimes, like tonight, she takes long walks in the moonlight too! Just saying!"*

"You are so wrong Steve!" Pizza Guy said. "Why do you think about girls like that?"

"And another hundred million points for Pizza Guy!" Sophia thought. *"That's two hundred million for Pizza Guy and a negative two million for Steve the Letch."*

Steve laughed, took a long drag on his cigarette then dropped it on the ground and crushed it out with his shoe and said, "Maybe she'll order another pizza sometime when you're riding with me and you can check her out some more!"

"I hope so!" Pizza Guy said. "I mean, I know where she lives, and her name is Sophia!"

"Aw! He remembered my name!" Sophia thought. *"Another hundred million points for Pizza Guy!"*

"Mount up, dude! We gotta get you home!" Steve said.

They got back into the car, cranked up the radio as Bryan Adams was lamenting about the summer of sixty-nine.

When they backed out onto the chip and sealed road, Steve gunned the car's engine and sped down the road toward town. Sophia waited a minute or two before standing up; she wanted to make sure they were gone.

"Pizza Guy thinks I'm cute, that I have nice legs and likes short hair even though he likes my long hair! I wonder if he would think I look good now?" Sophia thought.

The mud from the ditch wasn't like the mud she had smeared all over herself earlier in the day. The ditch mud was more like thick, muddy water, it would need to be washed off, but it would be easier to remove than the mud bath mud had been.

"You were almost seen…AGAIN!" Polly Pragmatic said.

"But I wasn't, so it's all good." Sophia replied.

"He was right in front of you! You could tell his face turned red when they were talking about you. He could have…" Pragmatic Polly began before Sophia cut her off.

"He could have had his way with me?" Sophia asked. *"I doubt that! I am covered in mud, and like you said, when that letch Steve was talking about my boobs, Pizza Guy's face turned red. He was embarrassed. And he <u>didn't</u> see me!*

I am tired of living in the 'what if'! I am going to live in the 'what is'! I am fine! Nothing happened! They didn't even know I was here! Now I am going back to The Grove to wash the mud off!" Sophia thought.

"Good! You are not at the bridge and that is the safe zone." Polly said.

"You're right Polly." Sophia said. *"I need to go back, and while I am walking, I am going to listen to one of Laura's tapes."*

She picked up her phone and flashlight and began walking back to the bridge while she listened to Laura's tape that was labeled "02-08-1964".

~ ~ ~ ~ ~ ~

Popping.

Crackling.

"Okay." Laura said. *"I have sooo much to tell you!"*

Popping.

Crackling.

"So, last night, Friday night, Jerry took me to the Winter Sports Banquet up in Ridgeway Center and I lettered in basketball again! I was so excited! Bill Morris was there and was being his usual jerky self, but in spite of that, I had a really good time!"

Popping.

Crackling.

"During the banquet it started to snow, and it just kept getting worse and worse. Ridgeway Center is something like fifty miles from here."

Popping.

Crackling.

"Jerry tried really hard to get us home, but the snow was just so bad. We finally had to stop in a little town, and I do mean little, called Freemont. There was a twenty-four-hour diner/motel there right off the highway and we were going to stay there until the storm stopped, but the diner was closing because of the storm."

Popping.
Crackling.

"I called Mom and Dad to let them know we were okay; they were glad we stopped and that's when Jerry told me the diner was closing. He also told me there was a room at the motel we could stay in if we wanted it. I guess the owner knew we were in trouble, so he just let us stay there for free."

Popping.
Crackling.

"Diary, last night I asked my parents if it were alright for me to spend the night in a motel with my boyfriend!

Let me tell you, that was something I NEVER thought I would EVER do! But I did and they were okay with it. They told me after I got home that we didn't have much of a choice and they trusted Jerry and me to do the right thing."

Popping.
Crackling.

"After we were in the room, Jerry did the sweetest thing. When I realized that I didn't have anything to sleep in, well, he didn't either. I guess we could have slept in our dress clothes, but I think my wool skirt wouldn't have been all that comfortable. Jerry went to the car and brought in his gym bag. His dad had let him take the car to school and he forgot to put his clean gym clothes in his locker. Thank goodness for that! He had two pairs of shorts and two tee shirts. He had one other thing in there, but I will not be discussing that!

Anyway, we changed clothes and Jerry did something else really sweet! There was only one bed and he said that I got it. Then he took the cushions from the couch and an extra blanket that was in the motel room's closet and made himself a pallet to sleep on the floor."

Popping.
Crackling.

"It stormed really bad last night; you could hear the ice and sleet and snow hitting the windows. I think it might have even thundered too! And the wind was something else, I had never heard wind actually howl, but it sure did last night. I'm glad we stopped and I'm glad I was with Jerry."

Popping.

Crackling.

"Diary, I need to tell you something."

Popping.

Crackling.

"Jerry was on his couch cushion pallet on the floor right next to the bed and I was able to reach down and hold his hand! After we turned off the lights, we started talking and..."

Popping.

Crackling.

"And I asked him to sleep with me."

Popping.

Crackling.

"He thought I was asking him to have sex and he said that he wanted to, but he was waiting for when we were married!"

Popping.

Crackling.

"He really said 'we'! Diary, I knew Jerry was special! I mean most guys would have...well...tried for a homerun if you know what I mean, but not Jerry. He got really flustered and I think kind of embarrassed.

I told him that I wanted him to sleep next to me, but not sleep with me. Does that make any sense at all? I told him that I was waiting too. I told him that what I said did sound like it meant something else and for him not to worry about it."

Popping.

Crackling.

"So, last night Jerry and I did sleep together, but we didn't sleep together. And I really liked being able to snuggle with him and fall asleep with his arms around me! With his blanket on top of the one already on the bed and us cuddled up together it was nice and toasty warm last night!"

Popping.

Crackling.

"But something did happen last night."

Popping.

Crackling.

"I woke up at about three in the morning and Jerry was right next to me with his arm draped across me snuggled up close and his hand was up my shirt! He was sort of... rubbing with his fingers!"

Popping.

Crackling.

"I was shocked at first, but when I looked at him, he was really deeply sound asleep. I said his name several times, but he never flinched. He just kept breathing slowly and steadily and his fingers kept doing what they were doing!"

Popping.

Crackling.

"I took his hand out of my shirt and when I finally woke him up and told him what he had been doing, he was so embarrassed! In fact, he started to cry because he was so upset by it. I think he thought I was going to break up with him and never speak to him again or something. I really felt sorry for him. I mean he was asleep when all that happened there is no doubt in my mind about that. So, I hugged him and told him I wasn't mad or anything and he calmed down. I did make him laugh when I said, 'You got to second base, and you don't even remember coming up to bat!'"

Popping.

Crackling.

"We talked for a while, but he kept apologizing about touching me. Finally, I told him that if he said he was sorry one more time I was going to get mad. He apologized for that too and we both laughed, then we just snuggled until we fell back asleep. Diary, I have never slept better in my life!"

Popping.

Crackling.

"This morning Jerry got up and took a shower then went out and cleaned off the car while I took my shower. He told me to take my time because he had looked outside, and the car was covered with snow and there was frozen sleet underneath that too. He said he thought it would take at least an hour to get everything cleaned off,

I was still in the bathroom when he came in to warm up and I didn't hear him. Before I took my shower, I had laid out my clothes on the bed and I really thought he was still going to be outside cleaning off the car, and I wouldn't have to worry about him being in the room."

Popping.

Crackling.

"I came out of the bathroom and around the corner not wearing anything AT ALL; not even a towel and Jerry was standing there and saw EVERYTHING!"

Popping.

Crackling.

"Diary, it doesn't seem like I get to make very many choices about anything that really matters. Those choices are made for me. But I made a choice this morning when that happened. It probably wasn't the smartest thing I have ever done, but it was my decision and my choice!"

Popping.

Crackling.

"When I saw him, I felt my face turn red, and I saw his did too but neither one of us looked away. For a moment it seemed like time stopped and all I could see was Jerry looking me over. I don't blame him one bit because had it been him standing there totally naked, I would have looked too.

Like I said, I made a choice, two actually. The first was coming out of the bathroom without anything on when Jerry could have been in the room. The second choice I made was what I did next."

Popping.

Crackling.

"I said, 'Jerry, take a good look. Because the next time you see me like this will be on our wedding night!' Then I walked over to where he was standing, his mouth was still wide open from the shock of it all, I guess. I said, 'On our wedding night you will get to do more than just look; I promise!' Then I reached up and grabbed his face, pulled him close and I kissed him like I had never kissed him before!"

Popping.

Crackling.

"When I was done, I said, 'Until then, you'll just have to use your imagination!'

Jerry said, 'Right now, there's no imagination required!'

I have to admit that I laughed out loud when he said that because he was absolutely right! I told him to '...enjoy this preview of coming attractions!' and he laughed!"

Popping.

Crackling.

"I went over and started getting dressed and he asked if I wanted to do that in private. I laughed again! I said, 'It's a little late for that don't you think Jerry?'"

"Yeah, I guess it is, so just take your time!" He said.

"My face flushed a little darker red, I could feel it, and we both laughed! Then Jerry <u>did</u> step outside for a few minutes."

Popping.

Crackling.

"We got breakfast in the diner then headed home after I called Mom and Dad and let them know we were on the way. The trip back was interesting to say the least, we giggled a lot and I think both our faces were red for most of the trip. If the heater and defroster had stopped working, the car would have still been warm from the heat from our faces!

When we finally got back to my house, he asked if he could tell me something, and I said sure. What he said was, 'I'm sorry I saw you without your clothes on Laura, but I'm not sorry either. I hope that doesn't make you mad or make me sound like a pervert or anything.'

'I'm not mad Jerry. It was kind of my fault what happened, but....'

'But what?' He asked.

'Did you like what you saw?' I asked.

His face turned red, he grinned and said, 'I wish I could see you like that every day for the rest of my life!'

'Once we are married you can! I promise!'

His face turned even more RED, I laughed, gave him a kiss, and reminded him what else he had done during the night and to not worry about it, then I went inside.

I hope what I did doesn't make me sound slutty or anything. I didn't mean for him to see me without anything on, but once he had I figured it didn't really matter!"

Popping.

Crackling.

"Someday diary, I am going to marry Jerry Collins and on our wedding night he and I are going to play a special game of baseball. I guarantee that he will hit the best homerun of his life; a grand slam!"

Popping.

Crackling.

Silence.

~ ~ ~ ~ ~ ~

"Wow Laura! When you make a choice, you really go all out and make a choice!" Sophia thought.

Chapter 29

When she got back to her campsite, she tossed her phone and earbuds onto the cot then waded across the pool to the waterfall where she washed the mud from her body.

Once that was done, she went to the fire ring. The fire was still burning, but it had died down considerably. Sophia tossed on four more logs and waited for them to catch. While she waited, she poured herself a cup of tea from the thermos and watched the flames, thinking, until her cup was empty.

"I think if I had a boyfriend like Jerry and he saw me without clothes on." Sophia thought. *"I would do what Laura did. I mean he had already seen everything so why get all crazy about it. It's not like they did The Big Monkey Ooo-Wah-Doo or anything!"*

Sophia considered putting the camp cot back in the tent, but when she checked the weather app on her phone, she saw the low temperature was predicted to be seventy. So instead, she got her fleece blanket, wrapped it around herself and looked at the sky through the circular opening of the sinkhole.

"I will be sleeping under the stars tonight!" She thought.

It was one-fifteen a.m., and her eyes were starting to get heavy. Before drifting off, she set the alarm on her phone for five-thirty, plugged it into one of the portable battery packs and closed her eyes; she was asleep almost immediately.

~ ~ ~ ~ ~ ~

"Sophia?" Laura said from far away. "Sophia, wake up!"

Sophia's eyes opened, but she didn't see Laura.

"Where are you?" Sophia asked.

"I'm over here." Laura said.

Sophia looked at the crescent shaped pool and saw Laura sitting at the edge of the pool wearing a dark navy blue and white striped bikini.

"WOWZAH!!!" Sophia said. "And you had two babies?"

Laura laughed. "This is fifteen-year-old me, Sophia, remember?"

"I wish I looked as good as you do." Sophia said.

"Sophia." Laura said. "You look amazing!"

"Well, you look pretty amazing yourself!" Sophia said and got up and went over and sat next to Laura. "What's up?"

"Just checking on my little risk taker." Laura said. "Why did you ride most of the way out here totally nude tonight?"

"Because I could!" Sophia said.

Laura laughed. *"Just so you know, those dates that I circled on your calendar are for the times when no one but you is between the bridge and the cemetery."*

"I figured that out, but I wasn't seen so it's all good!" Sophia said.

"You almost were seen." Laura said. *"Three different times."*

Sophia laughed. *"Don't you remember what you told me?"*

"What was that?" Laura asked.

"You said, 'Sometimes you have to do something a little crazy to prove that you are actually sane! Riding my bike out here and then walking back out to the chip and sealed road with nothing on and almost being seen proves that." Sophia said. *"But I bet that's not the reason you popped into my dreams again, is it?"*

Laura smiled. *"No, not really. I just want you to know when you are not between the bridge and the cemetery, you can get into trouble if you're not careful. But a mermaid would know that, right?"*

Sophia laughed out loud! *"I'm glad it was that little boy who saw me and not the older one. I mean he is starting high school and it would be more than just a little awkward to see him after he had seen me."*

"If that had happened, what would you have done?" Laura asked.

"I probably would have just talked to him." Sophia said. *"I mean, he would have already seen everything. But as someone who came out of a motel bathroom with nothing on, you would know that, right?"*

"Touché'!" Laura laughed. *"But I had known Jerry for almost a year and a half."*

Sophia giggled then asked, *"Would you like to see something?"*

"Sure!" Laura said.

"Come on." Sophia said and slid into the water.

They waded across the pool to the waterfall, but instead of walking through the pouring water, Sophia took Laura around the side of the falls and slipped behind them.

"This is the Art Gallery." Sophia said. *"And that is my first...uh...sculpture."* She pointed to the plaster casting.

"Now it's my turn to say WOWZAH!" Laura said. *"How did you make that?"*

Sophia told her even though she knew Laura already knew how it was made; she was, after all, having a dream and Laura knew everything she knew.

"Look at the back." Sophia said.

Laura read what Sophia had written, she even traced her finger across the words.

"What are you going to do with it?" Laura asked. "That is too pretty to leave back here behind the waterfall."

"I'm not sure." Sophia said.

"Why do you call it "Choices"?" Laura asked.

"Because I made a choice to make it, just like I made a choice to come out here the last few days and not wear any clothes." Sophia said.

"It sounds to me like you are doing something to get over being mad about having to move." Laura said. "Am I right?"

Sophia considered the question for a moment and realized that she was not nearly as angry as she had been. If she were honest, she would say the anger had started to subside once she had made the choice to take off her clothes, to make the plaster casting, and to cut her hair.

"You are." Sophia said.

"Part of getting over something is to take responsibility for what you have been telling yourself. Honestly, most of your unhappiness is coming from the things you think about." Laura said.

"Really?" Sophia asked.

"Yes Sophia." Laura said. "What have you been thinking about this summer?"

Sophia took a deep breath. "How unfair everything has been. Having had to move with, like, three weeks' notice. Missing my friends. Giving up my cheerleading spot. And not having a choice about any of it, but I think you already know all of that." Sophia said.

"What have you been thinking about while you have been out at the bridge and here?" Laura asked as she gestured at the Art Gallery, the waterfall and the rest of the sinkhole.

"That I like myself." Sophia said. "That I like not wearing clothes! That I have an awesome tan! And that I look amazing!"

"And?" Laura asked.

"And...Pizza Guy is totally cute, and he and I will probably be in some of the same classes!" Sophia said.

Laura laughed her sweet, melodious laugh! "Now you're talking!"

"So, am I cured of being angry?" Sophia asked.

"That's totally up to you." Laura said. "You can be bitter, or you can be better."

"You are right!" Sophia said.

"Now, what are you going to do with that?" Laura pointed at the plaster casting.

"I don't know." Sophia said. *"I really like how it looks, but it's not like I can show it to my parents. They would probably have a stroke if they saw it and knew it was me who made it."*

"Probably." Laura said. *"But if you had found it at that store a few doors down from the ice cream place...?"*

"Oh!" Sophia said. *"I saw an old oak shelf in the trash a couple of houses down on my bike ride out here tonight; I could mount it on that if I knew how to do that."*

Laura whispered in her ear.

"Really?" Sophia said.

"Really!" Laura said. *"Take a chance, make a choice!"*

"I think I will!" Sophia said.

Laura and Sophia left the Art Gallery.

"I have to be going Sophia." Laura said.

"Will I see you again?" Sophia asked.

"Certainly!" Laura said. *"And just so you know, with what I just told you, you won't get caught or be seen, so have fun!"*

~ ~ ~ ~ ~ ~

Sophia sat up with a start. She was in the sinkhole, but Laura was gone. She looked at the clock on her phone.

"That can't be right?" She thought.

The clock showed that it was one forty-five; she had slept only thirty minutes, but she felt like she had slept all night. She laughed knowing what she was going to do and knowing it would be the riskiest thing she had *ever* done in her life.

"Sometimes you have to do something a little crazy to prove that you are actually sane!" She thought.

She splashed her way to the Art Gallery and retrieved her plaster casting. When she got back to her camp cot, she wrapped it up in the two towels she had brought with her and placed her plaster clone in the dry bag, slipped on her tennis shoes and headed up out of the sinkhole to her bike and she rode back to the house!

~ ~ ~ ~ ~ ~

She rolled into the garage at two-ten, then scampered down the street and acquired the oak board she had seen there. Once back in the garage she used a large bottle of glue to mount the plaster casting to it, then she took a picture of it.

"It will be dry when I get home tomorrow." She thought. *"Actually, it already is tomorrow!"*

She started to get back on her bike but paused and opened the internet browser on her phone, went to her favorite online shopping site that had free shipping and designed and ordered an antique looking adhesive backed engraved plaque, hit the "checkout" button and was stunned to see that her order would arrive by eleven thirty a.m.!

The plaque said:

~ Choices ~
"Sometimes you have to do something a
little crazy to prove that you are actually sane!"

"It will be here before Mom and Dad get back!" Sophia thought. *"Too cool!"*

~ ~ ~ ~ ~ ~

She got back to the Grove at three-fifteen and laid back down on her cot and thought, *"Polly, that was, by far the absolute most stupid thing I have ever done! But man, it was fun!"*

Polly didn't answer and Sophia didn't care. She quickly tapped out a text message to her parents and set the delay so it wouldn't be sent until nine-thirty in the morning. The text told her parents what she had found at the junk store, that she thought it was pretty artistic and wanted to keep it and she included a picture. Then she plugged her phone back into the portable battery, pulled the fleece blanket over herself and fell into a deep, restful dreamless sleep.

~ ~ ~ ~ ~ ~

Sophia woke up refreshed and giggled when she realized that sometime in the night, she had kicked the fleece blanket off and was lying on her camp cot completely uncovered. She stretched and grabbed her phone that told her it was already seventy-eight degrees and seven-thirty.

"Oh man!" She thought. *"I missed seeing the sun come up."*

She changed the phone's alarm for ten-thirty. If her parents were going to be home by noon, she wanted to be at the house and ready to go get her haircut when they got back.

She sat up and looked at the crescent shaped pool. The waterfall splashing into it was loud, but the call of nature was louder.

Sophia went to the water's edge and dipped her toes in, which caused her to shiver and increased her discomfort, then she waded into the water. Her intent was to go only waist deep, but as she waded toward the deeper end of the pool, she misjudged where she was, stepped off the ledge and she went completely under!

"COLD! COLD! COLD! Oh, this is cold!" Sophia sputtered as she surfaced.

She considered getting out of the water, but because she was already wet, she made ten laps back and forth across the length of the pool.

"Sometimes you have to do something a little crazy to prove that you are actually sane." She thought.

She stepped out of the pool, wrung as much water from her hair as she could, then got her thermos out of the tent and poured herself a cup of hot tea. She considered wrapping up in the fleece blanket; the water had been cold, and she had goose flesh, but resisted the urge. Instead, she sat on the camp cot drinking her tea. When the first cup was finished, she poured herself a second and ate two of the hard-boiled eggs she had packed in the lunch box. She was not a big breakfast eater, so the eggs sufficed.

"I think I am done with swimming for a while." She thought. *"But I am definitely not done hiking! But now I need to take a shower! Then I'll put on the good old Tan Booster Ten!"*

She crawled back into her tent, dumped out the backpack and gathered up the toiletries she had brought along. As she headed to the waterfall, she picked up her phone and earbuds.

"And I think I'll listen to another one of Laura's tapes!" She said to herself. The recording was dated "05-17-1964".

~ ~ ~ ~ ~ ~

Popping.

Crackling.

"'So…' Laura said. "Jerry and I went to Prom!!! It was so much fun, and we were the only Sophomores there thanks to Amy and Will! But…'"

Popping.

Crackling.

"'There's always a 'but' isn't there? In this case, the 'but' was Bill Morris. He showed up drunk or stoned or both and tried to blame me for him getting kicked off the basketball team. Then he made some really inappropriate remarks to me saying my dress would look good wadded up on the floor in the back seat of his car! I'll become a nun before I would do anything like that with him!

Jerry tried to stop what was happening, but Bill sucker punched him and that really made me angry! I was probably the angriest I have ever been when he did that, so I took care of Bill Morris."

Popping.

Crackling.

"Diary, I kneed Bill Morris where it counted, and he dropped. A little while later the police came and arrested him. I have never seen anything like that in my life!"

Popping.

Crackling.

"After we left the Prom, Will and Amy and Jerry and I went to a place called The Roadhouse. Mom and Dad weren't too crazy about us going to a roadhouse, but after we explained it was just the name, they were okay with it. I think Dad called around and checked with some other parents before he said yes."

Popping.

Crackling.

"The Roadhouse was a pit. We didn't stay very long."

Popping.

Crackling.

"Morton's stayed open until two in the morning so anyone who went to Prom could come in for ice cream or a soda or whatever. We went there and shared a banana split then left."

Laura laughed out loud!

"I guess you could say, we split a split then split! Then the four of us drove out to the covered bridge. It is really becoming one of my favorite places! I'm glad Jerry took me out there and showed it to me last summer, otherwise I would have never gone skinny dipping or got a sunburn on places that should not get sunburned! Now that I think about it, that sunburn <u>was</u> Jerry's fault!"

Laura laughed!

"When we got there, Jerry and Amy and Will and I just sat in the car and talked.

Well....Jerry and I may have kissed too, but...

I finally got home around three! I have never stayed out so late, but when I got up Mom and Dad didn't say anything, so I guess it wasn't too late."

Popping.

Crackling.

"Diary, I had so much fun last night! And I realized again how wonderful Jerry really is. "I love him!" Laura said.

Popping.

Crackling.

Silence.

~ ~ ~ ~ ~ ~

The floor of the space she had named The Art Gallery made the perfect shelf for holding her toiletries. She stepped behind the waterfall and placed the items on the stone shelf then stepped into the pouring water.

When her shower was done, she exited the waterfall and climbed out of the pool. She sat on the camp cot and braided her hair like Laura had showed her.

"I won't be doing this for a while." She thought. *"It's going to be weird having short hair. I haven't had my hair above my collar since I was nine."*

When the braid was done, Sophia folded up the camp cot and slid it into the carrying bag, then put her book and the Tan Booster Ten suntan lotion into her drawstring backpack. She took down the tent and put it, and the other camping gear, back into the dry bag and carried it all to the top of the stone staircase where she had parked her bicycle.

"I'm going to make sure my tan lines are really gone. And I know where I am going to go lay out too!" She thought.

She shouldered the camp cot and the backpack, grabbed her phone and trekked down the stone path into the hot, humid, brightly sunny morning!

Chapter 30

Sophia unfolded the camp cot next to the apple-colored headstone, then covered herself with the suntan lotion. The sun was bright, the day was going to be hot, and her tan lines were going to be gone.

The suntan lotion absorbed quickly, and she took her copy of the book from the backpack and laid prone on the cot enjoying the heat of the sun on her back. From somewhere behind her she heard a sound that made her stomach sink and her face turn hot; it was a very distinct "wolf whistle".

"Busted!" Polly Pragmatic said from inside her head. "And you don't even have a towel! I told you so!"

"SHUT UP!" Sophia said to her inner self.

She laid the book on the cot and stood up, no reason to try and hide herself because she had nothing to hide with and whoever was watching had already seen her, so stepping behind the headstone would be wasted effort.

"I hope they like Goldilocks." She thought.

She looked around the cemetery for whomever was watching and whistling at her.

She saw no one.

The whistle came again.

"Hello?" She said. "Who's there?"

The whistle came again, and it sounded very close. Sophia made a slow three hundred sixty-degree turn looking for whomever was watching her. The knot in the pit of her stomach tightened and was joined by a coldness that began at her bare feet and rose to the top of her head. She did not see anyone and was starting to get a little scared. What she did see was a small bird sitting atop a headstone not ten feet from her. Its body was grey, and its head was yellow with orange spots on the sides.

"Hello?' Sophia said.

The bird hopped across the headstone and said, "Hello."

"Did you whistle at me?" Sophia asked.

The bird whistled again, and Sophia started to laugh, her trepidation instantly evaporating. She picked up her phone and took a picture of her feathered voyeur. She opened her internet browser and began searching for what type of bird she was seeing.

"Hello." The bird mimicked again.

"Do I look good Mister Bird?" Sophia asked as she searched.

Mister Bird wolf whistled again!

"Thank you so much Mister Bird!" Sophia said with a giggle.

Her first search did not turn up any pictures that resembled Mister Bird so she redid it, this time entering in: "Birds that can whistle". After hitting search, she was pleased to see a picture that looked exactly like Mister Bird on her phone's screen.

"Are you a cockatiel, Mister Bird?" She asked and was rewarded with another wolf whistle! "You really should learn to say WOWZAH!" Sophia said. Mister Bird just looked at her from atop the headstone. "Can you say 'WOWZAH', Mister Bird?"

Mister Bird wolf whistled again then very clearly and plainly said, "WOWZAH!"

"Thank you, Mister Bird!" Sophia laughed. "You really know how to make a girl feel good!"

Mister Bird wolf whistled again, said, "WOWZAH!" then took flight for parts unknown.

Sophia, giggling, returned to the cot, picked up the book and began reading again.

~ ~ ~ ~ ~ ~

She read about Jerry and Laura getting ready to have their senior pictures taken. When she turned the page, she found herself staring into Laura's face.

"Oh wow! Laura, your eyes are so beautiful!" Sophia thought. *"Wowzah!"*

She rolled onto her back and started to read about Laura's eighteenth birthday but put the book down when she saw it was August eleventh.

"I wonder." She thought and picked up her phone and the ear bud case. *"Isn't that the next date on Laura's tapes?"*

With her fingers flying over the screen of her smart phone, she quickly found the audio file list and saw the date "08-11-1965". She smiled, inserted the ear buds and pressed the virtual play button.

~ ~ ~ ~ ~ ~

Popping.
Crackling.
"This is going to be short because I don't know what to say... I am totally at a loss for words."
Laura was laughing and crying at the same time.
Popping.
Crackling.
"Diary....I AM ENGAGED!!!!"

Popping.

Crackling.

Crying.

"OH MY GOSH! Jerry asked me to marry him!!!"

Popping.

Crackling.

"I said YES!!!"

Popping.

Crackling.

Silence.

~ ~ ~ ~ ~ ~

"Oh wow! They got engaged right before they started their senior year of high school! They were so young!" Sophia thought.

She read about their senior year and the planning of their wedding.

She felt herself smiling as she read about the ceremony that had taken place on the Little Grand Covered Bridge!

Sophia felt her face redden just a little as their honeymoon was discussed, because after what Laura had said when recounting the events of being stranded with Jerry during the snowstorm all she could think of was, *"Grand slam!"*

She read about their first Thanksgiving and Laura's unplanned trip to the bathroom.

Then she read how on Christmas they told their parents they were going to be grandparents!

She read Laura's accounts as her pregnancy progressed. She loved what Jerry had said and done when Laura had broken down into tears before telling him they were going to have twins.

She read about how Laura and Jerry's lives changed once the babies were born, how much they loved being Stephen and Stephanie's parents and how quickly the babies became toddlers!

Sophia cried when she read about Laura and the kids getting stung by wasps on their second birthday.

"Those poor babies." Sophia thought.

She laughed out loud when she read what Stephen and Stephanie called the dandelions that had gone to seed when they visited a park the day after being stung.

"Dandyflowers would be a really good name for a book!" She thought.

Sophia stood up and walked around. It was nine o'clock and she had been lying out in the sun for over an hour, reading. She wanted to stretch her legs a bit before finishing the book.

She strolled around the cemetery looking at the headstones and grave markers reading the names and thinking about what all of these people had seen and done during their lives. Finally, she found herself back in front of Laura's headstone.

"What happened to you Laura?" She asked looking at the family picture. *"What happened to you and your babies?"*

Sophia laid down on the cot, picked up the book and began reading again. In just a very few minutes the questions she had asked the picture were answered and Sophia wept.

The emotion that poured forth was like none she had ever experienced. Her tears and sobs erupted and were greater and more intense than those when she had broken down in the old barn. The emotions were so intense, she thought for a little while that they would never end.

When they finally subsided, and it took a while, Sophia finished the book. She hated how the story ended, but she loved how it ended too. If what she had read about had not happened, there would not be a story.

"But I don't have to like it." She thought as she gathered up her things and walked back to her bicycle.

~ ~ ~ ~ ~ ~

At ten-thirty, she was almost back to the bridge when her phone's alarm went off reminding her to head back to the house so she would be there when her parents got back.

She rode across the bridge without stopping; she was thinking about Laura and what had happened to her in that long-ago summer of nineteen sixty-nine. She was also thinking about herself and what had happened to her this summer. She was so into her thoughts that she had just passed the old barn when she remembered she was wearing only her tennis shoes and suntan lotion.

"Ooops!" She thought and rode back to the old barn to put on some clothes.

It was a good thing too, because just as her tee shirt was sliding down over her chest, four pickup trucks drove by as they headed away from town. The truck's beds each contained no less than five teenaged boys that were most likely going out to help some farmers put up hay.

"That would have definitely been very awkward!" She said to herself.

"WHAT?" Her Polly Pragmatic voice said. "Are we finally becoming modest and actually do care if we are seen running around naked...I mean...NUDE?"

"Maybe just a little." She confessed to herself. *"But I will still go out to the bridge and most definitely to The Grove and go skinny dipping!"*

~ ~ ~ ~ ~ ~

She arrived back at the house at eleven o'clock. Before taking another shower, this time in her bathroom, Sophia checked the front porch and saw that her package had arrived, so she went to the garage, put away the camping equipment then affixed the brass plaque below her plaster casting and carried it to her room.

~ ~ ~ ~ ~ ~

She had just gotten out of the shower when she heard the van pull in the driveway. It was eleven fifty-nine.

"They are back and right on time!" Sophia thought.

Walking around the house totally nude was no longer an option, so she put on the loosest clothes she could find but did not put on any underwear. She had gotten used to not having anything on her body, so wearing an oversized tee shirt and loose-fitting shorts was a close second. She would, after all, have to be dressed when she went to get her hair cut.

"The things I must endure." She thought with a laugh!

Sophia had completely dried her hair before either of her parents had come inside which she thought was a bit odd, but her birthday was tomorrow, and they were probably hiding whatever it was they had gotten for her somewhere out in the garage.

The pocket door slid partially open, and her mother called to her down the hall.

"Sophia, we are back! Are you here?" Carol said.

Once the pocket door had been rediscovered, the unspoken rule was the area down the hall, especially her room, was Sophia's space and her parents would only enter uninvited if it were absolutely necessary.

Sophia poked her head out her bedroom door with a look of mock surprise on her face then ducked back into her room and loudly said, "You have to leave through the window guys, my parents are home!"

"Was it the entire football team Sophia?" Carol called down the hallway.

"Nah, just half of them. The other half are just too offensive!" She said stepping into the hallway grinning and pulling her hair into a ponytail.

Carol laughed! "Are you sure you want to get your hair cut?"

"Oh, here we go. She and Dad don't like the idea of me cutting my hair and they have decided not to let me cut it." Sophia thought.

"Yup!" Sophia said. "New town, new school, new hair, new me!"

"Well, let's go! We have to be there in ten minutes." Carol said.

"Where's Dad?" Sophia asked.

"I dropped him off at the post office." Carol said. "He had some things from his class to put in his office."

"How's he getting home?" Sophia asked.

"We'll bring him. He's going to meet us at the salon. It's only two blocks from the post office." Carol said. "Now, we need to be going. Do you have a picture of how you want it cut?"

Sophia held up her phone.

"Let's go!" She said.

~ ~ ~ ~ ~ ~

"First National Bangs" was located in an old bank building and someone had had some fun when naming the salon. The old lobby was absolutely beautiful with its early twentieth century décor. There were no less than a dozen overstuffed chairs and sofas sitting around where people could wait until their stylist could work their magic on them.

Sophia chuckled when she saw where the old teller windows had been; they had been replaced with sinks, styling chairs, mirrors and everything else needed to style someone's hair.

The old vault door was open, and she could see where lock boxes and cash had once been stored, shelves had been added to display various hair care products.

"Are you Sophia?" A lady asked as she got up from one of the styling chairs and walked over to her and her mother.

Other than the stylists, Sophia and Carol were the only other people in the building.

"I am!" Sophia said.

She thought about saying, *"This is she!"*, to irritate her mother, but didn't.

"I'm Doni! My mother works at the post office with your dad." Doni said, then turned to Carol. "And you must be Carol!"

"Thank you for getting us in so fast!" Carol said.

"I had a cancellation. Otherwise, it might have been two or three weeks before my next opening." Doni said. "So, what are we doing?"

"Just as second." Sophia said and pulled out her phone. "I want something like this."

She showed Doni several pictures of Calysta Bevier when she had been on America's Got Talent.

"I heard her sing when she was on that show!" Doni gushed. "And we can get your hair looking like that if you are sure you want it that short."

"I'm sure!" Sophia confirmed. "New town, new school, new hair, new me!"

"Well, all right!" Doni said. "Let's get to it!"

"One thing first." She said.

Sophia handed her phone to her mother and removed the hair ties. Her ponytail disappeared as her hair dropped and fanned out across her back.

"Take a before picture Mom." She said. "I doubt I have my hair this long again for quite a while."

"If you're having second thoughts…" Carol began.

"No second thoughts." Sophia said. "I just want a picture of how long my hair…*was*."

Carol snapped several pictures.

"And you are donating your hair so it can be used to make wigs for cancer patients, right?" Doni asked as she led her to one of the old teller window stalls.

"Yes!" Sophia said. "Someone should get some good out of it!"

"You'll get some good out of it, your haircut is free!" Doni said. "Now, I need to put your hair into a braid so we can get started."

"Hang on." Sophia said and she deftly began braiding her hair the way Laura had showed her.

"Where did you learn to do that?" Carol asked.

"You wouldn't believe me if I told you." Sophia said.

"Honey, are you sure you want to cut it all off?" Doni asked. "I mean you can do so much with all that hair."

"It's just hair. If I don't like it short, it will grow back! Besides, the folks with cancer need it more than I do." Sophia said. "Mom, take a picture of the braid too."

Carol snapped more pictures, then Sophia sat in the styling chair and said, "Let's do this!"

"Here we go!" Doni said.

She picked up a large pair of scissors and with a few quick snips the braid thumped heavily onto the floor.

"How's that feel?" Doni asked.

"Lighter!" Sophia said. "A lot lighter!"

Doni picked up the eighteen-inch-long braid. "I think a couple of wigs can be made out of all this beautiful hair!"

~ ~ ~ ~ ~ ~

For the next hour or so Doni worked her magic using scissors, gel, a curling iron and a blow dryer to get Sophia's hair into an easy to take care of style that closely resembled Calysta Bevier's. It would have taken less time, but Carol asked a lot of questions about hair related things and Doni explained them in great detail.

"What do you think?" Doni asked once she was done.

She stood behind Sophia holding a large mirror that let her see the back of her head while looking in the mirror in front of her.

"I think…" Sophia began as she turned her head from side to side looking at the front, back and both sides of her newly cut hair. "I LOVE it!"

"What do you think Mom?" Doni asked Carol.

"Sophia, that short hair will take some getting used to, but it looks _really_ good on you!" Carol said.

"What do you think Dad?" Doni asked Dan as he stepped up beside Carol.

"I'm going to have to get a shotgun!" Dan said. "The fellows will be knocking the door down wanting to ask you out!"

"I'll only talk to the ones with fancy names and who bring their banjos!" Sophia giggled.

"Banjos?" Doni asked.

Sophia laughed. "It's a long story!"

"Oh, okay." Doni said.

"Mom take some pictures! I want to text them to the girls and see what they think." Sophia said still admiring her new hair style in the mirror in front of her.

"No!" Carol said. "I don't think so."

"Why not?" Sophia asked. "I want to know what Leah and Laney and Audrey think about my new doo."

Carol, Dan and Doni, who had been standing shoulder to shoulder, moved apart. There, looking at Sophia with big smiles on their faces _were_ Leah, Laney and Audrey!

"Gorgeous!" Leah said.

"Fantastic!" Laney added.

"It is to die for!" Audrey finished.

Then, in unison, all three of them said, "WOWZAH!"

"Wha…?" Was all Sophia could say before the tears began.

She was totally off-balance with the shock at seeing her friends for the first time in weeks.

The three girls converged around the chair where Sophia was sitting and gave her the best hug she had ever had in her entire life!

"Just so you know." Dan said. "You are going to be stuck with these three hooligans until Sunday afternoon!"

"Really?" Sophia said through her tears.

"Yes, really! And you're going to have to celebrate your birthday with them too!" Carol said with a broad smile. "No arguments!"

Wiping her eyes with the backs of her hands and laughing Sophia said, "I'll do my best to get through it!"

"You three, spin her around and scooch in beside her, I want a picture!" Carol said to Leah, Laney and Audrey.

Leah spun the chair to face Sophia's parents, then moved to her right, Laney moved to her left and Audrey moved behind her. Carol captured the moment with Sophia's cell phone camera.

"Now." Doni said taking the phone from Carol. She had stepped aside and watched as Sophia was reunited with her friends. "You two get in there!" Carol and Dan stood behind Leah and Laney while the group photo was taken.

"By the way Sophia, my class in Columbia *was* a one-day class." Dan admitted. "When your mother called you and said it had been extended, we were on our way to Springfield. We had to finish up some things with the sale of the old house. Well, that and to pick up these three!"

"When we saw that your dad's training was going to be right before your birthday and that we needed to go back to Springfield to finish up the business with the house, we started plotting this little reunion!" Carol said.

"You two lied to me?" Sophia asked.

"'Lied' is such a harsh word." Dan said with a grin. "I prefer to call it a creative distortion of the truth to affect a planned outcome!"

"I'll remember that if I ever get accused of lying!" Sophia said.

Leah's stomach growled loudly causing her to giggle. "Sorry, but it's been a while since breakfast." She said.

"In that case." Dan said. "Let us begin the birthday celebration weekend festivities with a trip to Show Me Pizza! They do have a really good salad bar and the pizza is pretty good too! And since I didn't have to pay for a haircut…"

"Oh wow!" Sophia thought. *"What if Pizza Guy is there. This could be fun!"*

Pizza Guy was not at Show Me Pizza, but Sophia didn't mind. The salad was good, the pizza was better, but being with her three friends was the best!

Chapter 31

They arrived back at the house and Dan pulled the van in the garage next to his pickup where the six of them piled out.

"Before you go inside Soph there is something we want to show you." He said.

Sophia started to speak, but before a single word could come out, Laney covered her mouth with a piece of grey duct tape, Leah grabbed her hands and Audrey took a red bandana from Sophia's mom and blindfolded her.

"Not a word Sophia." Laney said.

"You do ask a lot of questions sometimes." Leah said.

"You are going to love this!" Audrey added.

Sophia giggled and Leah put her left hand into her mother's hands and her right hand into her father's hands.

"We never did find that white cane." Carol said. "So, your dad and I will have to guide you. Is that okay?"

Sophia nodded her head. If the five of them had felt it necessary to gag her, blindfold her and restrain her hands, whatever was coming had to be something special!

"Open the door Leah." Dan said. "Push eight, two, five, zero and five."

"My birthday!" Sophia thought.

With her parents at her side, they walked her towards the door that opened into the back half of the garage. Stepping through the doorway, Sophia felt the slightly humid air change and the scent of freshly sawn wood was even stronger than when she noticed it the night before while packing her camping supplies in the large dry bag. There was another smell that was familiar, but she couldn't quite place it.

"What do you think ladies?" Carol asked. "Should we take off the blindfold?"

"On three!" Audrey said.

"One!" Leah shouted.

"Two!" Laney cried.

"Three!" They all yelled.

Sophia's hands were released, she slipped the bandana from her eyes and removed the duct tape. She couldn't see anything except for what little light that was coming in from the front part of the garage they had just left.

"Oh goody!" She said. "You have captured total darkness in the back half of the garage. Where *did* you find Harry Potter's deluminator?"

The group laughed!

"Let me get the lights. Be careful Sophia, we wouldn't want you to burn out your retinas again!" Carol said.

The lights came on and her dad announced, "The Pool Room!"

Filling half of this part of the garage nearly front to back was an above ground swimming pool that was surrounded by a wooden deck! On the end of the deck closest to where they were standing was a large table and several chairs. There was also a large stainless-steel bar-be-que grill with a sign above it that read, "Welcome to Our Deck – Sit Long, Talk Much, Laugh Often!"! On the opposite end was a box that had a small set of stairs next to it.

"What is that?" Sophia asked pointing to the box.

"That, is a six-person hot tub!" Carol said.

"No way!" Sophia exclaimed. "A pool and a hot tub? For real?"

"Yes way!" Dan said. "A pool and a hot tub! For real!"

The open half of the garage was covered in a green, short napped plastic carpeting that gave the area an outdoor feel. There were five large, mismatched couches sitting around an extra-large coffee table. The couches reminded Sophia of the hair salon.

Mounted on the wall between two windows that had been covered over with thick brown paper was their old fifty-inch smart television. When they had moved from Springfield, they had purchased a seventy-inch model for their new and larger living room.

"I wondered what happened to that." Sophia thought.

Directly underneath the T.V. was a shelf that held a DVD player, a stereo system, the remotes for the various devices and the control unit for an old, but quite functional, speaker system Dan had found online for the ridiculous price of twenty dollars. He, or someone, had mounted the speaker system's eight speakers around the pool room.

"Just a second." Carol said and went over to the stereo where she switched it on, and "Happy Birthday" began playing in surround sound!

"Are you kidding me!" She asked.

"No!" Carol said. "Tomorrow is your birthday!" She switched off the music.

Sophia laughed! "I mean…" She said. "A pool and a hot tub?"

"The pool is four feet deep, twenty-four feet long, eight feet wide and…" Dan said, pausing for effect. "It's also heated so it can be used even in the winter-time!"

"Definitely not going skinny dipping at the spring in the winter now!" Sophia thought.

She mounted the stairs to the pool's deck with her friends and parents behind her. As she stood looking at the pool she asked, "How did you do all of this without me knowing about it?"

"We were going to tell you, but when you spent Sunday and Monday helping Maude Adelaide clean, I had the pool guys come over and do the work!" Dan said. "We knew you would be helping her all day, so we were able to get the pool guys out of here before you got back. I was really glad they didn't mind working on a Sunday."

"It only took them two days to do all of this?" Sophia asked unbelievingly.

"All of this was a discontinued floor model, so they were able to take it apart in large sections and reassemble it here in about a day and a half. They finished around two o'clock on Monday and I started filling it when they left." Dan said. "Bringing the pieces in through there made it really easy too!"

He pointed to the back of the garage and Sophia realized the back wall was actually a large garage door.

"I'm going to make a screen wall that will fit into the opening when the door is open so we can enjoy the summer breeze without the summer bugs!" He added.

"And that is a hot tub?" Sophia asked again looking at the box with the stairs next to it.

"And that is a hot tub!" Carol said. "Over there is a bathroom / changing room and shower!" She pointed to a walled off area on the bar-be-que grill end of the pool. "The bathroom and shower was already here, and your dad added the changing room. It will make using this area so much easier."

"You won't have to run across the yard practically naked to go in the house to change or use the bathroom." Dan said.

"Been there, done that." Sophia thought. *"But Dad, there was no 'practically' about it when I did it! And just so you know, the gutters make a pretty good shower when it's raining!"*

"Where did those bikes come from?" Sophia asked.

"Those belong to these three." Carol said. "I had to take them out of the van when I got back so you wouldn't see them."

"*That's* why it took you so long to come in the house when you got back." Sophia said.

"Yes! Now, I want a picture!" Carol said. "Girls, where are your phones?"

Sophia handed hers over. Leah pulled her phone from her pocket and gave it to Carol. Laney and Audrey searched for their phones but then remembered they had left them charging in the van.

"By the way Sophia, that picture of that sculpture you sent with your text this morning, what was that all about?" Carol asked.

Sophia spun her story and told her parents that she had put the sculpture in her closet if they wanted to see it.

"I'm not lying." Sophia thought. *"I am creatively distorting the truth to affect a planned outcome! And the outcome I am planning is one where I don't get grounded for the rest of my life!"*

"I like it, but I'm not sure where I am going to put it." Sophia said.

"Why not out here?" Carol suggested. "I kind of like it even if it's a nude."

"What are you all talking about?" Audrey asked. "A nude sculpture?"

"Hang on." Sophia said. "I'll be right back."

She went to her room and retrieved "Choices". Before taking it to the Pool Room, she draped a towel over it so she could have a grand reveal.

When she got back, she propped it up on one of the couches and said, "Ladies and Dad! I give you… "Choices"!"

Everyone admired the sculpture and speculated how old it was. Sophia didn't say much, she just listened and tried not to laugh.

Dan found a bracket that he mounted on the back of the oak board, and with the direction of his wife, his daughter and her three best friends, he hung it on the wall behind the hot tub.

"That is beautiful!" Leah said and took her phone from Carol and snapped a picture of it and handed her phone back.

"That is really life-like." Carol said as she admired "Choices". "Whoever made that is an amazing artist! How much did you pay for it Soph?"

"Would you believe fifteen dollars?" She asked.

"You got a bargain!" Carol said. "But now I want to take a picture of you four by the pool."

"Wait, wait, wait." Dan said. "You all need to hold on to this." He brought out a large inflatable palm tree pool float. "It came with the pool!" He said.

"Well, you can't have too many four-foot-long inflatable palm trees now can you." Audrey said.

Carol held up one of the phones as the girls took hold of the palm tree which Dan then used like a snowplow to push them backwards into the pool.

There were shrieks, screams and one elongated "Nooooo!" from Sophia that lasted until she disappeared under the pool's surface. The four surfaced looking much like cats that had been dunked in an overly large, yet nicely chlorinated rain barrel.

"You know what Dad?" Sophia asked dripping with water and sarcasm.

"What's that Sophia-Love!" Dan responded through snorts of laughter.

"Someday you will want one of us to sneak liquor to you when you are in The Home." Sophia said. "But after today, all you will be getting is prune juice!"

"That's a risk I am willing to take!" Dan said dodging some half-hearted attempts from Audrey to splash him.

"Mom, would you go get us some towels please." Sophia asked.

"I'll get your swimsuit too. The others have theirs in the van." Carol said.

"They do?" Sophia asked her mother.

She hadn't noticed anything in the van other than her three friends.

"They do!" Carol said. "I moved their stuff all the way to the back of the van so you wouldn't see it when we went to get your hair cut."

"I'll go get your bags out of the van." Dan said. "It's the least I can do."

"Get our phones too." Laney said. "We need to call the child abuse hotline!"

Dan laughed and went to the van and Sophia, Leah, Laney and Audrey pulled themselves up onto the edge of the pool.

"Well Sophia." Audrey said. "Your hair *did* look good."

"I don't care." Sophia said. "I'm just glad you three are here!"

She felt the tears begin to well-up and the lump begin to form in her throat, but this time those well-known feelings were different. They were not because she was sad or angry or hurt; those feelings had evaporated the moment she had seen her three best friends at the hair salon. No, these tears and this lump was because she was incredibly happy!

"Here you go!" Dan said returning from the van with three overstuffed backpacks, two cell phones and associated charging cords. He sat them on one of the sofas.

"We may let you live." Laney said.

"As our slave." Audrey added.

"Who brings us ice cream!" Leah said.

Dan looked at them then asked, "Don't you have anything to add Sophia?"

"I got nothing." Sophia said. "But I do agree with the ice cream idea!"

"We do have to get some groceries Dan." Carol said as she reappeared from the house carrying an arm load of towels and Sophia's swimsuit. "But we'll need to go somewhere besides the little grocery store here."

"It's three o'clock." Dan said looking at his watch. "If we went to Macon, we wouldn't be getting back until about five if we leave now."

"The sooner you leave, the sooner you'll get back." Sophia said.

"And the sooner you can bring us ice cream!" Leah said.

"Will you four be alright?" Carol asked.

"We'll probably drown." Laney said.

"After raiding the liquor cabinet." Leah added, which really surprised everyone. She was usually the more reserved one of the quartet of friends.

"And inviting the whole football team over!" Sophia said. "Even the offensive ones!"

"That pretty much covers everything." Audrey said. "We're doomed!"

"We will be back as soon as we can." Carol laughed as she and Dan headed toward the door to the front part of the garage and the SCR-MOM van.

"Let's get our swimsuits on." Laney said. "Dibs on the bathroom!"

"Oh, for Pete's sake Laney, it's not like we haven't been changing in front of each other since forever." Leah said.

"She's right." Sophia said. "But let me check one thing first."

She went to the doorway that opened into the garage to make sure her parents had actually left. Seeing they had, she pressed the button that closed the garage door.

"It's just us." She announced and peeled off her shirt.

Audrey gasped audibly, "Whoa Sophia!"

"What?" She asked. "You've seen me without a shirt on before. If you remember at our last sleepover, you saw me walking down the street without *anything* on."

"I know that." Audrey said. "But…"

"But what?" Sophia asked.

"But…" Audrey began. "You are tan all over, front and back. Where are your tan lines?"

"You've been laying out topless, haven't you?" Laney asked.

"She sure has!" Leah added. "I mean look at her! You naughty girl!"

"I have done more than gone topless." Sophia said.

Like she had done with her sweatpants on the fishing platform on her first full day of not wearing clothes; she loosened the drawstring that held her shorts around her waist and let them drop around her ankles before she kicked them to one side.

"You have NO tan lines!" Leah observed. "None at all!"

"Like I said, I did more than go topless!" Sophia said. "We have some catching up to do! I have some things to tell you three!"

Unlike what she had done on the fishing platform, she put on her bikini then bounded up the stairs to the deck, jumped into the water and announced in her best Delmar O'Donnell voice, "C'mon in girls, the water is fine!" The movie "Oh Brother Where Art Thou" and the Delmar character were both favorites of hers.

Laney, Leah and Audrey looked at each other, then quickly put on their swimsuits, mounted the deck and cannonballed into the pool. For the next hour they swam and talked, and Sophia told them what she had been doing out at the bridge.

~ ~ ~ ~ ~ ~

"You really spent, like, two whole days outside with nothing on?" Audrey asked. "I mean *nothing* at all?"

"All I had on was suntan lotion and a smile!" Sophia said. "By the way, that Tan Booster Ten stuff is the awesome sauce!"

"Why did you use suntan lotion?" Leah asked. "You get tan just by thinking about it."

"If I did that without some sort of suntan lotion, I would be fried!" Audrey said.

"You *are* fried Audrey!" Laney said.

The girls laughed and Sophia teared up again.

"I have missed this!" She thought. *"I have missed this soooo much!"*

After swimming, they showered the pool water off and changed into dry clothes. Then Leah, Laney and Audrey took up residence on the couches waiting for Sophia, who had been the last to get out of the pool and as a result the last to shower.

When she came back into The Pool Room toweling her much shorter hair, she was pounced upon by her friends who, as only teenage girls can do, produced seemingly from nowhere the various implements, sprays and gels needed to do a friend's hair!

Using photos of Calysta Bevier from the internet as their guide, they, in less time than it had taken Doni the hairdresser, had Sophia's hair back to the way it was before her father had pushed them into the pool.

"This hair style is going to take some getting used to." Sophia said.

"Why?" Leah asked. "You look amazing!"

"My hair was long since, like, forever." Sophia said.

"It looks good!" Audrey said. "I mean *really* good, and with that tan you've gotten…"

"What about it?" Sophia asked.

"Sophia!" Audrey said. "You are smo-double O-king hot!"

The girls erupted into laughter at Audrey's pronouncement.

"Where do you come up with those words?" Laney asked.

"They just come to me." Audrey said grinning. "It's a gift!"

"But you are right Audrey." Laney said. "Sophia, you are totally hot, and your new hair style just took it to the next level!"

Sophia giggled. "I _am_ the short haired hottie with the tan body!"

Laughter filled The Pool Room again just as the garage door opener began growling its announcement that Sophia's parents had returned. It was four-thirty when Dan entered The Pool Room and began flinging ice cream sandwiches at the girls.

"Here's your ice cream!" He said. "I still need to do something else for your birthday though."

"Thanks Dad." Sophia said. "Now get out. We are catching up."

"Oh. So, the four of you will be grilling the burgers then?" He asked.

"These burgers of which you speak?" Laney asked. "Would they happen to be the World-Famous Dan Young Super Yummy, grilled to perfection onion and cheese infused burgers?"

"The very same!" Dan said.

"They will be served with corn on the cob, fresh sliced tomatoes, a salad with the awesome pink salad dressing and boiled baked potatoes…if I were to get some help that is." Carol said from the doorway. "And we could eat pool side!"

Audrey volunteered to slice the tomatoes, make the salad and set the table while Sophia, Leah and Laney shucked the corn. After Dan filled a large stock pot with water, the four girls washed the potatoes, then Dan sat it on a large propane burner to heat. Carol's trick for quick baked potatoes was to boil them first, then let Dan finish them on the grill.

"We can boil the corn and the potatoes together." He said. "Make sure you put the corn and the potatoes in that." He gestured to the metal basket that he had taken out of the stock pot. "That way, you can take everything out and drain it. Now, I am going to fire up the grill and get the burgers ready!"

Chapter 32

When everyone was finished eating, Audrey, Laney and Leah cleaned up the dishes while Sophia approached her father with a request.

"Do you still want to do something for me for my birthday?" She asked.

"Yes." He said. "And I'm guessing you have something in mind?"

"Maaaaybe!" She said.

"What is it?" He asked.

"Since you interrupted our catching up time, here's what I want to do." Sophia began.

~ ~ ~ ~ ~ ~

The SCR-MOM van parked next to the entrance to The Grove at six forty-five.

"I cannot believe we are doing this." Dan said.

He and Carol were actually against Sophia's idea, but when they had retreated to the laundry room to discuss it, they both felt *not* doing it would plunge Sophia back into the funk she had been in since the move even with her friends present. They had both swallowed hard and returned to the Pool Room to tell her and her friends that they could go camping by themselves.

"Okay." Carol said. "Are all your cell phones charged?"

Sophia and her friends nodded yes.

"When do you want me to come and get you?" Dan asked.

"No later than six tomorrow evening, but probably sooner." Sophia said.

"Tell me again why we put all the camping gear in those trees?" Dan asked.

"Because there's a totally awesome sinkhole over there and it's where we are camping." Sophia said.

"I hope you are not trespassing." Dan said.

He had done an internet search and found that the land where the sinkhole was located was actually owned by the state conservation department and as such was public land. Nowhere in his search did he find any prohibitions against camping.

"Dad." Sophia said. "It'll be okay."

"I can't believe we are doing this." Dan said again as he rubbed the back of his head.

"Okay." Carol said. "Are you sure you have enough food for tonight and tomorrow?"

"Mom!" Sophia said. "We have plenty! I think the guy at the store thought we were preppers or something with all the stuff we got!"

"Okay. Okay." Carol said. "Don't get into too much trouble out here. Call us if you need anything and when you are ready to be picked up."

With that, Dan and Carol Young closed up the van, got in and went back to the house.

~ ~ ~ ~ ~ ~

The girls were amazed as they descended down the flat, smooth stone stairs to the bottom of the sinkhole where they saw the waterfall fed pool and the flat, smooth area with the fire pit at one end.

"Someone was here not too long ago." Audrey said pointing at the muddy footprints that went to the pool's edge.

"Those are mine." Sophia said. "Yesterday and last night when Mom and Dad were supposed to be in Columbia for Dad's training, I spent all day out here. Then I went back to the house and was going to stay there but then I decided to come back out here and go camping." Sophia said.

"You camped here last night?" Audrey asked.

"Yeah, I brought my tent, but I didn't sleep in it. I pulled my camp cot out and I slept out here." She indicated the area near the fire pit. "I had a fire, but I really didn't need it. It was really nice!"

"This looks like it would be a good place to camp." Laney said.

"It is! That's why I chose it!" Sophia said.

While they were setting up their campsite, Sophia told the girls about her rain-soaked, no imagination required bike ride back to the house and how she almost got caught on the front porch by the pizza delivery guy.

"Why did you take your clothes off in the garage anyway?" Laney asked.

"Because they were soaking wet, and the shirt and shorts were both white. The rain made them totally see-through." Sophia said. "The pizza guy would have been able to see *everything* whether I had them on or took them off."

"Naked Sophia, Pizza Guy could see! A-W-K-W-A-R-D! Pizza Guy drools and needs no imagination! And Sophia says 'Whatever, I'm dying of starvation!'" Leah rattled off in singsong rhyming fashion.

They all laughed!

"It would have definitely been awkward if I couldn't have gotten the front door open when I did." Sophia said.

"Was the pizza guy cute?" Audrey asked.

"He was *totally* cute!" Sophia said and felt her face heat up. "He had blonde hair and the bluest eyes I have ever seen! And he is our age; he said he was starting high school on Monday!"

"What is his name?" Audrey asked.

"I don't know." Sophia said. "But…"

"But?" Audrey asked.

"But…if I hadn't gotten the door open and he saw me, would I have had to give him a tip?" Sophia asked.

The others looked at her like she had just grown a second head then all four dissolved into laughter!

"I want to show you something." Sophia said going to the edge of the pool. "This end is super deep. I went down at least thirty feet and it is a lot deeper than that."

Sophia took off her shirt and shorts. Once her parents had agreed to the campout, she and the others had put their swimsuits back on under their clothes.

She dove into the pool's deep water and swam down as far as she could before her lungs demanded she return to the surface just as the others were jumping in to join her.

After Leah, Laney and Audrey had dove down as far as they could in the deep water, Sophia took them across the pool to the waterfall and stepped through the coursing water to the space behind it and entered The Art Gallery.

"Whoa!" Leah said. "This is so neat!"

Sophia, looking at the space said, "Yes, it is really neat!"

Laney and Audrey stepped through the waterfall and they too were impressed.

"Is this what you wanted to show us?" Audrey asked.

"Yes, it is!" Sophia said. "Isn't it amazing?"

"This is totally awesome!" Laney said.

"I want to tell you all something." Sophia said.

Audrey, Laney and Leah looked at her and waited.

"So, that sculpture we hung by the hot tub…" Sophia began.

"Choices!" Laney said. "That is so cool! I wonder how old it is?"

"I know, right?" Leah said. "Whoever the model was…I mean…I wish I looked like that! Did you see those abs? She must have been a goddess or something!"

"Definitely a goddess!" Audrey said. "A Greek goddess!"

"You're right!" Laney added. "Those abs are definitely Greek goddess abs!"

Leah, Audrey and Laney began discussing 'Choices' in great detail, why they liked it and what Greek goddess it could have been based on.

Finally, after several minutes, Sophia shouted, "Guys!"

"What?" Her three friends shouted back at her in unison, irritated at having their discussion interrupted.

"'Choices' is me!" Sophia admitted. "I made that plaster casting two days ago!"

"No way!" Leah said.

"*You* made that?" Audrey asked. "It's, like, a gazillion years old!"

"There's no way you made that Soph." Laney added.

"Leah, you have a picture of it on your phone, right?" Sophia asked.

"Yeah." Leah said and she called it up on her phone. "Here it is."

"Hold it up next to my Greek goddess-like abs." Sophia said making quote marks in the air. "Look familiar?" She asked as she tensed her abdominal muscles in the same way she had when she made her second dirt angel.

Leah, Laney and Audrey compared the picture to Sophia's abdomen and were blown away when they realized she was telling them the truth; it was her navel that actually convinced them.

They began peppering Sophia with question after question about how she had created it and moreover *why* she had made it.

Her explanation was simple, she told them her feelings about having to move, having to leave everything and everyone she had known her whole life, having had to give up her spot on the varsity cheerleading squad and about having no choice whatsoever in any of it.

She told them after the second time she had dropped her phone in the creek she made the choice to not only go skinny dipping to retrieve it, but to spend the rest of the day and all of the next day and part of the third day completely and totally nude…because she could.

"I wanted to make some choices." Sophia said. "So, I did…figuratively and literally."

"And you look amazing too!" Audrey said.

"I made another choice when I camped here last night too." Sophia said.

"What?" Her three friends said in unison.

"I took 'Choices' back to the house and glued it to that oak board at like two o'clock this morning, then I came back here and crashed on my camp cot." Sophia said.

"I've known you since the first day of kindergarten Sophia and I think there is more to your story." Leah said.

"There is." Sophia said.

"Spill it!" Audrey demanded.

"Yeah, what else did you do?" Laney asked.

"When I took it back to the house, I rode my bike there and back." She said.

"And?" Leah asked.

"Well, I didn't put on any clothes when I did it." Sophia said.

Audrey, Laney and Leah's jaws fell open with stunned shock before they started giggling at Sophia's admission.

"YOU rode your bike from here to your house and back out here at, like, two o'clock in the morning and you were totally naked when you did it?" Audrey asked.

"I did have my tennis shoes on." Sophia offered sheepishly.

Her confession brought on another round of laughter.

"Weren't you afraid of getting caught?" Audrey asked.

"Yeah." Laney asked. "I mean… Weren't you afraid of being seen?"

"Something told me that I would be okay, and I was." Sophia said.

"Actually, Laura told me it would be okay, and I wouldn't be seen." Sophia thought.

Audrey, Laney and Leah just looked at her and shook their heads.

"Hey, don't you remember what the little plaque on my sculpture says?" Sophia asked. "It says: 'Sometimes you have to do something a little crazy to prove that you are actually sane!' And I have more than proved that I am sane because riding my bike from here, back to the house and back out here while totally nude has to be the craziest thing I have *ever* done! Not to mention that I have spent the better part of the last three days wearing nothing at all!"

"Don't forget Pizza Guy!" Leah added.

"Yeah." Sophia said feeling her face slightly flush. "There's nothing like standing at the front door totally nude with ultra-bright L.E.D. lights lighting you up like a Christmas tree and not being able to open the door when the pizza guy is literally two houses away!"

"Sophia Elizabeth Young!" Leah began. "I just realized something."

"What?" Sophia asked.

"*You* lied to your parents about 'Choices'." Leah said.

"I did?" Sophia asked.

"Yes, you did!" Leah said. "You told them you bought it for fifteen dollars!"

Sophia giggled! "Lying is such a harsh term. Like my dad said, I prefer to call what I did a creative distortion of the truth to affect a planned outcome!"

"And just what was the outcome you affected by distorting the truth?" Audrey asked.

"That I didn't have to explain to my parents why I made a casting of my chest that they both love and now have hanging above the new hot tub!" Sophia said.

"Are you ever going to tell them that 'Choices' is really you?" Laney asked.

"Maybe after I am married, and I live in a different state!" Sophia giggled.

"Once you get a boyfriend and invite him over to swim, he will see 'Choices' you know." Leah said.

"And if we fall in love and get married, I will tell him on our wedding night that he got a preview of coming attractions and he didn't even know it!" Sophia said.

~ ~ ~ ~ ~ ~

The foursome made their way back to the campsite where they had arranged their cots. They had brought along the large easy-up tent that Sophia's parents used when they went camping, but decided not to set it up; they were well protected down in the sinkhole. Instead, they built a fire and roasted hot dogs, made smores and popped popcorn.

"What *are* we doing tomorrow Sophia?" Audrey asked.

"I want to show you the spring that feeds the creek." Sophia said. "We can go swimming there."

"Aren't springs really, really cold?" Laney asked.

"Yes, and the water is blue too!" Sophia said. "You will be fine, princess!"

Laney snorted and "Harrumphed" good naturedly.

"Hey!" Leah said. "I thought *I* was the princess!"

"No, Leah!" Sophia said. "*You* are the PRETEND-CESS! Big difference!"

Leah laughed along with the others then added a good natured, "I hate you!"

"When are we going to go out there?" Audrey asked.

"I'm thinking after breakfast." Sophia said. "We can pack some food so we can eat lunch out there if we want, but we can figure that out in the morning. Right now, I think we should play our favorite game! I have made an addition that should make it even more fun!"

Chapter 33

Sophia switched on the two L.E.D. lanterns that they had brought; they illuminated the campsite in a nice even white light. Then she pulled out the fleece blanket, spread it on the smooth stone floor of the sinkhole and took out some well-known items from her backpack.

"Ladies!" Sophia said. "The new and improved Truth or Dare!"

Her statement was met with applause from her friends. Sophia shuffled each deck twice, then gave the Truth cards to Audrey and the Dare cards to Laney. They shuffled them twice each before passing them to Leah to shuffle as well. Once everyone had each shuffled both decks twice, they were placed in the center of the blanket.

"Tell us about this new addition you came up with Soph." Laney said.

"I call it "Group Dare." Sophia said making quote marks in the air. "Let's say Leah draws the Group Dare card, it can be in either the Truth pile or the Dare pile; her dare would be for all three of us. And because it's for the group, if anyone refuses…all three have to do whatever is in here." She said.

Sophia held up a plain white envelope with the word "PENALTY" written across its front.

"I bet the skinny dipping one we opened the last time we played was the least risky penalty. I know the one I wrote is A LOT riskier than just skinny dipping." She said.

"Ditto." Laney said.

"Agreed." Audrey said.

Leah giggled. "Mine *was* the skinny dipping one!" She admitted.

"So, other than the Group Dare card, everything else is the same?" Laney asked.

"Yes." Sophia said. "Should we use the same player numbers as last time? Or do we need to re-roll?"

"Same." Laney said.

"Same." Added Leah.

"Same." Audrey agreed.

"Okay." Sophia said. "Audrey is one, Laney is two, I'm three and Leah is four."

"Who starts?" Audrey asked.

"Sophia does." Leah said quickly. "It's her birthday weekend!"

Audrey and Laney nodded their consent.

"Okay, here we go!" Sophia said and rolled one of the four-sided dice.

It bounced once and came up on the number one, a Truth card. She rolled the second die, and like the first one it bounced on the blanket, but it came up on the number three.

"Roller's choice! Who will it be? Who will it be?" Audrey said sounding like one of the carnival barkers from the fair.

Sophia laughed and looked at her friends, then used the same sing-song rhyme Audrey had used the last time they had played which had resulted in her ultimately having to retrieve her bikini from the middle of the street in her birthday suit.

"Eeney, meaney, miney moo." Sophia said causing the others to crack up laughing! "It's gonna be one of you! It could be Leah or Laney Sue. It could be me, but it's YOU!" Sophia pointed at Audrey!

"I think this is where I am supposed to say, 'Oh joy!'" Audrey said.

"Pick a really good one Soph!" Leah said.

"Oh, I'm going to pick the best one Leah!" Sophia thought. *"Don't you worry about that one little bit!"*

Sophia laid her hand with the group dare card carefully concealed in her palm on top of the pile of Truth cards. She had been practicing the sleight of hand maneuver she had found on an online video for a few weeks so it looked totally natural, and her friends wouldn't notice.

"Oh boy!" She said looking at the card in mock surprise.

"What?" Audrey asked.

"Yeah, what does it say?" Laney asked.

Sophia laid the card on the blanket; written in block letters were two words: GROUP DARE!

The girls looked at the card for a quiet moment before Audrey asked, "What's the dare Soph?"

"Do you remember the last time we played Truth or Dare?" Sophia asked.

The three girls nodded their heads.

"Do you also remember that I went into the bathroom next to the living room to put on my pajamas after we got back from Laney's pool?" She asked.

The three again nodded their heads. Leah, Laney and Audrey had confused looks on their faces, they didn't know where Sophia was going with her line of questioning, but they knew her well enough to know that she was headed somewhere that would most likely end in a dare none but her would like.

"There is a vent in that bathroom that let's anyone hear what is being said in the living room." Sophia informed them.

"Oh, oh!" Leah said.

"You!" Sophia said pointing at Audrey. "You used loaded dice that you switched when you went to the bathroom right before you rolled my skinny-dipping dare. You wanted to make sure you would get a dare and that you got to pick who had to do it!"

"Oooo!" Leah said. "She burned you Audrey!"

"Burned like bread that was left in a toaster way too long!" Laney added.

"And you two!" Sophia said turning her attention to Leah and Laney. "You both knew all about it and did nothing! You are just as guilty as she is!"

"How does *your* toast taste?" Audrey asked them.

"Scorched." Laney said with a giggle!

"Singed!" Leah added.

"Because of what you three did, I had to walk a block down the street to get my bikini out from underneath those very bright L.E.D. streetlights while wearing nothing at all." Sophia reminded them.

"You looked really good doing it I might add." Audrey said.

"Flattery will get you everywhere, but it won't get you out of doing this dare." Sophia said. "But you are right, I did look good! I have been told I look like a Greek goddess!"

The group laughed!

"Now that I think about it." She continued. "My double great grandmother *was* from Greece, so I really *could be* a Greek goddess!"

"The way you are with your laptop." Leah said. "You are actually a geek goddess!"

They all laughed again!

"What's the dare Soph?" Laney asked.

"The dare is this." Sophia said. "I dare the group to walk back to the covered bridge tonight wearing nothing but skin!"

"What?!" Leah gasped.

"You heard me." Sophia said. "You all are going to the covered bridge and back tonight totally naked! And that is spelled N-E-K-K-E-D... neckked!" Sophia grinned her most magnificent, devilish grin.

"How far is it again to the bridge?" Leah asked.

"Four miles." Sophia said.

"So, we will be out in plain view for four miles not wearing anything at all?" Leah asked.

"More like eight miles. You have to walk back too!" Sophia said.

"You are kidding!" Leah said.

"No, I am not." Sophia said. "Who knows, maybe some of the Podunksville Possum boys will be out driving around and they might get a Springfield surprise!"

"Now wait a minute!" Audrey said. "You had to walk maybe a block to get your bikini and we have to go eight MILES? That's not fair!"

Sophia picked up the Penalty envelope, held it out to Audrey and raised her eyebrow in a "You can always do what's in here" kind of look.

"No thank you." Audrey said.

"You are evil Sophia!" Leah said. "Pure evil!"

"It's a gift!" Sophia said. "A gift I like to call…karma!"

The four stared at each other for a long moment, then as only friends who have known each other for a long time can do, dissolved into fits of belly cramping laughter!

Sophia looked at her cell phone's clock. "It's nine o'clock, ladies! Shall we take that walk to the bridge?"

"I'm doing this under protest!" Audrey said as she took off her bikini top. "You only had to walk a BLOCK!"

"And you have zero chance of being seen, unlike me." Sophia said to herself. *"This isn't much of a dare, but it is fun watching you all squirm!"*

"Uh, Soph?" Leah asked after getting ready for the walk to the bridge.

"Yeah?" Sophia said.

"This is a group dare, right?" Leah asked.

"Yup!" Sophia said.

"You still have *your* bikini on." Leah observed. "Are *you* refusing to do the dare?"

"The dare was for…" Sophia started to say but realized her error. Giggling, she took off her bikini as well and the four of them headed to the bridge.

~ ~ ~ ~ ~ ~

"Sophia, wake up!" Laura said.

"Wha…" Sophia said groggily.

"Wake up, I want to talk!" Laura said.

Sophia rubbed her eyes, sat up and looked around.

Leah was sprawled across her camp cot with her blanket half on and half off. Laney had kicked off all her covers off and was lying in the center of her cot in a fetal position. Audrey was lying prone on her cot with her head buried underneath her pillow.

"Where are you?" Sophia asked.

"I'm over here." Laura said. "By the pool."

Sophia looked around and saw Laura sitting by the pool with her feet in the water. She kicked off her covers and padded across the smooth stone over next to Laura.

"Why do you keep waking me up?" Sophia said with a sleepy smile.

"Because this is a dream, and you are still asleep." Laura said and then nodded at the cots.

Sophia was at first stunned at what she saw, then remembered that she was dreaming, or at least she hoped she was dreaming because when she looked at the four cots, she not only saw her friends, but she saw herself as well.

"THAT is so weird." Sophia said. "But dang, I look good!"

Laura laughed! "Yes, you do Sophia! Just like a Greek goddess with a new haircut!"

Sophia laughed! "What's up?"

"Just a quick visit to see how things are going." Laura said.

Sophia got quiet for a moment then said, "Now that they are here, everything is perfect!"

"Did you enjoy your walk earlier tonight?" Laura asked.

"I did. They were all so scared that someone would see them!" Sophia giggled. "To bad I made it a group dare though. I hadn't planned on having to do the dare with them."

"Are you going to tell them you set them up?" Laura asked.

"Probably not." Sophia said.

"How will it be after they leave?" Laura asked.

"It will be fine Laura." Sophia said with a more serious tone. "I'm over being mad about having to move. School starts on Monday and I will be "the new girl" or "the postmaster's daughter", but what I won't be is angry. New school! New hair! New me! You know?"

"Good!" Laura said. "And your hair does look amazing!"

"Thanks!" Sophia said. "It's super easy to take care of, but I will miss braiding it."

"It's hair." Laura said. "You can grow it out again!"

"Very true!" Sophia said.

"I have to go. I just wanted to check in with you. Don't have too much fun at the spring tomorrow though!" Laura winked.

"The girls are looking forward to it!" Sophia said.

"I know." Laura said. *"And it will be...what is it that you like to say...it will be epic!"*

"I hope so!" Sophia said.

"Oh, I almost forgot." Laura said reaching around to the back of her neck. *"This is for you."* She placed a heart-shaped locket in Sophia's hand. *"I want you to have it!"*

"But..." Sophia started to say.

"No buts!" Laura said firmly. *"It's yours, and I need to be going."*

"Thank you very much!" Sophia said as she looked at Laura, then at the locket.

"You're welcome very much!" Laura said, then added with a laugh. *"You know, Jerry and I used to say, 'Thank you very much!' and 'You're welcome very much!' all the time. I never realized until right now just how annoying that really is!"*

Sophia laughed and asked, *"Are you sure you want to give me this?"*

"Happy birthday, Sophia!" Laura said. *"I'll see you later!"*

As with her other dream visits, Laura faded away and Sophia returned to the land of sleep.

~ ~ ~ ~ ~ ~

Sophia's chicken alarm began clucking at eight a.m.; she had set it after they got back from their walk to the bridge so they could get an early start on their day.

The others awoke and they all had a cold breakfast consisting of ham and cheese deli sandwiches, apples and water before getting ready for their trip to the spring.

"Sophia, did you know you talk in your sleep?" Audrey asked.

"I do?" Sophia asked.

"Yes." Audrey said. "You do."

"What did I say?" Sophia asked.

"I'm not sure." Audrey said. "You mumble. I only heard one thing clearly."

"What was it?" Sophia asked.

"You said, 'THAT is so weird!'" Audrey said. "Then you laughed."

"How far is it to the spring?" Leah asked.

"Like seven miles." Sophia said. "Four to the bridge and another three to the spring."

"We're doing some serious hiking today!" Leah said.

"Does everyone have their backpack?" Sophia asked. "Because if you don't, you won't have lunch."

Before coming to the sinkhole, Sophia had dug around in her closet and found three more Missouri State drawstring backpacks for her friends to use on their campout. She had acquired the bags the year before when Missouri State opened for the new fall term. It seemed like every campus organization would give you a bag even if you were not going to school there.

"We all have our backpacks...Mom!" Audrey said.

"We should take our shirts and shorts with us too." Laney said. "I don't want to burn."

"Probably not a bad idea." Audrey said and they all put some extra clothes in their bags.

"Is that a new necklace Soph?" Leah asked. "I've never seen it before."

Sophia touched the gold locket.

"Yeah...I...got it for my birthday." Sophia said.

"It's super cute!" Leah said as she closed up her backpack.

~ ~ ~ ~ ~ ~

They started walking back to the bridge at nine o'clock, talking about everything and nothing. They were laughing hard at something Audrey had said when the sound of an engine got everyone's attention.

"What is that?" Leah asked.

"It sounds like a car." Laney said.

Sophia heard something in the engine's sound that made her pause. It was definitely an engine and it was getting louder, but it did not sound like a car's engine.

"That is..." Sophia started to say but was cut off by a loud roar as a bright yellow spray plane flew over them. "...an airplane."

They watched as the plane zoomed out over a pasture then nosed up and banked around sharply to the right and came back at them down the road.

"Can he see us?" Laney asked.

They could see the big grin on the pilot's face!

"Apparently he can." Audrey said.

"What do we do?" Leah asked.

"We do this!" Sophia said and began princess waving as the spray plane passed over them.

"We should take off our tops and give him something to remember!" Audrey suggested.

"I dare you!" Laney said.

"I double dare you!" Leah said with a giggle.

"I triple dare you!" Sophia said.

"Okay!" Audrey said and reached for the fastener of her bikini top.

"NO!" Laney, Leah and Sophia yelled at the same time.

"We were joking Audrey!" Leah said.

"I can't believe you were going to take off your top and flash that crop duster!" Laney said.

"Audrey!" Sophia said. "You are turning into a hoochie momma!"

Audrey laughed!

~ ~ ~ ~ ~ ~

Audrey could be very brash, sassy and impetuous when she wanted to be. She was someone who did things that suited her and told things the way they were.

When she had first seen the pink bikini, she told her friends that she knew it had been made for someone who wanted to be a dermatologist. When they asked what she meant, she said, "To wear this bikini you have to be very comfortable in your skin, and I am very comfortable in mine!"

She told Laney, Leah and Sophia that during Spring Break, she had to have an EKG when she made an unplanned visit to the Emergency Room after she had started having intense pains in her abdomen and chest. Even though she was almost fifteen at the time and someone that age is highly unlikely to be having a heart attack, the doctor wanted to run a twelve lead EKG to rule out that particular issue.

When the college age male emergency room technician came in to apply the six chest leads to go along with the four limb leads that were already stuck to her forearms and calves, he said he would go get a female to put the leads on her.

Audrey asked him, "Is it your job to do it?"

He said it was.

"Do it then." She said without a trace of embarrassment or awkwardness.

Yes, Audrey Noble is very comfortable in her skin!

The plane roared toward them again as it made another pass down the road. Audrey, Laney, Leah and Sophia continued waving at the plane looking every bit like the girls in Frederic Soulacroix's painting "Spring Nudes", except they had on bikinis and were standing in the middle of a gravel road whereas the French girls in the painting weren't wearing anything at all and were dancing in a grass covered meadow!

On his next pass, the pilot dropped even lower. The plane's wheels were no more than ten feet off the ground. The propeller stirred up a cloud of dust that covered the girls and stuck to the suntan lotion they had applied before leaving the sinkhole. He waggled his wings and flew away.

"I bet that crop duster starts flying around out here a lot!" Laney said, then sneezed.

The others giggled in agreement.

"You know, I like walking around out here in my bikini!" Leah said.

"You do?" Sophia asked. "Why?"

"I do!" Leah said. "I have a pageant coming up in a couple of weeks and I want to work on getting a darker tan."

"That Tan Booster Ten is the best suntan lotion ever!" Sophia said. "I told you, it is the awesome sauce!"

"You know Leah, if you want to keep working on your tan, Mom just started her new job; she and dad leave for work before seven o'clock every morning and they don't get home until six." Laney said. "Brian is at college in Ohio, and…"

"And?" Leah said.

"And you and Audrey and I could lay out all day. We don't have to start school until after Labor Day…unlike some people!" Laney said looking at Sophia. "With that new fence, and with Brian gone, no one could see us, so we could even…"

"We could even…what?" Leah asked.

"We could even do what Soph's been doing out here!" Laney said.

"Oh great, I have turned you three into nudists!" Sophia said.

"Well, we got you started in your…what did you call it last night when we walked to the bridge?" Audrey asked.

Sophia laughed. "My grand adventures in nudity!"

"Yeah!" Audrey said. "We got you started when you had to get your bikini from out in the middle of the street! In fact, now that I think about it, once you took it off to do the dare, you never put it on again even when we snuck back to your house! You were totally naked and outside for like two hours that night!"

"And I looked like a Greek goddess too!" Sophia added.

Laney, Leah and Audrey laughed, then began planning how they could have their own grand adventures and work on their tans at Laney's pool before school started.

~ ~ ~ ~ ~ ~

They arrived at the fishing platform, dropped their backpacks, kicked off their shoes and dove into the water to rinse off the dirt the crop duster's plane had coated them in when he had buzzed them.

"How do we get to the spring?" Laney asked.

"We can swim." Sophia said pointing upstream. "We can take that path." She pointed to the rocky path she had taken on her trip to the spring. "Or we can do a little of both."

"What are we going to do with our stuff?" Leah asked.

"We can carry it with us." Sophia said. "Or we can hide it underneath those buckets. My vote is to leave everything here."

The others agreed and after stashing the backpacks, they began their journey to the spring.

Chapter 34

"Whoa!" Leah said when she saw the spring.

Her single word statement was the consensus of the others when they saw the blue waters roiling in the large pool just above the place Sophia had named The Narrows.

"That is the coolest thing I have ever seen!" Laney said.

After passing The Narrows, the group walked along the rocky path to the far side of the spring's pool. Sophia wanted to see it from that angle because the last time she was here, her visit was cut short when she had been mistaken for a mermaid.

The four friends stood gazing at the water for a long time just taking in the quiet beauty of the surging spring.

"Let's go skinny dipping!" Leah suggested.

"Now you want to go skinny dipping? What's gotten into you Leah?" Laney asked.

"I like making a choice for myself." Leah said. "I have everything decided for me, or at least that's how it feels most of the time. I love doing the pageants, but everything is planned out for me. I hate that part of it. There are days I just want to do something that is totally spontaneous and today is one of those days."

After a quiet pause, Laney and Audrey admitted similar feelings about the lack of choices in their lives. They also admitted how much they were enjoying the freedom they were having as they explored the creek.

The four friends looked at each other, grinned, peeled off their bikinis and jumped into the spring's cold, blue water where they swam for more than an hour.

~ ~ ~ ~ ~ ~

The rock where Sophia had left her cell phone and ear buds on her first trip to the spring was small, but it was big enough for all four girls to sit on when they decided to take a break. While they were talking and warming up from their swim, Laney made an observation.

"I think we have company." Laney said.

"What?" Sophia asked. "Where?"

Laney pointed through the trees that sat above the rocky outcropping directly above the spring. There were two figures moving towards them, one taller than the other, and both were wearing bright hunter's orange shirts which is what had caught Laney's attention.

"We have to swim over there." Sophia said and pointed to the rocky overhang. "There's a space we can all fit in and no one can see us, but we have to get over there FAST!"

The four girls, who were all adept swimmers, wasted no time in crossing the spring's cold water to the rocky overhang. Once they were safely on the shelf they waited. Within a minute they heard a small voice.

"Oh man!" A little boy's voice said. "They is gone!"

"You saw another mermaid?" An older voice asked.

"Oh my gosh!" Sophia thought. *"They're back!"*

"No, they were just girls that I seed." The little boy said. "They had legs, not flippers."

"Maybe they were mermaids who got legs just to see what they were like." The older one suggested.

"Can that happen?" The little boy asked.

"Sometimes." The older one said. "At least that's what I have heard."

"So, they were four mermaids?" The little boy asked.

"I bet they were!" The older one said. "I just wish I could have seen them!"

"They was way over there on the other side." The little boy said sincerely.

"Do you think we should go over there and check?" The older one asked.

"No." The little boy said. "They's gone."

"Sorry buddy." The older one said. "But you know what happens when you see four mermaids out here don't you?"

"Ice cream?" The little boy asked hopefully.

"Yes!" The older one said. "But because you saw four of them, you get a banana split this time!"

"I love mermaids!" The little boy announced.

"Remind me to get you a camera the next time we come out here." The older one said. "That way you can take some mermaid pictures so I can see them too!"

"Okay!" The little boy said. "Now, can we get that banana split?"

"Right after I check one more thing we can." The older one said. "Come on."

Sophia placed her index finger to her lips telling the others to stay quiet. After five minutes had passed, she finally whispered, "Okay. let's go."

The four of them slid back into the cold spring, swam across the pool and put on their bikinis.

"I've never been a mermaid before!" Audrey said.

"I have." Sophia said.

Then she told them of her first encounter and the four of them laughed and made their way back to The Narrows.

They made several trips through the rushing water enjoying it as it propelled them down the stream. After their tenth time through, Sophia suggested they head back; she was thinking about what Laura had told her, *"...when you are not between the bridge and the cemetery, you can get into trouble...."*.

~ ~ ~ ~ ~ ~

They got back to the bridge at two o'clock, retrieved their backpacks and went up to the bridge and ate lunch in its shade. As they were eating, a loud and obnoxious wolf whistle broke the peacefulness of the day and threw Audrey, Laney and Leah into a panic. Sophia however, doubled over with hearty laughter.

"This is *NOT* funny Sophia!" Leah shrieked. "Someone is watching us!"

"Why aren't you worried Soph?" Audrey asked.

She saw Sophia's relaxed, amused mood and realized all was not what it appeared.

Sophia pointed to one of the rafters of the covered bridge. Sitting there was a small grey bird with yellow and orange spots on the sides of its tufted head.

"A bird?" Audrey asked.

"That is Mister Bird!" Sophia said. "I met him the morning before you three got here."

"What are you talking about?" Leah said. "Someone is watching us!"

"She sounds like Polly." Sophia thought.

"Relax Leah, no one is watching us." Sophia said.

"Did you not hear that whistle?" Laney asked.

Mister Bird cut loose with another pitch perfect wolf whistle.

"There it is again!" Laney said.

Sophia pointed to the rafter again and Laney and Leah looked upwards at the little bird who was the only other being on the bridge.

"Watch this." Sophia said. "Wowzah!"

The little bird looked at Sophia and repeated, very clearly, "Wowzah!", wolf whistled again then took flight.

"That was the coolest thing I have ever seen!" Leah said. "Did you teach him to say 'Wowzah'?"

"Yes!" Sophia said. "And just so you all know that little bird made me think someone was watching me the other day. He kind of freaked me out until I figured out it was a bird and not a person."

"What are we going to do when we are done eating?" Leah asked.

"I want to go see that old barn we passed on our way out here." Sophia said.

"Why?" Audrey asked.

"Just curious." Sophia said.

~ ~ ~ ~ ~ ~

The walk was uneventful, well, as uneventful as four teenaged girls walking down a road carrying backpacks and only wearing their bikinis, tennis shoes and suntan lotion can be.

When they finally got to the old barn, they stepped inside and looked around. In the hallway was a staircase leading up to the hayloft.

"That's different." Leah said.

"This is the barn where Laura and Jerry had their freshman prom!" Sophia thought. *"This must be Jerry's uncle's place."*

"I thought barns only had ladders." Leah said. "My grandparent's barn does."

"I guess not." Audrey said.

"It's kind of neat!" Laney said.

"It is!" Sophia said.

They looked around for a few minutes then decided to head back to The Grove. As they were walking toward the road, a convoy of pickups loaded down with teenaged boys drove by and whistled and hollered when they saw the bikini-clad girls. The girls just laughed and, as they had done with the spray plane, they princess waved!

Sophia's phone came to life with a text from her father. "SOPH – HEADED YOUR WAY. ARE YOU READY?"

"KIND OF." She replied.

"KIND OF?" Dan asked.

"WE ARE AT THAT OLD BARN THAT WE SAW ON THE WAY OUT TO THE BRIDGE. I GUESS YOU CAN PICK US UP HERE?" Sophia texted.

"OKAY! SEE YOU IN A BIT!" His text said.

"Get your clothes on." Sophia said. "Dad is on his way to get us. When we get back to the house, I want to show you all something else."

"What?" Leah asked.

"A really cool park!" Sophia said.

~ ~ ~ ~ ~ ~

The girls were wowed by the red bricked wonder that was the Coombs House Park! They giggled as they took turns taking each other's picture standing next to "Venus de Milo" and the "The Little Mermaid" statues.

"If we could spend another day out at the bridge and the sinkhole, we would be as bronze as Den Lille Havfrue is right now!" Leah said.

"Some of us already are!" Sophia teased.

"And some of us haven't spent three days running around not wearing anything at all!" Leah said.

"Do you want to go back tomorrow for a few hours?" Sophia asked. "We could hang out at the fishing platform."

"When is that book thing you're going to?" Laney asked.

"Two o'clock." Sophia said. "If we get up early, we could spend four or five hours out there."

Audrey, Laney and Leah agreed!

~ ~ ~ ~ ~ ~

When they got back to Sophia's house, they were met by an amazing smell coming from the Pool Room.

"Is that..." Laney asked inhaling deeply.

"...the smell of..." Leah added.

"...grilling steaks?" Audrey finished with a satisfied exhale.

"It is!" Carol said, peeking her head through the Pool Room's door. "And there are a few other things you four might enjoy too!"

The meal was similar to the one they had enjoyed the night before with the major change being steaks as the main course instead of hamburgers. The other addition was Sophia's traditional strawberry birthday cake. She had had a strawberry cake every year since she was three; it was something she looked forward to every August twenty-fifth!

Sophia received an array of gifts from her friends and her parents, but the best gift she received was being together with her best friends and her parents and...well... maybe the Pool Room, which was totally awesome!

~ ~ ~ ~ ~ ~

After the eating and the opening the birthday gifts was over, the six of them played a long and fun game of Monopoly at the poolside table that finally ended at ten o'clock with Carol being declared the winner. She had dominated the game by having hotels on Park Place, Boardwalk and nine other properties! She won when she finally bankrupted Laney!

When the talk of going inside to go to bed began, the girls announced their plans to sleep in the Pool Room. They reinforced their case when they mentioned the couches and how they would give each one of them a comfortable place to sleep versus the floor in Sophia's room.

Dan and Carol readily agreed, which surprised the girls who had anticipated needing more discussion regarding their plan. What surprised them even more was when they were shown that each of the couches was, in fact, a queen-sized hide-a-bed containing an actual mattress instead of the usual thin piece of foam rubber that many sofa sleepers held.

"The couches aren't the prettiest, but the mattresses are brand new and will make great guest beds for when you three come up or anyone spends the night." Carol said.

"Like when the football team comes over?" Sophia asked, grinning.

"No." Dan said. "They have to sleep on the floor. That toughens them up!"

Carol and Dan went into the house and brought out sheets, pillows and blankets. They also brought out a large box.

"This was on the front porch with your name on it. I found it after we got home this afternoon." Carol said. "I forgot about it until I went in to get this stuff."

Sophia opened the box and found an envelope taped to the front of a three ringed binder that was laying on top of a white plastic bag. She took the envelope, opened it and inside she found five crisp twenty-dollar bills and a piece of paper with a note written on it.

"It's from Maude Adelaide." Sophia announced, then read the note. "Sophia – I did not forget you. Here's the money you were promised. Myrtle is fine, but still at The Home. I might need some more help. I'll let you know. You were a real help to this old lady, and you got me to thinking so I started writing some things down that you asked about.

You asked about me and Charley. You asked about Margaret. And you asked about Laura. I wrote down all that I could remember and put it in this here binder. Myrtle said she would do the same once she is home. The other thing is for your hope chest. - Maude".

Sophia picked up the binder and opened it; inside she found what looked like five hundred single sided, double spaced pages of neatly printed text.

"Wow!" Sophia thought. *"Maude wrote this?"*

"What is that?" Carol asked.

"Maude paid me for helping her clean, and she wrote this." Sophia said holding up the binder. "I never saw a computer or a printer in her house. I don't know how she wrote so much, so fast."

"Old folks can surprise you." Carol said.

"She also put this in here." Sophia said and tugged the white plastic bag free from the box.

"What is it Sophia?" Dan and Carol asked nearly at the same time.

"Whatever it is, it is squishy." Sophia said and opened the thick-walled trash bag and pulled out a beautiful quilt! It was huge! But when you are just five-foot-one inches tall, many things were huge.

"That must be a king-sized quilt!" Carol exclaimed. "And it is beautiful!"

The quilt was an assortment of creams, tans, taupes, dark browns, blacks and lilac purple pieces of colored fabric! On each corner was an eight-pointed star in dark brown, tan and taupe, centered on a field of cream. The center of the quilt held another much larger eight-pointed star on an even larger field of cream.

"Wowzah!" Sophia said.

Dan looked closely at the quilt.

"That is handmade." He said.

"How can you tell by just looking at it that it is handmade?" Laney asked.

"Yeah!" Audrey chimed in. "Are you, like, the quilt whisperer?"

Leah didn't say anything; she was too busy giggling at what Audrey had said.

"I can tell it's handmade by looking at the stitches." Dan said.

The girls leaned closer, and he showed them that the stitches were not the same size and they were not spaced consistently. If the quilt were machine stitched, each stitch would be identical in size and spacing.

"Wow!" Leah said. "You can learn something new every day, even from old folks!"

Dan and Carol laughed!

"Speaking of old folks, isn't it getting to be your bedtime? I mean you two aren't getting any younger." Sophia said.

"Yes." Dan said. "We need to be getting back to The Home!"

"Sophia? Would you like me to put your quilt on your bed?" Carol asked.

"Yes!" She said. "Thanks Mom!"

"Once the girls go home you should send Ms. Adelaide a nice "Thank You" note." Dan said.

"I'm already planning on it." Sophia said. "That quilt is totally cool!"

The Youngs hugged each girl goodnight, they had known Leah, Laney and Audrey since early elementary school and looked at them as their own kids.

"Don't stay up ALL night!" Dan and Carol said.

"We won't." Sophia said. "The book signing is tomorrow, and I don't want to miss it!"

After Sophia's parents had gone inside to go to bed, the girls turned off The Pool Room's main lights and turned on the strings of white L.E.D. lights that had been mounted across the ceiling. They gave the outdoor themed room the appearance of stars.

When they were sure Dan and Carol were not coming back, the girls initiated the hot tub and pool, sans swimsuits, for two hours before crawling into their sofa beds.

~ ~ ~ ~ ~ ~

The girls woke up at seven o'clock and went into the house to fix breakfast. However, the door leading into the laundry room was being obstinate, so they had to walk around to the front porch and enter via the front door.

They cooked, served, and devoured a large breakfast of scrambled eggs, bacon and sourdough toast that they made for themselves and Sophia's parents. Carol, grateful that she didn't have to cook so early in the morning, agreed to take care of the dirty dishes which allowed the girls to shower and get ready for their day.

Laney's parents called from Terra Haute, Indiana where they had spent the night. They said they would be arriving by one o'clock and asked that Audrey, Laney and Leah be ready when they got there; there would still be close to four hours of driving before they got back to Springfield. They were assured that everyone would be ready to go, but before leaving, Carol and Dan were going to provide lunch.

"Where are you four off to?" Carol asked when the girls met in the kitchen after showering.

"They want to go back out to the covered bridge and take some pictures." Sophia said.

"I will have lunch ready at one o'clock when Laney's folks get here." Carol said. "So, you should have all your things ready to go before you go to the bridge."

Audrey, Laney and Leah promised everything was already ready; they really didn't have that much other than their backpacks and their bicycles.

~ ~ ~ ~ ~ ~

At eight forty-five, their bicycle tires made the familiar "ker-tikity" sound as they crossed the wooden planks that made up the floor of the covered bridge.

They parked on the fishing platform side of the bridge, then used their phones to take several group photos to go along with the birthday party pictures they had taken the night before.

The one they all liked was one Sophia took. It showed the four of them leaning over the bridge's balcony and looking down. She had programmed her phone's self-timer to wait for a full ninety seconds which gave her time to scramble up the embankment, cross the bridge and get in position with her friends, her best friends, before the camera snapped a series of twelve pictures in rapid succession.

"Those are so cool!" Audrey exclaimed when she saw them. "Send them to everyone Soph!"

The photos were shared.

"Speaking of cool; I want to go back to the sinkhole." Leah said. "There's something I want to do."

"Do we have time?" Laney asked. "I mean it is, like, four miles."

"We have time." Sophia said. "We can ride there in twenty minutes. It's not like we have to walk."

Chapter 35

The bike ride actually took thirteen minutes; Sophia turned on the stopwatch app on her phone when they left the bridge just to see how long it did take. It probably helped when Audrey challenged the others to, "Keep up or eat dust!" before she began furiously pedaling her bicycle down the gravel and dirt road.

When they arrived at The Grove, they parked their bikes in the tree branch tunnel and descended into the sinkhole.

"Okay Leah, we are here. What did you want to do?" Sophia said.

"I want to see how deep that cave is!" Leah said.

"I think you forgot your scuba gear." Laney said.

"I did!" Leah giggled. "But I remembered I had these in my backpack!"

She pulled out a package of glow sticks and a roll of string.

"If we tie a rock on one of these, pop it so it glows, we can drop it in the water and see how far it sinks." She said. "Who knows, it may go so deep we won't be able to see it glow anymore."

"We would have to swim over there before we could drop it and watch it sink." Lancy said.

Leah began tying a rock to a length of string that she had already fastened to the glow stick.

"You're not afraid of getting wet, are you?" She asked.

"It's not even ten o'clock in the morning and you are going to go skinny dipping?" Laney asked.

"Sometimes you have to do something a little crazy…" Leah said as she snapped the glow stick and shook it rapidly causing it to brighten with a neon yellow radiance. "…to prove that you are actually sane!"

Audrey, Laney and Sophia watched as Leah took off her clothes then dove into the deep end of the pool carrying the weighted glow stick. When she was over the mouth of the submerged cave, she released it and watched as it descended.

"Can you still see it?" Audrey asked after she could no longer see it from her place on the smooth stone floor.

"Yes!" Leah said. "It is still going."

Audrey found a rock, tied it to, then activated one of the glow sticks, stripped off her clothes and joined Leah treading water above the entrance to the cave.

"You can barely see it." She said as she looked down at Leah's descending light. "That is a really deep cave."

"Shall we join them?" Laney asked.

"Actually, I don't want to get my hair wet." Sophia said. "It looks really good today."

"Hey!" Laney yelled to Leah and Audrey. "Sophia doesn't want to get her *hair* wet. Since she moved from Springfield, I think she's turned into a girl or something!"

Sophia sighed, then laughed. "You only live once! And it's only hair."

She joined her friends in the deep end of the crescent shaped pool.

~ ~ ~ ~ ~ ~

When they ran out of glow sticks, none of which they could see anymore, Sophia, Audrey, Leah and Laney swam back across the pool, climbed out of the sinkhole and made their way back into the world of bright sunshine where they crossed the road to a wide sunny, grassy area to dry off. As they stood there, they really did look like the Soulacroix girls from the painting!

Once thoroughly dry, they descended the stone steps one last time, got dressed and said, "Until next time." to the sinkhole. Then they got on their bikes and headed back down the road.

~ ~ ~ ~ ~ ~

Morton's opened early on Sundays to take care of the before church breakfast crowd. When Sophia and her three friends arrived, it was eleven o'clock and the biscuit and gravy folks were gone and most likely warming a pew.

"You brought friends!" Marion said as Sophia, Audrey, Laney and Leah entered. "And what did you do to your hair?"

"Yes, I brought friends." Sophia said. "And I cut my hair!"

"Turn around." Marion demanded.

Sophia spun, then faced her again.

"It looks really good!" Marion said. "That cut suits you!"

"Thanks!" Sophia said.

"Who're these three?" Marion asked as she gave a quick nod to the girls.

"These are my friends: Audrey, Laney and Leah." Sophia said. "They came up from Springfield this weekend to help celebrate my birthday!"

"I see." Marion said. "Well, nice to meet you! Now why don't you go find a table and I'll get your order directly."

The four took the booth closest to the juke box, grabbed a menu and looked at their choices.

"By the way." Sophia said. "I'm buying."

The door's bell jingled, and they paused in their perusal of the menus to see who was coming in, not that they would know anyone outside Sophia's family, but they were curious.

Unlike the deceased feline who met its demise because of its inquisitiveness, Sophia and her friends were rewarded for theirs with the arrival of six women.

They appeared to be somewhere nearing seventy and were talking and laughing. The tallest of the group announced none too quietly that, "The Terras had returned!" as they sat at the only table capable of seating them all which was beside the booth where Sophia and her friends were sitting.

"Were you all back for the reunion?" Marion asked from her place behind the counter.

"Yes, we were!" The tall brunette said. "The Class of Nineteen Sixty-nine is back!"

"And the Class of Seventy!" Two of the other women added with a laugh. "Jackie you always forget we weren't in the same class."

"Sorry, Paris. Sorry, Melissa." The tall brunette said, and the entire table erupted into gales of laughter.

Sophia realized that Paris was the librarian she had startled on the day she got her library card and her copy of the book.

"Are you all going to the book signing?" Marion asked.

"What book signing?" The brunette who had been called Jackie asked.

"Jerry Collins' daughter wrote a book about him and Laura. She will be at the library signing copies later today." Marion said. "You would think the librarian would have told you about something like that."

"Paris?" Jackie asked.

"It completely slipped my mind." Paris said. "We haven't been together in so long I just got caught up in catching up that I totally forgot."

"What is the book about? Do you know?" One of the six asked Marion.

"What I've heard is that it's about Jerry and Laura." Marion said. "But I haven't read it yet."

"I have." Sophia said injecting herself into their conversation.

She opened the drawstring backpack and pulled out her copy and showed it to the women.

"May I?" Jackie asked Sophia as she motioned toward the book.

"Sure, go ahead," Sophia said.

Jackie took the book and began to thumb through it, stopping ever so often to read a passage. One passage in particular caught her attention.

"Oh my!" She said to the group. "We <u>are</u> in here!"

"What?" The woman Sophia heard one of the others called Nikole asked.

"We are?" Someone else asked.

"Yes. We are." Jackie said. "Listen to this: *'Don't think I don't know it was you six who planned that." Laura said addressing the still giggling group while she wrapped up in a beach towel she had brought from home. "You all are terrors!"*

"'We aren't terrors." Jackie Logan said. "We are "The Terras!"'

The present day Terras dissolved into more gales of laughter.

"Oh!" Melissa said. "I remember that day! Laura tried so hard to be mad, but she couldn't. She was always one for a good practical joke."

"Or a not so practical joke." Chimed in the woman Sophia had heard called Jamie. "And you all know "egg-xactly" what I am talking about too! Is that in the book?"

Jackie flipped rapidly through the book's pages, paused, then smiled and said, "It sure is!"

Sophia laughed to herself. She knew all about the egg incident, but now she was actually seeing most of the participants. The book was passed around the table accompanied with chuckles as The Terras read about the scandalous event that had been the talk of the school.

"How long was Laura grounded?" Jamie asked. "I know it was a long time."

"I believe it was…" Jackie began, but paused as she tried to remember that particular event from over fifty years ago. "A month. That seems right. And Meg got a month too."

"Yes, that's what I got." Paris added. "That was the longest month I have ever lived."

"Agreed." Nikole added.

"But you know." Jackie said. "From what my granddaughter tells me, much, much worse things go on now."

"They do." Sophia interjected without really thinking.

She wasn't one to butt in on other people's conversations and the realization she had, embarrassed her.

"Sorry." She added quickly.

The Terras didn't seem the least bit upset that she had spoken. "What's school like here?" Melissa asked.

"Uh…" Sophia began; she was really regretting having spoken. "I'm going to be a freshman and I just moved here, so I don't know." She said.

"That was such a stupid thing to say." Sophia thought. *"They don't want to know your life story."*

"Just like Laura!" Jamie said with a bright smile that lit up her face.

"She sure is!" Marion added. "In fact, she is living in Jerry and Laura's old house!"

"THAT'S who you are!" Paris said. "I knew you looked familiar, but I couldn't place you. You're the new postmaster's daughter."

"That's me." Sophia said.

"Did you cut your hair?" Paris asked.

"I did." Sophia said.

"That's why I didn't recognize you." Paris said. "It looks nice by the way!"

After fifteen more minutes of reminiscing, Jackie returned the book to Sophia.

"Here you go!" She said. "Thank you very much!"

"You're welcome!" Sophia said taking the book from her.

"I wonder what they would have done if I had said, "You're welcome very much!" Sophia said to herself.

"We should go visit Laura and Meg while we are here." Jackie said. "It's been a while."

"You all can." Paris said. "I have to get to the library and get set up for the signing. Maybe we could go pay our respects after that?"

"We'll stop by the library and say hello to Erin too." One of the ladies said. "I haven't seen her since Meg passed."

~ ~ ~ ~ ~ ~

One o'clock came way too fast, and lunch was eaten much too quickly. Before any of them realized it, it was time for Audrey, Laney and Leah to head back to Springfield. Hugs were had, a few tears were wiped away, and promises were made to see each other during Christmas break, or sooner if they could arrange it. Then it was one forty-five and the rental van Laney's parents had driven to Ohio was moving down the street.

"Are you okay?" Dan asked Sophia as they stood on the front porch watching Audrey, Laney and Leah disappear from sight.

"I'm good Dad!" Sophia said. "This was the best birthday ever! Thank you for getting them up here so we could be together!" Sophia wrapped her arms around him, and they shared a comfortable hug.

"Almost time for that book signing isn't it?" He asked.

"Yes." Sophia mumbled into his chest.

"Would you like a ride down to the library?" Dan asked.

Sophia thought she would ride her bike, but then changed her mind. She would let her dad take her and her bike to the library then she would ride home once she was done.

"That would be nice Dad! Thank you!" She said. "But first I need to do something."

Sophia made a quick trip to her room where she quickly moved all of Laura's digitalized tapes to a small flash drive and slipped it into her pocket.

~ ~ ~ ~ ~ ~

Sophia parked her bike in the rack near the front of the library and went inside. There were twenty or thirty people standing around near the entrance, none of whom she knew. However, when Paris Spencer saw her, she came over, thanked her for coming and asked if she wanted to get her book signed.

"Absolutely!" Sophia said.

"Well then, let me introduce you to Erin!" Paris said.

Paris guided Sophia through the milling group of people, down a book laden aisle to a large open space at the rear of the library to a table where additional copies of the book were being displayed. Behind the table was a woman who was leaning down talking to a little girl.

"Erin?" Paris said.

The woman, Erin, picked up the child, placed her on her lap and spun the chair around.

"Hi durl!" Eva Ivey, also known as Little Miss Allbody, exclaimed. "I meaneded Sofa."

"Hi Eva!" Sophia said.

"Allbody loves me!" Eva said. "Sometimes you forgetted."

Sophia laughed out loud! "You are right Eva, sometimes I do forget."

"Nice to see you again Sophia!" Erin Ivey said.

"Nice to see you too!" Sophia said. "So, you wrote this?"

She held up her copy of the book.

"I did!" Erin said. "It took me ten years, but I wrote it. Have you read it yet?"

"Yes!" Sophia said.

"Was there any particular part of the book that really jumped out at you?" Erin asked.

Sophia smiled and felt her face get warm.

"Ah!" Erin said. "The snowstorm?"

"Yes, but because I know what happened the morning after the snowstorm before Laura and Jerry headed home. Wow – double – owzah!!!" Sophia thought.

"Yes." Sophia said. "The snowstorm!"

"Well, just so you know, that part took me the longest to write. I wanted to make sure I got everything just right for that part of the story." Erin said.

"I think you did a pretty good job!" Sophia said laying her copy of the book on the table in front of Erin. "I didn't want to put it down once I started reading it!"

"Thank you!" Erin said and picked up the book, flipped open the cover and wrote a quick note then handed it back to Sophia.

"Thank you!" Sophia said. "Ummm…?"

Erin looked at her with a "go on" kind of look on her face.

"Did you know that Laura kept a diary?" Sophia asked.

"Yes!" Erin said. "That is mentioned at the end of the book."

"No, what I meant to say was, did you know Laura kept an *audio* diary?" Sophia asked. "On old reel to reel tapes?"

"How do you know that?" Erin asked, clearly intrigued.

When Sophia talked about kicking the stack of boxes that were full of books while wearing only flip flops, Erin laughed. She listened with rapt attention as Sophia spent the next several minutes recounting the how and why of finding Laura's tapes. When she finished, Sophia handed Erin the flash drive.

"What's this?" Erin asked as she took the flash drive.

"That's Laura's voice!" Sophia said. "I digitalized her tapes and put them on that."

"Thank you!" Erin gushed. "I'm really interested to hear what's on them!"

"I think you will like what's on there." Sophia said, paused, then continued. "You know, before I found those recordings, I was not in a very good place, but Laura helped me." Sophia said.

"How so?" Erin asked.

"Just listen to the tapes and you'll understand." Sophia said.

"Okay! And I want to get your flash drive back to you." Erin said.

"You can give it to me the next time you see me at the park." Sophia said.

"That works!" Erin said.

"Oh, here's this." She handed Erin a piece of paper with her email address on it. "In case the recordings don't play, you can email me, and I can get you another copy."

"Would you mind if I made a copy of the recordings and sent them to Laura's parents?" Erin asked. "I'm sure they would love to hear Laura's voice again."

"Laura's parents are still..." Sophia began, but stopped when she realized how what she was about to say might sound.

Erin chuckled. "Yes, Matthew and Marylyn Butler are still living. They are both in their nineties and still going strong!"

"That's great!" Sophia said. "If you need more copies of Laura's tapes, I can make them for you. Her parents should have them."

"Thank you!" Erin said. "That's very nice of you!"

~ ~ ~ ~ ~ ~

Sophia laid her bike in its accustomed place in the tall grass. Her signed copy of the book secured in the left side pannier wrapped up in the drawstring backpack.

She jogged across the bridge and went down to the fishing platform. She was covered in sweat from the bike ride, but it was August twenty-sixth, and the current temperature was ninety-five degrees, so she was not surprised.

"You are going to get caught for sure!" Polly chimed in.

"Where have you been Polly?" Sophia said to her conscience. *"I've missed you!"*

"Oh, I've been around." Polly said. "Are you still taking off your clothes and running around outside naked?"

"*Yes!*" Sophia said to herself. "*Because sometimes you have to do something a little crazy to prove that you are actually sane.*"

Polly harumphed then went silent.

Sophia peeled her sweaty clothes off, but this time she hid them under one of the buckets before plunging into the Little Grand Creek's cold water.

She made several laps back and forth across the creek like she had done on her previous visits. Then, she swam to the middle and let the current carry her downstream until she was almost to the dam.

As the current's speed increased, she angled across to the bank and climbed out and walked downstream to the dam and watched the water and began thinking.

She thought about what had happened since school had gotten out for the summer.

She thought about how she had felt about the move and the things she had lost.

She thought about finding the tapes Laura, or someone, had hidden in the cubbyhole.

She thought about Maude Adelaide.

She thought about Pizza Guy and how cute he was!

She thought about the absolute astonishment she had felt when Audrey, Laney and Leah had totally surprised her for her birthday!

"*I had the best birthday ever!*" Sophia thought. "*I really needed to see the girls; I'm glad Mom and Dad went and got them!*"

She thought about The Pool Room and how blown away she was when she first saw it!

She thought about meeting Erin Ivey and realized that she already kind of knew her!

She thought about Laura's visits.

And she thought, no, she knew, she was no longer angry!

"*Those tapes are going to surprise Erin!*" Sophia thought. "*Who knows, maybe she'll write another book about Laura's diaries or even one about the recordings of Laura's voice!*"

She decided to walk back to the fishing platform along the path. It would be quicker, and she would be mostly dry when she got back.

The path made a slight turn to the left before exiting the trees and it was a good thing too. Just as she was about to step out into the clearing and make her way the last few yards to the fishing platform, Sophia saw several people standing on it.

"Busted!" Polly said.

"Hush." Sophia replied.

Polly laughed.

She crouched down behind a large bush that gave her cover but also allowed her to see the platform. It didn't take her long to realize it was The Terras standing right next to the bucket where her clothes were stashed.

They didn't talk much. When they did, their voices were so low, Sophia couldn't hear what they were saying even though she had a pretty good idea what, or who, they were talking about.

Sophia remembered that one of them had suggested making a trip to see Laura and Meg. As the minivan that was parked at the end of the bridge was facing back toward town, she guessed that they had paid their respects and had stopped at the fishing platform to remember their friends. After several minutes, The Terras climbed the embankment, got into the minivan and drove away.

Sophia retrieved her cell phone, she was glad no one had called or texted her while The Terras were standing next to the bucket it was hidden under. She checked the time; it was four fifty-three. She texted her mom and told her she would be home by seven-thirty and received a response that said, "IT IS A SCHOOL NIGHT YOU KNOW." This was followed with a smiley face and thumbs up emoji!

Sophia climbed the bank and headed west. She wanted to pay her respects to Laura and Meg as well.

"Sometimes you have to do something a little crazy to prove that you are actually sane!" Sophia thought.

Chapter 36

Once the Schwinn was secured in the bike rack, Sophia made her way to the high school's front doors, took a deep breath, let it out and entered. It was the second time she had been inside the building. The first was when she and her mother had come to enroll, get her class schedule and locate her locker in what the guidance counselor had called "the freshman hallway". On that day, the building was quiet, which was quite the contrast to how the high school sounded now.

As the doors opened, she was inundated with the clangs and bangs of locker doors being opened and shut and the clatter and chatter of voices. Sophia was also acutely aware that as she entered, she instantly became the focus of everyone's attention.

"Maybe shorts weren't a good idea." She thought, but then added, *"But if you got it, flaunt it and I got it!"*

~ ~ ~ ~ ~ ~

"Who's that?" A girl said.

"I think I saw her at the library yesterday." Someone else added.

"She's cute!" A boy said.

"Is she a senior?" Someone asked.

~ ~ ~ ~ ~ ~

Sophia crossed the lobby in front of the school's auditorium and headed down the freshman hallway that was lined with lima bean green colored lockers to number twenty-nine.

"Okay...forty-four, zero, thirty-eight." She said to herself as she spun the dial of the combination lock on the locker's door.

When she and her mother had found her locker, she opened it on her first try. However, on this attempt on her first day as a freshman the locker door would not budge.

Oh, come on!" Sophia thought. *"Are you related to our backdoor?"*

She reset the lock and then spun the dial again.

"One complete turn to the left to forty-four. Two complete turns to the right to zero. One complete turn back to the left to thirty-eight. That should open it." She thought.

It did not.

Sophia was usually patient, but today, when it felt like every person in this new school was staring at her as she struggled to open her locker, her patience was rapidly wearing thin.

"One complete turn to the left to forty-four! Two complete turns to the right to zero! One complete turn to the left to thirty-eight!" She thought and gritted her teeth.

The latch tripped but the door still would not open. Sophia tugged the door's handle a couple of times, but nothing happened. She yanked hard on the locker's latch and the door slipped from her hand as it flew open. There was a thunderous, vibrating crash.

She turned to her right and was surprised to see Pizza Guy standing next to her holding onto her locker door.

"You almost got me!" He said with an amazing smile.

"I am so sorry! Are you okay?" Sophia said as she felt flutterbys in her stomach!

"Yeah, I'm okay!" Pizza Guy said.

"I was trying to get my stupid locker to open, and I yanked on it. I guess that's when it flew open." She bit her bottom lip and looked as though she was going to cry. "I am sorry."

"Really, I'm okay." He smiled at her. "I caught the door. It didn't hit me."

"Are you sure?" She said.

"I'm sure." He said. An expression of sudden realization came across his face and he blushed. "You are the B.O.M!"

Sophia saw that he quickly glanced down at her legs then just as quickly returned to her face.

Sophia laughed. "I like to think so!"

"Oh, that was smoooooooth!" A female voice said.

Sophia looked and there was an extremely pretty blonde-haired girl with exquisitely beautiful sapphire blue eyes standing just behind Pizza Guy.

"Laura Kay, go AWAY!" He said loudly, but not in a mean way. The girl, Laura, giggled and crossed the hall to a group of girls.

"If that's your girlfriend..." Sophia started to say, but Pizza Guy interrupted her.

"Uh...no! That..." He motioned with his thumb toward the girl he had called Laura and, in a voice loud enough for her to hear said, "...is my *evil* twin sister!"

"I heard that." Laura said.

"You were meant to." Pizza Guy said and Laura and her friends laughed.

Sophia was relieved, she didn't want to start her first day with people thinking she was flirting with someone's boyfriend.

There was an awkward silence before Sophia asked, "So, what is your name, or should I just call you Pizza Guy?"

Pizza Guy laughed again!

"My name is Michael Ivey and that is my sister Laura!" He paused, then added, "I didn't recognize you at first Sophia because you cut your hair!

"I did!" Sophia said, pleased that he remembered her name. "Besides your name, is there anything else I should know about you?"

"I have a younger brother named Tori who is ten and my baby sister, Eva is extremely four!" Michael said.

"Is your mother Erin Ivey, the author?" Sophia asked.

"She is!" Michael said. "Have you read her book?"

"Yes, and I have a signed copy too!" Sophia said. "Have *you* read it?"

"Not yet." Michael confessed.

"You are mentioned in it you know." Sophia said. "So, I know a few more things about you!"

"I guess I should read it then." Michael said.

"Yes, you should! And your little sister Eva took me "fountain climbing" at the Coombs Park!" Sophia said.

The flutterbys had taken wing!

"That was you?" Michael asked. "She told us about her friend 'Sofa', but… That was you?"

"That was me!" Sophia said.

"Hey Laura!" Michael called to his sister. "This is Eva's friend…Sofa"!

"Nice to meet you…Sofa!" Laura laughed.

A bell rang and the milling crowd began to disperse.

"Five minutes until classes start." Michael said. "What's your first class?"

Sophia retrieved her schedule, looked at it and said, "Algebra. Room 103."

"No kidding, me too!" Michael said. "You know where it's at don't you?"

"No. It's my first day!" Sophia lied.

She had found every classroom she would be in when she had picked up her schedule. What she was doing was creatively distorting the truth to affect a planned outcome and the outcome she was hoping for was to keep talking to Michael!

They walked down the rapidly depopulating hallway and found themselves in another awkward silence.

Michael finally asked, "If you've read Mom's book and you know a few things about me; you should tell me something about yourself. All I know about you is your name is Sophia Young, you like beef, onion and mushroom pizza and you cut your hair."

Sophia stopped walking and looked at Michael. They were in the middle of the high school's main hallway in front of the school's auditorium.

She smiled and said, "I'm not allergic to wasp stings!"

~ ~ ~ ~ ~ ~

Sophia bounded up the front porch stairs at three twenty-two after putting her Schwinn in the garage and finding the backdoor was still up to its old tricks.

When she opened the door and stepped into the living room, neither of her parents were around. It had been their tradition to be together when she got back from her first day of school. She called them on her cell phone.

"Hey, we went to pick up some ice cream!" Her mom said after the first ring. "Did you go out the that covered bridge like you said you might?"

"Yes, Mom I went to the bridge. I went skinny dipping. I walked to The Grove and back and...I thought about Michael Ivey!!!" She thought to herself.

"I did, but I'm not there now." Sophia said.

"Where are you?" Carol asked.

Sophia looked around the living room, glanced at the pocket door that led to her bedroom and private bath. She smiled!

"I'm home!" Sophia said.

Epilogue

If there is such a thing as love at first sight, it happened to Sophia and Michael! There was a spark they both felt when he had delivered the pizza to her on the night of the rainstorm. There was definitely something more on the first day of their freshman year of high school!

But what happened with Sophia and Michael...hmmm?

~ ~ ~ ~ ~ ~

Dan Young's prediction, that within two weeks of starting school, their new home would begin hosting the new friends Sophia would make just like they had done in their old home in Springfield, came true, but it didn't take two weeks.

At two o'clock on the Saturday after school began, The Pool Room played host to fifteen teens; two of whom were Michael and Laura Ivey! They talked, played music, munched on the snacks everyone had contributed and enjoyed the pool and hot tub.

Sophia liked being with Michael and he liked being with her!

~ ~ ~ ~ ~ ~

By the time Homecoming came around at the end of September, they were a couple! Even though they couldn't officially date until they were sixteen, they were allowed to attend the Homecoming Dance together.

Michael wore tan slacks, a white button-down dress shirt with a navy and gold necktie and a navy-blue sport coat.

Sophia said he looked very handsome!

Sophia wore the little black dress her mother had gotten for her at the mall in Columbia, the heart shaped locket and heels that still didn't make her as tall as him.

Michael told her she looked beautiful!

He walked her home which was romantic and painful for Sophia. It was romantic because Michael was the guy she was falling for and she knew it! It was painful because the heels she had worn were brand new, tight and they hurt her feet. After a block or two, the heels came off and Sophia put holes in the soles of a pair of smokey grey panty hose!

Somewhere underneath a streetlight, this one was arc sodium and not one of the L.E.D. lights like they had in Springfield, Michael stopped walking, turned to Sophia, swallowed hard and asked her if he could kiss her.

Sophia swallowed hard and said yes!

He leaned down just a bit and she rose up on her toes just a bit and they gently kissed! The flutterbys swarmed as their lips met for the first time!

"WOW-TRIPLE-OWZAH!!!" Sophia thought!

~ ~ ~ ~ ~ ~

Halloween was a cold and snowy affair that interfered with the younger kid's tricking and treating. Four-year-old Eva and ten-year-old Tori were none too happy that their candy getting opportunity had been sabotaged by Mother Nature, but they did enjoy themselves Halloween afternoon.

Sophia invited them to come over with Laura and Michael to swim while she and their siblings decorated The Pool Room in the theme of and with the music of the Beach Boys for the Halloween party, she was hosting later that night!!

Instead of bobbing for apples, the party goers played a game where teams of two had to get a beach ball from one end of the heated pool to the other without touching it with their hands or touching each other.

Sophia and Michael were eliminated during the very first round, but they didn't care, they sat at the edge of the pool cheering on everyone else.

Without consciously thinking about it, Sophia's right hand found Michael's left hand and their fingers intertwined for several wonderful minutes!

~ ~ ~ ~ ~ ~

Audrey, Laney and Leah came up for a four-day visit on December thirtieth and finally met Michael. After some serious interrogation, he was deemed worthy!

On New Year's Eve, Sophia had planned on having a small party with the girls and Michael and Laura, to bring in the new year. However, Michael came down with a stomach bug, so only Laura could come which worked out just fine.

Laura, Audrey, Laney, Leah and Sophia had a sleepover in The Pool Room where they brought in the new year with a game of Truth or Dare! Ironically enough, Laura, like her namesake, had to make a snow angel in her bikini at the stroke of midnight when she received a dare from Sophia.

Laura was grateful for the hot tub!

~ ~ ~ ~ ~ ~

One snowy Friday night in late January, Sophia convinced her parents to take her and Laura to The Grove for a winter campout. Although the temperature was in the low twenties and there was nearly eight inches of snow on the ground, the sinkhole was snow free and in the forties. With a large fire in the fire ring and two heavy sleeping bags, she and Laura were toasty warm the entire night!

~ ~ ~ ~ ~ ~

The Kickapoo High School Spring Break was the same week as the Wildcat's Spring Break and Sophia, much to Michael's chagrin, spent four of the seven days in Springfield with the girls!

It was Sophia's first time back to her old neighborhood in nine months. It wasn't as weird of an experience as she had thought it would be. By the time she was packing up, she was looking forward to going …home!

~ ~ ~ ~ ~ ~

Sophia and Michael held the first ever "Freshmen Only Pool Prom" on the first Saturday in May. Everyone was requested to wear "thrift store chic" outfits that could get wet. A "grand promenade" was held, and after each pool prom participant had made their entrance to show off their attire, they either jumped, were pushed or pulled into the pool! It was a huge success!

~ ~ ~ ~ ~ ~

When school got out for the summer, Sophia secured a part-time job at Morton's working side-by-side with Marion. Michael got a job at, of all places, Show Me Pizza! He was told that once he got his driver's license, he could make deliveries once he had a car to drive.

~ ~ ~ ~ ~ ~

Sophia and Laura Ivey made the cheerleading squad at the end of their freshman year! After securing her spot, Sophia made herself stop calling the school "The Home of the Podunksville Fighting Possums" as she was now a Wildcat Cheerleader!

The squad went to cheer camp on the Missouri State campus in July where Sophia and Laura were named co-captains. They held those spots until they graduated high school.

After cheer camp, they stayed in Springfield for a few days and hung out with Audrey, Laney and Leah, where they may or may not have played Truth or Dare and they may or may not have snuck away from Audrey's house to go to Laney's and may or may not have gone skinny dipping!

~ ~ ~ ~ ~ ~

Sophia and Michael dated all through high school. There were some minor spats as there are in all relationships, but nothing of real consequence.

After graduation, they attended Missouri State, graduating Magna Cum Laude and both left college without any student loan debt thanks to the careful financial planning on the part of their parents and several nice scholarships!

~ ~ ~ ~ ~ ~

One week after receiving their diplomas while on a quick trip back home, Michael took Sophia to The Grove and down into the sinkhole. He knew it was a special place for her and he planned to make it even more special! As they watched and listened to the water drop into the crescent shaped pool, Michael dropped to one knee and proposed. Sophia accepted, then they both dissolved into a great laughing, crying, blubbering mess!

~ ~ ~ ~ ~ ~

Their wedding was in August the following year and as you may have already guessed, it was held at the covered bridge on the twenty-seventh!

Sophia had a difficult time trying to decide who to have as her maid of honor. She hated having to make *that* choice so instead of one Maid of Honor, she had FIVE Maids of Honor; Audrey Noble, Leah Sterling, Laney Williams, Laura Ivey and Eva Ivey, who had just turned thirteen!

For the wedding ceremony, Erin loaned Sophia a pair of pearl earrings and a pearl necklace. She told her they were the ones she had worn when she married Michael's father, Jack!

~ ~ ~ ~ ~ ~

The reception was held at Sophia's parent's house and it was attended by many friends and family members! Dan hired a band and built a stage over the swimming pool where they could play while the party goers served themselves from the two long buffet tables that were sitting where the five sleeper sofas usually sat.

When it was time to leave on their honeymoon, Michael and Sophia Ivey, with the requisite tin cans jangling behind their car, were chased through town by at least fifty cars with horns blaring!

They had told everyone that they were going to go to Columbia for the night. Then they would head to St. Louis to catch an afternoon flight to Florida where they would board a ship for a seven-day cruise through the Bahamas. Instead, they snuck back to The Grove where they had stashed some camping equipment and spent their first night as a married couple in the sinkhole!

~ ~ ~ ~ ~ ~

In the waning August sunlight, the newest Ivey family inflated a queen size air mattress using its built-in air pump. They built a fire in the well-seasoned fire ring, then looked inside the very old, but quite functional stainless-steel cooler that once belonged to Michael's grandfather, Jerry.

Inside, they found a beef, onion and mushroom pizza and bread sticks which they heated up over the campfire, a bottle of wine and a box of chocolate covered strawberries!

When Sophia saw the pizza and breadsticks she laughed and thought, *"Well, I did get my wedding ring so I guess Michael will finally get to meet Goldilocks!"*

After eating, Michael presented Sophia with a gold foil wrapped box that was just a bit bigger than a picture frame. When she opened it, she found a photo album containing twenty-five photos of a younger version of herself. In each photo, she was wearing...nothing!

"Where did you get *these*!?" Sophia asked.

"From my trail cameras. I saw these the afternoon before I delivered that first pizza to you." He said.

"So that's why your face turned red and why you were checking me out?" Sophia asked.

"Guilty as charged!" Michael said.

Sophia laughed. "Did you like what you saw?"

"No." Michael said.

"No?" Sophia asked.

"I loved what I saw then, and I love what I am seeing now!" He said. "You are definitely the B.O.M. Soph!"

"Did you know that every time you were in The Pool Room, I was nude and on display?" Sophia asked.

"What do you mean?" He asked.

"I made "Choices" the day I first went to the spring; the day these were taken apparently!" She said. "It was a preview of coming attractions!"

"That was you?!" Michael asked. "Why did you do that? Are you a nudist or something?"

"I did it because, sometimes you have to do something a little crazy to prove that you are actually sane!" Sophia said. "I am not a nudist. I just like being…comfortable! And just so you know, I plan on being comfortable around you A LOT!!!"

"Do you want to get comfortable now?" He asked.

Sophia set the photo album on the floor of the sinkhole.

"I have waited my whole life to get comfortable with you Michael!" She said. "Come here!"

DEDICATION

To Mom and Dad. I miss you both.

To my little buckeye daughter! I am so proud of you for being a part of THE Ohio State Marching Band (TBDBITL 141 & 142!!!). I don't know what the future holds for you, but you will do great things!

To my son, my tech geek and personal computer fix-it guy! I still don't know how you built your computer (which is actually two computers) but you did! I hope you find your niche!

To my dear friend Sandi Seitz. What I wouldn't give to be able to pick up the phone and say, "Ha-Row!!!!"

To my friend, the adorable and ebullient Miss Leah Coombs! What a wonderfully smart, articulate and charming young lady you are! Yes, "Leah Sterling" is based, in part, on you! The fictional Coombs House Park is named after your family! I will miss seeing you at the Young Authors Conference. Keep writing!!!

To Audrey Good! You are one of my favorite band kids and "Audrey Noble" is totally based on you!
I let your mom, read part of the story while I was still writing the book (something I have never done before). She said, "And every bit of that sounds exactly like something Audrey would do!!!"
You are most certainly comfortable in your skin. No one is going to walk all over you as you continue your journey in this thing called life!

Finally, to a young lady named Sophia Patrick, who died unexpectedly August 1, 2020, just before starting her senior year of high school at the much too young age of seventeen.
I did not know her, but when I would go to McDonald's to work on "Laura's Voice", I would see her when she and her friends would come in after an event at the high school.
When she died, I changed the name of the main character to Sophia, in her memory. ~ J.T.M.

www.ingramcontent.com/pod-product-compliance
Lightning Source LLC
Chambersburg PA
CBHW020337180626
46812CB00001B/240